Praise for Chasing Time

"A glittering fantasy with lush imagination and storytelling. Adrielle Maddox is a sumptuous young adult fantasy for readers to devour."
— L J Andrews, author of *Curse of Shadows and Thorns* (*The Broken Kingdoms, Book 1*)

"Adrielle is a heroine for all readers to embrace bold and ready to fling herself into the unknown, despite her realistic fears, ready to change things for the better for all humankind because, well, that's what is expected of us all. Adventure placed against a broad span of history, stirred with mighty imagination, Montana serves up a magical potion that will have readers cheering, laughing and shedding a tear."
— Judy Cairo, producer, Oscar-winning *Crazy Heart*

"Chasing Time is a grand entrance for this trilogy, sure to capture a large young adult audience, plus readers new to the genre. It features strong, relatable characters and deals sure-handedly with powerful emotions—most laudably, love, in all its facets. This is a really good story. Be ready for a great trip." — Donald E. McQuinn, author of *The Moondark Saga*

CHASING TIME

ADRIELLE MADDOX
1

CHASING TIME

MONTANA WAKEFIELD

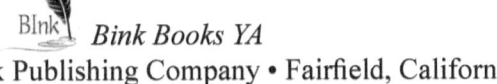
Bink Books YA
Bedazzled Ink Publishing Company • Fairfield, California

paperback 978-1-949290-96-7

Cover Design
by

Bink Books
a division of
Bedazzled Ink Publishing, LLC
Fairfield, California
http://www.bedazzledink.com

For Stan, who believed in me and in this story.
I'm so grateful to share my life with you.
I wish I'd found you at twenty. I love you.

Acknowledgments

Where do you start when there are so many to thank? My heart is overflowing. First and foremost, I'd like to thank Stan, you restored my faith in love. Taught me to never give up. And literally saved my life. Dreams can come true. You are amazing.

Thank you papa, Enrique, whose love of books rubbed off on me. Your creative spirit lives in me. I cherish our Sunday mornings growing up, when the five of us kids gathered on yours and mom's bed, excited to hear about your latest read. Your imagination and thirst for knowledge set me on my lifelong journey. Mama, Lucy, whose support and wise words always came when they were most needed. Abuelito Miguel, the clicking of your typewriter gave me my first memory of the birth of a story. My two grandmothers: Elvira, whose quiet resilience taught me how to love unwaveringly, and Pilar, whose eccentricity showed me it's all right to be yourself, even if others can't grasp how truly wonderful you are.

Laura, you are my oldest and best friend. My constant in this life. Your smile is the brightest beam in the universe. Alex, you are the pillar of support holding me up in my worst moments. Dan, thanks for your love, and the guitar that appeared miraculously one day when I needed music back in my life. Helena, your love of movies and stories are a constant reminder that we live vicariously through stories. Fatima, I treasure your bedtime stories— among them, "El Rey Midas."

Thank you to my three kids. I feel so fortunate to be your mom. Thank you for sharing your lives with me, and for putting up with my stories when they were only glimpses of possibilities. You taught me how different all of us are. Cassidy, your innocence, acceptance, and perseverance to achieve despite setbacks, are commendable. Monet, reading 6.1 grade level pre-kindergarten—you're amazing. Thank you for finally liking your name. I was a little worried when you and Mauve read the Baby-Sitter's Club series, and you came to me wanting to change your names to Mary Anne and Kristy. Lol. Monet, you always seemed to have it all figured out. I didn't find out till much later you were fighting to find your way. Mauve, you always loved the underdog. You were my popular kid because everyone loved you. And my first editor for Feathers. You were determined to win me that Mother's Day basket when you were in fourth grade, by writing an essay on why I was the best mom. I was so proud of you (and still am) when the call came saying you'd won. My little writer. You are full of surprises and talent. All three of you are.

Scarlatti, my furry baby, thanks for the snuggles and distractions when I needed a break.

Thank you, Don McQuinn, for teaching me the craft. Jeff Arch, for pointing me in the right direction with *Save the Cat*, and for telling me *Sleepless in Seattle*, my favorite movie of all time, took you thirteen years to write. Ditto for me, from the first Feathers draft to *Chasing Time*. I am in good company.

A huge thank you to my agent Betsy Green. Bedazzled Ink Publishing LLC. Liz Gibson, Claudia Wilde, and CA Casey. This wouldn't be possible without you. Thank you for believing in my story and sharing it with readers. Casey, you are an outstanding editor.

Last, but not least, thank you to all you writers and future writers who are my inspiration and have enriched my life with your endless imagination. Among them, Liane Moriarty, Stephenie Meyers, Earnest Hemingway, F. Scott Fitzgerald, J. D. Salinger, John Steinbeck, Margaret Mitchell, Anne Rice, John Grisham, Suzanne Collins, Ayn Rand, Cormack McCarthy, and Dr Seuss. And to you, future readers. I hope you love this story. In writing the Adrielle Maddox series, I learned the importance of striving to be our best. And accepting ourselves, though this might not be easy. I am forever grateful to all who have shown me love and kindness throughout my life. And to those of you who haven't, you helped me reach within myself to discover who I am. Answers often lie in the most unexpected places.

With my wings I could protect her, as a mortal I could be with her

prologue

ANGELO RACED UP the stairs two treads at a time, his heartbeat pounding in his ears. He reached the top of the turret in the castle and blew past the wooden door, the musky smell of incense slamming into him. Monika, the old woman, was there, in her darkened chamber, a bent silhouette staring into the distance.

"Where is she?" Angelo demanded.

Monika turned, the black bird on her shoulder frozen like a taxidermy prop. She raised her bony hand and slid off her hood. Angelo shuddered. She was as decrepit as the walls surrounding her. Her skin, a map of deeply etched wrinkles, was crepey and thin. A net of blue veins showed through the transparency. It was clear by the way her eyes washed over him she'd been expecting him, a cool acknowledgement this was an inevitable step in the unfolding sequence of events.

Clutched tightly in her right hand was her jeweled golden scepter. Though stories of its beauty and magic preceded it, nothing did it justice. The column, made of the finest gold, was solid and unyielding. A diamond the size of a fist was anchored in the heart of it; the stone's razor-sharp cuts dissecting the light. Despite being the bravest and strongest soldier in the Achaean army, Angelo's knees weakened at its beauty. He fought the urge to kneel in its presence.

Monika loosened her grasp on the metal rod and rotated it, unleashing shafts of light from the center gem. The room was instantly ablaze with colors. She extended a shaky arm and beckoned him with one gnarly finger.

"Look deeper into the heart of the diamond," she said, her voice a throaty croak.

Angelo leaned in, the heavy stench of death and decay clinging to the air. His raptor vision braced against the brilliance inside the stone and targeted a single crimson feather drifting along the stream of light.

"I see a feather. Crimson. But only one," he said.

"Yes, but it is brilliant and gleaming."

"And solitary. Does this mean she is still alive?" His heartbeat suspended as he waited for her reply.

"The skin of the fruit reflects the color of the feathers. You know what the Book says: *If you pass a beam of light through a prism, the light will split into all the colors of the rainbow.* The crimson feather signifies war, the first of the four seal judgments. Adrielle will have to master the four corresponding trials if she is to prevail. Only then, will she earn the Crest of the Traveller and fulfill the prophecy by becoming the white light, the culmination of all frequencies."

Angelo raised his eyes to hers. "But that is an unfathomable feat."

Monika's eyes bore into him, and he resented it. He steeled against her gaze, a myriad of questions chasing around his mind.

"She will need the *Book of Feathers*. Without it she will never survive," Angelo said.

"True."

Her confirmation squeezed at his chest, and he massaged the tightening. The thought of living in a world without her . . . He couldn't let that happen. He remembered her so vividly he could hear her voice and smell jasmine in her hair.

"Haden guards the ancient book. With that much power, he will never give it up. Not unless . . ." He paced about the room. *Unless Haden were to fall in love with her.* He didn't dare say it out loud. He clenched his fists, angered at the irony in this impossible complication.

He turned back to Monika and searched her face. "What about Domenikos?"

"Domenikos?" Her eyes darkened. Thin lids fluttered as she slowly shook her head. "He is aware she is the key to peace between our societies. He will do everything in his power to stop her."

"What can I do to prevent him from destroying her?" he asked, the weight of his fear almost crushing him.

She averted her eyes and stared into undecipherable space. Angelo's chest hurt. He couldn't breathe, and his eyes filled with tears.

Monika turned back. "Only her choices will determine her destiny. They will seal her fate," she said, her voice softening.

Damn. Angelo spun away from the light, afraid she might see his tide of emotions. He was determined to keep his secret. Some said seers opened windows to the future and past. Not knowing how much Monika could see was alarming.

He regained his composure. "How do I find her?"

"Follow the path your heart enlightens. You must hurry, the magic cloaking of the spell dissolves when she comes of age. At midnight."

Angelo gave a slight nod and changed to his natural bird form. He spread his silver wings.

"Adrielle is marked. Her skin and hair are as white as the light inside this stone." Monika raised her scepter high and struck the floor with great force. A thunderous rumble shook the room and all the colors fused to a blinding white.

Chapter 1

Florida – Present Time

A SINGLE SHADOW spilled out through a crack in the door into the hallway and stretched almost to her bedroom. Crouched beyond the light, Adrielle watched in awe and fear. There they were, huddled in her father's meeting room, their colorful feathers interwoven like tapestry, each bird indistinguishable from the next.

The sounds came all at once. Chanting voices and wind and a howling, a screeching whistle that seemed to call her name. The sound was so desperate and chilling it bit into Adrielle's core. She told herself she wouldn't scream.

Fire engulfed her on all sides, and she turned to run. She covered her face with her hands, her fingers tangling in her white hair. Something was pulling at her hands. She fought it, the heat of the flame biting her skin. Engulfed in the flames, she saw her mother's face.

A deep guttural sound escaped Adrielle's throat. She squeezed her eyes tight, her heart pounding against her chest.

"Adrielle! Adrielle wake up," someone said, their hands clamped firmly on her wrists.

Adrielle opened her eyes. Coco's round brown eyes locked onto hers.

"You're ok. You had another nightmare," Coco said, and waited for this to sink in.

The eyes staring back were troubled, but calm. Large chocolate pools of compassion. She took a moment to process they weren't her mother's, but her sister's. The freckles, like sprinkles of cinnamon scattered on the bridge of Coco's nose gave her away.

Adrielle looked frantically around the room, cold fear gripping her. The smell of molten wax and caramel clung to the air. She was burrowed into the crumpled sheets on Coco's bed, an open textbook beside her. She searched out ordinary objects to anchor her and confirm she was safe, an anxiety controlling trick she'd learned to use. There was Coco's dresser, her jewelry box. The leaning mirror. The pile of clothes on the floor. She was aware Coco was watching her. She turned back to Coco, this time feeling less anxious.

A sharp rap sounded against the glass. Startled, they turned to the window.

"It's only the storm," Coco said, stroking Adrielle's arms.

"No, listen," Adrielle insisted. "This isn't the first time I've heard it."

Coco walked to the window. "It's a big black bird, a raven I think. It must have hit the window." She returned to the bed and sat beside Adrielle. "I thought your nightmares had stopped."

Adrielle shook her head.

"Do you want to talk about it?"

"No," she said, pushing away the look of terror on her mother's face. "Just a dream."

Coco looked unsure but returned to her seat at the dressing table. She moved her can of soda off to one side and unfurled a long black carrying case containing her Sephora makeup brushes, then rifled through an assortment of beauty products: base, eye shadows, blush, mascara, and liquid liner. In the far corner, a caramel scented candle burned.

Adrielle closed her textbook and checked her phone for missed calls or texts. She sighed, disappointed.

"What's wrong?" Coco asked, watching her through the dresser mirror.

"Nothing. *Rien*," she said in French. "Josh was supposed to be here an hour ago."

Coco sighed, her bracelet-clad arms clinking as she picked up the can of Coke Zero and sipped at the fizz. "Come with me tonight."

"*Je deteste les parties—*"

"Really?" Coco lifted an eyebrow. "That's so annoying."

"What?"

"*That!* Speaking French just now. Most people speak English." Coco set the coke can down and pushed the bangles as far up her arms as they'd go. "These are so noisy."

"How can you stand them?" Adrielle asked.

"My bracelets?"

"Yeah, your shackles."

"Shackles?" Coco brushed her manicured hands over her forearms. "They're pretty. My camouflage, my scars are less noticeable this way."

Adrielle stood up and cleared the piles of clothes on the floor.

"I was gonna do that," Coco said, applying her new Fenty Beauty foundation with a brush. "Not sure what to wear."

"I can tell," Adrielle said, slipping the castaway dresses back onto hangers.

"Wish my skin was as perfect as yours."

"No, you don't. You know how people stare," Adrielle muttered, blinking at her reflection as she passed the mirror. She paused, gathered her long white hair into a ponytail, and slipped on the elastic hair band she wore on her wrist. "Better." She made a sour puckered face.

"We all have things we don't like about ourselves," Coco snapped, tugging at her polka-dotted robe sleeves. "Why is Josh standing you up again? I would've ditched him months ago."

"He's just late."

"Really? If that's the way you wanna see it. But of all days." She slipped her robe off and hung it on the edge of her mirror. "You excited it's almost your birthday?"

Adrielle shrugged. "I guess. I'm getting old."

Coco assumed the gimme-a-break expression.

Adrielle gazed at the pictures of their friends pinned on the wall by the dresser. Every one of them seemed to have carved a pathway for themselves. "I don't know what I'm supposed to do with the rest of my life."

"I know, right? 'Cause everybody else does. And you? You have no idea."

"You know what I mean. There's so much pressure. I'm applying to colleges, and I don't even know what to study. That seems out of sequence."

"Sign up for art or something. I look at your drawings and wish I were that good."

Adrielle shook her head. "What I mean is, I don't know where I fit in. It's like I don't fit in anywhere. I'm this blaringly white appendage everyone stares at."

"You're beautiful."

"Mom always said—"

"Mom?" Coco's voice softened. "Is that what this is about?"

"I miss her."

"Me too." Coco said, "but it's time to move on. Let the past go."

Adrielle checked again for messages and tossed her phone on the bed.

Coco wagged her finger. "Bad Karma. That's what comes if you dwell on painful things. Leave it behind, Adie." She swiveled on her makeup stool to face her mirror. "We can't change the past, but we can make peace with it."

"I wish I could. If only we'd . . ."

"Stop. We were just kids. The fire wasn't anyone's fault." Coco rested her head in her hands and closed her eyes.

"The nightmares are getting worse," Adrielle said softly. "It's every time I close my eyes now. They're so real. I feel this dark oppressive being getting closer."

Adrielle faced the window and struggled to keep her voice steady. "Everything turns cold and dark. No matter where I go, they're following me."

"Who is?"

"I don't know. Something terrible I can't get away from. It's like it's inside me. This dark presence that wants to take over. Kind of like death."

"Oh god, Adie—Mom's death hit you hard."

"You're thinking I should go back to that shrink," Adrielle said in a low and timid voice.

"You have to move on."

"There's no moving on from this. That's why my dreams are things I don't speak about."

"Try not to overthink. All we can do is live."

Adrielle shook her head. "For years I believed she was coming back. Even after they'd told us."

Coco drew in a long breath. "I didn't want to believe it either."

"Wish I could go back and change it. She was the only person who accepted I was different."

"That's not true. All that matters is what *you* think. I wish you'd confront life without living in the past. It's the only way we get to where we're supposed to be." Coco held Adrielle's gaze. "With your birthday tomorrow, I've been thinking about her too. I wonder all the time what it would've been like. Having parents." She crunched the Coke can, tossed it into the trashcan, and swiped at the corner of her eye.

"If Mom were here, she'd tell you you're going to have to make the choice. Either embrace who you are or spend the rest of your life hiding from it."

"That's the whole point, I'm not sure who I am."

Coco opened her bottom drawer and pulled out a shiny red box. "For your birthday. It's from Mom."

"Mom?" Adrielle said, taking the box but afraid to open it.

Coco nodded. "She made me promise if anything happened, you got this when you turned eighteen. She said it belongs to you." She sighed. "It was the last thing I grabbed." Her eyes drifted to her arms. She tugged at her sleeves.

Adrielle followed her gaze. The scars. "Oh, Coco . . . and you kept it from me all this time?"

"I was going to tell you years ago, but I was worried because of your nightmares. Don't even *think* about not opening it until midnight," she warned.

Adrielle lifted the lid off the box and gasped. Inside was a gold pendant watch on a long chain. She inspected the face closely.

"It's broken." Coco shrugged. "I took it to the watch repair at the mall but they couldn't fix it. They said they'd never seen one like it."

Adrielle slipped the chain over her head. Her breath caught. A rush of heat spread from the point of contact through her entire body and settled in the spot between her shoulder blades. Her hand went to it like a bee sting, but there was nothing there, only a piercing needling burn that disappeared as quickly as it came.

Chapter 2

Achaea, Greece – 241 BCE

THE CHANTING HAD stopped. Low murmurs drifted into the hall. Most of it was muffled, words she didn't understand. But her name was mentioned, and then a rush of commotion. Voices erupted like fireworks. Adrielle blinked, her attention secured on the meeting room.

She crept along the length of the wall. A floorboard creaked under her foot, and she froze, not knowing if she should run, or fess up. Afraid of getting caught, she backed up quickly and stumbled into something behind her.

She turned as a young man helped steady her. He was tall and hard, his sinewy arms like steel. He pressed a finger to his lips. Without warning, he grabbed her hand and pulled her further into the shadows. A warm sensation coursed through her body. Something about his touch was familiar. She jerked her hand away, embarrassed and angry someone had caught her watching, and pressed her back against the cold stone.

"Who are you?" she asked in a hushed tone.

He shook his head and with a deliberate motion, turned his attention to the meeting room. Adrielle also turned, and they stood there for what seemed a long time.

Adrielle looked back at the young man—to apologize, to ask what they were doing in that room, and he was gone. Only a silver feather lay in his place. Adrielle picked it up. It sparkled in the dim light. The tiny barbs glittering like diamonds.

The absence of sound roared overhead. She turned toward the meeting room. Everyone there had disappeared too. All that remained were the candles, layers and layers of molten wax. Vaporous coils of smoke replaced the flame from minutes before, and the smell of melted wax burned in her nose.

Achaea, Greece – 231 BCE
Ten years Later

A HARROWING, INTRUSIVE sound exploded into the night like a canon tearing up the hillside and penetrating the thick castle walls into the small bedroom where Adrielle lay sleeping. Loud and piercing, the clanging noise infused into her subconscious.

Desperate to cling onto shreds of her dream, Adrielle pulled her pillow tightly over her head. "What is that sound?" She moaned, willing it away. But the brash vibrations swelled in her ears until they became an undeniable force.

Adrielle reached to nudge Haden, thinking he knew what the harrowing sound was, but the spot on the bed was cold. Through filtered moonlight, she saw the bottom sheet was stretched taut, the damask quilt folded neatly back the way she left it for him at night, meaning, he hadn't been to bed. Shivers of panic tingled in her veins. She fought to keep calm; panic would only cloud her mind.

She raised her head off the pillow and concentrated. *A bell?* Yes, that was it.

More alert, Adrielle scanned the room. Her silk robe was draped over the foot of the bed. Her green velvet dress was on the chair at her bedside, where she'd taken it off the night before. She picked up her leatherbound journal on the night table beside the bed and examined her last entry. She exhaled; everything was exactly as she'd left it.

Everything *looked* right, at a glance, but somehow it felt different than when she'd gone to bed. She closed her eyes, desperate to search her mind for answers as she retraced her steps from the night before.

It didn't make sense. She'd been certain all she'd wake to was the comfort of Haden's embrace. But now this: the tolling bell, an unslept bed. She feared something terrible had happened. That, like the dusting of ash after a volcano eruption, there would be no containing the aftermath.

Adrielle pushed her hair off her forehead and rubbed her eyes. She could barely make out Haden's silhouette. He was a frozen statue across the room, staring out the window. A wedge of moonlight illuminated one side of his face. A deep furrow was carved on his brow.

She studied the way his shoulders slumped, the way his eyes probed about in the dark. He wasn't passively staring at all. He was on alert. And he was wearing his cloak.

Adrielle grabbed her dressing gown—an early wedding gift from Haden—and draped it around her shoulders. Whatever the problem was, there had to be a solution. She sucked in a quick breath as her feet touched the cold stone floor.

She wandered over to him and stood, her eyes following his to the town-site below. Instead of the usual hazy glow cast from the occasional oil lamp in the dawn light, embers ignited and spun like fireflies into the dark, illuminating the town square into a massive fireball. Adrielle shivered.

Haden slipped his arm around her waist.

"What's—?" She saw Domenikos by the tower and sucked in a paralyzing breath. She had to run.

She concentrated on keeping her breath slow and steady as shivers caused her teeth to chatter. Haden tightened his embrace, their eyes meeting briefly. Before she could read what was in them, he gently kissed the top of her head and turned back to his surveillance.

How could she have been blindsided? Plans for her upcoming wedding had been enough to blanket the encroaching danger.

Seemingly overnight, a vibrant city filled with children's laughter had become a graveyard massacre. Wailing children and women's lamenting screams filled the air.

When radicals smuggled into the city in droves, Haden had warned her about the possibility of a coup. He'd said as the leader's daughter, she'd need to escape for safety. But she wouldn't hear of it. She'd rationalized this was her home. Now she realized how naïve she'd been.

These radicals were cunning and calculating rivals. Like wolves in sheep's clothing they hid under the protective shield of the Achaean Act with the pretense of seeking refuge. Instead they sought out those with hostility toward the Act, those who felt their inherent freedoms had been compromised because of it.

Most didn't understand if the Achaean Act wasn't strictly followed, the threat of total annihilation for Achaeans was real. This was the very reason it was set into place years ago by the Unity, the leaders of Achaea. The Achaean Act was the last chance for peace between mortals and Achaeans.

Not long after the radical infiltration, hushed whispers of discord circulated amongst the people. They festered, destroying the general sense of kinship and camaraderie. Contrary to popular belief that budding opposition would fizzle out, under the expert guidance of a true deviant, Domenikos, the hostility erupted into chaos. Anarchy. Betrayal.

Naturally, there would be no wedding now; it would be a miracle if they could escape with their lives. Adrielle wished she'd listened. If only she could turn back time.

As though reading her thoughts, Haden squeezed Adrielle's hand.

The contagion of terror was even more visible in the first rays of daybreak. Far below Haden's castle, Domenikos stood in his natural Achaean bird form, with his wings spread wide. Elegantly poised and coolly calm, his intimidating stance challenged opposition. He looked as if he was fiercely aware of his surroundings and ready to pounce.

The three Tribunal leaders, wearing heavy iron collars with inner sharp spikes, were tied to one large stake next to Domenikos. The collars were chained together and bound so tightly, if one were to try to hang to avoid impending torture, the other two would strangle to death.

A mound of dry wood covered the foot of the stake.

A crowd was already gathered in the sliver of the rising sun. Domenikos pulled out his prized knife, the one with the silver filigree hilt. It was his hunting knife. His torture weapon. He twisted the needle-like blade until the metal glinted in a ray of morning light.

The crowd hushed. They watched in horror as Domenikos paused, a brazen smile stretching across his face as he savored the moment. He was an expert showman, and *torture* was his specialty.

Only Haden, as the keeper of the sacred *Book of Feathers,* and the three Tribunal leaders now on the stake, were privy to the entirety of Domenikos' audacities, for all crimes or acts of treason committed by any Achaean, were recorded within the book's binding.

Domenikos plunged his blade deep into the first Tribunal's side—Aaron, the strongest and most revered Achaean leader. Adrielle's father.

The flapping of the banners was the only sound as Adrielle, along with the crowd below, stared in disbelief. This harrowing silence was broken by a gurgle of blood rising into Aaron's mouth as he choked. He folded at the waist, wrenching on the collars on the other two Tribunal leaders. Deadly spikes bit into the other Tribunals' flesh, but they kept steady expressions, as if determined to accept their fate with dignity.

Domenikos raised his bloody knife to the crowd, savoring his victory.

Adrielle's legs buckled under her. Haden lunged and caught her while she gasped for air.

Unwilling to accept this fate, Adrielle staggered to her bed and collapsed onto it. She stared angrily at her hands, trembling excuses for appendages. She shoved them into her pockets. Nestled in the silky fabric, she felt the crisp, sharp, edge of an envelope. *What?* She tore open the envelope and read.

> Adrielle—your life is in danger. The answers you seek are in the ancient writings. Only you can delve under the surface and determine what is real, for the truth is hidden by perspective.
> ~A.

A? She re-read the words, trying to decipher what they meant.

"Save yourselves and fly away!" Domenikos taunted, his voice carrying up into the tower room.

Note in hand, Adrielle returned to Haden's side. Domenikos was lighting the mounds of gathered wood at the foot of the stake, making good on his promise: that each impending torture would be more heinous. Giant flames licked at the three Tribunal leaders' feet. He heated heavy tongs in the fire and pressed them onto their armpits, holding it there until their skin seared and blistered. The Tribunals' agonized screams split through the silence.

"I can't watch my father—" Adrielle turned away.

Haden vowed vengeance under his breath.

A sound came from the hall. Footsteps. Adrielle gazed at the slightly ajar door. A stealthy shadow in the hall approached. Adrielle shoved the note into her pocket and took a step toward the door.

"Get away from there," Haden barked.

The shadow in the hall stopped moving.

Haden strode to the elaborately carved table at the foot of their bed where a large leatherbound book lay. Adrielle stared at it. In disbelief. Where had it come from? The words, *The Book of Feathers* were written in highly stylized gilded font, with a four-feathered crest embossed underneath. *Were the ancient writings the note referred to in this book?*

She'd heard stories of this book, of its alleged mystical powers, but until now believed it was a myth. Why did Haden have it? Had her father given it to him? Allegedly, it dated back to the first Achaean, thousands of years before man. Rumored to be a collection of ancient manuscripts containing the hidden secrets of time travel.

Haden traced over the embossed feathered crest with his fingers. He looked her in the eyes. "We need to get you out of here."

Their eyes held, the air heavy with things unsaid.

"There is no turning back," he said. "Domenikos will have sealed off the city walls."

Feeling powerless, Adrielle twined her fingers through his and squeezed tight.

Haden bent over the book and leafed through the pages. "This is it." He faced Adrielle and chanted the words of the spell in a low rhythmic murmur.

The screams from outside silenced as though time itself stood still. Haden reached between his shoulder blades and scraped at a small spot near the center of his back until a feather came loose from beneath his skin. Adrielle watched spellbound. He pulled out a crimson feather, placed it on her palm, and folded her trembling fingers until they curled around it and her nails cut deep into her skin.

"This belongs to you," he said, lifting a long gold chain hidden under his cloak. "It's a chronometer, a tool that will enable you to travel anywhere. Guard it at all cost." He placed it around her neck, and a shock surged through Adrielle.

She trembled in fear as the light escaped her body, lit up the tower room, shot out like lightning, and split the sky.

Haden pulled Adrielle close and pressed his forehead to hers. "I'll find you."

WITH HIS BACK pressed against the stone wall in the hall outside Adrielle's chamber, Angelo had a slivered view of the bedroom. He scanned the details of the room with his mind in search of the mystical book.

There it was, on the table at the foot of the bed. Angelo clenched his fists. He was too late. Adrielle may be safe for now, but only for a time. She might never survive without the book. And without the chronometer, he doubted he'd ever find her again. *Damn.*

IN THE DARKENED room with invisible boundaries, the woman stared into the vast nothingness. She felt his dark and sinister presence approaching.

"Tell me where she is," Domenikos said.

She sat unmoving and said nothing.

Are you afraid I'll hurt her? You must know by now, there's only one thing I want."

"You are a liar. There's no end to what you want—I know you better than anyone. Do what you will with me, but I'll never tell you where she is."

Domenikos slapped her face, his thick gold ring ripping her skin. She could feel blood tracking down her cheek. She flinched, and he paced around her.

"Let's go," he said to his henchman. "We're wasting our time here."

"What should we do with *her*?"

"I don't know yet. Leave her for now," Domenikos said. He jerked as if struck by lightning and lost his balance, swaying for a moment.

The henchman eyed him. "You okay?"

"More than okay," Domenikos said. "We're in luck."

"How do you mean?"

The corner of his lips turned up. "I've found her."

"Are you sure?" the henchman asked.

"Completely. I feel her strength pulsing through my veins."

"Strong enough to track her?"

"Let's go." Domenikos laughed. "This is turning out to be a welcomed surprise."

Chapter 3

FLORIDA — PRESENT TIME

DOWNSTAIRS, THE GRANDFATHER clock chimed eight-thirty.

"It can't be," Adrielle said, tapping the glass on her cell phone with her black fingernail. "I don't understand. Something must have happened."

"Text him," Coco said.

"No way." Adrielle flopped onto her back. "I'd look desperate. Like I thought he was standing me up."

"He is."

Adrielle folded her arms behind her head and stared up at the ceiling. Coco had replaced a bare bulb with a delicate glass chandelier.

"Don't."

"What?"

"*That.*" Coco gestured with the hand holding her kabuki brush. A fine mist of powder scattered and drifted to the floor. "Pretend it doesn't matter."

"It doesn't."

"He isn't worth the trouble."

"He'll show, you'll see," Adrielle said, hoping like mad he would. She raced over her last conversation with Josh . . .

"We're celebrating my birthday tonight, aren't we?"

He hesitated. "Sure, I'll be by later."

"What time?" she pressed.

"Oh, I don't know . . . I've got some stuff to take care of first."

"Seven?"

"Yeah, maybe? Sure. Seven. Be ready," he said, stroking her face. "Eighteen huh?" He leaned in for a kiss. "We'll ring it in at midnight."

A text chimed into Coco's phone. She skimmed it and groaned. "And why am I not surprised?"

"What?"

Coco reread the text. "It's Veda."

"And?"

Coco hesitated. "I hate for you to find out like this."

"Oh, god. Now I'm worried."

"Josh just showed up at the party."

"No way." Adrielle jerked up, the knot in her stomach hardening.

"Veda wouldn't make that up."

"She's gossipy."

"Not about that."

"He said he had an errand."

"Unbelievable," Coco said, stepping over the hairdryer on the floor and heading for the pile of clothes in the center of her room. "It's just like you to give him a pass." She dug deep underneath until she reached the perfect dress. "Here." She tossed it to Adrielle. "There's only one way to find out."

Adrielle held up the dress, a clingy black shift dress with a plunging neckline. "It's pretty, but too revealing." She tossed it back to Coco.

"That's the point. Adie, you *gotta* call him out on this. It's not cool." Coco stepped into her walk-in closet and clicked through her hangers. "I smell Scarlett behind this," she shouted, her voice too loud. She re-appeared in a blue mini skirt and a blouse with long sleeves, her expression serious. "Don't go soft on him." She held Adrielle's eyes and tossed her the dress. "We're getting to the bottom of this."

There was a soft knock on the door.

"Everyone decent?" Layla asked. She poked her white-haired head into the room and held up a small package. "This came for you, Adrielle." Her eyes drifted to the mound of clothes scattered on the floor and then swung to Coco. "Oh my," she breathed in sharply. Coco's bra was visible under her sheer blouse. "It's—" Her face reddened, a wide toothy smile forming on her face.

Adrielle and Coco stifled giggles. They'd often discussed Layla's conservative taste. But it wasn't just her reaction that made them chuckle. Layla's new dentures, designed to give a more youthful smile, made her front teeth larger and looking like a caricature.

She shuffled to Adrielle and handed her the package.

"Thanks," Adrielle said, inspecting the brown paper wrapping closely. "How did it get here? There's no stamp or return address."

"It was on the front step when I got home. Oh"—she held up a crooked arthritic finger and shook it—"I have something else for you too."

Layla shuffled to the door and waited for it to latch behind her.

"Did you see the look on her face?" Coco chortled. "She looked straight at my boobs."

Adrielle ignored her and turned back to the package. "Strange"—she wrinkled her brow—"kind of looks like my writing."

"You sure you didn't leave it there yourself? You know, the secret admirer just in case?" Coco asked, opening the doors on both sides of her stand-alone jewelry case.

"In case of what?" Adrielle asked.

"Insurance. In case Josh doesn't get you anything."

Adrielle picked up a pillow and tossed it at Coco, who ducked, and seemingly undaunted, continued rifling through layers of necklaces. She selected three beaded chains and slipped them over her head. "They cover my chest. We'll see if this satisfies the warden."

"Shh . . . she'll be back any minute."

"So?"

"So, you'll hurt her feelings. You're sore because she's always on your case. *And* she's probably right. Your wild streak's gonna get you in trouble."

Coco shimmied up to her full-length mirror. She pivoted around and planted her fists on her hips. "Well?"

"Doesn't rattle," Adrielle said, shaking the package near her ear.

"I meant my jewels! Open it already."

"Better. And no, it's not officially my birthday until midnight. This present is gonna wait." She cupped her hands around the package. "Bet it's a book." She set it aside.

"Can't believe you'd get excited over a book," Coco said, tucking lip gloss into her cross-body bag. She found a stick of gum in the side pocket and popped it in her mouth. "Hurry." She slipped the purse over her head. "We want to catch him red-handed."

"You're so dramatic." Adrielle laughed. "I'll go. But only because I'm gonna prove you wrong." She took her t-shirt off and picked up Coco's dress.

Layla pushed open the door and stood in the doorway.

"Those stairs have gotten steeper," she wheezed. "Oh good, I'm just in time." She held up a wire hanger with a clear plastic covering. "I took measurements from your clothes. Tailored it in here and there. And sent it to the drycleaners." She fumbled to remove the plastic, her knotty fingers not co-operating.

Adrielle and Coco exchanged a look as Layla shuffled to the bed.

Underneath the plastic was a long white dress yellowed with age. "It's white brocade." She gave them a toothy smile. "And look, it even has a matching jacket." She placed it all on Adrielle's lap. "I was every girl's envy when I wore it. And since it's your eighteenth . . . well—"

Coco choked on her gum.

"Thought you could use a nice outfit for your birthday celebration," Layla said, a whiff of Chantilly perfume wafting as she settled down next to Adrielle.

"She couldn't," Coco stammered.

"It's my pleasure." Layla grinned.

Coco stared back and forth between her slinky black dress and the white brocade.

Adrielle shot her a warning look. "Thanks." She ran her hand along the yellowed fabric. "It's beautiful."

Coco winced.

"You really like it?" Layla beamed.

"Yes, thank you," Adrielle said, avoiding eye contact with Coco, who was making quick slashing gestures across her throat.

"I thought you might." Layla stared at her bony hands. "Guess these old fingers have some use after all." She squeezed Adrielle's knee, stood up, and took a moment to massage her lower back. She looked at the pile of clothes on the floor and then to Coco. "I'll get out of your way so you can get to it. Don't stay out too late, wouldn't want you girls to get into trouble."

"You've got to be kidding," Coco sputtered as soon as the door closed. "Thanks Layla. It's beautiful. You can't actually wear that."

"I'm not hurting her feelings," Adrielle insisted, taking the dress off the hanger and unzipping it.

"You can't." Coco winced. "Everyone will—"

"They already do."

THE SMELL OF cigarettes and booze slammed into Adrielle like a cement wall. The house seemed to be room-to-room kids holding red plastic cups. Adrielle followed closely as Coco wove through the entry toward the living area.

Normally, Adrielle found loud music irritating and was surprised to find it more of a relief. The noise level made it impossible to continue her internal dialogue.

Josh wasn't a player. But why hadn't he called?

Veda, an Asian American with a penchant for gossip, beelined to them, nodding at schoolmates along the path. Her eyes widened at Adrielle's dress then caught Coco's glare and stifled a laugh. She hooked her arm through Coco's and with a flip of her shiny black hair, led the way to Kate, Dave, and Liz, who were clustered at the other end of the room, red cups in hand.

Adrielle noticed her friends were dressed in jeans and t-shirts. She should have known Coco always overdressed. Feeling out of place, she surveyed the room and was relieved to not see Scarlett nor Josh.

"Whoa," Dave said, his eyes stopping on Adrielle's dress.

Liz smacked him on the chest.

"Ouch." He rubbed the spot. "*What* in god's name are you wearing?"

"Guess I underestimated this," Adrielle muttered. She was used to blatant stares, but people were doing double takes and laughing.

Coco leaned into the others. "Layla's coming out dress. Adie didn't want to hurt her feelings." The others exchanged knowing glances.

"Shut up. It's the cutest thing ever," Kate said. She was a pretty Irish-Catholic redhead with petite features and bright blue eyes. "Look, how it accents her eyes."

Adrielle lowered her eyes quickly.

"Shhhh . . . no one say anything about the ugly dress," Liz said, her slurred speech too loud.

Coco crossed her arms and shot her a warning look.

"Why did you make her?" Liz persisted.

Coco gasped.

"You outta your mind?" Liz sputtered, flailing her arms. "You know how sensitive Adrielle is about her looks."

Veda rolled her eyes. "Ironic isn't it, coming from someone who doesn't give a squat about appearance."

"Not fair. I care." Liz licked her fingers and smoothed down her unruly curls, then pushed up her thick, black-rimmed glasses.

Dave pulled her aside. "Forget about it. Veda's still sore you refused her makeover."

"Tweezers aren't my thing. And makeup? Don't get me started."

"It was Layla's. She tailored it," Coco said.

"Oooohhh," the others chirped.

Kate leaned in. "Love that thrifting thing. You look beautiful, Adie."

"That's what I meant. She's hot," Dave explained.

"How would you know?" Liz asked, taking in his pressed canary yellow shirt with tails neatly tucked into his belted madras shorts.

"I may be gay, but I'm not blind," he snapped, and the two began an on-going quick-witted banter.

"Did you see the albino?" one of two girls *en route* to the kitchen sniggered.

"Yeah, she lives with a cat lady," the other said.

"Cat lady?"

"Ya. Her mom died in a fire, and the courts sent her to live there. Her sister too. I think she's got twenty of them."

"Ewww gross."

"I'm going to the bathroom." Adrielle wove her way through the crowd.

"Who invited the Albino?"

"Didn't she start a fire? Burn up her mother or something?"

"Think so—her sister has these scars. So gross."

Scarlett. Adrielle fumed. She wandered to the end of the bathroom line, pretending not to notice the side jabbing reactions.

Josh? She stepped toward the center of the room. *Oh my god, oh my god.* He was in the corner with Scarlett.

She backed away and tripped over someone. A stranger's hand steadied her, then encircled her waist and lead her down the hall.

"Hey, wait a—" Adrielle struggled between protesting and the relief she felt as the stranger pulled her into a small parlor room.

"What do ya think you're doing?" She met his green eyes, then peeked through an opened door and was relieved to see it was a bathroom. She walked in and locked the door.

Scissors. I need scissors. She riffled through drawers and cabinets. There they were, in a first aid kit. She exhaled. The cuticle scissors were small, but sharp.

Adrielle snipped at the fabric of her dress just above the knees until chunks of the brocade material dropped to the floor.

How could I have been so stupid? Long dresses are useless relics. She threw the excess fabric into the trash and inspected the hemline in the mirror.

Good God. The jagged hemline resembled Charlie Brown's smile. It needed a total redo. She undressed quickly, smoothed the fabric out on the floor, and trimmed the dress as best she could. She recut the hem, then slipped the dress and jacket on. *Better.*

She poked her head out the door, relieved to find the guy was gone and braced for another onslaught of derogatory comments. She hated the gossip circling around school. Arguably, her group of friends made for an unseemly alliance, but their friendship was thick and cemented, their bond welding tighter with each passing year. Across the room her friends were laughing and enjoying themselves. *Good,* the focus would be off her.

The others looked up in time to see the trail of snickers as Adrielle passed by.

"Wowza" Dave sputtered, "You cut the bottom off."

Adrielle felt her cheeks warm.

"Dude, you ok?" Coco asked.

Liz balled up her fists and pointed. "Josh is over there, in the corner with Sssscarlett. She's such a bully."

"Shhh—" Dave scolded.

Liz jabbed him. "Why shhh? Everyone knows. We've all been her targets."

Rubbing his chest, Dave continued his banter with her until Kate shot them a warning look. "Behave."

"Are you going to confront him?" Coco whispered to Adrielle.

"God no, I . . ." Adrielle shook her head. Confrontations of any kind made her nervous. She looked down at her knobby knees. *How could she—in her getup?* She fought off fresh tears.

"To Adrielle's birthday," Liz said, raising her red cup in toast.

"You two want a drink?" Veda asked Coco, running her fingers down her silky hair. "She's seen him, so the worst is over. Oh-my-god." She giggled. "Three o'clock. Look what Erika's wearing. Friggin' ugly."

"Snap chat that shit," Dave agreed. He turned to Liz. "Did I tell you? The Stella McCartney on *Project Runway* was awesome."

Kate signaled that Coco and Adrielle still didn't have drinks.

"Oh, sorry." Veda turned toward the kitchen.

"I've got this," Coco said, placing a hand on Veda's arm and disappearing into the crowd.

COCO MANEUVERED BETWEEN bodies, wedging her way up to the large granite island.

The entire surface was cluttered with junk food and liquor bottles. She passed over the booze and reached between two Goths for the bottle of Coke Zero.

"Allow me," one of them said, beating her to it. He lifted a red cup from the stack and unscrewed the Coke. "Embellishments?" He waved his hand over the assortment of liquor.

"Designated driver," she said, mesmerized by his long lashes.

"One can't hurt, can it?" He flashed a radiant smile.

She shook her head and studied him as he poured. His snaggle tooth could be considered cute, but it also resembled a fang.

"Two please," she said.

He filled one cup and waited for the fizz to subside. "One for sis?" he purred.

His voice had the haunting quality of an owl. He met her eyes and shifted them to the room where Adrielle was. He raised one eyebrow.

"Not the perfect birthday, is it." He slid the plastic cup to her and picked up another one.

Sis? Birthday? Coco shivered. She wanted to ask *how* he knew but didn't want to engage in more conversation. She turned away and gazed at the crowd.

Under ordinary circumstances, she may have found him attractive. But tonight, an alarm blared. Of one thing she was certain: she hadn't seen him before.

"Here you go." He held out the second drink. She didn't take it right away.

Even in the dim lighting, she could see the flashes of green in his eyes as he gazed at her with a wry expression. He wore his hair without a part, slicked straight back to accentuate his milky white skin. Though he was Goth, definitely and clearly Goth, he could have been a model for a foreign fashion designer. Not only was he fastidiously groomed, he was totally bad ass. The faint traces of facial hair pebbled on his jaw and upper lip gave him a rugged, sexy, appearance.

Still, there was something about him that was strange for a Goth. He was too smooth. Too debonair. And she couldn't get past how quickly his attention had breezed toward Adrielle. Collecting her wits, she took the second cup and turned to the living room.

The Goth's stare burned a hole in her back. She maneuvered awkwardly to Adrielle, concentrating on not tripping over her shoes. He'd rattled her, and in the overcrowded room, her four-inch stilettos felt like she was toddling on cobblestones.

How had he known? Even under close scrutiny, most people never made the sister-connection. Looks-wise, Adrielle and Coco were as different as sisters could be. Where Adrielle's hair was white, hers was ebony.

And what was up with the birthday remark? After a bout with online bullying, Adrielle shut down her Facebook profile, so it was impossible for him to know that way.

Coco handed Adrielle her drink, Coke splashing over the rim.

"What's wrong? Your hand's trembling. Did you see Josh? Scarlett?" Adrielle asked.

Coco leaned in. "No—nothing like that. Don't look now, but the creep at the island knew we were sisters. *And* he mentioned your birthday."

"Which one?" Adrielle asked. "Oh." She lowered her gaze; her face turning pink.

"I said—don't look," Coco snapped.

"Sorry—but he's staring right at me."

"Who is?" Liz asked, pressing her cheek against Adrielle's and following her gaze to the Goth's hard stare.

"Don't know him. Never seen him before," Adrielle mumbled.

"What's rattling you?" Kate asked. "Don't know that I've ever seen you two like this."

"Like what?" Coco snapped.

"Disheveled."

"Over there," Liz said, her voice booming as she pointed toward the kitchen. "The Goth. He's staring."

Dave pressed her arm down.

"Shhhhh," Adrielle and Coco hissed.

"Does anyone know him?" Liz asked, lowering her voice a notch.

Veda, Kate, and Dave looked toward the kitchen. From where they were standing, they had a clear view.

"Nope."

"You guys." Coco placed a firm hand on Veda's shoulder and pivoted her away. "You're being too obvious."

"To be clear . . . nobody knows him?" Liz persisted, pushing her thick glasses high up on the bridge of her nose and squinting. "*Them,* I mean. There are two of them staring now."

"I told you, *no.* Never seen either one. The taller one knows it's Adrielle's birthday. And that we're sisters."

"Goths," Kate said dismissively. "So creepy."

"Why?" Dave snickered. "Because it's Florida and they only wear black?"

"His voice," Coco whispered. "It's *too* smooth. *Too*—I don't want to know. But trust me on this—something's not right. Look—no don't look—he's leering at Adie like he's going to gobble her up." She shuddered and ducked behind Dave.

"I agree." Liz said, slipping her hand into her handbag. She pulled out her mace. "He could be a predator."

Veda laughed. "Not so strange given what she's wearing. Everyone's gawking."

"Hot," Dave insisted. "Even with the retro thing, Adrielle's definitely hot."

"Not like that. Stalker style," Coco persisted, glancing back to the kitchen. "Oh no." She gasped, stretching her neck to see past the crowd. "Where'd they go? They couldn't have vanished. Any of you see them?"

"Nope," everyone said.

"Chillax." Kate giggled. "Everyone's so uptight. What happened to having a good time?"

"Kate's right. Everyone chill," Veda said. "Adrielle can handle herself."

ADRIELLE WASN'T SO sure. Tonight was turning into one huge mistake.

"Wish I'd brought the selfie stick," Dave said, scrolling through his pics.

Veda jabbed Coco on the side. "Guess who just went upstairs?"

"The Goths?"

"Noooo." She glanced at Adrielle.

"Ooooooh—" Coco winced.

The knot in Adrielle's stomach tightened. She'd been wrestling with what to do since she'd seen Josh. Why would he lie? "I'm going up." She handed Coco her cup, the Coke spilling over the rim and onto her dress.

Coco grabbed her arm. "You sure about this?"

"No, but I'm going."

She looked up from the bottom of the staircase. The treads seemed to go on forever. *Why hadn't she thought this through?* She tugged on the hem of her dress. Now it was uncomfortably short. And she was hot, the fabric clinging to her like saran wrap. She peeled off the matching jacket and ditched it on the bottom post.

Determined to break up with Josh, she headed upstairs.

"WE HAVE TO stop her," Haden said, seeking out Monika's gaze from under the folds of her eyelids. Like coved hoods, they made her ebony eyes appear darker.

"Haden, even *you* can't stop this," Monika said. "Let history play out the way it was meant to. Neither you nor I can stop the journey she has embarked on."

Haden pressed the weathered leatherbound book to his chest. He regretted the moment he'd sent her back. He regretted everything.

THOUGH THE MUSIC was blasting throughout the downstairs, the upstairs hallway was surprisingly quiet. Adrielle stood on the top tread, staring down the length of the hallway, and tugged at the hem. *What was she doing?*

The exterior of Scarlett's house appeared large, but the reality overwhelmed. Nothing, not even Scarlett's constant boasting over her family's wealth, could have prepared Adrielle for a home this grand.

The decor was formal and stuffy. The hallway itself was wide and seemed to roll on forever with the mirror-like effect of a parlor trick. Along the length were gilded side tables with silver frames and freshly cut flowers in leaded glass vases. Flanged on either side of the tables were Louis XIV style antique wooden chairs.

The walls dripped with moldings and were lined with dozens of oil portraits. On any other occasion they could have been inspiring to Adrielle who loved art, yet at this moment they made her feel claustrophobic.

Adrielle wiggled her nose. The thick aroma of potpourri saturated the air. She stepped on the Persian runners, probably handmade, and tiptoed along the desolate hall, feeling like an intruder, her heart pumping in her ears. It was like being in a museum after hours. At any given moment she fully expected a hand to clamp down on her shoulder and yank her out.

More than once she considered turning back, but how else would she get to the bottom of this? She continued down the hall, concentrating on making as little noise as possible and wondering why no one else was around. She reached the first door on the right.

Using any distraction possible to postpone the inevitable, Adrielle pulled on the collar of her dress. She stood primly in front of the door. Sparkly glass knobs reflected a myriad of colors in the light. She marveled at the glossiness of the white paint, and the elaborate and intricate molding around the door. This was quite possibly the fanciest home she'd ever been in. Certainly a world away from her own, like the chipped gray paint on the newel post at the bottom of the stairs she dusted every Saturday morning as part of her chores.

She pressed her ear to the wooden door and heard a faint noise on the other side.

She could do this. Was that them on the other side? Were they making out? God, what would she say if they really were inside? Would she confront them or pretend she was looking for a bathroom?

She stared at her shaking hand on the glass doorknob, her white-knuckled fingers trembling. *Dang.* She hated that about herself; how transparent she was. And how scared.

She almost lifted her hand off the glass handle and walked away, but the pull to know the truth was too strong. In one jarring move she turned the knob and stepped inside.

Adrielle stared at the scene and choked down a gasp.

Scarlett and Josh were blindfolded and standing back-to-back in the middle of the room. Thick yellow ropes knotted their wrists and ankles together. Both Goths from the kitchen stood at either side of them.

The taller one with the wide-set green eyes smiled, his snaggletooth gleaming as she walked in. From the look on their faces, they'd been expecting her. He raised a knife to Josh's neck and pressed the sharp edge across Josh's throat. The blindfold loosened.

"No," Adrielle squealed, rushed forward, and skidded to a halt, trembles shooting through her arms and legs. She locked gazes with Josh. His eyes had the fear of a trapped animal.

The tall Goth smirked, the green of his irises burning. He seemed to know she was disoriented and was enjoying every bit of it.

"We've been expecting you," he purred, his voice rolling through her like a steam roller and setting her hair on end.

Chapter 4

Achaea, Greece — 241 BCE

FOR THE FIRST time in his life Haden felt alone. Hopelessly and utterly alone.

With the carnage in the town site over, and immediate danger on hold, the stillness of the day bellowed out to him. He stood at the foot of their bed, regretting he'd propelled Adrielle into the future.

Desperate to keep Adrielle safe, he'd done the unthinkable—he'd given her his swing feather, the most powerful in his wings. This feather of distinction was bequeathed at birth and placed him at the head of the Achaean army, empowering him to watch over the *Book of Feathers*. It was impulsive, yes. But in his defense, it was the only way he could think of to protect and give her strength as he sent her forward.

With time burning a hole in him, more time than he cared to think of without her, he tried to picture Adrielle as she'd looked the morning he'd asked her to marry him. If only memory could conjure her up.

He realized now, in his hurry to save her, he'd overlooked one fatal detail. Without the chronometer, there was no sure way to find her. Determined to uncover a solution, he'd spent every waking moment since her departure, scouring every spell in the *Book of Feathers*, only to find he was doomed.

Due to the sheer volume of statistical possibilities, it was near impossible to find her. But if Adrielle was to use his crimson feather and attempt her hand at time travelling, the infrared light emitted by travelling might detect her location. What were the chances of that? She had no inkling of the power harnessed in his swing feather.

He thought back to the morning he had asked her to marry him. He'd promised himself he would wait. There was a wedge of sunlight glowing on her face. Right there. He stroked a spot on the bed linen. The sun was just appearing and somehow, it always found her first. He sucked in a long inhale. He believed foolishly he could freeze that moment. Memorized every detail: the color of her hair as it fanned out on her pillow. Her smell. Even now, if he closed his eyes, he could feel the heat coming off her body as she lay next to him.

A loud rap at the door startled him.

"Who is it?" he grumbled.

"Angelo." Angelo strode into the room. "The remaining councils are convening in the cave. We must hurry."

Haden raised his hand, demanding a moment to collect himself. He stood up and thought about how he'd planned to wait until sunset to ask her, so they could spend the day together at the lookout and watch the waves crash onto the rocks below. She always loved that. But as she lay in his arms, he realized he couldn't wait.

"Haden—you coming?"

He nodded. "I was thinking about Adrielle. Life with her would have been perfect. She was wise beyond her years and far too stubborn for her own good. She was *all* I wanted."

"Stop it. You speak as though she's dead."

He turned to Angelo. "God no. I couldn't live if that were so."

ANGELO PASSED THE window that looked out onto the charred remains of town. Hearing Haden speak his feelings out loud ripped at his insides. He sucked in a breath and turned a blank face to him.

"I think now how empty I was, the years I spent as a traveller," Haden continued, "but I didn't know it until that moment. She taught me more about love and longing in that short stretch than I've ever known. How it feels to be alive for the very first time."

Angelo's chest tightened. Waves of guilt twisted inside as he watched Haden wrestle with the same emotions and fears he himself felt. "I'm sorry. I know you've never been good at compromises."

Haden nodded. "'Tis true. I'm not as strong as you are, my dear brother."

Haden picked up a silk ribbon from a pillow on the bed and fumbled to tie it around his wrist. "Will you?"

Angelo bit his cheek as he tied it around Haden's wrist.

"Tell the others I am on my way," Haden said, straightening the collar of his cloak as he stood.

Angelo walked out of the room, the intensity of Haden's feelings for Adrielle tormenting him. Before this, he hadn't wanted to accept they were real. That their engagement was real. It was much easier to believe Haden was following Aaron's orders. That it was all for duty.

HADEN CAST A quick look around and took several long strides to the foot of the bed. He lifted the *Book of Feathers* from the table and turned his back on the past.

Chapter 5

Florida – Present Time

WITH HER EYES frozen on the knife at Josh's neck, Adrielle bellowed, "Let him go." She was surprised at her forceful tone.

"Is that a command or a plea?" the Goth challenged, his voice thick with mockery. He raised his eyebrows and ran his tongue across his lips, then pressed the blade further into Josh's neck.

"Nooooo!" Adrielle screamed, raising her hands.

The Goth chuckled, his eyes drifting to her fingers.

She tucked her shaking hands under her arm pits, angry at being so transparent, and stumbled backward.

"So . . . *you* are giving the orders now?" the Goth asked. He removed the knife from Josh's neck.

Josh choked out a long exhale.

Adrielle took a calming breath. She had to keep focused.

The Goth slid his eyes to hers. "Tell me, Princess, did you really think you could hide from me forever?"

He raised his knife and held it close to Josh's neck. His expression said he was enjoying seeing Adrielle on edge. He pressed the metal tip into Josh's flesh. One tiny drop of crimson blood popped out and trickled down Josh's throat.

"Don't." Adrielle lowered her gaze to her toes. She couldn't watch. "I . . . I don't know you."

"But you do." The Goth beamed. "Though I must admit, it's been some time."

"There's some kind of mistake." Adrielle glanced at him and then at Josh. Josh's face had drained of color. "Please don't hurt him. I've never seen you before."

"Do you believe that, Brix?" The Goth exchanged a glance with the other Goth.

Brix, a slighter, paler, version of the first Goth, smirked, then jerked his head side to side.

"Tsk, tsk . . ." The Goth set his foot on the seat of a chair and wiped the blade on the knee of his black jeans, leaving a smear of Josh's blood.

The stain twisted Adrielle's stomach. *This is not the time to get squeamish.* She swallowed hard, the urge to scream escalating. She raised her eyes to him, unprepared for his hypnotic pull. How was it possible he could suck her in—in one gaze? Was he a psychopath?

She had to break the spell. She'd watched enough *CSI* to know showing fear could do no good. Any reaction at all could set him off.

She glanced at the door. Could she make a run for it? Could she save herself if she couldn't save Josh? What about Scarlett? Would someone come to the rescue if they heard her scream?

"Doubtful on all counts," the Goth said, as if he read her thoughts. He jerked his head left to right like a machete. "No one is going to save you darling." He twirled the knife handle until the glint of the metal shone into her eyes and cut Josh and Scarlett's blindfolds with a daring swoop.

Adrielle blinked, doubly shocked he'd known her thoughts, and pulled away the blindfolds. Josh stared back at her, terrified, his wide eyes, questioning.

Behind him, Scarlett's usually pretty face was distorted; pink and swollen like a party balloon squeezed out of shape from the bottom. Her bloodshot eyes trailed blue mascara down her face.

Adrielle masked her fear and turned boldly to the Goth. "What do you want? I'll do anything."

"Anything?" He grinned like a Cheshire Cat, the points of his eyebrows rising slightly. "Give me"—he pointed to Adrielle's chest—"that!"

"This?" Adrielle asked, gripping her watch.

"Yes, that. Your necklace," he said. "Then I'll disappear forever."

"My necklace?" Adrielle gasped, twining her fingers tightly around it. "What do you want with a broken watch?"

The Goth touched the edge of his blade to Josh's neck. Josh moaned. His perspiring upper lip quivered.

"Stop it. It's yours," Adrielle squealed. She lifted the necklace off her neck, and a gut-wrenching sensation of loss overcame her.

The Goth's eyes twinkled like a leprechaun's lust for gold.

"The knife. First give me your knife," Adrielle hissed, dangling the watch.

The Goth lifted the blade away from Josh's neck. Josh's eyes locked onto the blade suspended inches away.

"The ropes—cut them both free," Adrielle ordered, shaking the chain for dramatic effect.

"As you wish." With two swift slashes they were unbound, the ropes curling onto the floor.

A swoosh of relief passed between Scarlett and Josh. Josh pushed his damp hair off his forehead and rubbed his wrists.

Scarlett, apparently frozen with fear, stood unmoving at his back.

The Goth placed the knife flatly on the palms of his hands to proffer it for the exchange.

A loud gong shook the room.

"A grandfather clock?" Adrielle muttered, looking around the room. The gong continued to boom.

Adrielle stared at her watch. *How?* The sound was reverberating from inside her necklace, it spun with tremendous speed until it looked like a globe.

Adrielle raised the pendant to eye level. She stopped the motion, lay the watch onto her palm, and turned it over to expose the face. The second hand was gliding along smoothly, counting down the seconds to midnight.

"It's working?" she mumbled.

"Domenikos, hurry," Brix yelled, his voice brittle with alarm.

"Now that I've found you, you will never be free," the taller Goth said.

Horrific visions of her nightmares filled her mind: the smell of burning flesh and smoke and the onslaught of piercing screams.

"Stop it," she yelled, cupping her hands to her ears. The room was filled with smoke. She searched the room for fire, but it was impossible to see anything. She squeezed her eyes shut as the sting of hot flames took her back to the night of the fire.

She clutched at her chest. With the watch wedged tightly between her heart and her hands, she wished for time to stop. For everything to stop.

Please . . . she wished, with every ounce of will.

From the corner of the room, a soft hum swelled. A voice, chanting. The words were indiscernible, even as the voice grew louder. Then a sudden rap shook the floor with tremendous force.

Everything stopped. The pain. The smell. The burning.

Adrielle opened her eyes. The smoke was gone.

"Bravo." Someone in the corner clapped. "You have impressed us all by finding her, Domenikos, but it is too late."

In one startling swoop, the Goth slid the blade along Josh's throat. Scarlett's piercing scream filled the room as a gush of blood splattered out of Josh's neck and mouth. His eyes rolled back into his sockets, and he fell to the floor with a heavy thud, a ghastly expression frozen on his face.

"Oh my god. Oh my god," Adrielle gasped, her throat tightening in fear. The watch slipped through her fingers and dropped to the floor as she turned to pounce on the Goth. She soared through the air and fell with a thud on the spot where the Goths had stood.

They're gone? How? Only a sulfuric smell remained.

One final gong shook the room.

Adrielle ran to where Josh lay in a lifeless heap.

From the corner of her eyes, she saw Scarlett slithering toward the door.

"I am cursed," Adrielle whimpered.

"Not cursed," the voice in the corner said.

Adrielle's and Scarlett's gazes interlocked before they turned together toward the blinding light illuminating the corner of the room.

Adrielle blinked away spots caused by the bright light. She made out a silhouette of a small woman, her back rounded with age, standing eerily still.

"Come hither, child," the woman crooned. "The time of reckoning has come."

Scarlett stood frozen by the door.

Adrielle stepped slowly toward the old woman.

She was dressed in purple robes, fluttering behind her. A black bird was perched stiffly on her shoulder. Her knotted fingers wrapped tightly around a gem-encrusted golden scepter. She extended her other hand, a brown package sitting on her palm.

Adrielle recognized the package at once. "Is that?" *Adrielle* was written in elaborate black calligraphy. "OMG it is. How did you get that? I left it on my bed."

"I've kept it safe for some time now and expected you to open it earlier this afternoon," the woman said, holding the package up for Adrielle to take. "I'm merely returning it to its rightful owner."

"So, it was *you* that sent it?"

"Yes."

"Why? And how did you get it from my room?"

"Kraaa, Kraaa." A deep guttural sound spewed from the bird. It fluttered and spread wide its black wings. Adrielle ducked as the bird swooped around the room. She'd never seen such a large bird. Its broad wings had finger-like feathers at the tips.

"She won't hurt you," the woman said without looking at the bird. "Take it," she commanded, lifting the package higher.

Adrielle stood firmly in place. "They killed Josh," she said, her voice tremulous and angry. "Why?" She turned to the door. "Where did they go? They're all gone. Not just the Goths," she locked onto the yellow ropes curled in a pool of blood, "but Josh and Scarlett too." She turned back to the old woman. "Did any of this really happen? Is Josh really dead?"

"That's up to you, dear," the woman cackled.

An icy shiver rolled from Adrielle's neck down her back. It wasn't an un-abandoned laugh, light and heart-felt like Coco's, but something dark and sinister.

"Who are you?"

"Perhaps the better question is: *who are you?*"

Her words were chilling. She'd wrestled with this question so many times. The old woman's eyes dropped to the package. "Here."

She pressed it into Adrielle's hands. Adrielle resisted the impulse to pull back. The woman's hands were snake-like, her skin wrinkly like crepe paper.

"Some of the answers you seek are inside," she said, her eyes boring into Adrielle's. "Others you will have to find on your own."

Adrielle tore at the brown paper, exposing a weathered book. "A book? I knew it."

"Not just any book. It's a journal."

Adrielle ripped off the wrapping. It had a simple binding, hand sewn, made of worn leather darkened with age. She opened the cover. The pages were thin and yellowed; the edges uneven and curled from use. The text was in tidy calligraphy similar to that on the brown paper wrapping and loaded with inked markings scribbled in the margins.

"Some of the writing is so faded I can't make out the words," Adrielle said.

The woman waved her hand to urge her on.

. . . With my wings, I could protect her, but as a mortal, I could be with her . . .

"What does this mean?" Adrielle asked, meeting the woman's gaze.

The woman blinked. Her hooded eyes resembled the bird's, black and cold, the expression solemn.

"Read on," she commanded.

Achaea, Greece- 241 BCE—Haden: Fear hangs in the air like an invisible cloak. Already, smokestacks of humans tied to the stake dot the horizon and the acrid smell of burning flesh fills my nostrils. People are frantic to put an end to their fear, to extinguish the shadows that haunt in the night. This frenzy, fervent as fire, inhales everything in its path. And the shadows, one of the many after-effects of the great divide, will never stop. Cast by Domenikos' army, they are now as much a part of the light as the dark.

"Domenikos?" Adrielle blurted. "Wasn't that—" She pointed to where the Goth had last stood and cringed, seeing the cut ropes, still knotted and twisted on the wooden floor. "I'm sure that's what the other Goth called him. And you did too—that *was* you—wasn't it? The voice?" She gazed at the old woman. "Domenikos," she whispered, a cold shiver running through her.

"Yes." The woman bobbed her head slightly. "Read on."

Perhaps once, many centuries ago . . . there was a chance . . . but now . . . ahhh . . . though I've always believed regret is wasted in the face of adversity, it weighs heavily on my mind.

Shrieks of countless souls fill the air, but only one haunts me now. I watch from my tower above, horror stricken as flames lick at her toes. Her wavy locks dampened by sweat, hang down low on her sides as heat begins to consume her flesh. My heart is bursting with anguish. My head throbbing as she writhes in pain. And all the while I try not to think about the inhumaneness of it all.

The custom of basting humans in grease so they will not burn too quickly has spread as savagely as the fires that consume.

"The fire . . ." Adrielle grabbed a handful of her dress's brocade fabric and twisted it in her fist. She thought back to the night her mother died. She hadn't wanted to throw away her mother's clothes, even though they were scorched and ruined from the flames. Contrary to logic, she'd always believed her mother would return. She inhaled a long breath and, pushing painful agony away, continued to read.

For days I have wrestled with myself. I realize now there is only one escape from the fate that engulfs her. I sweep over the landscape of fireballs, the fire burning so bright I have to shade my eyes. Even as I reason, I am unable to silence the voices in my head: You will lose her forever . . .

Perhaps. But I know now what I must do. I must break the sacred oath.

Only when her fingers curl around my feathers do I exhale. She is safe for now, I think, feeling hollow as her body deflates into thin air.

As she read, the words empowered her. She locked onto the old woman's gaze with tearful eyes. She wanted to ask about . . . *Haden* . . . but couldn't force herself to speak his name.

Chapter 6

SOMEWHERE IN BETWEEN

"WHY?" ADRIELLE ASKED, in a sudden burst of anger. "Why are you giving me this now?"

The old woman smiled. "A promise."

"How do I know if this is real or fiction? It could be a story with no truth behind it. There are too many missing parts to make sense of it." Adrielle shook her head. "Pieces. That's all this is. Pieces I don't know what to do with."

"You will. Memory will return, now that the time of reckoning is here."

Adrielle felt the rising dread of something terrible about to happen.

She clutched for her necklace. "It's gone," she cried, feeling a hollow ache. She remembered how the necklace had slipped through her fingers when the Goth demanded it.

She dropped to her knees and searched the floor. "Nothing." Suppressing rising panic, she pressed her cheek against the wood floor and flattened her hand on the Persian rug. What if her watch had disappeared along with the Goths? And what about Josh? Fear raced through her veins.

The old woman stood motionless as Adrielle continued the hunt.

She caught a flicker of the shiny gold patina peeking out from beneath the bookshelves.

It must have bounced, she thought, scuttling over to pick it up.

Adrielle extended her arm underneath, but the watch was inches too far.

She scanned the room for something, anything, to reach the watch.

There. On the end table next to the sofa was a pointy letter opener fashioned like a small knight's sword. She thrust the letter opener under the bookshelves until she managed to scoop a link of the chain and pulled only the chain out.

Panicked, she scanned the floor. *There*, she exhaled with relief. The watch had ricochet not far from where she had stood.

She secured the watch back on the chain and clasped it, a feeling of calm washing over her as she slipped it over her head.

Then something struck her. The second hand on the face was not moving. Nor were the hour and minute hands. She looked up at the woman.

"It stopped working at midnight. Well, there you go." She shrugged. "It's broken. Everything's back to the way it was."

"No." The woman shook her head. "Not everything."

"I don't understand how it worked at all. Coco said she tried to get it fixed. Even the clock repair couldn't fix it. And I'd set the hands to ten-ten. How then, did it run to midnight?"

The woman's expression remained stoic. Her eyes were shiny expressionless marbles set into hooded lids.

"And the gonging? Where did that harrowing sound come from?"

"Kraaa. Kraaa," the bird on the woman's shoulder cawed.

Adrielle flinched. "Coco said this watch belonged to my mother, but I have a memory. A faint one, but a memory, of a dream I had long ago. Someone named Haden gave this to me as an early wedding gift. But . . . he isn't real. A real person I mean—is he? He's a character in my dream?" She frowned as she stared down at the book.

"Oh, he's a character all right," the old woman said. "The watch is working perfectly. You have a choice to make. Time has merely stopped until it's done."

"Hang on . . . you can't mean that literally—that time has stopped until I make a decision."

"I do."

Adrielle stared at the woman. Maybe the sound hadn't actually come from the watch. She inspected the room in closer detail. It was a study, the far wall lined with bookshelves. Maybe there was another clock.

"There." Third shelf down, tucked between two leatherbound books with gold leaf writing, was a small glass dome covering a brass clock. The kind often seen in older homes, fancy, with spinning wheels. She tread carefully toward it. Oddly, it too had stopped at midnight. She tapped on the glass with her black fingernail, double-checking to see if the hands had just stuck.

"Midnight," she said, approaching the woman and stopping a few feet away. "It doesn't make sense. It's stopped at midnight too."

The large bird perched on the woman's shoulder sat eerily still. If she hadn't seen it fly, Adrielle would have thought it was stuffed. A macabre prop set there for drama. The beady eyes, round and shiny, blinked periodically and followed her every move like a cliché in a horror flick. It was giving her the creeps.

"What am I missing here?" Adrielle asked.

The woman held her stare, then set her gaze back onto the book still in Adrielle's hands. "In there." She gestured with the bob of her chin. "The book holds clues to who you are. Your necklace, another."

"How could this watch possibly be a clue?" Adrielle asked, growing more and more impatient and inspecting the watch face closely.

"That is not any ordinary watch, you see, it is a chronometer."

"A chronometer? What's that?"

"An instrument used to measure time in minute increments."

"Well, whatever it is, it's broken."

"No, it most assuredly is not."

Adrielle closed her eyes and willed her temper to settle.

"I told you, time is merely paused until you make your decision."

Adrielle shook her head in frustration.

The old woman raised her brows. "We're going round and round and getting nowhere. You are really stubborn."

Adrielle studied her watch. "This has been a long day, and I don't understand anything you're saying. You're like Rumplestilskin, talking in riddles and making no sense."

"Riddles? That device is unique. It can stop time, but it also has the capability to transport you to *any* specific time and place. It can send you to a past time, or propel you forward into the future. Whichever direction you choose to go." The woman closed her veiny lids and sighed. "It is quite exquisite really. The only one of its kind."

Could the woman be a fake? A party favor Scarlett had hired?

The more she considered it, the more it made sense. This must be what Josh had to take care of, a kind of birthday initiation. The whole Goth thing had been just that, a prank. Scarlett's prank that everyone else was in on. By now, everyone was probably tweeting about it. And by Monday it would be all over the school—how the albino girl had fallen for it.

Whose journal is this? Why do I have such a memory of Haden?

"Choose. Embrace your destiny or keep hiding forever."

"Hiding? I'm not hiding. I'm here, as visible as you are."

"That is part of the problem. Haden propelled you to this time to keep you safe. But that is impossible now that Domenikos has found you. Listen carefully. This is not the epoch you were born into." Her dark eyes glowed until she resembled a jack-o-lantern. She lifted the scepter and struck the ground so hard the entire floor shook.

The bird on her shoulder made a ghastly shrieking noise and spread its wings into a broad span. It swooped around the room in wide circles until the woman motioned for it to return to her shoulder. She caressed the bird's black feathers in one long stroke.

"Who are you?"

"In time you will know."

"So, with this thing you call a chronometer, I can go back in time? To any time span I choose?"

"Not time span, a precise time."

Adrielle guffawed. "Meaning minutes and seconds?"

A hard scorn settled on the woman's face.

"Okay, okay . . . say I play along."

"This is not something you play at."

"Say I believe you." Adrielle rolled her eyes. "Does this mean I can time travel back to change things?"

The woman nodded.

"I can change anything? Anything at all?" Adrielle asked, excitement mounting inside her.

The woman nodded.

"I can't believe this necklace has that kind of power. Imagine, going back to fix things." She grinned. "Awesome."

"Beware." The woman held up a knotted finger. "There are consequences. Physical laws you must adhere to."

"What kind of consequences?"

"It causes a paradox. Tamper with the past, meaning anything whatsoever, and there will be a ripple of events."

Adrielle's mind was racing. She wanted to believe this was all a game, because that would mean Josh was still alive. But she wanted to change the past desperately.

"You could cause a paradox in the time continuum. Or as some call it, the *butterfly* effect. As you will see, the chronometer is not to be toyed with. If you decide to use it, you must learn how to use it well."

"Can I save Josh's life? If he's really dead, that is."

"Perhaps. There is always that chance. But in trying to save his life, you may lose your own. Everything is at risk now."

Adrielle thought hard for a moment. She held the shiny gold timepiece tightly in her hands. "And my mother . . . can I save her?" she asked, raising her eyes to the woman's.

"Save her?" The woman laughed. "Oh, she does not need saving, Adrielle." She stared at Adrielle silently.

That didn't make any sense. "My mother died in a fire. What do you mean she doesn't need saving?"

The woman gestured to the book.

Adrielle held it up. "This book—Haden's journal I suppose? How do I know if these things actually happened?" Adrielle didn't need her confirmation. Since the woman had appeared, memories of past events before she was born had begun filling her mind. She brushed her fingers over the book's worn binding. "*Haden,*" she whispered, "if he's real, how could I have forgotten him?"

A yearning to change the past swelled inside her, so intense, she became weak and grabbed the nearby table to steady herself.

The woman watched her without speaking. She seemed to know Adrielle was remembering.

"All along, Coco thought it had been mama's necklace, but I have a memory of that last day with Haden. Domenikos was in the square. The Tribunals were burning at the stake. I still don't understand one thing though . . . The memories I have, are conflicting with this journal entry."

Adrielle flipped through the thin pages, her fingers brushing over the ornate script. "Now I'm remembering Haden turned to a page in an old book—what was it called?—oh yeah, *The Book of Feathers*. He chanted, he put this watch around my neck. But it says, '. . . *I watch from my tower above, horror stricken as flames lick at her toes. Her wavy locks dampened by sweat, hang down low on her sides as heat begins to consume her flesh.*'" She looked up at the woman. "Clearly, I am burning here. But that's not how it happened."

The old woman smiled. "Which time?"

"This is getting complicated. How do I find this guy, Haden?"

"Heed my words. If you use this power, you must be prepared to risk everything. From this point onward, *nothing* will be the same."

"I don't have anything to lose."

"Are you certain about that?" the old woman asked. "Things rarely turn out the way one expects. That is both the joy and the sorrow of life."

"I'm sure."

"Look deeply into the eye of the diamond. If your decision still stands, it will be so."

She lifted her scepter and tapped it on the floor. A beam of light glowed from the jewel in the crown of the scepter and a myriad of colors exploded and reflected throughout the room.

Adrielle's eyes stung as though she was staring straight into the sun.

"Concentrate on the images in the center of the diamond," the woman ordered.

Diamond? Adrielle gasped. It was the size of her fist. She forced her eyes to stay open and didn't dare blink until the swirls of colors blended and formed recognizable images.

She saw the trees lining her street, and then her house in perfect detail as if she were physically there. Then, remarkably, she popped inside her room, coconut sunscreen tingling her nose.

Her room was messy; her clothes scattered and piled high on the floor. She winced, scolding herself for being a slob. Her guitar was propped in the corner with a ream of loose-leaf paper and scattered pencils. A minute later Coco bounced in the door.

Coco, she winced, *how would she ever explain this to her?*

She looked deeply into Coco's eyes. It was amazing. Instead of seeing herself as though she were outside her own body, she'd transitioned inside as if she were actually standing there in front of Coco and saw the tiny flecks of mascara speckled on her face. It didn't feel like she was upstairs in Scarlett's house, looking inside the scepter crown. It felt like she was home suddenly.

When her eyes locked onto Coco's, she realized her mascara wasn't just speckled, it had tear-streaked down her face. And her eyes were red and swollen. She was about to ask what was wrong when *poof*, Coco vanished.

Now she was outside her body again, watching herself undress. It was dark outside; the streetlight was shining in through the window, and she was getting ready for bed.

She pulled off her t-shirt and added it to the pile of clothes on the floor.

It was the first time she'd ever had a full view of her back without the use of a mirror. Adrielle leaned in closer to the scepter crown. It was so odd to see herself, inside it. The red birthmark that had appeared the night of the fire was still there. In fact, it looked a brighter red.

"What's that mark?" she demanded. "Why did it show up the night of the fire?"

"The mark of a traveller. The time of reckoning is here. Make your choice."

"No more riddles," Adrielle yelled. "I want the truth."

"The truth is earned and comes at a great cost."

Adrielle squinted. "This is what I want—I want the truth."

"Once you embark on your journey, you can never go back."

Adrielle held her ground. She gazed sternly into the old woman's eyes.

"Very well then. Your choice is made." The woman banged the scepter hard on the floor. Loud gongs shook the room as though giant Cathedral bells were tolling. The black bird flew up, spreading its wings wide.

The swirls of images inside the diamond crown exploded out into the room, filling the space around her. The images faded until they dissolved into sparkles and disappeared like stardust.

Simultaneously, a burning sensation seared in her back. Adrielle reached around, her fingers trembling as her fingertips brushed over the red mark. It wasn't smooth as it had always been, how it had felt when she'd showered that morning. Now there were pointy pricks coming out from under her skin.

"What is happening?" she asked, terrified.

The old woman watched silently as Adrielle picked at the protruding bump with her fingernail and pulled. Her fingers trembled as she brought a red feather up to her face. "A red feather?" Vibrant images of Haden wrapping her fingers around a crimson feather flooded her mind. "Is this *that* feather? The one Haden gave me?"

"You remember more than I thought."

"How could this have come out of my back? Out from under my skin?" she demanded.

"If it is the truth you seek, then it is *your* journey and yours alone. It is not for me to tell you anything more than this: The feather you hold in your hand has the power to do many things. It can be a curse, or your biggest advantage. Depending on perspective."

Adrielle swiped at her forehead. She felt dizzy. She backed up to the sofa, grateful for something to lean against.

"How can anything that is a curse be an advantage?" she asked, staring at the feather in her fist. The feather was a brilliant crimson color with a glittering sheen like finely milled diamonds.

"Don't be afraid. There are only two mistakes you can make on your journey. Not starting it, and not seeing it through."

The old woman began to fade.

"Wait! Don't go." Adrielle tried to grab onto the woman's hand but her hand passed through as if she were a hologram. "How are you no longer physically here?" she hollered, but the woman was already gone.

Everything in the room jiggled; the windows like cellophane bent and twisted. Solid walls dissolved into patches of colors.

Adrielle pressed her hands to her head. Then her body twitched and convulsed. Shuddering waves rolled through her, one after another with no reprieve. She bent over and heaved. The acrid bile reminding her she hadn't eaten.

Where one moment she was burning up, the next she was ice cold—her teeth chattering senselessly.

She thought of birds and the repetitive high-pitched noises they made when communicating and quickly pushed it out of her mind, convinced whatever bug she'd caught had a hallucinogenic side effect.

She wiped her mouth with the back of her hand and rubbed her hands over her arms, hoping the friction would draw some warmth.

She was tired. So very tired. Pillaged of all her strength she closed her eyes.

The last thing she remembered thinking was: *Where is Coco?*

Chapter 7

Achaea, Greece – 241 BCE

A SINKING SHIP couldn't evoke more dread than Haden felt, as he and Angelo stepped into the darkened cave. Nestled high on a cliff north of the city, this deep cavern jutted in from the edge of a rugged coastline and was invisible from below. Because flight was its only means of access, it was designated long ago as the meeting place for the surviving travellers, if havoc were ever unleashed upon the world, and their peaceful society were in upheaval. The limited access ensured the surviving travellers would still have the capacity to travel and be equipped with the necessary valor needed to execute a survival plan for the Achaean race.

Angelo looked around the room. "This is it? There are no others?" he asked Astraia, the black-feathered traveller.

"This is it," she confirmed, her green-flecked eyes expressing the sorrow each one of them felt.

Unbelievably, this musky cove had once been the meeting place of the most courageous leaders, in their attempt to avoid this very paradox.

"Haden, as the leader of the Achaean army and keeper of *The Book of Feathers*, I think we must state for the record—that we three are the sole survivors," Astraia said. "The only ones left to uphold the Achaean Act."

"You mean all three thousand twenty-six Achaeans have disappeared?" Angelo asked.

Astraia nodded. "It goes unsaid, but again, must be noted for the record, that Domenikos, the fourth remaining Achaean, is not present. He must be hunted down and executed for treason. The calamity he has caused is of catastrophic scale. Unmatched in the history of our existence."

"I am well aware," Haden agreed.

"With the slaughter of the three Tribunals, we must, each one of us, fulfill our prospective obligations as the four remaining travellers of the Apocalypse. We must not rest until we have vengeance."

Astraia reached for the mark in the center of her back, scraped along her skin's surface, and pulled at a pointy nub until a shiny black feather came loose. She held it up for the others to see.

"This is my swing feather." She gazed at Angelo, and with a nodding gesture, bid him to do the same.

Angelo hesitated and glanced at Haden. He reached for the space between his shoulder blades and scraped at a similar crested mark until he pulled out a silver feather. His swing feather was long and gleamed in the wedge of moonlight.

With the nod, Astraia acknowledged his feather's beauty. She turned to Haden, who looked at her with somber concern. He paused before reaching onto his back, then pulled out a bright red feather and held it up.

"That is not your swing feather," she said. "Haden, what have you done?"

Haden flexed the muscles of his jaw.

She sighed. "It is done then. The plan is in motion."

"She's not the one," Haden insisted. "I only used it to ensure her safety."

"Ahhhh . . ." Astraia shook her head. "So your love for her has rendered you blind." She turned her gaze to the weathered manuscript clutched tightly in his arms. "Show us the book."

Haden hesitated. Up until now he had been the sole keeper and protector of its secrets.

"It contains our instructions."

He looked down at the book.

"Haden," Astraia warned, "we need to work together."

Grudgingly he laid it on the ground in the center of the cave. They crouched close to it, respectful of its powers. Within the bindings were ancient secrets about to be exposed.

Haden opened the weathered cover. Inside, yellowed pages were crowded with history and tradition. Brilliant illustrations depicted the history of their race. He turned to a page a third of the way in, where a silk ribbon tied around a lock of pale hair was wedged into the spine. He paused before reaching for the lock, aware Astraia was watching him.

Angelo flinched as Haden picked up the pale strands of hair and rubbed them between his fingertips.

In his hurry to the cave, he had forgotten to remove the lock. He ran his fingers along the inked script and found the desired text . . . *How could I have made such a mistake?* Needing to prove Astraia wrong, Haden read aloud:

Out of devastation, a leader like no other will arise. Unmatched in integrity and wisdom, the path to embrace their true destiny will be thorny and difficult. They must overcome the four trials in order to earn the four corresponding swing feathers: Red for War, Black for Justice, Silver for Conquest, and Pale Green for death.

If successful in exposing the truth and bringing justice to the Achaean offenders, they will gain the necessary strength and wisdom to free the immortals from bondage. This leader will be able to reclaim lives. By ensuring a future for the Achaean race and their posterity, this leader will be venerated for their achievements and claim their rightful place as the leading traveller: endowed with the power to bend time and saddled with the responsibilities that position brings.

However, if the leader fails, they will spend eternity as a prisoner, in the clutches of their rival.

In the silent cave, hushed musings multiplied as each of them sorted through the unexpected revelations.

For quite some time, Haden had suspected Adrielle to be the one. As whisperings of the coup had infiltrated the town, she'd shared valuable insight only possible from a true leader. That had been one of the reasons he'd given her his swing feather.

"What about the feathers? What color will they be?" Astraia asked.

They eagerly turned back to the book.

The feathers will be unprecedented. A culmination of all the colors; the leader will become a prism, which will allow them to float undetected through time.

They looked at each other in astonishment. As travellers, they could travel through time, but not always undetected.

Astraia spread her arms wide and shed her humanesque appearance.

"What are you doing?" Haden asked, "It is forbidden."

"I have long forgotten what it feels like to be free. These words have awakened my craving to roam the earth as we once did." She turned and walked to the edge of the precipice.

"Where are you going?" Angelo asked.

"To find her before he does. Clearly, she is our only chance to live unadulterated."

Astraia transformed into her natural Achaean state, spreading her black wings wide, and flew out of the cave into the night.

"WE BLEW IT," Brix said. His face scrunched to a crumpled pout.

"How easily you give up. You knew this at the start, that it would be a long game," Domenikos insisted, pacing around the room.

"So, what now?"

He stopped with a sinister expression. "We break her down link by link."

"And what about her?" Brix asked, pointing to the blonde quivering in the corner.

Domenikos turned. He ambled over to her until she lay at his feet and cocked his head. "Tell me . . . do you want to live? Or do you want to die?" he asked in a low humming purr.

"Live. I want to live! Please don't kill me," Scarlett cried, crouching down low to the ground and cowering under him.

Domenikos laughed.

"Toss her in with the others—for now," he said. "We'll deal with her later."

Brix grabbed a handful of her perfectly highlighted hair and dragged her behind him. Her tanned skin scraped along the jagged stone floor, leaving a trail of blood.

Chapter 8

Florida – Present Day

"SHE SHOULD BE back by now." Coco said, biting into the rim of her red plastic cup. She was debating whether to swear off the deal she'd made with herself, to give Adrielle more space, or not. She cast one final glance around the room. "She's not answering my texts. And I don't see her anywhere."

"Relax, she's a big girl," Veda said. "Give her space."

"This isn't what I was thinking when I asked her to come along. In my mind, I anticipated catching Josh in his lie—red-handed with Scarlett, then Adrielle breaking up with him on the spot and spending the rest of the night celebrating. But the whole evening's been off from the get-go."

"I know, with those super creepy Goths and everything." Kate shuddered. "By the way, where did they go? It's like they vanished into thin air." She stretched high on her tiptoes to see over the crowd. "Yep, definitely gone. Strange. I never saw them slip by. Did you guys?"

They shook their heads no and continued to peruse the room.

"That's it," Coco said, scrunching her cup and tossing it into a nearby trash bin. "I'm going upstairs. The suspense is driving me nuts."

"I'm in," Veda and Kate blurted at the same time.

"I'm starving," Liz chirped, following behind. "Can we get dinner afterward? To celebrate? Or grab some TB?"

"TB?" Kate asked.

"Taco Bell," Liz answered with an are-you-kidding-me look.

"Oh, I thought it was to be decided."

"That's TBD—never mind," Liz said, shaking her head. She nudged Dave. "You in?"

He shrugged. "Okay, sure—this party's pretty lame."

They wove a path toward the stairs, the smell of cannabis mottled with booze and pungent cigarettes hung in the air and tickled their noses. They passed a group of girls hovering around the foot of the stairs, and Coco heard them whisper, "That's the albino's sister."

"Losers," Veda said, flipping them off as they jabbed one another and burst into giggles. "I'm so over people like that."

Coco breezed past them. "Mean girls. Never gonna change them."

"No, but they don't even know us. They should know better," Veda added.

Coco shrugged. "Not our job to teach 'em." She'd learned to ignore off-colored remarks because people always responded negatively to Adrielle's looks. Granted, Adie *had* looked stranger when she was younger, before she'd started wearing makeup. She was always too white, too skinny, and too odd. But now that she was growing up, she was transforming into a hottie, and some girls felt threatened by it, so the teasing never stopped. In fact, it got worse.

"Look, her jacket," Kate said, slipping it off the bottom post. She too, was badgered by other girls because of her curvy body. Understandably, they were jealous that guys were all over her.

"Gee, I wonder if Scarlett isn't the reason Adrielle didn't come back down," Veda said.

"Just what I was thinking," Coco confided. "I'm starting to feel like coming here was a mistake. I really hope she didn't get bullied."

Every tread they climbed heightened her sense of doom. What should have been a celebration was quickly turning into a nightmare.

They reached the top landing, and Coco raised her hands as a signal for the others to halt.

"What's wrong?" Veda whispered.

"Listen."

"I don't hear a thing," Kate said.

"Exactly, it's too quiet," Coco said.

They looked at one other—Coco's feeling of unease reflected in their eyes. As their gazes drifted from one oil painting to the next and absorbed the elaborate moldings and soaring ceilings, their noses became saturated with the fragrant lemon oil and potpourri.

"I don't know, I'm getting this weird vibe. And it's like, creeping me out," Coco said.

"You're right," Dave added. "There's an unnatural stillness."

"Money," Liz sputtered. "It's how the other half lives."

"Not really money, it's the oversaturation of rich details," Dave clarified. "Order, history. Culture. All marinated in one whopping overdose."

"You're right. It's like a museum," Veda added.

"Sorry, but no wonder Scarlett's such a bitch," Liz said. "Her home is the set for a horror flick."

"Isn't it though?" Kate giggled. "Like, it's so spooky. Look at my goosebumps." She brushed her hands up and down her arms. "It's like we've been transported into an Oculus Rift."

"Shhh." Veda shot her a warning look.

"Like the eerie stillness before an earthquake or a tsunami," Dave said.

"Nothing natural about this," Liz commented, her eyes dropping to her fingernails. "Chewed stubs. I may have to break down and get that manicure. Damage control."

Kate burst into giggles, breaking into full-blown chortles.

They all turned to her. "Shhh . . ." Their faces contorting to annoyed scowls.

"Sorry, like, you guys know I can't stand suspense. It's making me, like, super nervous." She bit her lower lip and inched closer to Veda.

They listened again, no one daring to speak. *Nothing.* No voices. No noise. Which was even more uncanny because of the wall of noise they'd just left downstairs.

"Hate this," Dave said, sticking his finger in his ear and jerking it around. "My ears are plugged, just like they get in an airplane."

Liz smacked his chest. "Don't be such a schmuck. You sound like a wet dog."

"Stop with the jabbing already. If you keep this up, I'm going to have to get body armor," he complained, rubbing his chest.

"You're such a drama queen."

"Seriously. I'm getting sorer by the minute."

They whispered, debating which one of the doors lining both sides of the long hallway to try first.

A loud thud came from the other side of the first door.

Without hesitation, Coco turned the doorknob and went through the doorway. "Adrielle!"

"What?" the others shrieked. They rushed in to where Adrielle lay unconscious on the floor and formed a tight protective circle around her.

Coco dropped to her knees and turned Adrielle's face upward to get a better look. She patted her cheeks lightly.

"Is she all right? Please let her be all right . . . should we call someone? OMG! What could have happened?" they cried.

Adrielle didn't open her eyes right away.

Coco lifted her lids, but her eyes rolled backward. "Oh my god, she's out cold."

"Dave's right, it's a scene right out of a mystery novel," Liz murmured, casting a suspicious glance around the room.

Coco gave her a look. Liz should never drink. She was being impossibly annoying.

"I'm just saying." She shrugged. "Look at that. Clues." She pointed at the floor next to Adrielle. Brown paper wrapping was torn and discarded in a crumpled pile. And close by, a leatherbound book lay open.

"The package?" Coco whispered, recognizing the wrapping. She slipped her arms around Adrielle's shoulders and lifted her head off the carpet. The foul smell of vomit attacked her nose. "Oh, Adrielle . . . you've been sick."

"Ewww, gross," Kate squeaked, taking a step back. "Look, it's all over her dress."

"There's another smell too," Liz said, twitching her nose like a bloodhound. "I can't quite pinpoint it, but it smells like those shops downtown—"

"We smell vomit, and you smell—" Veda said smirking.

"Incense? Yes, that's it," Liz said, sniffling. "Hate that it clings to my clothes and skin."

"Really? Could you guys be any more insensitive?" Coco said, anxiety pitting her gut. She turned back to Adrielle and swept the hair off her forehead. "Oh, Adrielle . . ."

"Sulfur too. Why would I smell that?" Liz asked. She scrunched her face in deep thought.

"Maybe someone tooted," Kate said, biting down hard on her hand to keep from giggling.

"And how old are we?" Liz snipped.

"Both of you stop," Veda chided. She crouched next to Coco to get a closer look.

Seeing Veda's facial tic in overdrive, Liz mimicked it behind her back, which made Kate giggle even more.

Coco and Veda stared at her.

"Sorry." Kate took a couple of steps back. "It's just when you do that thing with your—"

"You're unbelievable," Veda said, shaking her head in disgust. "You know I can't help it. My ticking is worse when I'm nervous."

"I said I'm sorry." Kate winced. "It was Liz's fault." She turned to Liz and pressed her lips into a very deliberate rebuke.

"She looks sick," Coco breathed, leaning over Adrielle. She patted her cheeks lightly until finally, her eyelids fluttered open.

"Oh, thank goodness." Coco inhaled a sharp breath of relief. "You're gonna be okay," she said, not entirely convinced.

Adrielle struggled to sit up. "Oooh . . ." She groaned, pressing her hands to her head.

"Take your time," Veda said. "You must have had too much to drink."

"It was Coke—that's all," Coco sputtered.

"Are you sure?" Liz asked. "I'm just saying. What if the creepy Goths spiked her drink?"

Coco shot her a warning look. Liz was on her nerves.

"With a ruffy?" Kate exclaimed.

"It's not a dog." Liz grunted. "It's r-u-f-i-e. Rufie."

"Yeah that."

Coco shook her head. "No way. I watched them pour the Coke straight out of the bottle."

"Maybe she's right. What if it was already spiked? You know, like they might've already put that date drug in?" Kate suggested.

"Flunitrazepam?" Dave asked.

"Ya, I guess? Is that the one that makes it so you won't remember?"

"Remember what?"

"I don't know, whatever happened here?"

"Guys, I drank the same thing. Shut it down." Coco was getting more and more irritated and wished they'd all just drop it. "We don't know what she remembers yet. We haven't even asked."

"Should we?" Dave asked, motioning toward the door. "We could wait outside."

"No, it's okay," Coco insisted.

"Maybe if I hadn't said anything about Scarlett and Josh, this wouldn't have happened," Veda pressed.

"Stop it. All of you," Coco said. "This has nothing to do with us."

"Let's get her onto the sofa." Dave slipped a hand under Adrielle's armpits. "Grab her feet."

A waft of barf floated up as they moved her.

"We'll need a clean washcloth," Dave said. "Wet and cold to clean her up a bit."

"I'll get it," said Liz, spotting a door.

"I feel like crap," Adrielle said with a moan as they settled her onto the leather sofa. With her head in her hands, she rocked slightly. "What happened? I've got a mother of a headache. I must have hit my head really hard."

A sigh of relief came from everyone.

"I was just about to ask," Coco said, partially masking her concern. "Dude, we found you on the floor knocked out. You okay?"

"I'm fine, I think," she said, twisting her neck side to side.

Coco picked up the book and held it up. "This was on the floor. It's the package, right?"

Adrielle nodded.

"Why did you bring it?"

"I didn't."

"Guess we know what it is now." She handed it to Adrielle.

"Ouch." Adrielle let go of the book and pressed her hands against her head.

"Maybe you shouldn't move yet. Could be a concussion," Dave advised.

"Josh." Adrielle shuddered.

"It's from Josh?"

"No." She pushed the book away and attempted to stand, but her legs gave way.

Coco pressed her hand down on Adrielle's shoulder. "Hang tight, I don't think standing's a good idea."

Adrielle eased back down. "Guess not, my legs feel rubbery." She tipped her head back and closed her eyes while Coco rifled through the book. "Looks totally legit. Like it's genuinely old."

"You have no idea," Adrielle said.

"Who's it from?" Coco asked. "Josh?"

Adrielle shook her head. "No, it isn't. I already told you."

"Well—who then?" Coco flipped through the pages start to back. "It doesn't say." She held it out to Adrielle.

"Not now," Adrielle said.

"What?"

"It's—" She looked confused. "None of this makes sense—not if I think about it."

"What are you talking about? *What* doesn't make sense?" Coco searched the floor for the discarded wrapping.

"There." Adrielle pointed to a spot. "That's where they were tied up."

"Who?"

"Josh and Scarlett."

Liz returned with a cool washcloth. "Close your eyes and rest," she said, laying it onto Adrielle's forehead. "I think she's hallucinating. Must be a concussion."

"I'm not," Adrielle objected, taking the cloth off and sitting up. "When I walked in, the Goths were holding them hostage. They wanted my watch, and I was about to give it to them, when this gonging started. That's when the woman appeared in the corner." She rubbed her forehead. "They disappeared just like that."

"Adie . . ." Coco grumbled. "It sounds like you had one heck of a nightmare."

"No, I was awake. I know it sounds crazy, but it's true. All of it."

"You didn't eat anything—did you?" Liz asked. "Like mushrooms I mean?"

"Mushrooms?" Adrielle gasped.

"Ok, ok—just using the process of elimination. There's chips and stuff downstairs, should I get you some?" Liz offered.

"No." Adrielle grabbed at her stomach. "I can't stand the thoughts of food right now."

"Party's over. Let's get you home," Coco said.

Adrielle nodded. "Home sounds good." She started to stand and fell back onto the sofa. "I'm dizzy. My head feels like a spinning top."

"Some color's returning to her face," Liz said, pressing the cool washcloth onto Adrielle's forehead.

Coco watched Adrielle, only partially alarmed now. She wondered if she had built up her birthday so much that no matter what happened, it would be a letdown.

"What about Josh? You said you saw him?" Veda said.

Adrielle stared at the ceiling, barely shaking her head. "They must have gone into another room."

"Shhh," Kate hissed, giving Veda the hard stare. "Leave the poor girl alone. How far does a girl have to go so they get the message? Adrielle is in no condition to face what was an obvious boyfriend-dump."

Liz opened her mouth as Adrielle stood up. "Aghh," Liz choked and waved her hand.

"Adie, you don't look so good," Coco worried.

"Thanks a lot," Adrielle said, hunching her shoulders. "I just need a minute to figure this out."

"Figure what out?" Coco asked as she went to the door.

Veda was checking the hall and started down the stairs.

"Ok, here's the thing . . . Josh is dead," Adrielle said.

Chapter 9

Florida – Present Day

"DEAD? AS IN D-E-A-D dead?" Kate squealed. "As in—my aunt Harriet we buried last summer—dead?"

Veda clonked up the stairs, her platform sandals echoing into the room.

"I'm serious." Adrielle blew a puff of air from her lower lip and collapsed onto the sofa.

"Dear God, she really does have a concussion," Liz blurted.

"It feels like a giant weight is lifted off my shoulders. I'm over keeping secrets."

"Secrets?" Everyone sputtered.

"Look, guys, I swear. I don't even know where to begin explaining what happened when I walked into this room. You'll never believe it. Never."

"Go on," Dave urged.

"I—sheesh—am I the only one feeling hot here?"

"Adie, quit stalling," Coco urged. "You're leaving us hanging."

"Ok. But keep in mind you've been warned. Here's the thing. I don't expect you to believe me." She swiped her forehead with the back of her hand. "'Cause I'm not sure I do."

"We get that." Liz circled the room, her nose twitching like a bloodhound. "Why don't you start by explaining why I can smell fire?" She stopped walking. "And perfume. It's strongest over here." She pointed to the floor where she was standing at the far end of the room. She singled out a strand of her curly locks, and brought it up to her nose, sniffed it, and frowned. "I knew it. The smell's already latched onto it."

Liz opened her large leather bag and fished out a small atomizer of Kate Spade *Walk on Air* perfume, the fragrant mist swelled into the room as she pressed the nozzle.

Veda rolled her eyes.

"Do you have to do that?" Dave groaned, flailing his arms around and coughing.

Liz shot him a look of disapproval and sprayed another squirt in his direction before re-zipping the bottle back into the center compartment.

Unfazed by his reaction, she picked the book up from the sofa and leafed through it.

"*Who* would give you this?" she asked, holding it up for everyone to see. "It's someone's diary and it looks ancient."

"I know. Really," Coco agreed, peering over Liz's shoulder at the yellowed pages. "Someone dropped it off for her earlier today."

Dave un-scrunched the brown paper wrapping lying on the floor and inspected it. "There's no return address. Toss the thing over."

Adrielle watched him study a few pages. If he authenticated it, the others would follow.

He shook his index finger. "This is probably the only other person besides Adrielle that's into calligraphy. It's even neater than hers. Totally old school."

"What's calligraphy?" Kate asked.

"Penmanship," he explained. "The root of the word, *Kali* comes from the Greek language and means beautiful, and *graphia* means writing. In the first century, the Roman alphabet—"

"Really? We're doing this?" Veda asked, pointing at Kate.

Kate's jaw hung open.

"I'm sorry, this is so—" Veda burst into an uncontrollable laughing fit. "Too bizarre. Dave, I've told you before, your trivia's wasted on us." She sat down.

"Ahem." Liz pushed her eyebrows together until they resembled a wiggly worm over her eyes. "Did you find out who it was from?" She took the book back from Dave.

"This might be Adrielle's wildest hallucination," Veda said. "I think you banged your head and dreamt the whole thing up."

"Shhh. Adrielle . . . what do you mean by Josh is dead? Exactly?" Liz looked at her over her glasses. "Do you mean like dead to you 'cause he cheated? You can't possibly mean *dead.* As in not coming back dead."

"Well, I guess that all depends."

All eyes turned to Adrielle.

"Oh boy." She squirmed, feeling the pressure of being the focus of attention. "I don't know where to start."

Coco put a reassuring hand on Adrielle's arm and gave a gentle squeeze. "Sweetie, why don't you start at the beginning."

"K." Adrielle swallowed. "Ahem. So, I put my ear to the door but still couldn't hear a thing."

"And?"

She took a sharp breath and hiccoughed a sob. "So, I walked in and—"

Dave sidled beside her. He gave her a reassuring pat on her head and ruffled her hair.

"She's not a dog for goodness sakes," Liz complained, swiping at his hand.

Adrielle stared straight ahead, avoiding eye contact and concentrating on controlling her voice. "That's when I saw them—the Goths."

"I knew it. They screamed trouble." Coco folded her arms.

"They had 'em tied up. Josh and Scarlett."

"Where?" Liz asked, looking for signs of a tussle.

"Over there." She gestured to the spot, then rubbed at her wrists as Josh had done. "These thick ropes were—they're gone. I saw the knife, tight against Josh's neck. They were gonna cut his throat if I didn't give them this." She lifted her watch.

"Mom's watch? Why would they—?"

"You didn't give it to them?" Veda asked.

"I tried—but these gongs started ringing."

"Wait. Gongs?" Coco asked.

"Yeah. I couldn't figure out where the sound was coming from. It was from my watch, which didn't make sense."

"None of this makes sense," Dave said.

"This booming . . . ahhh." Adrielle held her head in her hands. "My head feels like a watermelon splitting open."

Coco's face fell.

"This isn't funny. Not even a bit," Veda mumbled.

"They have medication for this kind of thing—it'll be okay," Kate offered.

"Medication?" Coco said.

Dave shrugged. "Don't get mad, if she needs help—"

"People, stay focused." Liz pursed her lips into a thin line, her sharp eyes glancing around the room. "Hmmmm . . . Adrielle, you said he was dead. How?"

"The Goth. He slit his throat. They were both here."

"Where did they go?"

"Disappeared."

"Both of them?"

"Yep."

"You actually believe that? That everyone disappeared?" Coco asked.

Adrielle nodded.

"Then what?" Liz asked, walking over to the spot Adrielle was pointing to.

"Everything. Everything happened at once."

"Meaning?"

Adrielle stared up at Liz wide-eyed.

"Go on."

"There's not a spot of blood, Adrielle. If this was a crime scene, there would be blood splatters," Veda said. "If you want us to believe you, there has to be some evidence."

"Believe me? I don't care if you believe me. It's the truth."

"Stop it. Can't you see she's traumatized?" Coco said, her brow wrinkling with worry. She settled down next to Adrielle and slipped her hand into hers.

"There is evidence," Liz said. "I smell fire and perfume here in the corner. Why don't you tell us about that?"

"The old woman," Adrielle said. "A seer or psychic or something. I thought it was a joke but then . . ."

Adrielle recounted how the old woman and the raven had appeared, and how when she banged her scepter into the ground, she'd been able to see inside her bedroom at home. She told them everything except the part where she'd pulled the feather out from her back.

She leaned forward. Kate pulled Adrielle's collar down, and before Adrielle could stop her, ran her hands along the skin.

"OMG Adrielle, this is so gross," Kate exclaimed. "What is it?"

THE NIGHT AIR felt cool on Adrielle's face. She sat awkwardly forward in the front passenger seat of Coco's Jetta. Her back was raw, as if she'd been rolling in a haystack, and the hay had gotten stuck in her clothes and was pricking her back. If she leaned against the seat, it felt even worse.

Coco stole a sideways glance. Adrielle didn't dare say more until she'd had a chance to mull everything over. There was a lot to consider. Coco had been working at the mall since she was fifteen and saved every bit she could to backpack through Europe with her. Adrielle found out she'd planned on surprising her with flights by accident, after she'd seen her searches on her laptop. But this changed everything.

The others, Veda, Liz, and Dave sat motionless in the back seat.

"Who wants to get dropped off first?" Coco asked as they neared the 189 exit off the I-95.

"Dropped off?" they grunted.

"I've already texted my mom," Veda said. "She's with Kate's mom, and they're cool with us sleeping over."

"Good idea. You in?" she asked Dave, reaching for her phone.

"I guess," Dave said. "My parents are in Vegas. And what happens while they're in Vegas, stays between us."

"Good. I think we need to keep a close eye on Adrielle tonight," Liz whispered.

"You okay with that?" Coco asked Adrielle, who only shrugged. "I guess it's settled then. We'll hang in my room tonight. But we'll need to be quiet." She met Liz's gaze in the rear-view mirror. "The warden."

"Why're you all looking at me?" Liz asked. "*I'm* not going to make a peep."

"Good. Layla goes to bed early and the last thing I need is to deal with her."

THE PORCH LIGHT was on when they pulled into the driveway. They slipped their shoes off by the front door and tossed them in a pile and followed Coco upstairs.

Adrielle went to her room and changed into her pajamas. She paused at Coco's door and leaned against the doorjamb. Though she wouldn't admit it, it was comforting not to be on her own tonight.

"You okay?" Coco asked.

"It looks exactly the way we left it," she said, already in the mindset that everything would be different.

"Of course it does, Adie—sheesh."

Adrielle entered the room. Ironically, she felt like *this* was the dream. She picked up her books still scattered on Coco's bed and stacked them neatly on the bookshelves, then drifted to the mound of clothes in the center of the room and made a half-hearted attempt at moving them over. She walked over to Coco's dresser and lightly touched Coco's empty Coke can.

"Did you really expect everything to have changed?" Coco laughed.

"No, I guess not. But—after seeing the house in the center jewel, I thought it would *feel* different."

"Oh, that." Coco sounded disappointed. "So, you're sticking to your story."

"It's the truth," Adrielle said, realizing how outrageous it sounded.

"I call the pink pillow." Kate emerged out of Coco's closet with an armful of sleeping bags. She tossed one over to Liz, handed Veda another, and set hers on the floor beside her.

"What about me?" Dave complained.

"Hang on." Coco pulled out the trundle bed and grabbed extra blankets and pillows. "Here. You guys can toss for the bed. Adie and I will share mine."

"You can have it," Dave said to Liz, striding over to Coco's reading chair by the window. "I'll sleep in this chair. Or maybe not." He picked up a string of lacy panties spread over the top. "Uhh, where do you want these?" He hooked them onto his finger and looked around the room.

"Give 'em here," Coco snapped, snatching them out of his hands and stuffing them in a drawer. "They're clean you know. I just hadn't put my laundry away."

"Hadn't noticed," he said, his eyes drifting to her clothes on the floor.

"Shut up." She tossed him a pillow and after a flurry of fidgeting and grunting, everyone settled in.

"Goodnight, everybody." Coco exhaled, turning off the light on her night table.

Adrielle turned onto her side and pulled her knees up in fetal position, her knees almost touching Coco's. They hadn't slept in the same bed since they were younger and doing so now evoked a swarm of memories.

"You okay?" Coco whispered.

Adrielle nodded. A wedge of moonlight filtering through the window gave the room a peaceful glow, but even in the dim lighting she could see Coco was scared. She looked back at her with the same expression as the night of the fire.

"Adie," Coco whispered, wrapping her fingers around Adrielle's hand. "Don't worry. We'll sort through this." She closed her eyes.

Adrielle felt so drained, her mind started to doze off.

"I'm still hungry," Liz said.

"Can't you wait?" Dave asked.

"No, my stomach is growling."

"There's food in the fridge." Coco yawned. "Just don't make any noise."

LIZ CREPT INTO Coco's room, using her phone light. The room was dark, she could barely make out her friends huddled under blankets on their sides. She heard the slow cadence of their breathing, but she was too wired to sleep. She wanted to talk about what had happened. Dave was already curled up on the chair, snoring. She climbed into the trundle bed and pulled the blanket up around her chin.

Her mind was reeling. From the time they entered Scarlett's den, it was like a bad dream. Adrielle's story didn't make sense. She was really shaken up. Poor Adrielle. What a way to celebrate a birthday. She lay back on her pillow and closed her eyes. There had to be more to it. Something they were missing. *That book looked really old.* Liz wiped the crumbs off her chin and sat up. She squinted through the dim light and saw the book on the dresser. Maybe she'd have a look. Phone in hand, she tiptoed out of bed and picked it up.

"Interesting," she whispered, sitting on Coco's chair. The binding was hand sewn; the handwriting too curvy to make out most of the words without more light. She turned on the phone's flashlight app and began to read.

"Holy shit," she whispered.

"What now, Sherlock?" Coco hissed from the bed.

Liz swirled away from the dresser. Coco was sitting up. "Oh, you're awake?"

"I am now."

"Good. Cause this book says, 'Achaea, Greece 241 BCE.' It's a journal. It can't be real, not in this condition."

"Are we sleeping or investigating?" Kate asked, sitting up too.

"Go back to sleep." Veda moaned. "I'm exhausted."

Kate lay back down.

"Sure, the leather's pretty worn, but there's absolutely no proof this is legit. I mean—that would make this a couple of thousand years old, right? That would be impossible."

"What are you doing?" Veda snapped, pulling her sleeping bag up around her neck. "Get in your own bed."

"I'm scared," Kate whined, scuttling back into her sleeping bag and zipping it up. She shimmied along the floor until she was tight next to Veda.

"God, how old *are* you?" Veda complained.

"Well, you know Tae Kwon Do."

"So?"

"You can fight your way out of anything, if something happens."

"Stop it. Nothing's gonna happen."

"What about all this talk about dying? And what Adie said about—?"

"Kate, it's not real," Veda said. "Adrielle just hit her head."

Kate scrunched deeper inside her bag until only the top of her head was visible.

"Then what was sticking out of her back?" she breathed.

"This," Adrielle said.

Liz shone her phone-light toward the bed. "Is that a feather?" She buried her head back into the book.

"Yep," Adrielle said.

The only sound was the fragile papyrus as Liz flipped frantically through the pages. Back and forth and back. "Ah-ha. Found it. It says here this *Haden* character puts a feather in the girl's hand—who incidentally is called Adrielle. Lemme see it."

Adrielle handed the feather to Liz, who inspected it closely.

"It shimmers," Liz said as she ran her fingers along the barb and pulled on the vane. Some of the downy barbs came off. She tucked them into the journal for a bookmark and handed the feather back. "Can't believe this came out of your back."

"OMG," Kate squealed, scrunching her knees up to her chest. "What if it's contagious?"

"Shut up," Adrielle hissed.

"What's going on?" Dave groaned, rubbing his eyes as he awoke. "Is it morning?"

"Go back to sleep, Kate's just creeped out," Veda said.

"Oh," he exhaled, wrestling with his pillow and punching it into shape. He laid his head back down and within seconds was snoring.

"It's true. He put it in my hand," Adrielle whispered, her voice coming out soft and breathy.

"Who did?" Coco asked, bolting up.

"Haden," Adrielle breathed.

"Uh, guys." Liz choked. The sound of her chair hitting the floor echoed in the room as she tripped over it. "This can't be good."

"Who's Haden?" Veda asked.

Liz pointed to a long, elongated, shadow coming from the window.

"I am."

Chapter 10

Florida – Present Day

"AHHHHHHHHH." DAVE'S BLOOD curdling scream filled the room.

Adrielle opened her eyes. In one leap, Dave bounced from the chair by the window onto Coco's bed. Kate and Veda followed, the four of them huddled in a tight ball, holding pillow barricades with their backs pressed into the headboard.

"Die demon, die," Liz hollered from the corner by the closet. She crossed her index fingers in a makeshift crucifix and held them up.

Haden swung his eyes toward her. "It's not demon, it's Haden. H-a-d-e-n," he said dryly.

Adrielle's heart pounded. Something in his voice cut to her core.

Liz flinched. She looked surprised it hadn't worked. She stuffed her chubby hand in her pocket and pulled out a can of pepper spray.

The others watched in horror as Haden cast a quick look around the room. His gaze drifted over the mound of clothes on the floor and trailed onto the bed where they were huddled, their arms encircling one another.

"How did you get in?" Coco snarled, pressing Adrielle safely behind her. They were at the foot of the bed, ready to make a run for it.

Haden stood just inside the window with his legs shoulder width apart and arms crossed. He was tall and muscular, with slicked-back dark hair and a chiseled jaw. He spotted Adrielle and stood immobile, the intensity of his stare making her uncomfortable.

She squirmed, stealthily trying to get a better look at him while staying safely behind Coco. Was this the Haden in the book the old woman gave her?

"How did you get inside?" Coco said, raising her quivering voice. "There's no trees or trellis. I locked the window."

"I'm not here to hurt you," Haden said, turning his gaze back to Adrielle.

"That's not what I asked." Coco straightened.

Adrielle glanced behind her. Kate was cowering like a leaf, clutching onto Veda with both hands.

"Our dad's a cop. He's just down the hall," Dave threatened, his thumb pointing toward the hall. "You should know he's got a gun."

"Nice try." Haden smirked, his dimples deepening. "I don't think Layla could make it up the stairs in time."

Coco sucked in a breath. "You know about Layla?"

He shifted his focus to Adrielle who stood directly behind Coco. "I'd hoped, but—"

Adrielle froze. There was a spark of excitement he couldn't seem to contain. Why was he hoping to see her? The warm reception in his expression when his eyes met hers threw her off.

"Hello? This isn't the least bit uncomfortable," Liz blurted. Pressing her back against the wall, she inched along it until she reached Coco's bed.

Haden took a bold step toward them. The gang huddled closer still. Kate clawed her way to the back and ducked down low, using the others for a shield. All Adrielle could see was the swirl of her auburn hair gathered into her messy bun.

"Your friends are scared," Haden said flatly. "I'm *really* not going to hurt them. I only came for you." He fixed his eyes on Adrielle.

"Me?"

He had an intensity in his eyes. An urgency. He nodded. "Yep. Let's go."

"She's not going anywhere," Coco snapped. "How dare you assume?"

Adrielle pressed her fingers into her skull. What did he want with her?

"Are you all right?" Haden asked, his voice turning more genial.

With a quick inhale Adrielle nodded.

Coco wrapped her arms protectively around her.

With Haden distracted, Liz shoved her can of pepper spray into his face and pressed the release. He scooped Liz up with one arm like she was a featherweight, until her feet dangled high in the air.

"Let me go—let me go!" she protested, kicking her legs while pummeling him with her fists.

Haden sighed and raised his eyebrows as he watched her curiously for several moments. He cocked his head. "My, you *are* feisty!" He turned his attention back to Adrielle. Adrielle shook her head.

"Very well then," he said. "I'll let you go if you promise to behave."

Liz swallowed hard, her eyes wide with alarm. Haden sat her down gently. Liz scurried like a rodent to the others. Haden sniggered, the green in his eyes flashing. He turned back to Adrielle. "Better?"

Adrielle nodded. How strange, he seemed to want to please her.

"Good. We need to go now," he said, extending his arm for her to take. His hands were strong, calloused. Fighter's hands. There was a scar along the top extending to his wrist. Adrielle scooted closer to Coco.

"You can't take her," Coco insisted, wedging herself in between Adrielle and Haden.

"He's taking her?" Kate shuddered. "He can't."

"Shh," Veda warned. "I think he can do pretty much whatever he wants."

"What about her home-sickness?"

Haden looked past Coco to Adrielle, his tone turning more serious now. "We don't have much time. You should know he's coming for you."

"Who is?" Coco rebounded, her fists balling up at her sides.

"Domenikos. And this time, he won't fail."

"Dome-who?" Liz blurted.

Haden's eyes flashed. "Your demon."

"That guy? The one that killed Josh?" Liz said.

"Yes."

Adrielle was angry and afraid. She saw in her mind Josh fall to the ground, and Domenikos' smug look of victory in one endless loop. She didn't want to see Domenikos ever again. He was the thing of nightmares. She raised her eyes to Haden. If Domenikos was after her, she had a better chance with Haden.

"You're in danger, Adrielle." Haden shifted his focus to the window and back to her.

"Where did they go? I'm not sure what happened. I turned away and they were gone. Scarlett too. How did he do that?" she demanded. Discordant chatter broke out between her friends.

"Why is she in danger?"

"Who is this Domenikos?"

"Why does she have to go?"

"Where is he taking her?"

"What's going to happen to her? To us?"

In the commotion, a surge of memories assaulted Adrielle, so palpable, they swallowed the sounds around her until she couldn't hear her friends' voices. Were these images real or a hallucination? She pressed her palms against her head and searched out Haden's gaze. He had a look of worry and angst on his face.

"Are you remembering?" he asked, watching her closely.

Adrielle didn't answer. She was being bombarded by too much hellacious information.

"Adrielle, I—this must be a shock. The spell I used—it was for your own good."

"Spell?" What was he saying? "What do you mean?" Adrielle asked, the space between her shoulders burning.

A high-pitched whimper escaped Kate. Adrielle turned to see her grab at her windpipe. She made the sign of the cross.

Veda looked shocked. "Really? You told me you didn't believe. That you only went to church for your grandma."

"Shhh . . . I was too hasty," Kate trembled, pressing her fists to her mouth.

Adrielle turned back to listen.

"It was necessary for you to survive," Haden said, sucking in a quick breath. His face had paled. "Believe me when I say it was your only escape. The only way possible to keep you alive." Haden shook his head. "He would have killed you then. And knowing what I know about you."

"You don't know *anything* about me," Adrielle sputtered.

Haden flinched. Then his eyes saddened. "Don't I?"

"You were going to be married—" Liz shot.

"Shhh!" everyone shushed.

"I'm only saying. It's in the journal."

"Shhh," Dave and Veda said.

Haden threw a sharp sideways glance at them and turned back to Adrielle. Holding her gaze, he said, "It's true. But dammit, Adrielle, we don't have time for this now." He raked his hands over his hair and sucked in a deep breath. A rush of words pelted out. "Transporting you here suppressed most of your memories, but we can get them back, Adrielle, we can. And we'll return to the way we were. Our dreams—all of them—are possible now." He took a long stride toward her.

"Stay where you are," Veda demanded squirming out of Kate's clutching grip. She shuffled to the front of the group and positioned herself in a Tae Kwon Do sparring pose.

"Is she joking?" Haden asked, making a low sound of amusement.

Kate shook her head. *"No.* Definitely no."

"Hmmm." He grunted, raising his eyebrows and swinging his attention back to Adrielle. "Things really have evolved in these modern times. Women are a lot tougher."

"Or so they think," Dave muttered, pulling on Veda's camisole and jerking her back to their cluster.

"I told the old woman I wanted the truth," Adrielle said. "She thought there was a way I could get Josh back."

A mixture of anger and jealousy flashed in Haden's eyes. "Perhaps. But this isn't about him. It's about us."

"There is no *us!*" Adrielle insisted. "I don't know you."

"But you do," he said, his eyes trailing down the chain hanging around her neck.

Adrielle coiled her fingers around her watch.

"I'm happy to see my gift travelled successfully with you," he said, grinning.

"Your gift?" Coco sputtered.

"Yes, I—"

"He did—" Liz interrupted, her head bobbing like a dash adornment. "It's in here." She pressed her index finger on the cover of the journal.

"That's outrageous. It's Mom's," Coco said, giving Haden a venomous stare.

"—wedding present. It says so in here—"

Dave jabbed Liz in the side.

"Shut up, Liz. Stay out of this," Coco yelled.

Liz pressed the book to her chest and looked hurt.

Coco turned back to Haden. "It's a lie. It is!"

Haden strode past Coco, placed his hands around Adrielle's arms, and brought her in closer. "Adrielle, listen to me. Please."

Adrielle glanced down at his hands. They looked strange on her skin, but his touch felt familiar.

Haden shook her gently. "The only way to the truth is by coming with me."

Could she believe him? Adrielle tried to remember something, anything, that would guide her. The old woman had said Haden propelled her to the future—to keep her safe. She also said it was impossible now.

"If you don't come, Domenikos will destroy everyone in this room. He'll use them as bait, tightening the vise until he gets what he wants."

"I don't know if I can trust you," Adrielle said.

Haden looked hurt. He squeezed her biceps.

"Ow," Adrielle said, trying to wriggle out of his grip but his hands were steel traps. His eyes were blazing now, as though everything hinged on this moment. She swung her gaze to Coco.

"Don't listen to her," Haden said, pushing his face into Adrielle's. "Listen to yourself. Somewhere inside you, you have to know what I'm saying is the truth."

A sharp pain stung her between her shoulders. Adrielle sucked in a sharp breath and held the air in her lungs for a long moment.

"If you want the truth, I can take you to it."

She exhaled. "I'll come."

"Adie!" Coco cried, terrified.

"I need answers Coco. It's now or never," Adrielle said. "I have to see where I fit into all this."

Disappointment settled on Coco's face.

Outside the sky cracked with thunder. Hard rain pelted through the open window onto the wood floors. Coco started to edge around Haden to clasp the panes shut. Before she had the chance to reach the window, a lightning bolt split the darkness. A black bird swept into the room.

"Kraaa, Kraaaa," The bird cawed.

"What is that?" Coco scowled, ducking as it circled the room. Dave and Veda swatted at it.

Kate closed her eyes and crouched even lower. "OMG. It's like that Hancock movie!"

"Hitchcock!" Dave spat, picking up the tennis racket leaning against the wall in the corner.

"No don't, it's—"Haden started.

Dave had hit the bird so hard it fell limp to the floor.

"Dear God, what have you done?" he stammered, sounding genuinely upset. He lifted the little wings and watched in horror as they dropped down like lead weights as he let go. He leaned down and pressed his ear to its chest, being very still as he listened for the beating heart.

Everyone watched cautiously.

"Thankfully, you haven't finished her off," he exhaled.

"Her?" Dave and Veda snorted.

He slipped the bird into the palm of his hand and gently rubbed it. "Kraaaa." The bird raised its head. "Oh, thank god. She's going to be okay."

"Why is he saying it's a her?" Dave whispered.

"Because its Astraia," Haden said.

The bird transformed into a young black woman.

"Holy shit." Dave glared, his hands trembling around the racket he still held high in the air.

The woman, who appeared to be in her early twenties, stood up, stretched, and rolled her head around until a loud crack was heard.

"Astraia," Haden acknowledged with a slight nod. "Delighted you made it."

"Hoooooly sheeters." Liz pushed her glasses up on the bridge of her nose. "Did everyone see that?" She exchanged a quick glance with Dave, then Coco. She blinked, took her glasses off and wiped them, and then slipped them back on. "And he knows her too. This wasn't in the book, but—it can't be good."

"Can't be," Coco whispered, slowly shaking her head.

Dave swallowed. "I think I have to use the little boys room." Liz grabbed his t-shirt and reeled him back. "You're not going anywhere," she breathed through barred teeth.

Kate opened her eyes and squeezed Veda's hand.

"Ouch," Veda yelped. "Let go."

"Sorry, *who* is that?" she whispered.

"Never mind," Veda said, turning her attention back to Haden. "You're better off keeping your eyes closed."

"Have you seen Domenikos?" Astraia asked; worry etched all over her face.

Haden shook his head.

"Angelo?" she asked, searching the room. Her eyes traced over to Adrielle. Adrielle squirmed, feeling the heat of her stare. "That's her, isn't it?"

Haden threw a sideways glance and confirmed with a slight nod. "Yep."

Adrielle cringed. How much stranger was this going to get?

"Angelo's somewhere out there," Haden said, pacing to the window and leaning out. "We need to go, and fast. Keeping one step ahead is our only advantage. Funny, I don't see him—dear God!" he gasped, taking a large step back. "Up there." He pointed. "Hundreds of them."

Astraia squeezed in between Haden and Coco to get a clearer view. "Oh-oh. It may be too late."

"Look at all the birds," Coco exclaimed. "The sky is covered with them."

Countless black birds were silhouetted against the low hanging moon. They whirled in ever-changing patterns, twisting and changing direction.

"Oh my god," Kate squealed from the bed. "I told you—it's Hancock."

"Hitchcock. Hitchcock," Dave said.

"C'mon," Haden said, clasping Adrielle's hand. "We need to go *now!*"

"Are you outta your mind?" Coco protested, wedging in between them.

"We're going," he snapped, grabbing Adrielle's wrists and pulling her toward him. His eyes flashed. "Time's up. I can't explain now, but *you* are the only one with the power to stop him."

"You can't possibly be considering this. He's a stranger," Coco said angrily.

"They're coming by the swarms," Astraia hissed, still leaning out the window. "We have to find Angelo."

Haden slipped beside her to search the sky again. "He was right there when I came in." He pointed to the outside ledge. "Never mind him. He'll show up eventually."

"One of Domenikos' gnomes must have—" Astraia said.

"No. He's too smart for that."

"Go! I'll wait here for him."

"You're staying *here?*" Haden asked. He seemed surprised.

"Only until Angelo comes. We need to confer with him and plan our next step."

"Very well." Haden turned to Adrielle. "Let's go!"

"What? No!" Coco shrieked.

Adrielle stood still. Haden seemed so sure Domenikos was coming for her. Could she believe him? If so, she wasn't ready to face him. Not yet.

"Don't go," Kate said, her voice quivering.

Adrielle studied her friends. They were scared. All of them except Liz, who pressed the book tightly to her chest and had that look she got whenever her mind was putting together pieces of a puzzle. If Haden was right, she couldn't risk their lives.

"You can do this," Haden said, wrapping his arms around her. "You're the keeper of the chronometer."

Adrielle shivered.

"Don't listen to him," Coco said, her voice breaking.

Adrielle took Coco's hands and squeezed. "Stop mothering me." She blew her bangs up, and they fell back onto her forehead. "It's just like you said. Embrace who I am or spend the rest of my life hiding from it. I need to get to the bottom of this."

"You've never listened to me before."

"I haven't, have I? God. What a pain in the butt I've been."

Adrielle turned to Haden and swallowed hard. She didn't know how this worked, but she was ready.

Haden gestured toward her friends and made a slight face. "They really care about you. You know, you might never get back here."

Adrielle acknowledged with the bob of her head. "That's what the scepter woman warned."

"Monika? You saw her?" Haden was surprised.

"I didn't know her name, but yeah. She warned everything would change." Adrielle gave her friends a nod and turned back to a teary-eyed Coco. She squeezed Coco's hand and fought away tears. "Te quiero."

If this was her destiny, she would embrace it.

Chapter 11

Florida – Present Day

"UHHH, GUYS." KATE pointed shakily toward Astraia. "The creepy bird-girl is still here."

"It's Astraia. As in the scales of justice," Astraia said indignantly.

Coco, too stunned to comment, could only stare at her.

Dave snapped his fingers. "Oh that's right. Astraia was the Greek goddess of justice. After the world became wicked, she left the earth and became the constellation Virgo."

"I've never been a goddess. And I'm still here. I'm Achaean," Astraia corrected.

Dave thought for a moment. "Not sure what that means."

Astraia seemed put off at first, but then studied Dave curiously. "We are an ancient species, superior to humans. Our natural form is bird-like, but we can change to look like you. And we can time travel. Think of us as bird-people."

"So, Achaeans are shapeshifters?" Dave asked.

"In a way." Astraia wandered to the window and gazed out.

"Where did you come from?"

Astraia looked over her shoulder at him, her expression showing a rush of irritation. She was clearly on edge about the friend she was expecting. "We evolved, like everything else. We're not mythological creatures. At one time we roamed freely like dinosaurs. Most people forget many species became extinct. We survived and blended in."

Why was David going on about it with her? Coco chewed on her thumbnail. This didn't feel right. Her friend Haden took Adrielle, and now they were expecting someone else? For all she knew, this was a home invasion, and they would all be held as hostages.

Coco glanced at Liz. She was mystified too. Without taking her eyes off Astraia, Liz dug in her handbag and replaced her inhaler with a Twizzler. She chomped on it nervously.

Dave tapped her hand lightly, and the candy dropped to the floor. "You're dieting."

"Five second rule," Liz growled, picking the licorice up and blowing on it three times.

"Should we—be afraid of you?" Veda asked, jumping into a sparring position. "I know Tae Kwon Do."

Astraia turned her attention away from the dark sky only for a moment. "I'd forgotten how amusing you mortals can be. That won't get you far with Domenikos. *'Pain for amusement's sake'* is his motto."

Liz stopped munching mid-chew. "Domenikos? As in the Goth that sliced Josh's neck?"

"The one and only," she said, continuing her patrol.

A small choking sound came from Liz as she wrapped her fingers around her throat.

Coco, trying to figure out what was happening, asked, "What does he want with Adrielle's watch?"

"I assume by watch you mean chronometer," Dave interjected.

"Yes." Dave could be so irritating. Coco took two bold steps to Astraia but keeping a safe distance away from her. "Supposing that's what he's after, killing Josh must have been a scare tactic."

"Domenikos doesn't do scare tactics. It was a direct threat. That's why Josh is dead," Astraia said. "Whoever is in possession of the chronometer, masters time."

"You mean time travel?" Dave clarified.

"Yes."

"Woowsa. That's pretty powerful. People have killed for a lot less," Dave said.

"The watch is Adrielle's," Liz said. "It's in the journal—it was Haden's wedding gift."

"Damn it, Liz," Coco chided. "That journal is useless."

"Let me see it," Astraia said.

Liz held it out grudgingly.

Astraia leafed through it and handed it back. "Looks like some of it is in Haden's handwriting. It could have valuable information."

Coco was surprised Astraia gave it back. She returned to the window and studied the sky.

"Where—*is*—Angelo?" Astraia's voice was terse and agitated. "We need him. Domenikos will be here any minute."

"Is he going to kill us?" Liz asked.

"That all depends on Adrielle. Not if she owns up to her position."

"What do you mean?" Coco asked. Astraia seemed serious. She didn't like the idea of Adrielle being connected to any of this.

"Right now, I'll bet Haden's showing her what will happen if she doesn't get involved. Hopefully they don't mess anything up on their little time travel expedition."

"What will happen?" Coco asked.

"Wait a minute, are you saying they've gone back in history?" Dave asked. "That time travel really is possible?"

"Yes."

Dave slapped his hand to his forehead. "Holy cow. That's so dangerous."

"There was a ban placed on travelling," Astraia said. "Some objected, but it was the only solution for co-habitation between our species. Domenikos was the leader of the opposition. He killed our leaders, the ones who upheld the law."

"If you're a superior race, why doesn't the government know about you?" Coco said. "And what does this have to do with Adrielle?" All of this was outrageous. But the bird transformation really confused her. It looked so real. And how did Adrielle and Haden vanish like that?

Astraia turned to Coco, her seriousness disarming. "You must already know Adrielle is different. She is the link between mortals and Achaeans. Destined to take her place as the time keeper."

"Time keeper? You had me until the destiny thing. I don't believe in it," Dave said.

"Believe what you will. It doesn't change the truth."

"So why the chronometer?" Coco interjected.

"The chronometer is her tool. It can take her to a specific place or time. If it gets in Domenikos' hands—" Astraia lowered her eyes.

Coco glanced at the scars on her forearms. She thought about the fire. How her mother made her promise to give the chronometer to Adrielle. Coco chewed her nails again, a habit she'd kicked in the seventh grade.

"Your manicure," Veda whispered.

Coco slipped her hands under her armpits. This was heavy stuff. She paced the room. The strappy heels she'd worn to the party were lying in her path. Frustrated, she kicked them into her closet.

"What if Adrielle doesn't co-operate?" Liz asked.

Astraia made a quick slashing gesture across her neck. "If she's lucky."

"Yick, that's a treat-spoiler." Liz meandered to the small trashcan by the dresser. She unfolded the wrapper she'd saved and spit her candy into it. She was about to toss it in, and instead kicked the metal trashcan with her Sperry deck shoes. She tossed the candy in her handbag and spun around to Astraia. "What *exactly* do you expect Adrielle to do?"

Astraia took so long to answer, Liz's attention turned to the dresser. She picked up an eyeshadow palette. "Coco, why is there so much makeup? It looks like an Ulta store."

Everyone began talking at once. Coco leaned against the wall. She listened to the buzz and fought to sort through questions churning in her head as Liz played shuffleboard with her perfume bottles.

"Everyone stop!" Coco grunted through barred teeth. She leaned in so close to Astraia her breath felt icy on her skin. "All I want to know is where did Adrielle go? And when is she coming back?"

Kate put up her hand. "Excuse me, if we're all asking questions, I want to know what was sticking out of Adrielle's back?"

Everyone turned to Astraia.

"It's a badge," Astraia said. "The first stage of her transformation."

"Are we talking cell modification?" Dave asked, alarmed.

"Like in the Fly movie? Or Spiderman?" Kate whimpered. "She'll never get a boyfriend."

"Shhhhh," Everyone, including Astraia, hissed.

"WHOA, TAKE A look at this." Dave summoned the others to the window. "See that glow? It's St. Elmos' fire."

"Saint who?" Kate asked.

"Not a person, its plasma. A form of matter found in stars that's sometimes caused by lightning, or high temperature flames. An electric field causes ionization of the air molecules, roughly 1000 volts per centimeter, and it sets off a bright blue or violet glow."

"Sorry I asked," Kate mumbled, turning back to her fashion magazine. "Listening to you is kinda like watching the news. Or nail polish drying. I'm not sure which is worse."

Coco and Veda joined Dave at the window.

"Looks like fireworks," Veda said.

"This is so rare," Dave exclaimed. "The conditions needed are a high voltage differential between clouds and the ground underneath. Sometimes thunderstorms bring it on, but, like I said, extremely rare."

"Let me see," Astraia said, wedging her way to the window. She leaned out to study the sky. "Hate to disappoint you, but the colorful glow is also caused by an overload in Achaean travelling. Which doesn't make any sense."

"I'm with you," Kate said, looking up from her magazine.

"Ahem. As I was saying, I don't understand. The glow is too bright for the three Achaeans that are left."

The sky darkened. "Where did they all come from?" Coco asked, mesmerized as thousands of birds filled the sky.

"What do they want?" Veda asked. "It's creepy."

"Awesome. It's a murmuration," Dave said, wedging his way back to the window. "Look it up."

Kate held up her iPhone to ask Siri. "A murmur what?"

Coco didn't like seeing the alarm on Astraia's face. "What's going on Astraia?"

"Domenikos—he must have gotten a hold of a spell and taken the other Achaeans as slaves."

"Why are they coming here?" Coco asked, closing the window and locking it. Her heart pounded and her armpits felt damp. Calm down. Her panic attack wouldn't help anyone.

"That's not going to keep them out," Astraia warned.

With a harsh tug Coco pulled the curtain shut. "What do they want? Adrielle's gone now."

"Domenikos is smart. He knows it's only a matter of time before she returns."

"And then what?" Dave asked. "If she comes back, he whisks her away?"

"Something like that."

Veda's face paled. "He's going to use us as bait."

"She's not even here. Who knows if she'll *ever* come back—" Kate dabbed at her eyes with a Kleenex, saw it was already soaked with tears, and tossed it into the trashcan. "Sorry Coco," she said, her voice shaking. "But you heard that guy she left with. It might not even be possible."

Coco went to gnaw on her fingers and stopped. She'd destroyed her nails. She tucked her hands into her armpits. "So, what do we do?"

"Sorry, this is unprecedented," Astraia said. "Anything goes."

"What about your friend? Why isn't he here yet?" Veda asked.

"Angelo? I don't know. At this point, all we can do is wait."

"Ahhh . . . I'm *so* hungry. We never did have dinner." Liz tucked her pencil and sketchpad away. She was sitting on the floor just outside the closet, surrounded by food wrappers, her legs stretched out in front.

"Really?" Dave shook his head. "How can you eat at a time like this?"

Coco had watched her kick off her Sperry's and dump her purse upside down, then go through all her reserve snacks while sketching Astraia, probably in case they needed to describe her to the police.

"You know I always stress eat. I'm nervous, so deal with it." She stuffed empty wrappers back into her purse and sat it on her lap.

Dave sighed.

"What do you keep in there anyways?" Coco asked. "It's like this bottomless pit."

They all started laughing. Liz licked her finger and rubbed on a darkened stain on the leather.

"Pull us out a seven-layer burrito," Veda coaxed.

"I wish." Liz giggled, flattening out her handbag. "Wish I'd bought some of that jerky when we were in line at Walmart. Maybe I should go downstairs? There was some stuff in the fridge."

Dave turned to Astraia. "Do you think that's a good idea? I mean . . . is it safe?"

Astraia shrugged.

"I'll take my chances." Liz jumped up. She pulled down on her t-shirt when her tummy poked out underneath, and mumbled, "It shrunk in the dryer." She grabbed Coco's pink and black polka dotted robe hanging on a hook in the closet. "Can I borrow this?"

"Sure," Coco said. "It's one size fits all."

Liz slipped it on and tied it in around the waist. She pulled out the mace from her handbag, aligned the sprayer so it was ready to deploy, and slipped her purse strap over her shoulder.

"OMG. You're taking your purse?" Coco guffawed.

"You never know," Liz said, her voice deadly serious. "Be right back."

Meanwhile, Veda was playing with her iPhone, completely oblivious to everything.

"What are you doing?" Coco asked, after Liz stepped out.

"Facebook creeping. Jill just updated her status. She's in a relationship with Rob, you know, that geeky guy at the party."

"You're kiddin' me." Kate laughed. "Never would have guessed."

"Didn't I tell you? She was acting all slutty. Didn't you see that spandex thing she was wearing? Look, she posted selfies."

They scrolled through her profile and spent a good while creeping on various sites.

"Liz should have come back by now," Dave said, his voice filled with alarm. "I told you guys she shouldn't have gone."

"She's probably still eating." Veda chuckled.

"No. Definitely no. She would've come back with stuff. Plus, I texted her. I'm going down," Dave announced, pacing toward the door.

Astraia stiffened. "I don't think that's a good idea. If by chance they've taken her."

"Taken her? I thought you said it was okay for her to go down?" Coco fretted.

"I never said that."

"I should've just gone downstairs with her." Dave groaned.

"It won't do any good if we all get separated. I'll come down with you. The rest of you sit tight." Astraia glanced over her shoulder at the sky. "If Angelo pops in, tell him I'll be right back."

"Pops in?" Kate huffed, sidling over to Veda after they left. "She makes it sound so, so typical."

Coco parted the window curtains and looked out. "Holy shoot. They're gone. All the birds are gone!"

"Can't be, can it?" Veda said, glancing up from her phone. She went to the window. A chill seeped in from outside, causing the windowpane to fog. "Damn. Not a spec in sight. I wonder what that means?"

"It means they took Liz," Astraia said, reappearing in the doorway.

Dave was behind her, his jaw hanging open. He stepped in front of her, lifted a container with a half- eaten rotisserie chicken for everyone to see, and burst into tears.

Chapter 12

London – November 8, 1888

LIZ FOUND HERSELF standing under a streetlight, the dim yellow glow illuminating a cobblestoned street. Lining the boulevard were narrow attached row houses that looked exactly alike and reached as far as she could see. There were no cars zipping past. The street was deserted.

It was a bitter night, the cold damp cutting into her bones. It felt like midwinter, not a Florida summer night. Where was she?

Damn, it was cold. Her breath came out in jagged little puffs and quickly disappeared the way it had when she was a girl growing up in Jersey. She put her fists up to her mouth and blew warm air.

This couldn't be happening. She squeezed her eyes shut and re-opened them.

Still here, she blinked. *If you panic, you'll be toast*, she told herself, thinking of every low-budget film she'd ever seen.

Liz folded over the two sides of Coco's pink and black polka-dotted robe, re-tightened the belt, and lifted the collar up tight against her neck. She had to be brave. She pulled her purse strap snugly over her right shoulder. Thank goodness she had her purse. She rubbed her arms up and down. Clues, there had to be clues. She reviewed what she remembered.

Her hand was on the fridge door. She was dead set on sinking her teeth into the rotisserie chicken on the bottom shelf; her mouth had been watering for it since she'd seen it earlier. Oh yeah, she'd sat the container on the counter and began picking at it, ripping at pieces of meat and stuffing them into her mouth before anyone came down.

She ran her tongue along the front of her teeth, then over her back molars; a piece of chicken was caught in between two molars. *So, it had happened! But how did I get here? In this strange place?* Fear set her on edge.

She remembered a warm sensation had started in her chest. It coursed outward until it swam through her veins. It was a numbing tingly feeling, not unlike drifting to sleep. She'd passed it off as heartburn, which made sense. She'd been eating so fast.

Hoofs and the sound of grating wheels startled her. A solitary horse and carriage clipped around the corner and echoed. It was headed her way.

Gah. Horses? Carriages?

She ducked under a tree on the boulevard and leaned up against the trunk. Had she travelled through time? Could that tingly sensation be what one feels when passing through time? Or was she dreaming?

Admittedly, this wouldn't be the first time she'd fallen asleep eating. Once before she'd woken herself up chewing imaginary food; grinding her teeth so hard she'd chipped a tooth. Her jaw was tense and tight. It clicked as she wiggled it side to side. Boy, she really had to start wearing her mouth guard.

She tucked her hands under her armpits and watched the carriage until it disappeared around the corner. She was alone again. Few stars twinkled in the sky. She smelled horse manure. Where was Dave when you needed him? This didn't make sense.

If she was painfully honest, it was bad news the minute that guy appeared. That weird, smug, guy that hauled Adrielle away. *Haden,* he'd said he was. No, she'd known it before. The minute she'd started reading that old journal.

Liz reached into her handbag and fumbled, shoving empty candy wrappers around. "Jumping jellybeans," she cursed, why hadn't she dumped the wrappers into Coco's trash? She hadn't wanted everyone to see how much junk she'd consumed. But, *whateva,* as Coco would say.

Thoughts of Coco set her emotions spiraling. What if she never saw her friends again? Hot sloppy tears blurred her vision and fogged her glasses. She hated when that happened. She slipped them off and used her robe to rub the glass until it gleamed, then slipped them back on, pushing the frames up tight against the bridge of her nose. Better. She peered through the lenses at her surroundings. *Wow.* Even the yellow glow of the streetlamp looked real.

She reached for her phone. No reception. Of course not, that would be too easy.

She scoped up and down the street. No one was around. What now? She swallowed a lump. She had to find a way back on her own.

She fumbled in the pit of her purse for her notepad and pencil. Yes! She smiled, feeling the crisp edge of the cover. She'd secured it to Adrielle's journal with her black hair elastic. Almost afraid to pull out the worn leather book, she lifted it out and raised it up to the streetlight. She tugged at a knot of hair clinging to the elastic until it came off and snapped the elastic around her wrist.

The answers had to be in there, didn't they? She rifled through the journal pages back to front, her fingers skimming the paper with a feathery touch. So much writing to go through, all in old-style calligraphy. There was a piece of hard candy stuck on one of the pages. She pulled on it and it left a mark and took some of the surface writing off. *Dang.* She looked around to make sure no one was watching, blew on it for good measure and stuffed it in her mouth—who knew when the next meal would come?

Under the dim streetlight, Liz found solace in the inked words; the foreign locale not as jarring in the face of a stirring mystery. Despite everything, excitement budded. She had a real full-fledged mystery to solve. She devoured the narrative while keeping her ears pricked for sounds. A heavy raindrop pelted onto the page and the ink began to run.

Oh no . . . She blotted it with the palm of her hand, wiping the excess ink onto her robe. She raised her eyes to the sky. A storm. The night sky was so dark she hadn't noticed the rain-laden clouds overhead. Pulling the bathrobe over her head, she stuffed the journal and her notes back in her purse. At least she was wearing her gray Sperry topsiders. Thank goodness she hadn't listened to Dave's party-fashion sense. Heels would be useless. She'd gone with her gut and worn her comfortable walking shoes.

"You've been blessed, Lizzie-bear." She smiled, the words rolling off her tongue in a whisper. Just like her grams used to say—well, technically, as Kate's Irish-Catholic grandma used to say. It stuck because Kate started to say it. Kate, the believer.

Seeking shelter if the storm got worse would be difficult. She'd have to knock on doors. Try to explain. *What exactly?* That she was stranded in another lifetime? In her fuzzy pink and black robe?

She wondered if anyone had noticed she was gone yet. Specifically, if Kate knew. Because that meant Kate was saying her prayers right about now, and she could use every bit of help she could get.

Liz wondered if the others knew Kate's secret. She hid it well. The only reason she knew was because she'd caught Kate reading the Bible. Once, during library-quiet-time at school. Kate had tucked it into a *Cosmo* for camouflage. So she was pretty sure the others didn't know. At the time, Kate exchanged a look with her that said, *please don't tell.* And Liz had kept her secret. All this time, she'd never told anyone. Because she also had a secret.

For years, she'd dreamt of being an investigative journalist the way other little girls dream of being a Victoria Secret model.

For this reason, Liz carried her pad and pencil at all times. She even titled a section in her notebook: *top ten unsolved crimes*, detailing the main facts, on the odd chance she ran into info that might solve them. All day long she'd take notes, observations, thoughts, sketched, doodled, recording anything that may become relevant, in hopes that one day, she would transform into a successful news anchor like Rachel Maddow. Or maybe even Katie Couric, her hero. The first female news anchor to front her own show.

Only Dave discovered the truth about her aspirations. Over homemade brownies, one late night during *Project Runway* binging, they'd shared their fears, hopes, and dreams. She chuckled, feeling a hollow pit. He was her one true confidant. Leave it to Dave to spell out her one flaw that would hinder her success—her outward appearance.

There was no denying that in contrast to other successful anchors, Liz was too fat, too messy, and too—well, she hated using the urban term *gender ninja*—she'd seen it written on the bathroom stall in red lipstick: LIZ IS A GENDER NINJA!!!

She sucked in a breath. That stung. She'd had to look it up. Google said it meant gender indecipherable. Probably left there by Scarlett. She'd never forgotten how it made her feel. Or the red smear she left when she tried to wipe it off with toilet paper. That was how she was perceived by the mean girls.

Dave saw her swollen eyes and pried it out of her. Together they'd concocted a plan to reach her goals. Dave was the one person in the world who believed if she stuck to the plan, one day she'd be smart enough, pretty enough, and courageous enough, to chase her dream.

From around the corner, a tall strawberry-blonde woman appeared. Liz's heart spiked. She sank into the shadows. The only way to ward off fear was to think of this as an investigative assignment.

Beside the woman, was a man with a pale complexion. She followed them as they crossed the boulevard and turned onto Dorset Street. The man's attire struck her as strange. He was wearing a long dark coat with a white astrakhan collar and dark spats that covered his light button up boots. *Spats?* An uncomfortable tightness squeezed her chest.

If Dave hadn't taken that course on fashion, she might not know that men wore cloth spats over their boots in the late nineteenth and early twentieth century to protect them from the mud and rain. By the mid 1930s, they were considered old fashioned.

She had the odd feeling he was someone to notice. She looked at the man's face. It was too dark to see clearly. For some reason, he looked familiar. *Impossible.* He carried kid gloves in his right hand, a package on his left.

The woman wore a long dress with a white apron. She was laughing as they neared the streetlight, the yellow glow gleamed on the man's horseshoe pin secured to his necktie. Just as she was about to get a good look at him, he pulled his felt hat over his eyes. If she didn't know any better, she would have thought he did it on purpose. But she was well hidden behind the tree.

He wore a massive gold chain tucked into his waistcoat. The chain was familiar. His moustache thick and—gross. No wonder they went out of style.

The couple strolled past her, arms interlinked.

They turned down Dorset Street. Liz tracked them, ducking behind every tree. She strained to hear every word.

He calls the woman Mary Kelly. She scribbled it onto her pad. *Mary Kelly.* The name had a ring to it. Why? As she walked, she rifled through her notepad, dodging potholes and squinting to see her notes in the dim lighting. She flipped back, and back, and back, pausing whenever they did, to skim over the "Thames mysteries," or "Embankment murders," and then further back, until she saw the name *Mary Jane Kelly* scribbled in red ink, in the section titled: *most horrific unsolved crimes.*

No . . .

Her stomach twisted the way it did when she'd devoured too many Doritos and her stomach complained. She gulped. It was plain as anything in her notepad . . . under number three, halfway down on page twenty-two, she'd doodled the words "Jack the Ripper." And right beside it, *victim: Mary Jane Kelly*, his last known murder. She'd even sketched a sharp pointy knife on the inside of the page.

"No, No, No!" Her heart raced. She flipped frantically back and forth, certain she'd had a talk with Dave about that last murder. What was is it he'd said?

There. In green ink—a gag gift from Dave on her birthday because he knew she hated green—they'd googled the details and discussed the written account: *The whole of the surface of the abdomen and thighs was removed and the abdominal cavity emptied of its viscera. The breasts were cut off, the arms mutilated by several jagged wounds and the face hacked beyond recognition of the features. The tissues of the neck were severed all round down to the bone.*

Liz rounded the other side of a nearby tree, bent over, and heaved. She wiped her mouth with her sleeve and stared at the regurgitated chicken with chunks of red licorice mixed in. She'd never eat licorice again. Not ever.

Up ahead, the pair stopped in front of a doorway.

Could he really be Jack the Ripper? The woman was pretty. Twinkly blue eyes, reddish blonde hair with a large bust. She reminded her of Kate.

How did the pieces of the puzzle fit? Both the Thames murders and the Ripper murders happened around the same time. The old-fashioned row houses, the clothes, the cold damp weather. England. She had to be in England.

Somehow, she must have traveled back. November 8th, 1888. That's when it happened. By the next morning, November ninth—*hours from now*—this girl would be toast. Mutilated beyond recognition. The pit in her stomach churned.

Kate would say there was a reason she was here, in this place, at this time. She didn't believe in destiny. She'd had a whole discussion with Dave about it. He'd said the only thing that got you to where you'd be in the future, were your choices. She wanted to believe Kate. God, was she supposed to stop it?

Liz fought to remember an etched drawing she'd seen online of the man who'd last been seen with Mary Jane Kelly. She pulled out her phone. *Dang.* She shook it. Of course, there was no signal in the past.

She turned back to study the couple. This time, the man lifted his head and stared back. It all came in a flash. The green flecks, that insolent grin. *OMG,* it was *him.* Domenikos.

Liz fumbled in her purse and found the mace. Making sure the sprayer was pointed correctly, she yelled, "Run, run for your life. The man beside you is Jack the Ripper. He's going to slaughter you!"

Domenikos smiled.

Someone pulled on the back of her robe and caught her by the wrist. "What the hell are you doing?" he seethed, swiveling her around.

It was Haden, a fierce glare on his face.

"I need to stop him."

"No, you twit! You *can't* stop him, not if you ever want to see Adrielle again."

Chapter 13

London – November 8, 1888

WHERE WAS HADEN? And why had he brought her to London only to leave? The cold wind snapped against Adrielle's skin and thrashed her white hair like a whip behind her. She shivered, raising the lapel of her collar and buttoning it before shoving her hands in her pockets. It was cold. Damn cold. Leaning into the wind, she quickened her pace.

Long strides drove her along the Thames River toward Pimlico, to gain information on the "Embankment murders." During breakfast, at a café Haden had taken her to, she'd browsed through the paper, skimming articles containing details of the recent serial killings. *The London Times* was littered with them. Dismembered bodies had been turning up along the banks. Though Adrielle had no proof Domenikos was behind it, a burning ache in her gut told her she was on the right path.

She reached the corner of the London tower and paused to watch the reflection of the stars on the Thames, then placed her hands on the stonewall and stared deep into the water. It looked cold and turbulent and mysterious. Though beautiful, it was more rugged than the Seine. There was a damp, unfamiliar smell that clung to this river.

Adrielle had never traveled before all of this madness, much less been to London or Paris. Jacksonville was as far north as she'd ever gone, and Orlando as far south. Now, halfway around the world, she was seeing things she had only ever dreamed of. The wanderlust bug was biting hard, and thoughts of travelling the world were growing more and more appealing.

Haden had explained about Domenikos, the Achaean species. Even time travel. She had so many unanswered questions. She reached inside her coat and felt the cold metal of the chronometer. She was surprised Haden allowed her to keep such a valuable tool, considering it was the one thing Domenikos wanted. She'd offered it up to Haden, partly out of fear for having to defend herself against Domenikos again, but Haden insisted it was to remain with her at all times.

She glanced down at it, taking pleasure in the delicate gold hands that ticked their way around the face. It was late, it said, well past midnight.

Few strangers ambled by. Adrielle gave a simple nod. It seemed to suffice well, to exchange greetings. It was soothing to see basic human courtesy remained intact, though she was in a different time period.

Across the street, the corner shop sold winter attire. She crossed the cobbled boulevard and stood in front of the window. Her platinum hair reflected in the glass. It seemed to glow in this gray city.

There was a particularly pretty fur bonnet, paired with black kid gloves, on display inside the store. It looked like fox fur. Unfortunately, because of the late hour, the store was closed.

What she wouldn't give for a pair of gloves. Her fingers were cold, stiff, and chafed. She wouldn't be surprised if she got frostbite. She balled her fists and looked up and down the street. It was deserted. The glass would be easy enough to break. She was pretty good at copying some of Veda's Tae Kwon Do moves, all she had to do was put all her weight behind a high kick.

Adrielle was contemplating what Coco would do when she caught a reflection. Two shadows moving stealthily toward her. Who? She couldn't be sure, but she had the rising dread of something terrible about to happen. She ducked into the doorway and pressed her back against the door. From the alcove she had a clearer view. Two men. The rounded end of a club poked underneath one overcoat.

Paralyzing fear washed over her. She might not be able to outrun them.

Mimicking what she'd seen in movies and TV, she wrapped her hand with her coat and punched it against the windowpane. Momentarily shocked, she stood frozen, watching shards of glass shatter to the ground. Then she reached inside to unlatch the lock, entered quickly, and grabbed a large, jagged shard as a weapon.

The edge of the glass cut into her skin. She winced, a spurt of blood oozing out. She pulled her sleeve to cover the gash and to make it easier to hold the shard's jagged edge. She entered the store and followed a walkway to the storeroom, then hid behind boxes of inventory.

Their footsteps were not far behind. Light pads on the wood. The creaking of the planks gave them away. With a sharp intake of breath, Adrielle raised the glass shard over her shoulder.

In the dim light, elongated shadows crept closer. Gone from her mind were the gloves and bonnet from the display. This was survival. She thought about the murders. The girls in the embankment that had lost their lives, and she wondered if this would be her last memory.

A cold hand reached out of the darkness and grabbed her mane of hair.

With the ferocity of a wild animal, she plunged the shard into the man's arm. A yelping screech filled the room and the grip on her hair released. Boxes crashed to the floor.

Adrielle tensed, ready to lunge. The shadows of the figures flickered along the wall as they moved away from her. Their hushed cries grew weaker. Crushing glass by the front door told her they were on their way out. She exhaled. Safe for now. But for how long?

Adrielle tiptoed along the wall, a packing knife she'd found by an empty container clutched in her hand. She snatched the black bonnet and gloves and bolted out through the doorway. She couldn't stay here, and it wouldn't do any good to stick out. Her white hair was as bright as a lit flare.

Half expecting someone to shout at her, Adrielle turned back to the path, devouring the street with her eyes. It looked deserted, but she couldn't be sure.

While running, she pulled on the bonnet and gloves. She wondered what her friends would think. She knew what Coco would think. It was wrong to steal. But she'd be proud of her too.

Adrielle pushed fear to the back of her mind. She needed to keep her head. Crossing the fair distance across town would sap her energy. She slowed her pace to a lengthy stride.

What did the others think of her disappearing like that? Would she ever see them again? She hoped so.

Her one regret? The book. She wished she'd tucked it into her pocket, if it even worked that way when it came to travelling. She didn't know if anything on her was transported—they had it both ways in movies. But this was real life. She'd have to ask Haden.

The old woman at Scarlett's party had said that the book contained answers to her questions. She smiled . . . Liz, with her overactive imagination and love of mysteries, had already been devouring the pages.

Ahhh . . . a wave of nostalgia punched her gut. She winced, sucking in a long breath. She'd expected it, the homesickness. In fact, she was surprised at how long it had taken for it to hit. She was the only one of her friends that had never been on a sleepover because of it. A surge of anxiety came over her. She squeezed the memory of home into a deep corner of her mind and focused on the path ahead. She couldn't get weak. Not now. The only thing to do was trudge on.

"THERE YOU ARE. Where have you been?" Astraia wailed. "Babysitting this group of—I don't know, *teens*—I guess you'd say, is not part of my job description."

"We're not teens, we're adults." Veda objected.

Coco winced. This was not the time to get testy.

Astraia raised a brow.

"Technically, it's true. We're eighteen. All of us except for—well, I guess Adrielle is too," Dave said, his voice weak.

Coco shot him a look. Why did her friends have such big mouths?

Astraia flung her hands up in desperation. "See what I've had to put up with?"

"Never mind all that. Where's Adrielle?" Angelo asked impatiently as he scoured the room.

"With Haden."

"Haden?" Angelo sucked in a sharp breath. "How did that happen? The plan was for all of us to meet here."

Plan? They planned this? Coco studied Angelo's cherubic face and chipped at her nail polish. He was handsome. More handsome than the other one. But there was a resemblance around the eyes.

"I don't know. He just . . ."

"Where did he take her? I can't believe you trusted him with her."

He couldn't be trusted. Coco knew it. She bit her tongue to keep from screaming out.

"It's not like I had a choice, Angelo. You know how he can be. Especially when it comes to her."

"This doesn't sound good," Coco whispered to Veda. What did they all want with Adrielle?

"I know," Veda said, pulling out her phone surreptitiously. She switched the camera view from selfie-mode and started recording.

"What are you doing?" Coco snapped.

"No one will ever believe this. Not if we don't record it."

"Unbelievable." Coco lunged for the phone and snatched it out of her hand.

"You are such a buzz kill," Veda grunted.

"How can you think of posting at a time like this? Honestly. Sometimes I think all you care about is talking snark."

"Well? What is it, exactly, that you'd like me to do?"

"Figure out a way to get them back. Both of them."

After she said it, Coco realized Angelo had been watching their entire exchange.

"Two are missing?" he said.

"Mhmm." Astraia nodded. "Domenikos' minions must have snagged the other one when she went downstairs."

"She never came back," Dave said, holding up the chicken container. His expression twisting with a wave of gloom.

Angelo frowned, then trekked to the window and stared into the night. "See that glow? There's a lot of activity going on out there."

Astraia strode to his side. They stared into the sky for a long moment. "Yeah, something's definitely going on."

"A Doppler effect," he said. "You hear that? A lot more travellers than we expected. And they're getting closer. We need to find Adrielle."

Travellers? Coco felt as though she'd been punched in the stomach. How many were there? What was going on?

"Can I come with?" Dave asked. He rubbed at his knees as he stood.

"No."

"C'mon. She's my best friend. I have to get her back," he grumbled. "And my legs have gone to sleep from sitting here.

"You don't get to complain. Remain still and behave." Angelo pivoted to Astraia, his expression turning dour. "This is just a setback. Everything is still in play."

Everything? My god, this *had* been planned. Coco searched her mind, trying to think back to the night of the fire.

"What about them? Can we just leave them here?" Astraia asked. "You said yourself, they're getting closer. It won't be long before they arrive."

Kate clutched onto Veda's arm, crouching into as small of a ball as she could.

Angelo skimmed over their faces and stopped at Coco. "How much do you know?"

"Only what Adrielle told us. Something about going back to change the past."

"And Domenikos?"

"Nothing—ah, Adrielle said he killed Josh. That he sliced his neck. Is it true?"

"Perhaps. But I bet otherwise," Angelo said.

"You mean he's still alive? Or did Adrielle imagine it?"

"No, that's not what I mean at all. I'm saying that killing him like that—so easily, I'd believe it more if he'd tortured him."

"Torture?" Coco exchanged a look with Dave. What were they up against?

UNEVEN COBBLESTONES PRESSED on the heels of Adrielle's feet. She ran along the riverbank. Crisp air biting into her cheeks. As she ran, her mind drifted.

Even if she got to Pimlico and asked around about the murders, what would that do? She wasn't here to solve those murders, she was here to save her mom.

From the start she'd wanted to find a way back to the night of the fire. That's all she'd wanted as far back as she could remember. But Haden had first taken her to Paris to witness Hitler's atrocities. Maybe to prove he could time travel. And then he'd brought her to London, only to mysteriously disappear.

Why the detours? What was Haden up to? She didn't want to go anywhere near Domenikos. In fact, the opposite. The further the better.

Adrielle stopped running. She braced her hands on her knees to catch her breath and stared up at the dark sky. She felt alone. Small, in the scheme of things. She paced along the riverbank, drifting until she found a quiet place. Her gut told her she was going about it all wrong. First, she'd save her mom. Then she'd worry about Domenikos and Josh.

Making sure she was still alone, she pulled on the leather gloves, finger by finger, and slipped them off. She took the chronometer from her pocket. *You'd better work.* She cradled it in her hands and stared into its face.

Adrielle held it up to her forehead and closed her eyes. *What now?* She felt stupid. She needed the book. Yes, that was as good a start as any. She squeezed her eyes shut to conjure up an image of the simple binding. The worn leather cover. And that ornate handwriting.

Surprisingly, Liz, her frizzy bed-head hair and skewed glasses on the tip of her nose, popped into her head.

It struck her as odd that Liz would appear in her mind, since she'd been missing Coco like crazy. Then she had a thought. Liz had been the only one to take the book seriously.

Nothing. She didn't feel a thing. This wasn't the way it was supposed to be. Then, heat seeped from the watch to her hands and arms and swam thickly though her veins, startling her.

She opened her eyes a crack. There she was, wrapped in Coco's pink and black polka dotted robe—the one she'd picked out for her last Christmas.

"Lizzie-bear?" Adrielle squealed. "Is that really you?"

Chubby un-coordinated arms flung around Adrielle's middle. "Adie, oh Adie," Liz choked. Something dropped to the ground and rolled along the cobblestones.

"Yikes, my mace!" she screeched.

Liz turned and ran ahead, the robe hanging off one shoulder and tie fluttering behind in the breeze. Butterflies swirled in her stomach. Lizzie. Thank goodness. She blinked away tears.

Adrielle was about to call her, tell her to forget about the mace, when out of the corner of one eye she caught a movement across the street from inside a doorway. Someone was watching her. Her heart spiked.

"Oh no. Not the Goth," she said.

Domenikos gave a small nod and smiled a wry smile. Then with his arm around a woman with ginger blonde hair, watched her and Liz for a long moment, as Liz skipped back toward her, waving the mace in her hand.

His sardonic smile spoke volumes. Cold sweat trickled down Adrielle's back. Domenikos made sure they were both aware of him, before disappearing inside the doorway with the woman.

Out of nowhere, the sky became dotted with black-winged birds. Shrill cawing screeched in the air as swarms gathered and swooped. The whoosh of flapping wings. They grazed Adrielle's ears and sent shivers down her spine.

"Let's go, go, go, Adie. Now!" Liz yelled, tugging on the collar of her robe to cover her head. She sprinted back to Adrielle's side, her arms thrashing. Fingers coiled around the mace. Like a dog on a dead run, she clung tightly to Adrielle, almost knocking her over.

"Make them stop," she cried, pressing her body against Adrielle's as the large black birds picked at her hair.

Thousands of birds dove straight at them. Adrielle screamed, cowering under the swarm. She covered her head with her arms. All she could think of was going home.

DOMENIKOS STARED AT the lifeless body on the floor and felt nothing. The eyes remained open; a combination of fear and hope reflected in them and seemed to transcend their mortality. But he knew better.

He was no longer surprised by a victim's last-minute bargaining. The promise of eternal life was usually enough for them to pledge their perpetual devotion and alliance. At the final moment, they were so tied to the mortal experience they gave little thought to what was actually being bargained: their eternal freedom. His promises of continued existence beyond the veil brought them the needed security net to finally let go.

It was a shame that adherence to their beliefs, whatever that entailed— be it of an afterlife or a code of existence, was truly rare. Usually those set guidelines formed during a lifetime of experiences were swept away like cobwebs when all the cards were on the table.

"What should we do with the bodies?" Brix asked.

"Dismember them and toss them in the river."

"Like the others?"

"Yes, Brix, like the others. Unless you can find some other use for them."

"No. I'll do the honors," he said, pulling out his hunting knife. "Can I keep the skin?"

"Let Vladik take care of it. I need you to check on the others before we meet Haden."

Domenikos wiped his dagger on his pants and slid it into his sheath.

"Domenikos, did they give in?"

Domenikos nodded yes. He turned away, the bodies forgotten before he reached the door.

"STOP TAUNTING HER," Haden demanded. "She's not your plaything."

"Nor yours," Domenikos said, his right hand resting on the hilt of his knife. "In any case, it's none of your business."

"She's promised to me," Haden said, anger rising in his chest. "That makes her mine."

"That's one way of looking at it." Domenikos smirked.

"You are infuriating. You're only making things worse for all of us."

"By that you mean— for you?" Domenikos sneered. "We have a deal. Get me what I want, and I will consider it."

"You're going against everything we believe in, Domenikos. This can't go on."

"We shall see." Domenikos took out his knife and slid his blade along the palm of his hand. "Would hate to see that lovely white skin stained with blood. But there are worse things, I suppose." He raised his eyes to meet Haden.

Haden didn't wait for him to finish speaking. He had to find Adrielle.

Chapter 14

Florida – Present Day

ADRIELLE AND LIZ appeared on her front doorstep, in a pretzeled position, their arms interlinked. The August humidity and heat clinging to their skin. They untangled their arms and legs and sat upright.

Liz was the first to stand. Adrielle watched her shake her legs, testing her balance, first by putting all her weight on the right leg, then the left. When she had her equilibrium back, she slipped the robe off and looped it over her arm. She slid her purse high on her shoulder and tugged at the strap to make sure it was secure. With her free arm, she pushed back her mop of hair, angled her glasses squarely on her face, and pushed them up to the bridge of her nose.

"I think Dave's right, I should cut my hair," she said, turning to Adrielle.

"That's it? That's all you're going to say?" Adrielle stood up and dusted herself off in one quick movement. "I feel like I've just gone through the spin cycle." She turned to get a good look at her surroundings. Layla's ceramic smurfs peaked out at them from under the Petunias.

"Awesome! "We're in my front yard," Adrielle squealed. She stared at the house, completely transfixed by details she'd never noticed before: the stucco arch way, the way the light hit on the brass door knocker they'd given Layla for Christmas, the potted plants that needed watering—those were new. "How did that just happen?" she whispered. "I wished for home and here we are."

"I dunno, but for the record, I didn't know that was coming," Liz said.

"Me neither."

"That bird attack, it was . . . let's just say . . ." Liz looked over her shoulder and then up at the sky. "I'm only just now feeling my face muscles start to relax. I hope that's the closest we come to those things." She shifted her purse higher on her shoulder and looked up at the house. "Let's go in, I feel weak. I need to eat."

"You need to eat? Unbelievable."

"Can't wait to see what's happened since we left."

"That's more like it," Adrielle said, beginning to relax into herself again.

Strangely, the light on the porch was not burning the way it normally did. Adrielle made a mental note to pick up a new bulb at Walmart for Layla and tried the door. It was locked. She glanced down at the chronometer. "Too late to knock, its after two in the morning."

"Really? You don't think they're all still up?"

"Hmmm . . . maybe? But I don't want to chance it. Layla gets pretty cranky without her sleep."

"Ok, so, what now?"

"Spare key." Adrielle gestured to the side of the house with an open palm. She skipped over to where they'd been hiding the key since fourth grade, in the planter with the painted red gardenias.

"Hurry," Liz called from the front. "I have to pee, too."

"Hang on, the key's missing. I'll try the sliding door," Adrielle called out. She ambled to the back. The shed door was open. There were empty flower pots stacked next to it and half a bag of left-over potting soil. Layla must have been distracted. She always made a point of putting her gardening tools away. Before trying the sliders, Adrielle looked through the glass and winced. *What is going on?*

Everything was different. Instead of their worn overstuffed flowered sofa and matching floral border, there was a tufted dark leather sofa, a large square ottoman, a giant-sized flat screen TV hanging on the wall and an open-concept kitchen that was to die for. *This can't be good.*

Afraid to make any loud noises, she tiptoed back to the front where she'd left Liz. "Oh, thank god. You're still here," she exhaled, clasping onto Liz's arm.

"Of course I am." Liz blinked. "Did you get the key?"

Adrielle felt sick. She shook her head.

"What's wrong?" Liz asked.

Adrielle opened her mouth, then closed it again. There was no easy way to say this.

"Adie? You okay?"

"No." She took four large strides to check the house numbers on the garage, already knowing they were right, then walked out to the curb to double-check the street sign.

Palmetto Drive. 34 Palmetto Drive. Yep, it was right.

She wanted to scream, to yell at someone for playing this sick joke. But there was no one to blame. She traipsed back to the front and read the doorknocker engraving. It said Thompson, not Bevans.

"What's going on?" Liz pressed, meeting her on the porch. "What are you doing? I really, really, have to pee."

Adrielle pointed to the knocker.

"Oh boy." Liz let out a slow whistle and pushed her glasses firmly up. "I remember when you and Coco ordered the engraving."

Two minutes later, the two stood motionless, staring through the patio doors into the family room.

"Holy caramels!" Liz exclaimed.

"Caramels?"

"You're right, this calls for stronger language. Hot chili peppers."

Adrielle remembered years ago Liz made her grandma a promise she'd never use foul language, and since then, found other words for self-expression. Adrielle covered her face with her hands and moaned. "Oh, Liz, I'm afraid to go upstairs."

"Me too," Liz confessed. "But let's go anyways."

"Okay. But . . . what about the doorknocker? This might officially be considered breaking-and-entering."

"Go!"

They tried the patio doors and luckily, though they were locked, the old jimmying them up-and-down worked. They entered the house and crept through the dark. It smelled of apple pie and cinnamon. There was a night light on in the kitchen giving off a soft glow. The granite counters had a wax-like shine that gave the impression they'd never been cooked on. And there was no appliance clutter or spaghetti sauce splatters from last night's meal either.

Gone was the homey, cluttered, fixer upper that was their home. This décor looked like an HGTV makeover, or a builder's model home.

"Guess Layla's changed her motto from 'if it ain't junk, load it on the counter' to 'less is more,'" Adrielle said, a pit solidifying in her stomach. They walked around the kitchen island and headed to the front foyer.

How long had they been gone? The bald carpet leading up the stairs to the bedroom had been replaced with wood, which was throughout the downstairs. And there was a large grandfather clock in the entry on the wall opposite the stairs. The girls exchanged a look.

"Maybe Coco finally talked Layla into renovating," Liz offered.

"Maybe," Adrielle whispered, "but I have the feeling this isn't home anymore."

"There's only one way to find out," Liz said.

They tiptoed upstairs. Adrielle was relieved the floor plan was the same. Their bedrooms were to the right, and Layla's on the left.

They paused at Coco's door. "Coco?" Adrielle called timidly. She was afraid to open the door.

"Go in already," Liz urged, giving her the slightest push with the tip of one finger.

Adrielle resisted. "I feel silly. I mean—"

"What? You want me to go first, you big chicken? It's your house."

"I'm not so sure," Adrielle whispered. "I'm scared. I think—I don't know what to think. Let's listen."

"Ok then, I'm going to use the hall bathroom," Liz said, disappearing into the second door down.

Maybe Liz was right. This was stupid. It was her home. Coco's room had always been like hers. When they moved into the house and decided which room they'd take, they agreed it was best if Coco took the larger of the two bedrooms because she was such a slob. A larger room would help with clutter, and actually, Adrielle preferred the cozier smaller room.

"C'mon already," Liz insisted, reappearing at her side. "Don't be a wuss."

"Okay, okay." Adrielle took a bold step in, stopped and frowned at the glow from a large TV lit the room. Layla had always been against having a television in their room.

Liz peered over Adrielle's shoulder. "Cool! The HD image is so clear it's almost like we're really there—Oh no." A red blinking news band informed there'd been a bunch of fires. "Strange, that kinda thing happens in California, not in Florida."

The springs on Coco's old bed squeaked. "I was afraid you'd never come," a husky voice said.

His voice sent shock waves through Adrielle's body.

"Who's there?" Liz demanded. The click of the light switch echoed, and light flooded the room. Liz was already clutching her mace.

Adrielle stiffened. There was a guy lying casually on the bed. The same guy who'd led her down the hall at the party. He'd rescued her from the bullies. "It's you."

He didn't flinch.

"What are you doing in our room?" Adrielle said, suppressing a vat of anger. She looked past him. "Coco?"

"She's not here."

"Where is she? Where are the others?"

"I don't know."

Adrielle didn't dare move. She watched him watching her for a moment, trying to decide if he meant her harm. She reasoned if he did, he would have already done so.

"I don't believe we've officially met," he said, extending his arm. "I'm Angelo."

Adrielle just stared at his arm.

"You remember me from the party," he said, "but you may not recall we already knew each other—momentary amnesia being one of the side effects of travelling."

So, he was a traveller. "Where's Coco?" Adrielle said, searching the room. The TV was muted, tuned onto the news channel.

Adrielle was aware Liz seemed less concerned now, though she kept one eye on Angelo and another one on the TV, which was bombarded with footage of the fires.

"Look, I'm not going to sugar coat it for you. I think Domenikos has her."

"What do you mean by—*has her?* Do you mean in the same way he has Josh? And maybe Scarlett? Are we talking dead?"

"No, I'm pretty sure she's not dead. That wouldn't work well as a bargaining tool."

"Oh my god. How do I get her back?"

He didn't answer right away.

"And the others? Does he have *them* too?" Liz panned to the TV, partially distracted by the news story.

"Don't know. My bet is if he doesn't already, he may soon."

"Why would he take them?" Adrielle asked. She shouldn't have left. She put everyone at risk. "And how do we get them back?"

"That's what we need to find out. Once a mortal is displaced, there's only a small window for them to travel back to their natural time placement, before it's too late."

Adrielle grunted. "I'm afraid to ask what you mean by *too late*. This thing just keeps getting worse."

"I mean when you time travel, the fabric of time makes a gap, and the longer you stay away the more things get displaced and change. Eventually, the gap closes, and they can't get back, no matter what they do. They remain trapped wherever they are."

"Holy drumsticks!" Liz exclaimed. "That could explain the new décor. What about the fires? Is he responsible for those too?"

Angelo shrugged. "Arson *is* one of his specialties."

"You mean he just goes around randomly taking people *and* setting fires?" said Liz.

"Not randomly, everything Domenikos does is calculating."

"He's some piece of work." Liz dug in her bag and pulled out a writing pad. "What about motive? Aside from wretched deviance. If he's as calculating as you say, he must have one."

"I think by now, you're beginning to understand what he's capable of."

"Dave—jeez, I miss him so much. We need everyone back. That includes Scarlett." Liz made a point of meeting Adrielle's gaze. "No matter how much you don't like her, Adie."

"Let's get back to Coco and the others," Adrielle said tersely, irritated by Liz's comment. None of them liked Scarlett. She looked down at her watch and turned back to Angelo. "If this is what he wants, he can have it."

"No. He can never have that. Then we'd all be screwed," he said.

"But if it's the only way to make him stop." She gestured to the TV. "Looks like thousands of innocent people are paying the price."

"We have to find another way. That chronometer would give him the power to control time. If he gets a hold of it, you can count on him using it for the wrong reasons. Think this through."

"There's no question in my mind, if that's what it's going to take to get Coco back, and everything else back to normal."

"There is no normal. Don't you get it?" He was getting worked up. "Once he has the chronometer, there will never be a normal again. Ever. Everything is changing because travelling causes a chain reaction. We're at an impasse unless you come up with a plan."

"Me? Why me?"

"You're the link between the species," another voice said from behind.

They spun around.

"Haden! Where did you go?" Adrielle burst out. She was both relieved he was there, and furious at him too. "You took me to Paris, told me how dangerous Domenikos was, and left me in London where he was." She turned to Liz. "I was attacked." She uncovered her hand to show them the gash in her hand. "It's gone, I sliced my hand fighting them off, and there's no trace of the cut." She stared at her hand unbelieving. "How?"

"You've taken a trajectory to another future," Angelo explained.

"Look, you travelled London because that's where Domenikos was, and you were concentrating on finding Domenikos," Haden said.

"I was?" She pressed her eyebrows together. "Maybe, but, I thought he was in the foyer at the Paris Opera? You said he was." She turned to Liz. "

That's where Haden first took me. Where he explained about time travel. We saw Domenikos conspiring with Hitler."

Liz looked uncertain.

Haden tapped Adrielle's shoulder. "Focus. He *was* there, and then he was gone. Even if on the surface you thought Domenikos was still in Paris, your inter-travel sub-conscious knew he'd already left. It guided you to him. That's what happens when you track someone."

"That's a mouthful," Adrielle said, thinking back. "You're right. I *was* wondering where he'd gone. So—you're saying there's a built-in radar that guides you when you travel?"

"Yes. You need to hone your skills," Haden warned.

Adrielle laughed. "I don't have any skills." The idea was ludicrous.

"You do, Adie. You speak dozens of languages. You're intuitive, smart—" Liz grew more and more excited.

"Those things definitely help, but mostly you need to concentrate on perfecting your *travelling* skills. The technicality of it all."

Adrielle planted her fists on her hips. "How do you propose I do that?"

"It's fairly easy," Haden said. "You clear your mind of everything else and think of where you want to go. Or think of a person, or an event. The chronometer and feather do the rest."

"My feather? The red one I pulled out of my back?"

Angelo and Haden exchanged a look.

"What?"

They shrugged.

They were hiding something. She'd get it out of them, eventually. "Clearing my mind is not as easy as it sounds. At any given time there are a million thoughts running through my head. Why don't I just let the chronometer do it?"

"That's a tool. You'll need to learn how to use it," Haden said, clenching his jaw. He looked exasperated. "You're responsible for—"

"How very noble of you. Go ahead and blame everything on me. Let's see . . . the end of the world. Genocide. Anything else you'd like to add?" She was fuming now.

"Really? We're doing this?" Liz said. She dug in her handbag and pulled out the journal. "It says here . . ." She turned to a page she'd dog-eared and began reading. "'Continued abuse of travelling will eradicate one or both of the species. Therefore, the enforcer will need to use the required tools for everyone's protection: the chronometer, the feathers, and the *Book of Feathers*.'"

"I'm the enforcer?"

"Looks that way," Angelo said.

"Shut up! Seriously?" Adrielle turned to Haden, who confirmed.

"Listen up," Angelo said in a quiet, measured, voice. "Each tool has a purpose." He searched out Adrielle's gaze. "You with me?"

"I'm all in." Haden said. "The chronometer will take you to the exact time. And the feather—"

Liz held up a finger, "Technically, it says *swing* feather here, that being the longest and most powerful of a bird's feathers."

"Let me see that." Adrielle began reading over her shoulder. "You're right, it says the swing feather is what makes the travel possible."

"About that—" Haden said.

Angelo shook his head. "This isn't the time."

Liz continued reading, "The enforcer is the only one capable of establishing peace, the only one who will be able to travel through time undetected."

"And the link to both species." Angelo said.

"It's you, Adrielle, whether you like it or not," said Haden.

"Well, I don't like."

Haden frowned. Adrielle knew she was being stubborn. But she didn't like them putting all of this on her. "Look at this room. You can't deny things have already changed. Did either of you do anything that might have caused this?"

Adrielle crossed her arms and thought about what the old woman said.

"Let's see." Liz pulled out her cell. "I tried saving the girl. The one from Jack the Ripper. She scrolled down the results page on her safari search. "Thank you Verizon, thank you Google," she said, with a wide grin. She started reading and cringed. "Mary Kelly was still slaughtered. Guess I didn't change anything after all." Disappointment settled on her face. She looked at Adrielle. "Did *you* do anything in the past? Anything that may have caused all this change? Not that I'm complaining or anything—this is going to do wonders for our movie night—*if* we ever get everyone back, that is." She held her hands up to rest her case.

Adrielle glanced down at her hands, remembering how cold she'd been. She'd stolen the hat and gloves. She pushed a corner of her kid gloves further into her pocket. Haden threw her a quick sideways glance and smiled. Could he know? She felt a rush of guilt.

"Let me explain. Someone was after me. I—"

"Never mind all that. What's done is done," Haden said. "I think by now we're all familiar with the repercussions of even the slightest change. As far as the attack? I think it's safe to say they were Domenikos' henchmen. You can expect more of that, from here on in."

That was the last thing Adrielle wanted to hear.

"It's time to switch the playing field and concoct a plan," Haden said.

"Adrielle, why don't you think of a time and place and see if you're capable of coming back here without creating any impression waves," Angelo said. "That means, go back as a spectator but *don't* touch a thing."

Adrielle's face grew warm. She hated being the center of attention and being put on the spot even more. "What if I can't—?"

"You have to," Haden insisted.

"But if he's—"

"Adie, stop it! Just think of Coco. Think of what *she'd* do," Liz said.

Adrielle closed her eyes and imagined Coco. She was so strong and capable and . . .

Warm tingles flowed through her veins, and she was back at the party on the eve of her birthday. This time she was seeing it as a 3-D movie. They were huddled, all of them. Liz, Dave, Kate, and Veda. And she was there beside Coco, wearing that awful dress. Coco was right. It looked even worse second time around. Coco returned from the kitchen with drinks, and she was talking about the Goth, worried about the strange way he'd looked at her. She'd been right all along.

Adrielle watched herself—she'd been so pre-occupied, worrying about Josh. It was all she could think about. She allowed herself to get lost in the moment. The smell of booze and weed. Cigarettes. Chatter and laughter came from all corners. The popular girls were laughing at her. Angelo appeared out of nowhere. He led her away from the taunting mean girls.

This time, she absorbed more details. She marveled at the paintings on the wall. There was a Renoir. A DaVinci. *Could that be a real Da Vinci?* She studied the signature. Maybe. It looked authentic enough, but so did most forgeries.

The experience was surreal. She continued watching as she reached for the doorknob. She pulled herself back, not wanting to be in the same room as Domenikos. Not ever again. Her limbs got tingly, the sensation rushing to the rest of her body.

"YOU'RE BACK. WELL done," Haden said, a wide smile spreading on his face. He gave her shoulder a squeeze.

Adrielle blinked, she felt as if she'd been absorbed into a television show and regurgitated. Liz and Angelo were staring at her. She remembered Angelo better now. He was wearing the same blue t-shirt as the night of the party. She met his eyes fleetingly. The way he looked at her now—it was almost as though Angelo knew what she was thinking. She looked back at Haden, who wore the smug look of superiority.

"Did I change anything?" she asked, glancing around the room.

"Don't think so," Liz said. "The crawl on the TV is still updating the fires. You vanished and boom—you were right back. Where did you go?"

"To the night of the party, before any of this happened."

"Don't fool yourself thinking that was the beginning," Angelo warned. "This entire span of events has been in play longer than you can imagine."

"He must be right. The journal dates back thousands of years ago." Liz shook her finger. Adrielle marveled how easily she'd picked up Dave's habit. "I have this one question though, I can't quite figure out."

"Which is?" Haden asked.

"Two really. The first being, where and what is this *Book of Feathers?* And second, what are all those birds that keep showing up? Can they all change shape like that girl that transformed? Astraia? Is she a shapeshifter?"

Adrielle caught Haden and Angelo's silent exchange. What weren't they letting on?

"That's a lot more than two questions," Angelo said. "Haden, why don't you do the honors. Up until now, he's been the protector of the *Book of Feathers*, and the only one privy to its contents."

Haden raised an eyebrow with a cocky expression.

"I saw the book for the first time just before Astraia ended up here. If you can believe the rumors," Angelo continued. "It contains sacred spells that give the one in possession of the book an unfair advantage over everyone else. Feel free to clarify for us, my dear brother. Is any of this true?"

"Brother?" Adrielle asked. "For real?" She took a bold step toward Angelo and studied his face.

He was cute, that was for sure. He had a speckle of freckles on his nose and the top of his cheeks. Even though his hair was blonder and curlier than Haden's, there was a resemblance.

"I can see it now. Those green flecks you both have. The Goth had them too. Is he also your brother?"

"Not mine," Haden said, turning quickly to Angelo.

Adrielle felt the tension thicken.

"Sure, he's Achaean, like us. That's as far as the similarity goes," Haden said.

What weren't they telling her? She turned to Liz, who only shrugged.

"It's true," Haden said. "The book contains powerful spells. That's why Domenikos wants it. If he gets both the Chronometer and the *Book of Feathers*, we're doomed. All of us. You understand?"

Adrielle nodded.

"Good. We need to work together and set a plan in motion."

"Work together? As in *all of us?"* Liz asked, turning to Adrielle. She leaned into her and whispered, "They obviously don't know you don't work well in groups."

"What? Adrielle frowned.

"Do we have a problem?" Haden asked, looking pointedly at Adrielle.

"Not on my part," Liz said, raising her hand in mock salute.

Adrielle could only shake her head.

"Ok then." Liz grunted, returning to the journal.

With a clear memory of the birthday night, Adrielle thought of the beginnings of a plan. "Chronometer aside, would Domenikos stop if he were to get a hold of the book?"

"Perhaps, but that will never work," Haden said.

"Right. 'Cause he'd have access to all the secrets. Unless . . ." Liz said, glancing up at one of Adrielle's paintings on the wall.

"Exactly, Liz. I don't mean give him the *real* book. I mean give him a fake. A forgery," Adrielle explained.

"No way. It's too risky," Haden said. "We'd need a perfect copy. The wording on the spells would have to be changed so they wouldn't have any power, but still sound credible. It contains drawings, illustrations. It would have to be flawless. Completely believable. And Domenikos is not easy to trick. Trust me, when I say, he is the *king* of trickery."

Adrielle turned away. It could be done. She wandered to the window. The sky was dotted with birds. They were almost out of time. She couldn't stop thinking about the paintings hanging in Scarlett's upstairs hall. She turned to the others. "Let's say we get the illustrations *and* the calligraphy looking exact—if he's never seen the actual authentic book—how would he know? Am I right in assuming that?"

Haden confirmed with a nod. "Domenikos has never seen it."

"Then I'm pretty sure we can pull it off."

With an unsmiling shake of his head, Haden said, "Pretty sure is not good enough."

Liz hesitated before lifting the journal. "Adie is the best at calligraphy. Her writing is just like this. You can't tell her script from any medieval manuscript. She aced that assignment in art class."

"This isn't art class." Haden was getting angry.

"That painting over there." Liz pointed at the wall. "Adrielle painted it for Coco. She's really good."

Angelo smiled. "That's because she had the best teacher. But Haden is right. There is too much at stake. This isn't some grade in art class. This is for the world's future. Mankind and Achaeans alike. We can't take that risk."

"I thought you said *I* was the link. That it was up to me?"

"Yes, but—"

"I'm doing it. And I know just the artist." Adrielle grinned. "I need to travel back to talk him into it."

"Adie! How is that going to get everyone back?" Liz asked. "Don't be so impulsive. You're not supposed to change anything. If you go back in time—" She raised her hands in surrender. "I'm just saying—look what happened after you went to London. And you'd need to go to the exact time and place. You don't even know how to."

"That's the easy part," Angelo said. "I'll help her hone her skills."

Adrielle was relieved he was coming around.

"Maybe Adrielle's right. If we can trick Domenikos into believing."

"Trick Domenikos?" Haden scoffed. "You say it so off handed. Like, oh, we're going to trick Domenikos now. Get real, Angelo."

"Hear me out. If he thinks he has the real thing, he'll let his guard down, and we can take him down then."

A look of worry settled on Haden's face. He paced to the window, placed his hands on the window frame, and looked up at the sky. "All right. But this is easier said than done. When you are in the midst of it all, everything you are going to have to face, you need to remember one thing, Adrielle." He turned to her, his words a little slower, a little quieter. "*You* are the link. This is something only *you* are capable of doing. No one else can face Domenikos and make him believe. You'll need to believe it yourself. Be all in. *Really* in. Not just with your head, but with your heart and soul too. It means you are risking everything. Mankind and Achaeans, for this *one* thing. It's the only way you'll be able to pass all the tests that will be placed in your path."

"Got it. Now let's roll. Who's coming with?" Adrielle felt lighter. Happy even, they'd listened.

Angelo and Haden stared at her with apprehensive expressions.

"Too risky," Angelo said. "He'll know what we are up to if he sees us with you. Sorry, but, you have to go it alone."

He was right. She ran her fingers over the length of the gold chain and stared at the little gold hands on the face of her watch. She could do this. She sucked a deep inhale and blew out from her bottom lip. "Wish me luck."

"No, no, no. There you go again. There is no luck," Haden said. He touched her arm gently. "Remember—when we transport ourselves along the timeline, we have the option to be physically present, or be an observer without disturbing anything. It's safer if you're not a participant. Hitler couldn't see or hear us as we watched. It was as if we weren't really there. The event happens in real time, and we are observing. Flies on the wall. When Domenikos appeared, he heard us. Don't forget, travellers can spot other travellers, even if they're travelling as spectators."

Adrielle's heart raced. The thought of facing Domenikos. Maybe she'd overestimated her ability.

"Don't worry. Think of a time, and the chronometer will do the rest. And remember, nothing of importance can be altered."

"Gotcha." Adrielle glanced at Liz. "One last hug for good luck?"

"Definitely," Liz said, stuffing the journal back into her handbag. "Oh, shouldn't you have a quick look at the *Book of Feathers*? So you know what it's supposed to look like?"

"OMG, you're right. I've never even seen it," Adrielle realized.

"You have," Haden said. "A long, long, time ago. You probably weren't aware of it at the time."

"Who has it now?"

"I have it secured in the past," Haden said.

"Tell me exactly where you left it, and I'll get it," she said.

Haden rubbed a spot under his heart, near the sternum. He took a deep breath and exhaled. "You sure you can do this?"

"I have to try."

He glanced at Angelo and cast his eyes downward.

Angelo squeezed Haden's shoulder. "It'll be ok."

"Very well then. If you go back to the day I sent you here, the *Book of Feathers* is in the tower room. You'll see I am holding it as we bid our goodbyes."

Adrielle nodded.

"Since you'll be travelling as a spectator, you'll have to wait until I send the 'you from the past,' forward in time."

"Understood."

Haden cleared his throat. "Uhh"—he clenched his fists—"there is a moment—right after—when I experience a break down. You must be quick about it, before the *me* from the past, realizes what you're up to. Or I'll be unable to let you go. Remember, as an Achaean, I may be able to see you in travelling form. So stay out of sight."

"Thank you," Adrielle said, touching his arm lightly. She'd seen enough images in her head after reading the journal entry to go back to that time continuum. He was right. It wouldn't be easy. The turmoil of emotions in that short time span could be detrimental.

"Bye, Lizzie bear," she said, extending her arms.

Liz hugged Adrielle with her chubby arms. Adrielle could sense Haden and Angelo trying to meet her gaze. She was certain they didn't know what she was up to. Before they could object, Adrielle and Liz travelled to the past.

Chapter 15

AcHaea, Greece – 241 BCE

THE SOUND WAS harrowing. Intrusive. It exploded into the night like a canon, tearing up the hillside and penetrating the thick castle walls into the small bedroom where Adrielle lay sleeping.

Adrielle awoke with a start, warm tingles pulsing through her body. The sound of the bell was loud, piercing. It jump-started her heart like a defibrillator.

A thought came to her then; the town bell hadn't rung in over one hundred years. The toll was the sign of a monumental event. And then, in a forceful overwhelming way, it hit her: *She was back. Here, to the place she'd fled from. That there'd been other failed attempts.*

Familiar surroundings confirmed it. Adrielle listened to the brash vibrations of the bell ripple in the cavern that was her bedroom. The sound swelled in her ears and became an undeniable force. She brushed her hand against the linen sheets, the fibers soft against her skin. Wait, something was wrong. Her hands were solid, not translucent. She wasn't a spectator, as they'd planned. She was a participant. It meant the future as she knew it hinged on her. She may lose the one thing that meant the most to her in the entire world. Coco.

Doubt spread until her limbs quivered. A sick feeling twisted her stomach. She had to stop the fear. Stop focusing on failure. From this moment on, everything would have a severe impact on her future and everyone else's.

Needing a moment to collect herself, she concentrated on breathing—in and out. In and out—until the trembles subsided.

She sat up, dangling her legs off the edge of the bed. She wriggled her toes. Before lowering her feet, she hesitated, remembering how cold the stone floor would feel on the bottoms of her feet.

Determined to go through with the plan, she absorbed the chill and turned toward the window where she knew Haden would be standing, looking down on the town square.

He stood as she remembered, his face solemn, worry etched on his brow. His clothes, the heavy cloak on his shoulders, reminded her he hadn't slept. Ready to leave at a moment's notice.

Adrielle was more aware, this time around, he was planning an escape for her. She also knew there would be no escaping a confrontation with Domenikos. He would find her. And she would have to fight him with everything she had. She shuddered.

Undeniably, as she glanced around the room, everything was already different. Memories of her past—of Florida—became fused with memories of the present, 241 BCE. They laced with memories of other failed attempts.

Funny, how aware she was of time. How easily plans could get derailed.

No doubt Domenikos was below in the center of town, vying for leadership. Crucifying the Tribunals. The souls of—was it three thousand Achaeans they'd said? The fate of so many lives hinged on her now. Everything hinged on her. *Damn.* She glanced back at Haden, her body tingling with stress, knowing it wouldn't be long now.

Draped casually on the foot of the bed was a pale mauve robe. She reached for it, feeling the softness of the cloth. A memory of when Haden had given it to her flowed seamlessly from it to her. Wow. She drew in a long breath. This would be tricky. Sorting out what was past and what was present was not easy.

She wrapped the robe around her shoulders and strode toward him. She wondered if Domenikos would be expecting her. Everything was more difficult now that she was aware of the consequences. She almost preferred to be blindsided. There would be no anticipation that way. The fear of failure wouldn't gnaw away at her.

Adrielle stood beside Haden, shivering. A dim light filtered in from the window. Smoke from the town-site wafted in and tickled her nose. Haden pulled her in close and nestled her in his arms. The expression on his face showed he understood the robe did nothing to ward off the cold. Nothing would avert the chill radiating from what was transpiring. It was the death of an era. Of her father.

If this were like the other attempts, in minutes, Haden would be chanting the spell that would propel her forward in the future a couple of thousand years. It would cause temporary amnesia, the side effect of travelling. But they'd tried that before and it hadn't worked. She'd have to change something.

"It's time," he said, taking her hand and intertwining his fingers with hers. They walked toward the table at the end of the bed. Adrielle's eyes drifted to the weathered book that sat on the top. She felt her heart skip. The candle beside it had molten wax that had run into the candle dish, beading onto the table and exposing a burnt wick. *Fire.* Yes, Domenikos liked to use fire for destruction. But fire had other uses too, not all of them bad.

The knock on the door came sooner than expected. It threw off her timing.

"My sweet, could you get that?" Haden squeezed her hand.

"Of course." She slipped her hand out of his and strode down the long hallway leading to the door, looking back only once to see what Haden was up to, before opening the large wooden door.

"Angelo? What are you doing h—" Before she had a chance to finish, a barrage of emotions sent her heart into a tailspin. She knew then, what he'd meant when he'd said, "there's no question we've officially met." Of course: they were lovers.

"I had to see you, to warn you."

Adrielle wrinkled her brow. "No, it's not supposed to be this way," she whispered.

"Who is it, Adrielle?" Haden called from inside the room.

Angelo pleaded with his eyes. He leaned into her and whispered, "Don't go through with it. There's something you need to know."

Adrielle's gaze dropped down to his shirt, the same blue t-shirt he'd worn in Florida, when lying casually on Coco's bed.

"My love?" Haden's voice carried across the cold vacuous hall.

"It's no one," she answered Haden, gesturing to Angelo's clothes and pointing to the exit at the end of the hall. He had to leave. If Haden saw his clothes, he'd know something was up.

"No one?" Haden asked, his voice full of alarm. The echo of his quick footsteps warned he was rushing toward her.

Adrielle turned to look.

"Oh, it is only the maid," Haden said, looking past her, a relieved look on his face.

Adrielle turned back to see why he'd suddenly grown calm. Angelo had disappeared. Liz was standing in his place. Alarm and relief blasted through her. *Lizzie-bear*, wearing Coco's bathrobe wrong side out so only the black lining showed. Adrielle grunted.

"Now, sweetness . . . that is no way to address the help," Haden chided. "They can't all be as fair as you, now can they? Run along. You can make up the room later."

He turned on his heels and slipped his hand into Adrielle's. "Hurry love, there's no time to waste." He clung onto her hand and pulled her back to their bedroom. "We are almost out of time."

As he dragged her, Adrielle realized this Haden from the past had no memory of present-day Florida. It hadn't happened yet. All she could do was stare back at Liz in disbelief. "Where did you go?" she mouthed over her shoulder.

Liz mouthed back, "I was right behind you, and then—" She flailed her arms wildly up and shrugged.

ANGELO RE-APPEARED BEHIND Liz. In an attempt to look more like a monk than the carefree surfer from moments before, he had changed his clothes to a floor-length brown robe.

"Stay here and don't move, if you want to stay alive," Angelo warned Liz. "Domenikos will be coming up those stairs in about a nano-second."

Liz nodded. With her frizzy curls and inside-out robe, she had the grungy look of a disheveled teenager.

By the time Angelo entered the small bedroom, Adrielle had already gone. He worried about her wellbeing and regretted not being able to speak with her.

The Haden from the past was sitting on the edge of the bed, Adrielle's pillow pressed to his face.

Haden sucked in a long inhale. Without looking up, he set the pillow gently on the bed. "I promised myself I would wait—the morning I asked her to marry me. The sun was just appearing and there was a wedge of sunlight glowing on her face. Of course"—he smiled—"it always found her first. She looked so glorious in that moment, I could not contain my love any longer."

While Haden was lost in the past memory of Adrielle, Angelo turned his attention to the small table at the foot of the bed. There was an empty spot next to the candle with the melted wax. The *Book of Feathers* was gone.

AS LIZ PEERED into the castle bedroom, a hand clasped tightly around her mouth and pulled her back into the hall. She tried to scream but all that came out was a squeak. She wriggled to break herself free, but arms encircling her were stronger. Out of the corner of her eye, she saw a feather tattoo of the palest green color that circled the unbending, steely biceps. It was no use; those arms held no mercy.

Deep fried mozza-sticks. Oh, Dammit to hell. Liz cursed wildly. Her handbag, which normally hung over her shoulder, was out of reach. What could she do without it? The last thing she remembered thinking before everything went black was, *God. Where was her mace when she needed it?*

LIZ CAME TO and couldn't be sure how long she'd been out. The pounding in her head reminded her of the caffeine bender she'd gone on with Dave, the weekend she'd stayed over at his house, when his parents decided to make a quick getaway to Vegas for their twentieth wedding anniversary. They'd stayed up all night binging on *Project Runway* re-runs and OD-ing on Monster energy drinks.

Liz pressed her hands to the sides of her head, which felt like a pulsing watermelon. She rocked back and forth in pain, but why was she in a fetal position?

She opened one eye first. Directly in her field of vision was a blur of pink. She stared at it, aiming both eyeballs dead center until the pink haze sharpened to the large stain on the outer flap her of her knock-off Kate Spade leather handbag. It was swaying back and forth like a pendulum.

A ping of regret hit her, as it did every time she remembered how careless she'd been with the salsa, when she juggled eating Mexican and driving on I-95.

Focus, she scolded herself. Shaking her head like a wet dog, she committed to using the giant chrome lobster clip Veda gave her for Christmas as a focal point. As her eyes adjusted to the arc of the swing, the pummeling in her head calmed. She raised her eyes to the top of the strap.

Holy hell! The finger on which her purse swung had chipped maroon nail polish.

Domenikos' laughter filled the room. "Well, well. We caught ourselves the not-so-little, Lizzie bear!"

"Go to hell." Liz snarled, swiping unsuccessfully for her handbag.

"This something you want?" he taunted, jiggling her purse up and down while managing to keep it barely out of reach. She wanted to sock him in the mouth for making her feel like a recovering alcoholic on the third day of rehab.

Domenikos shook his head. "Tsk, tsk, tsk. Someone's been bingeing." He reached inside her purse, exposed a handful of empty candy wrappers, and crinkled them for effect before tossing them high in the air. He waited until the wrappers settled on the ground before meeting her gaze.

Liz cringed. Ashamed he'd exposed her bad habit.

Someone in the corner gasped. "Liz, you didn't!"

"Dave?" She twisted around, anxiously looking around the room. There he was, sitting cross-legged in the chair by the window, wearing his ridiculous green and blue plaid madras shorts and pink RL polo. She'd never seen anything so beautiful. "Omigod—it *is* you!" She scurried to get up. She was so happy, she thought she'd burst.

"Not so fast." Someone behind her pushed down on her shoulders. Liz landed hard on her butt. "Ouch," she yelped, rubbing the sore spot. "What the hell?"

"Ahem," Domenikos said, his leering face pushing into hers. "I have the floor."

"Still here, huh?" she mumbled, staring into his dark green flecks. A roll of repulsion swarmed over her. "Wha—what are you going to do with me?" She absorbed the pale green tattoo on his arm, remembering too well the unyielding steel of his biceps. "You've made a mistake. I'm only the sidekick. The sprinkles, not the frozen yogurt."

Domenikos sneered. "I'm going to give you the same proposition I've given everyone else."

In a blink they were back in Coco's bedroom.

"Ha—how did ja do dat?" Liz yelped.

Astraia, the *bird-girl* with the Miley Cyrus attitude stood at Domenikos' side, her arms folded and legs in a wide stance. At the foot of Coco's bed, Kate was pressed against Veda, suction-cupped to her and whimpering like a puppy.

"Is this real?" Liz asked, the squirt of perfume she'd tried on earlier tickling her nose. On top of Coco's dresser, the perfume bottles were in disarray. The empty Coke Zero can was still there. Everything seemed to be in order. Coco's clothes were piled on the floor in a heap. Even the new flat-screen TV they'd watched the news on earlier was gone, magically restored to its pre-flight-out-of-date-wide-backed model.

"Really?" Liz said, disappointment pitting. "You couldn't have left the TV?" She reached for the remote. "Who watches Dr. Oz anymore?"

Domenikos laughed, yanking back the remote so it was out of reach. "Me. I keep up with you mortals' idiosyncrasies."

"Don't lump me in on that bunch," Liz said.

On the screen, Dr. Oz was hovering next to a plump blonde woman—mid-thirties—with super-sized nail tips and overdone makeup. She was devouring something leafy in a metal bowl and moaning in ecstasy.

"I thought this might be to your liking. Very well then." He switched the channel to the news. Liz sensed him watching her as she read the crawl.

—the city is in turmoil. More murmurations sweeping throughout the state of Florida. The birds were first sighted in the city of Palm Coast and continue to gain in number. Reports of these black-winged birds coincide with the disappearances of forty-three Palm Coast residents, including four fatalities. Authorities are ordering a mandatory evacuation. Again, it is not known where these birds originated, but take every precaution. The murmurations are extremely dangerous . . . "

Domenikos was beside himself, a look of accomplishment swelling on his face. Liz bolted to the window. The fresh air felt good on her face. Her heart spiked as she saw the sky was dotted with birds. She turned to Domenikos, her stomach churning in revulsion. "Is this invasion your version of *War of the Worlds*?"

"Something like that," he said. "It doesn't have to be all bad. I want the chronometer."

"What does that have to do with me?"

"You are my bargaining chip. Once it is in my possession, everyone will be released."

"Everyone? As in all of us in this room? Or are there others?"

"Bring Coco back," Kate whimpered. "He took her. She's gone."

"What did you do?" Liz said.

Domenikos chuckled. "Aren't you an inquisitive one, *Lizzie-bear!*"

"You don't get to call me that."

Domenikos pressed his lips in thought. Liz could feel his rage simmering. *How could she not have noticed Coco was missing?*

Domenikos reached in his cloak and slid out a silver dagger. It had a thin blade and needle-like point. His teeth gleamed as he grinned.

Oh, oh. This can't be good. Adrielle had told her about the knife and warned her he would use it. She needed to escape. Astraia stood between Kate and Domenikos, poised to flee.

Where was Dave? There, in a chair behind Kate. "Can we lighten the mood here? How about a little mindless TV? *Project Runway* anyone? Or the Victoria Secret fashion show?" Liz said, meeting Dave's gaze and holding it. Circling her hands around her breasts as if adjusting her bra, she raised her eyebrows expectantly. Dave smiled . . .

The 2014 Victoria Secret fashion show—Since watching the episode, Liz had adopted the circling-her-hands-around-her-breasts gesture to mean: create a distraction. While Ed Sheeran was front stage crooning "Thinking Out Loud," Taylor Swift and Arianna Grande were duking it out backstage over who would wear the two-million-dollar diamond encrusted Fantasy bra. They caused so much commotion that long-time model Lily Aldridge snagged it out from underneath them. Before either was the wiser, she strutted down the runway in it and stole the show.

Dave gave a small nod, signaling he'd play along. Liz felt all worked up.

"Is that my Kate Spade bangle?" he shouted to Liz. "It is—" he yelped, bolting out of his chair and jumping onto Liz in a mock fight. Within seconds they were a jumbled ball of arms, legs, hair, and teeth.

The chaotic rumble caught Domenikos off guard. Liz managed to snag back her purse and reach inside for the journal, where she'd snipped a tiny piece of Adrielle's feather to use as a bookmark. She hoped the instructions in the journal worked. She concentrated harder than ever before—*gosh, why did she have to be such a stickler for details? Who cared where he'd gotten the knife?* She couldn't be sure where she was headed to now.

Chapter 16
Florence, Italy – 1504

LIZ AND DAVE landed in the center of town in a knotted mess. They untangled their limbs and waited for the tingly disoriented feeling to subside, and the momentary amnesia to dispel.

Liz held her breath, quickly surveying their surroundings. *It worked!* A flutter of excitement churned in her stomach. She laid a hand on Dave's shoulder and squeezed. Good, he was here too. Wherever *here* was.

The marketplace was awash with sights and smells. The chatter of commerce floated as people bartered for goods. Carts wheeled by, loaded with colorful vegetables and supplies. Dead chickens with their heads still attached dangled from long metal rods and resembled laundry hanging on a clothes wire. Each chicken looked frightingly similar to Liz's cat right after his bath. They were strung up by their feet, plucked, and basted with an oily marinade that dripped onto the cobbled street below. The smell permeated everything and dominated even the pungent smell of spices. It was almost enough for Liz to become a vegan, that was, until an image of a juicy fat burger popped in her head, and her stomach complained she hadn't eaten.

Beside her, Dave had a *Holy Shit* moment. He dusted himself off and stood. "Where are we?" he asked, but before Liz had a chance to answer, his face lit up in ecstasy. "Look at that." He pointed. "Eye candy everywhere."

Liz hadn't seen him this happy since Vera Wang unveiled her designer collection for Kohl's department store. She followed his gaze. People were wearing the most luxurious garments.

"Do hear that? They're speaking a foreign language. I wish Adrielle were here. What's happened?" Dave asked, all that lightness and joy growing serious.

"I swiped a piece of Adrielle's feather, and I guess it worked."

"Where are we?" His eyes widened.

"Not sure," Liz said. There were surrounded by jovial people, rosy cheeks and bright eyes reflecting their mood. Surprisingly, not one of them dawdled. Everyone was in a bustle.

"Can we get back?" Dave asked, the reality of the situation cementing itself.

"I dunno. Don't care, as long as Domenikos doesn't have us," she said.

They stood in the center of the commotion, absorbing their surroundings, inhaling tantalizing smells, until Dave's attire began attracting attention.

Liz suspected Dave was so blown away he couldn't think straight. He didn't seem to care what they thought of his plaid madras shorts.

"We gotta figure this out," Liz said, and pulled him into a doorway where they could watch unnoticed.

They stood there for a long time, on sensory overload, until Liz had an uncontrollable impulse to twitch her nose. She pushed against the tides of people and followed the sweet aroma of rosemary to a cart thick with spices and herbs.

"Where are we going?" Dave asked.

"I smell food."

He plodded alongside her, eager to get a closer look at the next cart down, which was filled with enticing fabrics. Yards of sheer silk in rich vibrant colors were draped and looped onto it and billowed in the warm breeze.

Nearby, in between the two carts, a group of round-bellied men were engaged in a heated discussion.

"Why Michelangelo, of course. Who else could sculpt like that, with that level of skill?" one of them asserted.

"You know I've always been a fan, that is *not* what I am saying. Only that Leonardo is a much better painter," the bald-headed man insisted, kissing his fingertips like they were dipped in honey. "I cannot wait to meet him later this afternoon."

Liz and Dave exchanged a look. How could they understand the language? "DaVinci?" they cried in unison, sounding like two schoolgirls who'd just been given a backstage pass to Drake.

"Of course!" one of the men responded indignantly.

"Leonardo Da Vinci is coming here?"

"None other. He is on the board to decide on the placement of the David."

"We're in Italy!" Liz and Dave squealed.

Suddenly, the bald-headed man who seemed to dominate the conversation, took notice of Liz. "Where have you been hiding, my lovely goddess?" He took hold of Liz's hand and before she could pull it away, his greasy lips were planting a slobbering kiss on it.

"It is true," one man continued to the other. "Today marks the completion of the statue of David, and the beginning of the festivities. Da Vinci is among a team of consultants summoned to Florence to decide on David's placement."

"Holy shit. It's 1504," Dave whispered to Liz, then turned to one of the men enthusiastically. "I can tell you where David ends up. The Piazza della Signoria, in front of the Palazzo Vecchio."

Liz cringed. Dave's Italian was not perfect, but passable. He was such a showoff. So much for blending in.

The men laughed.

"No one can tell you that, it has not been decided yet," one of them exclaimed. "But yes, there is much debate as to where David's final resting place will be. In any case, we will not have to wait much longer to see where."

"Ahhh," Dave continued, raising his nose and taking on the air of a highly sophisticated art connoisseur. "Where might we find this Da Vinci?"

"In Michelangelo's studio, of course."

A small glint passed from Dave to Liz. "Which is?"

"Follow the road to the Ponte Vecchio." The man gestured with his hand.

Both Liz and Dave stared wide-eyed. The man spoke incredibly fast and the language barrier disappeared as he relayed the information.

"If it pleases, my lady, I can accompany you," the bald man offered. "My name is Francesco del Giocondo." His bow was so deep his nose almost grazed the ground.

Though Liz no more wanted to lead this man on than a toad, she couldn't contain herself. Putting on her best flirty Kate imitation—a cross between Scarlett O'Hara and Marilyn Monroe, she batted her eyelashes and said, "oh, I couldn't—it would be so much trouble."

The man, like putty, bowed again. "Bella donna. What is your name?"

"Liz," she replied, fanning her face. She wished he'd stop ogling. Under his scrutiny, her skin grew warm.

"Lisa. Ah, mi donna Lisa."

Liz didn't bother correcting him. What did it matter? It could be argued that Lisa was Liz, she supposed. And the way he said it, mmmmm . . . it sounded so much more romantic. She smiled, slipping her glasses off her face and tucking them into her purse.

For the first time in her life, Liz felt feminine. Adored. She was thrilled he loved her curves. Because in the twenty-first century the standard for beauty was generally model thin, she'd never before taken the time to imagine what it would be like to attract that kind of attention. The kind of attraction that came so easily for Scarlett, or Kate, with her large breasts. This was so far out of her realm.

Then the budding realization that she cared what anyone else thought, sickened her. Why did she need his approval? How easily it loosened the heavy chains society and physiology had draped on her. Liz was starting to understand what it felt like to be liberated, free to be sexy and flirty, and feel good about her physical image. She felt herself outwardly blossom into the playful woman she'd always suspected lurked inside.

Dave was watching her and seemed overcome with joy. "What is happening? You have the confidence of a runway model," he said, tears in his eyes.

"Ahh—I understand now. You are of"—he waved his hand with a flimsy limp wrist—"their type." He pressed his finger to his lips as though to say it was their secret. He took hold of Liz's hand, slipped it through his arm, and patted her hand gently with the unbinding infatuation of a lovesick crush.

As they walked side-by-side in that haze only those who have felt it can understand, he smiled rapturously at her. Liz felt joy.

Dave followed a few steps behind them. When Liz looked back, she could tell by the look on his face he was in deep conflict. She pushed away the nagging thought this sudden interruption in the time continuum would cause serious repercussions. And yet, his face was that of a child in a candy store. He soaked up the surroundings Liz knew had been the coveted longing of his arduous studies in history. An impossibility, until now.

The Arno River was a snake of pale-green waters. Thin Italian Cypress trees lined the shore and reflected on the water's surface with the blurred haze of linseed oil in a romantic landscape painting.

They walked along its banks, inhaling the sweet smell of the lush vegetation, captivated by its beauty, until they reached the Ponte Vecchio where they took the second right, as the first man had instructed. When they reached a fork in the small cobblestoned road, they turned again and finally reached their destination.

They stood in front of a door, a heavy iron doorknocker greeting them. There was nothing out of the ordinary that would indicate this was the dwelling of an artist of esteemed heights, as one might imagine. The wood was aged and weathered. The marble threshold bowed with use. In fact, it looked similar to all the others along this winding ancient path.

Francesco released Liz's arm and bowed once more, taking her hand to his mouth and this time placing the softest sweetest kiss on it.

"We will meet tomorrow? Yes? By the Palazzo Vecchio at mid-day?" he asked.

"Yes, I will meet you then," she said.

He exhaled, and reluctantly let go of her hand. His eyes remaining locked onto hers as he disappeared into the crowd down the street.

"Liz, are you making dates with strangers?" Dave teased.

Liz didn't respond. She was still numb from Francesco's affection. Her mouth had gone dry. She stared at the top of her hand, hanging on to the memory of his slobbery kiss like a badge of honor.

"I'VE FOUND THEM," Brix said. "They are in Italy. 1504."

"And?"

"And . . ."

"What are they up to, Brix?"

"I don't know. So far, they just are. There doesn't seem to be any apparent plan. They are taking everything in."

"Taking in the sights? Hmmm. It is unlikely they would just pop up there randomly. They had to have something particular in mind to have arrived there—keep an eye on them. Make sure they don't leave. And report any changes directly to me."

"What about Astraia?"

"Don't worry about her. I'm watching her carefully."

"And the others?"

Domenikos smiled, his snaggle tooth gleaming. "This is the best part. How intricately they all fit into my plans."

THE DOORKNOCKER WAS centered high on the door. It looked ancient; a gargoyle face made of a heavy bronze metal staring out at them.

"Go for it," Liz urged, stepping back onto the street and waiting expectantly for Dave to make a move.

"Here goes," he said, giving one loud rap.

The sound echoed inside the house. They waited several minutes, nervous and excited all at once. When no one answered, Dave tried again.

"Can I help you?" A slight young man of about twenty, carrying a basket with various breads, sausages, and vegetables, had come along the street and stopped at the doorstep.

"We're looking for Michelangelo," Dave said, stepping back to get out of his way. The young man shook his head. "Not here." He took out a long skeleton key from his pocket and inserted it into the keyhole. "He will not be back until later tonight."

"Oh," Dave said, a surge of disappointment surfacing.

"Can I be of help?" he asked, his lively eyes surveying Dave's pink shirt and shorts. He bit back a smile and waited, shifting the basket from one arm to the other.

"We'll come back," Dave said, flushed with unexpected unease. They'd been so enthralled with the idea of meeting Michelangelo they hadn't even discussed what to do if he wasn't home.

The young man nodded slightly and slipped through the doorway. He was about to latch the door when someone called from across the street.

"Salai, is Leonardo not in?"

"Leonardo?" Liz and Dave mouthed.

At the mention of Leonardo, a flutter of excitement imploded inside Dave. Liz looked back. She appeared to be trying her best to mask her enthusiasm when she recognized Francesco's voice. Clearly, she was still shaken he'd taken to her so effusively. Dave watched as she waved limply at Francesco, who was leaning on a lamppost smiling at them both. Liz turned away quickly, her face growing a rosy pink.

Dave, enjoying every minute of her discomfort, jabbed her lightly. But it was more of a nervous reaction than anything else. He never liked to let on how much anything he truly valued meant to him. *Project Runway* was one thing, but meeting Leonardo and Michelangelo—quite another. As if being transported to a world he'd only imagined through books wasn't enough, life was suddenly full of possibilities. Their importance in history made it difficult for him to contain his delight. This experience was beyond even his greatest dream.

Salai nodded his greeting to Francesco. "He's in the studio, working on some sketches. Would you like to see him?"

"Yes, I think I will. I may have a new commission for him."

"ADRIELLE?" KATE SQUEAKED, peeking through her fingers. "Where did she go? Where did everybody go?" She pressed up against Veda when she saw Astraia was standing by the window, her eyes shifting between the outside, and to them.

"Shhh," Veda hissed.

"Well, are they dead?" Kate asked, petrified they would be next to disappear. "Did they agree to the Domino guy's proposition?"

Veda turned around and shook her head gently. "Will you be quiet? No one has agreed to anything."

"Not yet they haven't," Astaia said. "But the way I see it, you don't have much choice."

One Week Later
Florence, Italy — 1504

THE SMELL OF Linseed oil and turpentine was eternally ingrained in Liz's nose.

"Ah-ah-ah-ah, no moving, Lisa," Salai, Leonardo's assistant scolded.

"But I'm feeling hungry. Can't we have more grapes?"

"Very well then. Let him finish the mouth and you can take a break."

As Leonardo concentrated on painting the curvature of her lips, Liz went back to envisaging about her boyfriend. Perhaps he was not handsome, by her friend's standards, but she could easily overlook this because of his doting nature.

Even though he was considerably older than her, the wide span of their age difference was not frowned upon here, as it was in modern day Florida. In fact, it was very commonplace for a teenaged girl to marry an older man—even considered desirable—as long as he was fully capable of supporting her.

Francesco, she'd learned, came from a good family. He was a successful Florentine silk merchant by trade and loaded. Liz couldn't believe he'd commissioned Leonardo to do a painting of her. She was daydreaming about him and their upcoming wedding day when Michelangelo walked in the studio. Leonardo finally put his brush down, and Liz took a much-needed break.

The two artists began discussing the portrait and Leonardo's use of the background. Watching them interact with one another made it clear they were better friends than history books relayed. And Liz was grateful she was seeing it firsthand.

If Leonardo hadn't been at Michelangelo's studio the day they arrived, she might not have been offered a place to live. Or been able to have her portrait painted by such a famous artist. It was Leonardo who suggested to Michelangelo that he let her stay in the back room while he painted her. He'd said he was certain if Francesco had taken the time to walk her to Michelangelo's studio, she was someone to treat well—because Francesco never did that sort of thing. Nor did he go about commissioning paintings for a stranger. He insisted if they were to be married as time unfolded, it would not be good to have Liz stay in the same home as Francesco. As it turned out, Francesco asked her to be his bride not long after she arrived.

Liz stood up from the stool, her butt stiff and sore from sitting. She stretched from the waist down to the floor, downward dog style, then stood up and did a standing back bend, before turning her head side to side until she heard it crack.

Both Leonardo and Michelangelo watched. More than once they'd commented on what a free-spirited girl she was, if not strange. But Liz didn't care. She had bigger worries.

Since accepting Francesco's marriage proposal, she'd been consumed with how she'd break the news of her wedding to Dave. Francesco asked her to marry him in a moment when she'd felt particularly vulnerable, and the words slipped out before she had the sense to stop them. He'd been so elated, she hadn't the heart to tell him she only wanted to see how it felt to say yes. She'd always thought that was a question she'd never have the luxury of answering. And with the ensuing hubbub, how could she say no now?

Regretfully, Liz pushed the memory away, as she had the previous two days. Dave would never understand her reasoning or split-second decision to stay.

Liz nodded goodbye to Leonardo and Michelangelo and headed for the kitchen, where Salai was preparing a plate of cheese and fruit for lunch.

The moment she stepped into the kitchen, she felt herself relax. This kitchen was where she came whenever she needed solace, because it was the place she most felt at home. Though the architecture was naturally more rustic than she was used to, and Salai took care of the cooking, she could identify with its purpose. To feed. Sustain. Invigorate. Whom ever came up with the adage, "home is where the heart is," certainly got it right. This kitchen pulsed with life.

Wedges of sunlight spilled in the bright wood-beamed room that smelled of lemons and garlic. She loved that the ceramic bowls stacked along the back wall shelving, directly opposite the large bright window, were piled high with fruit and assorted vegetables and resembled still life paintings vibrant with energy.

The room itself could have been a painting. It sparkled with rich hues and textures. Just being here brought joy to her heart. But it was the lingering smell of cooking she found truly inviting. She missed her mother's home cooked meals, and it brought comfort knowing that like in her own home, there was always a pot of stew on the stove.

Liz lifted the lid off a heavy cast iron pot and inhaled deeply. Stirring the contents with a large wooden spoon on the counter, she recognized today's meal of cooked rabbit in a tomato-basil sauce loaded with carrots and potatoes. They had it often because it was one of Michelangelo's favorites. And it made her ravenous.

Without even thinking, Liz reached for one of the bowls, and before Salai had a chance to stop her, had devoured half a bowl full.

Salai paused, knife in hand, and said rather sharply, "Customarily we sit while we eat. The rabbit stew will not be ready for another hour."

"In that case," she replied, looking over her shoulder, her hand stopping mid-air, "I'll take some fruit and cheese with me."

Salai looked as if he was going to object, but he nodded and continued to cut cubes of cheese and fruit. She sat her bowl in the sink and went to stand next to a carved wooden chair by the center table, where she could watch him closer. Salai dropped large portions of fruit into a small basket with a checkered napkin.

His dark curls were unruly like hers. He wore his like a crown of ringlets. Secretly, she believed they looked alike, with his Romanesque nose and long arched eyebrows. Leonardo had suggested she pluck her eyebrows for the portrait, and Liz was seriously considering it.

As she waited impatiently for Salai to finish packing her lunch, she dug into her handbag and pulled the ancient journal out. She read the journal whenever she had a spare moment. She'd read through the book several times, but the calligraphy was so ornate it was difficult to understand. The margins had tiny notes crammed into them that she liked to study. She pressed on, deciphering what she could and taking notes on her own well-worn yellow notepad.

There were several historic references she'd dog-eared and needed to discuss with Dave, seeing he liked history as much as she liked food. She wanted to find out why the piece of feather she'd snipped from Adrielle transported them here, but no longer worked to get them out.

Dave was getting antsy. The initial excitement of having time travelled was starting to wear off, and he'd begun worrying they were trapped. They'd been here too long with no news from anyone, and no sign of Adrielle.

Salai watched her surreptitiously. Liz could feel his stare whenever she was distracted. She sensed he was getting used to her eccentricities, and they got along well, although she was different from other women of these times. He'd told her once, the wealthier the patrons were, the more demanding they became. Liz had no wealth to speak of, but her alliance to Francesco gave her equal standing.

Francesco del Giocondo's offer to marry Liz was rumored throughout the city. It was on everyone's mind. Upon commissioning Liz's portrait, Francesco inadvertently advertised he was a wealthy silk merchant with a penchant for art, because it was a well-known fact that Leonardo demanded a hefty fee for his portraits. Talk about the handsome sum he was paying only fueled how very accomplished he was, and what a desirable catch he'd be for any young woman. Though Liz preferred to keep her engagement quiet, the news soon buzzed through the city.

Salai finished packing the lunch. He handed it to Liz, and she took every morsel of food out of the basket and stuffed it haphazardly into her handbag. "It will be easier to carry this way," she said, in retort to his frown, without adding she'd planned on sharing it with Dave when she met up with him in the market. Salai nodded, taking the empty basket back, watching her covertly as she sashayed out of the room.

The narrow streets of this Italian city were no longer a puzzle to Liz. She'd always had a knack for finding her way, and the seven days they'd been in Florence was enough to become familiarized with it.

Liz loved the romance of a leisurely stroll along the path on the edge of the Arno River, but today, she was in a hurry. She wove around the streets, the scenery she normally savored blurring into inconvenience, not stopping until she reached the banks of the water. She indulged in one quick inhale of joy at seeing its beauty and quickly followed the trail to the Ponte Vecchio where the market displays began.

There, at the foot of the bridge, Dave sat on a wooden crate, his foot swinging back and forth while watching the people walk by. At seeing him from a distance, the aloofness with which he watched the crowds, caused a ping in her stomach.

Liz paused mid-step. She pressed her hand to her breastbone and caught her breath. Of course, he was going through withdrawals. This was the longest span she remembered that he hadn't watched an episode of *Project Runway*. And the longest he'd been away from Veda's continuous flow of gossip that kept them all up to date on the current goings-on of their peers.

When she spotted him, saw how rumpled his pink polo was, and how unkempt his blonde hair was without the bi-weekly trims, she was no longer sure she could stay in Florence.

This was insane! He didn't fit in to these times of long neglected hair and un-manicured nails. How could she ever have thought he'd fit in here? Or that she could say goodbye to her BFF?

Clearly, she cared about Francesco. But she'd said yes in a moment of impetuousness. Francesco had been so attentive; she'd become dazzled by the feeling of being desirable to someone. Anyone. All she wanted to do now was wrap her arms around Dave and tell him she'd made a huge mistake.

She glanced down at her feet. Thankfully, she hadn't given up her Sperrys when Francesco presented her with a trunk full of hand-sewn silk shoes encrusted with semi-precious stones and leather soles. Liz picked up the hem of her mauve silk dress, one of his other lavish gifts, and ran toward him.

"Lizzie, what's wrong?" Dave cried out as he saw her approach on a dead run. He jumped down from the cart and darted her way.

By the time she reached him she was so out of breath she could barely speak. "Noth—ing. I just—"

"What's happened? I don't think I've ever seen you run before."

It struck her that he was right. She never ran. Ever. She swiped at her tear-streaked cheeks, trying to hide a bout of emotion and sucked in large gulps of air. She bent over at the waist, resting her hands on her knees.

"I'm getting married," she blurted. "I'm sorry I hadn't told you."

He stood up and she fluttered her hands in front of her in a very Florentine way, to cool down.

"Oh Lizzie, I heard. I thought you'd lost your mind!" he exclaimed, his eyes roaming over her and drifting to her hair, the only part of her now that was still unruly. "The whole time I was thinking, who does that?" He took a moment to smooth his own hair. "Well?"

"Well?"

"Do you love him?"

"Fried frog legs," Liz cursed. "I don't know?"

"You don't know?"

"No. I—I thought I did but . . . seeing you here." She bit her lip. "We're not so different, he and I. But I could never leave you and he'd never fit in, in Florida. Everyone would think I've gone completely insane!"

"At least there's some improvement," Dave chuckled, "seeing as we've graduated from deep-fried mozza sticks."

She laughed.

"Any-who," he said, puckering his lips and rolling his eyes, "you don't have to have it all figured out just yet. Any breakthrough on the time travelling thing? We have to get out of here." He looked at her expectantly.

She hated to disappoint him. "No. I can't figure out why the feather worked and now it doesn't. Let's sit." She gestured for him to sit on a strip of thick grass at the river's edge.

He plopped down, and she ballooned her dress out around her like a collapsed parachute as she sank to the ground.

He winced. "The grass is going to stain the silk. It's still moist with dew."

She punched him in the arm. "Ah well. There are worse things in life." She leaned back on her fists behind her. She didn't want to elaborate that Francesco kept her in constant supply of silk. Dresses, blouses, skirts . . . robes. Anything she wanted. She thought back to her paltry closet at home stocked with Old Navy sweats and frayed jeans.

The river current flowed downward toward the bridge, and they relaxed into a mindless lull. They watched ripples form on the surface as a fisherman cast his net. Overhead, a bird dove into the water. It resurfaced with its catch and flew off. The fisherman shook his fist in frustration and recast his net.

Liz reached into her handbag and dug out her journal. She squirmed until she was comfortably cross-legged and turned to a page she'd dog-eared.

"Listen up, Sherlock, it says here the travel spells are in the *Book of Feathers*—an ancient manuscript full of secret rites. It's been carried down since the beginning for the Achaeans. That's the book Adrielle was trying to get a hold of when we jumped to that castle place I told you about. Remember?"

Dave's stomach growled and he made a small groan. He eyed her purse. "Got any food in there? I'm starving."

"Help yourself," she said, feeling terrible she hadn't offered.

She thought of the fruit bowls overflowing at the studio, and Salai with his constant food preparation. She slid her purse toward him. His fingernails were dirty and broken. She felt a stab of guilt as he dug inside and pulled out a handful of cheese cubes and an orange. Dave hadn't been allowed to stay at Michelangelo's. It was only Francesco's commission of her painting that landed her the accommodation.

"You doing ok?" she asked, wondering where he slept. She was afraid to ask.

"Sure," he said, tossing a couple of pieces of cheese in his mouth. He almost swallowed them whole. He stared into the river. "There's a dry spot under the bridge where I sleep. No one seems to care."

Liz swallowed a lump. "I do. Let me talk to Francesco."

"No, I told you we can't keep changing things. You've changed too much already."

He was right. She laid a hand on his shoulder. He looked sad. "We need to buy more time. I think if we could find that book, it could lead us to Adrielle."

Dave looked pointedly at her. "And then what? Meet up with whomever has it and shake him down?"

Wow. She hadn't seen him so touchy in a long time. "Something like that. On the upside, Adrielle may already have it. If she does, the three of us can figure the rest out."

"Hmm. What about the others?" Dave said, peeling the orange. He brought it up to his nose and inhaled the sweet fruity scent. "Why are oranges so much better here?"

Liz shrugged. "I wondered that too. I can smell its sweetness from here." He tossed the peel back into her purse. "I can't stop feeling awful about how we left everyone in Coco's room with Domenikos."

"I know, me neither. The worst part is I couldn't sleep last night because of it. It was like I was bombarded with all these details I'd forgotten about."

"Like?"

"Like when I was busy checking out Coco's bedroom—just before we came here—and Domenikos said he was going to give me the same proposition he'd given everyone else. He never answered when I questioned him about what he meant."

"Oh, right. I remember that. But no worries."

"What-do-ya-mean, no worries?"

Dave swallowed two large orange segments at once and laughed as the juice sprayed out onto Liz's dress. She winced, searching her bag for a napkin. She pulled it out and handed it to him. "You were saying?"

"That I was there before you and Adrielle arrived, remember? When you were in London." Dave leaned back onto his elbows and watched the river flow by. Now that he'd eaten, he seemed more relaxed. "His little proposition was to skip death and go into some sort of suspended existence. Become his minion for life."

Liz threw a sharp sideways glance at him. "Sheesh. That's what you call no worries?"

"Well, no one took him seriously. Including me, I guess."

"That's what worries me," Liz said, sitting a little straighter. "You didn't see what he did to that poor girl in England. C'mon, you're the history buff here. Mary Jane Kelley? The name ring a bell?"

Dave's eyes widened. "No way. Jack the Ripper?"

"Yes way." Liz nodded emphatically. "When we were there—Adie and I—well, not technically when he was, you know, doing the deed." She imitated the *Psycho* shower-stabbing scene. "But before. We saw him with her. Adrielle and I watched as he took the poor girl into a room. And I tried to warn her but—all of a sudden, we popped back into Coco's bedroom."

"Hmm." Dave bit his bottom lip. He frowned a little.

"It's almost like we keep going back there. Like *that* is the place where we know we'll find him."

"Liz, that's it. What if that's the one constant we can always go to?"

"Like a portal? Coco's room is a portal?"

"Maybe? I don't know. I mean, look, everyone seems to meet up there: you and Adrielle kept going back there. Domenikos showed up there. Angelo. Haden."

"And that creepy bird girl." Liz gave a slow whistle. "Maybe you're right."

"That doesn't explain how or why we ended up here," Dave said.

"Uhhh." Liz grimaced. "I think I can explain that one."

Dave flashed her a questioning look.

She held a finger up, the way Dave usually did, and he smiled. "Remember how we had that talk about my being a little ADHD?"

"Yep."

"Well, I couldn't help but wonder where Domenikos got that knife from, when he pulled it out. Now listen, before I lose my train of thought," she said, seeing that Dave was about to embark on one his you-need–to-focus tirades. "I've gone over this again and again in my head. It says in the journal the chronometer is the only sure way of pinpointing where exactly you travel to. Let's suppose Adrielle still has that. It also says Achaeans can travel through time because they have the feathers. And that's how we got here, with this little piece of Adrielle's feather." She reached in her cleavage and held it up. "For the record, it's the only safe place I could think of," she explained, anticipating his reaction and holding it up to the light.

In the sunlight the feather sparkled like it was covered in glitter.

"Hmm . . . I've never noticed before how shiny it is. Only the color."

"I know. It's an exquisitely detailed plumage," Dave said. "The red is so deep it's almost black, but definitely red. Crimson red."

"The feathers on Astraia were black when she was a bird. Before she turned. Remember?"

"How could I forget. OMG it was creepy."

"Really creepy."

"What color do you think Domenikos' are—saying he has them?"

"Feathers? Of course he has them, or he couldn't travel. Anyways, he's one of *them,* isn't he?"

They sat on the grass, eating the lunch and digested the information.

"Green," Liz blurted.

"Green? Why green?"

"I don't know. It makes sense. He has that pale green feather tattoo on his bicep. I saw it when he grabbed me." She tossed another piece of cheese into her mouth and swallowed. "It's nice not to worry about my weight. Have you noticed the women here are voluptuous?"

Dave choked on a grape. Liz was starting to worry she'd have to do the Heimlich maneuver when he sputtered, "Liz, the weight thing, that should be for yourself. Your personal health. Not for anyone else."

"I know," she said, staring into the water.

"Anyway, about the other thing, I have it. The four horsemen of the Apocalypse. That must be what it's referring to in that journal. Quick, read it to me again—you'd dog-eared it."

"Are you kidding me?" Liz said, her face falling as she looked down at the book. There were at least forty pages she'd dog-eared.

"It said something about a test to conquer each of the feathers, if that helps. It was the crimson feather that appeared on Adrielle's back. I think it may be the first of a series. If each feather represents a test, then red could be for war: the first in a sequence of seal judgments. The four horsemen could have corresponding feathers."

Liz put down the journal and turned to her own yellow pad. "Let me try this instead." She flipped through her notes. "Here, I've cross-referenced it to page 134." She turned to the corresponding page in the journal and read:

The ruling traveller must overcome all four judgments to embrace their destiny. Red is for war, the calming of the conflict between the societies. Silver is for conquest, the subjugation of enemy forces. Black is for the scale of justice, to right what is wronged. And finally, death, the pale rider; pale green. To conquer death.

They exchanged a look and read on.

When the four feathers are earned, the ruling traveller will pass through time undetected. If the ruling traveller rejects their destiny and the four feathers are not collected by the first solar eclipse after the first feather is earned, the time portals will remain closed and all will remain as is.

Liz rubbed at the spot by her heart. There was a squeezing sensation that didn't exactly feel like heartburn. "Dave."

"Yeah?"

"Do you think Adrielle really is the ruling traveller?"

"Yeah. It looks like it."

"Hmmm."

"And what do you suppose it means? *The time portals will remain closed and all will remain as is?*"

"I think that means we'll be stuck here indefinitely."

"WTF."

"Lizzie!"

Liz shook her head sharply. "I can't do it. It's not fair to either one of us. I'll have to break it off right away."

"Listen to me," Dave said, placing both hands on her arms and shaking her gently. For the first time in her life, Liz saw fear reflected on Dave's face. "You understand that backing out now could be detrimental to our health. I mean, by commissioning the portrait, he's bloody well gone and told the whole town he's bought you."

"No one's bought me!" Liz snapped, resenting the insinuation that Francesco wanted her for a girl-toy, instead of fallen in love with her.

"Wake up, Lizzie, the women's rights movement didn't start until 1848."

"And?"

"We need to be cautious. Especially since we could very well end up here for the rest of our lives. Dammit to hell, Liz, women here don't have the upper hand. Not even close. And right now, he could be your best bet for survival. By asking for your hand in marriage, he's given you more leverage than you could ever have dreamed of, on your own merit."

Liz considered this for a moment. "You're right. Guess I'll pretend to go along with it for now." She smoothed out the skirt of her dress. "Ok then." This was getting more and more complicated. "Let's just say the crimson feather is earned, and because Adrielle already has it, at least it makes sense she has it, since it came out of her back. And it says here the keeper of the *Book of Feathers* earns it. She would only need three more feathers before the solar eclipse."

"Right-O. So how do you suggest we find out when that is?"

"Leonardo. He's the only visionary who might believe us, and the only one smart enough to figure it out."

"Ok. About that other thing . . ."

"What thing?"

"The reason we're here? Before your ADHD kicked in?"

"Hmm."

"You know, about the knife."

"Oh yeah. Domenikos must have gotten it here. Do ya think?"

"Yes, I definitely think. That's the only thing that makes sense to me."

"But where?"

"Well now," Dave said, folding his hands neatly into his lap. He smiled, his eyes twinkling. "I'm not sure yet. But we've got two things figured out on our list."

THE SOUND OF a knock at the door resonated with a boom. Though almost inaudible, in the monastery, it may as well have been a bomb. Adrielle jumped, the ink spilling on her page and dribbling in spatters as her quill dropped to the floor.

She looked up. An elderly wiry-haired friar stood in the doorway, holding a tray of food. Without uttering a word, the monk laid the tray on the small table and backed out with a slight bow.

Adrielle smiled. A steaming bowl of consume soup was just what she needed. Outside the stone walls, the wind howled. It was freezing out in the yard and the cold air seeped in around the leaded windows.

She blotted at the spilled ink with a cloth and sighed, half of her morning's work ruined. Setting the work aside, she cradled the hot bowl, relaxing into the warmth, and breathed in the steam. Then she sipped the hot broth until it filled her insides.

She was thankful for the vow of silence this order had taken. A cursory search on the web had given her the location and time of a place where she could find refuge without being questioned. Where she could think without distractions.

The forgery required skill. After several attempts at recreating the near identical penmanship, she knew it would take longer to perfect than she'd originally thought. If she were to complete it in time, with any level of craftsmanship, she'd need help.

But first, there was something she'd been putting off that needed immediate attention. She set the bowl aside, let her fingers slide down the chain until the chronometer lay tightly in her hands, and squeezed her eyes shut.

Chapter 17

FLORENCE — 1504

IN HIS BIRD-LIKE state, Angelo squatted on the top of the Palazzo Vecchio, poised perfectly still like a carved gargoyle. The only thing moving were his eyes; his razor-sharp vision sifting through the crowd below.

He didn't know how it had happened, but he'd lost track of Adrielle. Since she was in possession of the *Book of Feathers*, it meant she was now its sole protector, which made her Domenikos' target. No matter how much he was against this entire thing, Adrielle was in the hot seat. He couldn't stop it. The wheels of destiny were set in motion. She'd have to find her own way out of this.

Stupidly, he hadn't warned Adrielle about the time crunch. He'd been waiting for the right moment. Until they were alone. The opportunity had never come. The tightening in his chest reminded him if he didn't find her soon, her friends could rapidly become a fading memory. By his calculations, they didn't have much time before the solar eclipse.

Angelo spread his wings wide. He soared into the sky, high over the city of Florence, toward the Arno river.

From this height, Angelo had a clear view of the center of Florence. The span of his wings was so wide he glided without much effort, concentrating on the scenery below. A crowd had gathered around the Duomo. As he neared, he saw it wasn't anything out of the ordinary. But there. Sitting along the banks of the river were Liz and Dave.

Angelo swept down over them and seized the journal from inside Liz's handbag. He secured it in his talons and flew into the hills beyond. He landed at the edge of a meadow, under a large tree where he could read the journal in private. Perhaps there was something in there that would help.

He realized right away how personal the journal was and felt a pang of guilt. Although the book belonged to Adrielle, Haden had also penned many entries. This was so out of character for him to violate their privacy like this.

He closed the book, taking a moment to process. What did this say about him? Written plainly on the pages, Adrielle expressed her innermost feelings with the understanding they'd be kept confidential. *If she ever found out . . .* It hurt. Even after pouring out his heart, his love for her, she had decided it was wiser to be with Haden. She'd been wrong. That hadn't changed a thing. Domenikos was still on the loose. And Adrielle's life was still in danger. He clenched his muscles until they ached.

That was the key point. Adrielle was in danger. He'd tried everything he could think of. He needed clues to find her. Protect her.

Everything hinged on the journal contents. Angelo re-opened the book and leafed through the pages, devouring the contents. There were details of events, places, explanations of the Travel code.

There, halfway down the page. Angelo re-read the passage three times, his heart pounding. He hadn't known of their covert alliance. He stuck a twig as a bookmark and closed the cover.

"WHERE IS SHE?" Angelo demanded of Monika. "Why can't I see her?"

"Look deeper into the heart of the diamond," she instructed, rotating the scepter until shafts of light spilled out from the center of the gem and filled the room.

"All I see is a red feather drifting along the shaft of white light. It is brilliant and gleaming and solitary."

Monika glared up at him. "Angelo, how many times must we go over the same sequence?"

"I need a favor," he said, his breath suspended.

"A favor? From me?" She cackled. "You know my allegiances cannot support any one of the four Achaeans."

"I am not asking for the kind of favor that would grant me an advantage. I only ask that you pass this along to its rightful owner."

Monika gazed down at the weathered book. A book once so full of life sat destitute in his proficient hands. "It is Adrielle's, is it not?"

Angelo nodded and stood very still. She searched his eyes to determine if his intentions were honorable, as he knew she would, and penetrated the surface greedily, absorbing his essence. Under normal circumstances, he would have covered his iris with his concealed eyelid, but he understood she needed to see past that. Not anticipating the feeling of vulnerability from her probing, Angelo flinched, fighting the impulse to retaliate.

The corner of her lips turned up. "Very well then." She extended her hand.

As Angelo passed her the book, his hand briefly touched hers and an electric current cycled between them, stunning Monika momentarily. Her eyes rolled backwards into her skull until only the whites of her eyes were visible.

"Monika, are you all right?" Angelo asked.

"Shhh." She hissed, raising her hand in protest.

She remained frozen in that catatonic state for several minutes. The silence was agonizing. Then, without warning, she banged the scepter hard on the ground. The diamond in the center of the crown lit up. Shards of colors exploded into the room, the light radiating so brightly Angelo could barely keep his eyes open.

"Go to her, Angelo," Monika said. "If you don't, she will surely die."

"I've tried. I don't know where she is!" he exclaimed, his heart pounding.

"There," Monika said, pointing her crooked finger into the center of the diamond. "Hurry, there is not much time."

He squinted past the intense light inside the gem, scoured the swirling colors, and locked in on shapes as they took form. "I see something. Damn, it's green."

"Go now," she yelled.

Angelo's third eyelid swept over his eyes and in one movement he transformed into a bird.

ALMOST AT ONCE the sky became dark. Like a fine mist of ink, heavy clouds banded into an oppressive shield that sprung rain pellets down like bullets.

"Let's go," Liz hollered, scooping up her purse and stuffing their remaining lunch inside. "Quick, give me the journal. I don't want it to get wet, the ink will run."

"I don't have the journal, you do," Dave said.

"That's not funny. Hurry up." She stood up and held her handbag open. "It's cobbled leather, and Kate Spade, I don't want it to get wet."

"It's a knockoff," he said.

Liz raised an eyebrow.

"Fine. I'm serious. You put it away when you pulled out the baguette. Look in the abyss of your purse." Dave wore an expression that said her insinuation he had it was infuriating.

Liz jammed her hand inside the bag and rummaged around. "OMG, OMG. It's really not here!" she wailed, squatting down on the grass and dumping the entire contents onto her full skirt. She rifled through the items, frenzied in panic. "Lip gloss, mace, wrappers. Rest of lunch. Pen. Yellow pad. OMG. It really, really, really, isn't here." Water droplets trailed down her face. "Double fudge sticks."

"No freaking way. Jeez, Liz, your vocab sucks."

The rain was coming down in torrents now. Sheets of water flattened her curly hair and dress, the silk fabric dissolving into a filmy sheath attached to her skin like plastic wrapping. She turned to Dave. "You did see me put it in there, right? I mean, I think I remember doing that, but I'm not sure anymore."

Dave nodded, a frightened expression on his face.

"I was afraid you'd say that." She stuffed everything back into her purse and stood up. She searched the ground frantically, the rain mixing with her tears and making it difficult to see. The contents of her stomach lurched up. She swallowed, raising her chin to the gloomy sky above. "God, no." She clenched her fists.

Overhead, far in the distance, she saw the tail end of a silver bird. She watched it until it disappeared.

"We're done here. Let's go. I've taken notes on pretty much everything that was in there, so it's probably okay." She fought to keep calm. "I mean, I hope it is. But this means someone or something else knows the value of its contents. Quick." She slung her purse into her armpit. "We need to get to Leonardo. A fresh mind on our side couldn't hurt."

THE STORM GREW worse by the minute. By the time they reached Michelangelo's house, they were soaked through to the bone.

They entered the house using the servant's side entrance, so they wouldn't soak the floors in the main area. Liz slipped her shoes off and lay them neatly under a coat hook. Already a large puddle of water was pooling at their feet.

Liz grabbed the bucket by the door and mopped up the water.

"Guess it's pointless to wish for a Kleenex," Dave said. He sneezed and snorted. "Not invented yet."

"Try my purse," Liz snapped, swishing the mop around. "You catching a cold?"

"I think so," he sniffled.

"Sit by the fire," Liz said.

He looked at fire in the stone fireplace. The logs in the firebox had burnt down, leaving coal embers glowing underneath.

"On the hook by the door," Liz said, without looking up from the kitchen floor.

Dave strode over to her purse, water swishing out of his sneakers. He dug inside.

Liz frowned, retracing his steps with the looped mop head. "Find them?"

"Zipped in the side compartment." He pulled out a single tissue, blew his nose twice, and stuck it in his pocket. The he shoved his finger in his ear and wiggled it. This wasn't a good sign. It meant his ears were getting itchy. "Hope you're not getting sick."

"I hope it isn't influenza. It's one of the big killers back in these times."

He was such a hypochondriac. "Are you hungry?" She wrung her hair out into the stone sink, where two plates with the remains of dinner were stacked. Her gaze drifted to the small rectangular table in the dining area. There were two empty wine glasses and a cutting block with an assortment of cheeses and dry fruits. Michelangelo had served an early dinner, and Leonardo had already retired to his quarters.

"I'm frozen." Dave shivered, his teeth chattering uncontrollably. He took off his sneakers and walked over to the fire.

"Here." She tossed him a towel dangling on a rack by the stove. "Once you're done, hang it there, close to the fire, to dry."

"Thanks," Dave said.

Liz watched him soak up his surroundings as he toweled off. When he was done, he hung the towel on the back of a chair as instructed.

"Mmmm. This feels *so* good," he said, taking a seat on the stone hearth and leaning into the warmth. He held his hands out close to the fire and stared into the flames. After a few minutes, he appeared more relaxed.

Liz took a seat next to him. "Can you believe this is really happening? I mean, every night I lay awake agonizing with stress. Wondering how long it's going to be before we're all back in Florida, where our biggest worry was who's going to have the next party. And what they'll have to eat."

"I know," Dave agreed. "The food part never entered my mind though. I hadn't realized how good we had it."

Liz didn't elaborate she'd never had it this good. Everything was so different here. She never would have imagined a boyfriend who lathered her with gifts. "Seems like a decade since Adrielle's birthday eve. Who could have guessed she was telling the truth when we found her upstairs at Scarlett's?"

Dave grew pensive. "Hey, do you really think Domenikos killed Josh? Was she wrong about that? Remember, we never did see a body."

"I don't know."

The creak of the front door startled them. They turned in time to see Michelangelo, a large block of marble cradled under one arm. He set it down on the floor by the entry and hung up his jacket.

Although small in stature, Michelangelo had broad well-developed shoulders and arms. He looked up at them and seemed surprised he wasn't alone.

His eyes were lively and vibrant. They were so intense, Liz hadn't noticed at first his nose looked as though it had been broken several times.

"Mona Lisa," he exclaimed, his face lighting up.

Liz felt fortunate he seemed exuberantly happy to see her. He had welcomed her, a stranger, into his home and been nothing but kind. He ruffled his hair with his hands, tiny droplets of water spraying out as he shook it.

"My friend, Dave," Liz said, gesturing casually toward him.

Dave nodded in acknowledgement. He seemed stunned. Michelangelo, the world-renowned genius, was his hero.

Dave cleared his throat. "Pleased to meet you."

Michelangelo nodded in reply. He turned to tug at his boots. "Have you seen the progress on Leonardo's painting? I'm heading to the studio if you'd like to take a look."

"That would be great," Liz replied. "I left before lunch and haven't had a chance to peek in yet."

Liz knew by Dave's expression he was in awe. He thought this was pretty cool. Awesomely cool. She'd seen his disappointment when they'd knocked at his house and he hadn't been home. Dave had been dying to meet him ever since. A large part of their conversations had been discussing when Liz would finally introduce them.

Dave hated groupies. Liz bit back a giggle at his struggle to calm down. He had a bad case of groupie syndrome, and he definitely didn't want to look like one.

Even though Michelangelo was only in his twenties, he was already a historic giant. One of the highest paid and influential artists of the times. The sculpting completion of *David* was revered as one of the most famous sculptures of all time. To be sitting in front of him now was undeniably one of Dave's most important moments.

"Dave?" Liz blurted.

Dave choked back a surge of tears.

"Are you alright?" Michelangelo asked. He seemed bewildered at seeing him so emotionally demonstrative.

Dave, overcome with emotion, could only nod.

"Come have a look then." Michelangelo gestured with his hand.

They followed him down a narrow hallway that led into the studio at the back of the house. Dave, apparently struggling to contain his excitement, skipped more than walked. Liz remembered when he'd written an essay on Michelangelo, the topic being "Who is your favorite person in history and why?" He'd written that in the twenty-first century, though there wasn't much solid historical support, general wisdom agreed the artist had been a homosexual. Dave was among those who believed he was, and he looked up to Michelangelo as a mentor, reminding himself in times of hardship that great things were possible. And here they were. Michelangelo was only a couple of years older than them, and he'd already accomplished so much.

At the end of the hall, they reached a small arched wood door with a wrought iron handle. The penetrating smell of oil paints and solvents burned at Liz's nose. Dave's gaze danced wildly around the studio. He was a child entering Disneyland, soaking up every detail.

The room itself was a fair size with whitewashed stucco walls and a raised wood beamed ceiling. Large windows lined the far wall. The raging storm outside darkened the interior so the room was lit with candles and oil lamps instead of natural light.

Considering Michelangelo used the room for both, sculpting and painting, he kept it considerably tidy. A straw broom was propped in the corner, where several buckets filled with dust and discarded chunks of marble were stacked.

Wood shelving on the far wall stocked sculpting tools and pieces of marble in various stages of completion. And in the center of the room, was a large wood easel holding Leonardo's painting. Beside it, a smaller square table with a double row of drawers was loaded with pigments and bottles of solvents, brushes, and a palette with gobs of paint.

Someone, probably Michelangelo, had started painting a fresco on one corner of one wall.

"Wow, what an incredible place to work," Dave said, his attention drifting over everything but not managing to rest on any one area because there was so much to take in. "I'm surprised with all the work going on, you get any sleep."

"Ah, so true." Michelangelo laughed. "The sleeping quarters are upstairs, through that side door." He pointed. "But I admit, sometimes I work here through the night. Lisa's and the servants' rooms are on the third floor, in the *dormatorio*. Mine is on the second, by the sala, the main living area. Right now, Leonardo is staying up there, so I, too, am bunking upstairs."

"There's so much art in this room, I hadn't even noticed the other door," Dave said. "I thought the main living area was downstairs, in the room we just came from, with the nice fireplace."

Small lines appeared at the corners of Michelangelo's eyes. "No, that is only the service area. The kitchen and work spaces. You must not be from here. Most of the homes here in Florence are set up like this." He frowned slightly. "Is your home far away?"

"You could say that," Dave replied, throwing a sharp sideways glance at Liz.

She was glad he didn't elaborate that since arriving, he'd been sleeping on the streets like a beggar. Both he and Liz had agreed not to press Michelangelo for a place to stay, fearing it may raise too many questions. Dave rubbed at a dirt mark on his sleeve. Michelangelo's eyes grazed over it and paused on the rip on his pants.

To avoid further discussion, Dave paced to the painting and peered at it. "Ahhh, ahhh," he gasped, his gaze jackhammering from it to Liz and back again.

"It is beautiful, is it not?" Michelangelo exclaimed. He seemed to be struggling to place Dave's reaction.

Dave was speechless. He turned to Liz and studied her face. Liz squirmed. He was making her feel uncomfortable. She was relieved when he turned back to the painting.

"Holy shit," he muttered under his breath. "This is the painting you've been sitting for? It's been a while since I've seen the printed color plate version in my Jansen art history textbook. It does not do this painting justice. Oh no. The colors here are much richer and vibrant. The skin is so translucent and dewy you can almost feel it."

"Scusi?"

Liz elbowed Dave.

"Amazing," Dave clarified. "Leonardo has captured her beauty. Both outside and from within."

"Ahh si . . . la Mona Lisa. Or the Gioconda," Michelangelo said, "as Salai calls it. He has told Leonardo this is his best painting so far. He would like to have it one day."

"I am sure he would." Dave gave her a quick sideways glance. "It is amazingly beautiful." He noticed the gown from the painting was laid over the back of a chair. He walked over and touched it, letting the fabric slip between his fingers. He turned to Liz. "And you wouldn't believe me when I said you needed a good tweezing."

Liz's hands went to her eyebrows. She felt her face grow warm. "Salai was trying to get me to do it this morning, but I wasn't sure. I guess Leonardo went ahead and painted them off."

Dave grew serious. He leaned into her and whispered, "Liz, you *do* understand this is *the* Mona Lisa, the famous Mona Lisa from the Louvre, right? Icon of the millennia. You know, from the *DaVinci Code*?"

"I know." She grimaced. "I was so afraid to tell you. I'm sorry. I didn't want you to think I'd messed something up."

Dave stared at her. She could only imagine the terrible things going through his mind.

"This proves we *have* changed history," she said.

"Or maybe it means we were already here. Once. You know, a time before. Since the painting looks like it always has." He leaned in closer. "I've never realized it was you before. Your hair is always so—and your eyebrows." He looked back at Liz and winced. "Let's just say they're distracting."

"Thanks a lot."

"No insult intended. Anyways, it's complicated. This time travel conundrum."

"Time travel?" someone said.

They looked up. Leonardo DaVinci stood in the doorway, wearing a flowing black robe to the floor, with a rope tied at the waist. His beard was long and wiry, similar to the way it was portrayed in his self-portrait.

"Don't let me interrupt. You had me at the words time travel. You must be a philosopher, like me," he said to Dave, matter-of-factly. He turned to Michelangelo. "Some of us do not like to venture beyond the known, but thankfully, there are others curious enough to imagine unknown things."

"Now that is not fair, my good friend. I only know what the church, la Santisima, tells us. Beyond that, it is not for us to know," Michelangelo responded.

"I am of the school that there are many things yet to be imagined and discovered." Leonardo turned back to Dave. "Now tell me about this time travel. I must learn everything there is. What do you know of it?"

Liz and Dave exchanged a look. Dave had a shocked expression. She knew he didn't like getting caught off guard, and they hadn't discussed how much they should say. Being asked about time travel by an ingenious mind, especially when they'd come here to discuss that very thing, was both exhilarating and frightening. Liz hoped they wouldn't get tossed on their ear.

"Michelangelo, come, let us sit and share a bottle of wine as we discuss such an interesting principle," Leonardo suggested.

Michelangelo looked as though he had never considered this concept being possible. What did he expect with Leonardo under his roof?

"Very well. Let us sit in front of the fire," he suggested, leading the way back through the hallway to the room with the fireplace. "You two look like the storm has shaken you up."

Michelangelo stirred the fire with a wrought iron poker. He added a couple of logs. "There, that's better." He sat the poker aside and took a moment to admire the flames as they reawakened. "Now let's move the table closer so we can enjoy the warmth."

With Dave's help, they repositioned the table from the far end of the room to in front of the hearth. They carried over the chairs. Leonardo poured the wine into small glasses. He slid over a filled glass for each of them and took the seat furthest from the fire.

"To the dolce vita," he said, raising his glass high.

The others raised their glasses, each toasting to life.

They settled around the table, and Leonardo set his glass down. He reached in his pocket and pulled out a small leather notebook.

"Ah, you have one of those too," Dave said, looking pleased.

"I never go anywhere without it," he said, thumbing through the pages until he came to a block of drawings crammed with tiny writing. He paused, taking several moments to review his past entries. He flipped through several more pages and stopped at a blank one. He pressed the journal open with the heel of his hand and pushed out of his chair to retrieve a jar of ink and a feather quill from the counter.

Liz stole a glance at Dave who looked like he was going cry with joy. They'd seen images of Leonardo's notebooks in the art books so this was an unexpected thrill.

Leonardo settled back down in his place. He dipped the tip of the quill into the ink jar, tapped it onto a blotting paper, and looked expectantly up at them, his eyes sliding between them. "Now, tell me what you know."

Dave and Liz exchanged a surprised look. Were they really going to tell him everything?

Liz kicked Dave under the table.

"Ouch." Dave jumped. "Why'd you go do that for? I didn't say anything."

"We need a moment," Liz hissed through gritted teeth.

"Why? He's our best chance for getting home."

"Home?" Leonardo asked. "That wouldn't by chance be Florida, would it?"

"Florida?" Dave and Liz squawked and stared at him.

"What do you know about Florida?" Liz asked.

Leonardo leaned casually back on his chair and turned toward the hall. "Adrielle? Will you come downstairs please? I think we have found your friends."

Chapter 18

Florence — 1504

THE MOMENT ADRIELLE crossed the doorway, Liz jumped out of her chair. She hurdled over the bucket with the mop, knocked it over, spilling water all over the floor, and almost flattened Adrielle to the floor. Adrielle fought to keep her balance as Liz wrapped her arms around her. She squealed like a newborn pig. Truth be told, Adrielle was just as excited to see her.

"Happy to see you too," Adrielle said, shifting her weight and repositioning to keep her balance. She tried to shake Liz off but Liz kept holding on. "How did you get here?"

"Busted," Liz said, finally releasing her embrace. She had the naughty look of a four-year-old who's both confessing and bragging about a misdoing. "I snipped a piece of your feather for a bookmark and voila."

"Interesting." Adrielle nodded, "I'd wondered if that might actually work."

"Oh, and I was thinking about Domenikos' knife when we were transported," Liz said. "I guess it means he must have gotten it here."

"Ahem. Ladies?" Dave stood up, his arms pressed to his sides. They followed his gaze to Leonardo who was waiting patiently for them to settle down.

"Have a seat my child," Leonardo instructed, sliding out the vacant chair next to him.

Liz picked up the bucket and made a half-hearted attempt at mopping up her mess.

"Who is this monstrosity of a child?" Michelangelo stood up so swiftly the top rail of his chair banged loudly on the wood floor behind him.

"Why the child has no color. She is a child of the devil," he cried, his arms flailing. His vibrant eyes bore into her like two lightsabers.

Adrielle froze. She'd gotten used to odd looks, they happened all the time. Most were of a curious nature, and it was understandable, because people seldom saw an albino. But no one had ever come out and accused her of being the devil.

Leonardo shot up to his feet. "Michelangelo, please, she is my guest." He walked to Adrielle and twined his protective arm around her thin shoulders.

Adrielle could see him quelling his outrage.

"How long have we known one another?" Leonardi asked. "Can you possibly believe I would mingle with the likes of the devil?"

Michelangelo stood transfixed, his mouth gaping open like a largemouth bass.

"Let us sit as friends and get to the bottom of this oddity," Leonardo insisted.

The room was thick with uncertainty. Finally, Michelangelo acquiesced after several moments and settled back into his seat. He folded his arms over his chest, his eyes flashing between Leonardo and Adrielle.

Leonardo paced back to his seat, but Adrielle stood stiffly in the doorway. She was still shaken up. Sitting was the last thing she wanted to do.

"Come have a seat," he said, rapping on the empty chair. "Tell him what you told me when you showed up this afternoon."

Adrielle glanced at Michelangelo. The only thing that might help was opening up to him and explaining the barricade she was up against.

Of course, this was easier said than done. She was a chicken. She hated confrontation. Her entire life was trying to blend in by hiding behind a façade of makeup and wearing whatever Coco's or anyone else's idea of fashion sense was. The one time she'd gone with her gut, at the party with Layla's out-of-style dress, she'd stuck out like a flare and been mocked for it. But there was no makeup or disguise she could hide behind forever. She was different, and like Coco had warned, the sooner she owned up to it the better.

Adrielle took the seat next to Leonardo and leaned on her elbows on the table. She pressed her fingers together forming a pyramid while she gathered her thoughts. She'd just tell it like it was. She glanced at Liz and Dave. They stared back expectantly. She felt better they were there. She took a deep breath and cleared her throat.

"It's true, I don't look like you." Her words flowed in perfect Italian, articulated like a native. "I don't have pigment in my skin. But that's no different than paint. It doesn't change who I am. So what, if I don't have color. If my hair looks white and my eyes are almost clear. The way I look doesn't make me a devil. I am still a girl. A human girl, trying to figure out where I fit in." She looked at Leonardo who nudged her on.

"*You* have talents in art and can do things impossible to others. I am not that different from you in that way. I can do things too, that others can't. And one of those things is travel in time."

Michelangelo sat unmoving. The stern expression on his face remained.

"Explain to him what you told me, about how it was that you arrived here. And why," Leonardo urged.

Adrielle inhaled another long breath and shot a look at Michelangelo. Would any of it make a difference? Michelangelo seemed to be made of stone. "Well, I am becoming what some call a traveller. Not a traveller in your sense of the word, meaning going on a trip from Venice to Florence by boarding a ship or a carriage. I can travel through time. I skip years ahead to the future, or behind to the past, to a time that has already passed."

"Madre Santisima! This cannot be," Michelangelo cried, once again rising from his seat. He was known for having a flaring temper and his was starting to blaze.

"It's true. As long as I have this." Adrielle reached in her pocket and pulled out a crimson feather.

Michelangelo, who had taken a large stride toward the door, turned around to face her.

She gazed resolutely into his eyes. "I will show you." She clasped her chronometer in one hand and the feather firmly in the other. "Tell me the date when you were given the commission to sculpt the David, and I will tell you more about it."

Michelangelo blinked. "I have never before seen eyes so pale. I can almost see through them. It is like seeing one of my sculptures awaken." He gazed at her for several seconds. "It was in 1501. That is all I will say."

"Okay then." Adrielle closed her eyes and before the others had a chance to blink twice, she left. And almost instantly re-appeared.

Everyone stared wide-eyed. She smiled, her eyes flicked to Leonardo who urged her on with a slight nod of the head. She turned to Michelangelo.

"The statue was originally commissioned by the Opera del Duomo for the Florence Cathedral. It was to be one of a series of large statues meant to fit in the cathedral's niches. Tall, about eighty meters from the ground. The consuls asked you to complete an unfinished project started in 1464 by Agostino Di Duccio, and later by Antonio Rossellino. Both sculptors rejected the marble because of its flaws. They thought it would make such a huge statue unstable. And so, it lay neglected in the courtyard of the Opera del Duomo for twenty-five years."

Michelangelo made a small grunting noise. "Leonardo, or any one of the thirty artists gathered to decide on an appropriate site for him, could have told you that."

"True. But you never told anyone why you decided to accept."

Michelangelo's face grew taut. "You have my attention."

"It was an overcast day when the consuls called you in. They explained they needed a religious subject for the statue. That the piece of marble they wanted you to sculpt had too many *taroli* or imperfections. That it had been rejected before. But they also said your talent was unequaled. They felt there was no one else who could undertake such a difficult request. And the marble was gleaming white. You accepted the challenge with enthusiasm but slept restlessly for many months. You weren't sure what to depict. And then one night, it came to you. You got up from your bed long after the sun had gone down and stood in the shadow of the stone, under the moonlight. It was then when you realized you had to sculpt David."

As she spoke, he watched her suspiciously.

"For forty days Goliath, champion for the philistines, challenged the Israelites to send out a champion. A single combat would decide the outcome. Only David, a young shepherd accepted the challenge, with little more than courage. His faith in God. His rock and his sling. Up until then, David had always been portrayed after the victory. After he had slain the giant. But *you*, Michelangelo, chose to show him before the battle. Tense. Concentrated. Relaxed but alert. In your David, you can barely see the slingshot he carries over his shoulder. You wanted to show his victory was because of his cleverness. Not sheer force. You wanted to show the self-confidence and concentration it takes to overcome an obstacle. And you did it, because that's how you see yourself. You accepted the challenge when others rejected it, in the same way David did."

Michelangelo looked shocked. "How can you possibly know that?"

"Because I was there. That night, as you stood in the shadow of that great stone and received your revelation, I was there too, receiving my own." Adrielle paused, the weight of her responsibility crushing down on her. This was more personal than she'd meant to get, but it was her only chance. She needed them to help with her plan. "Michelangelo, I have accepted a challenge that threatens mankind." Her voice quivered, and she fought to keep a torrent of tears at bay. "I have to overcome a giant of unspeakable evils with only my feather, my chronometer. And I have you two. I need you."

Michelangelo frowned a little. He seemed to be deliberating. The terse expression was gone. "How did I sculpt him?"

Adrielle bit back a smile. She couldn't say why, but she had the impression she was winning him over. "As a matter of fact," she pointed to his boots by the door, "wearing those most of the time." She stood up as high as her tiptoes allowed and leaned into the center of the table, her weight on her fists.

All eyes turned to her. Adrielle felt her face grow warm, but if she was going to solicit their help, she had to press on, prove to him without any doubt she could travel to the past.

"You worked in utmost secrecy, in the courtyard of the Opera del Duomo, where the stone was. Because it was in open air, you were wet a large part of the time, and wore those damn boots. Maybe that's where you got to the idea to make a wax model and submerge it in water. You let the water level drop as you worked and used different chisels to sculpt what you could see."

Leonardo slapped the table with his open hand. "Ahhhh." He shook a finger and laughed. "So that's how you did it." He dipped his quill in the ink jar and tapped the edge of the glass. For a moment, all that was heard was the tip of the quill brushing along the parchment paper.

Michelangelo shrugged off Leonardo's outburst and slid his eyes back to Adrielle. "Go on."

"You rarely ate. Or slept. When you did, it was in your clothes and usually in those boots."

Michelangelo collapsed into his chair, allowing it to cradle him. "How is this possible? No one else was there at the time. And I took every precaution to hide the masterpiece until the unveiling a few months ago. When I revealed it to the members of the Vestry board and to Pier Soderini, the *gonfaloniere* of the republic."

Leonardo raised one wiry eyebrow. "I take it this matter is now settled?"

Michelangelo nodded. He pushed his chair in. His expression intensified. "You know about my challenge, now tells us about yours—this giant of unspeakable evils."

"I know very little about him. He's committed horrific crimes; some I've seen for myself. He is Achaean, an ancient immortal that's not human, but looks it. And he can shift into a bird-like shape instantly and escape because he can time travel."

"This sounds like an invincible monster. How can you believe you can overtake such a beast?"

"Because I've been told I'm the only one who can. If he isn't stopped, he'll destroy the human race."

He knit his brows. "Who has told you this?"

"Others of his species."

"There are others?" He seemed surprised.

"Yes."

"Why you?"

"I don't know. I guess I have the things he needs."

"Which are?"

Adrielle pulled at the chain around her neck. "My chronometer for one. And that." She pointed to the doorway where a large book had fallen on the floor with Liz's unexpected tackle.

"That can't be!" Liz and Dave exclaimed.

"Yep. *The Book of Feathers*." Adrielle went to get it. She set the volume down gingerly and slid it to the center of the table where everyone could see.

The leather binding was hand tooled and weathered from age. There was an inscription on the front, LLAP, and underneath an embossed seal in the form of four intertwined feathers forming a crown. Each of the feathers had faint metallic coloring: pale green, crimson red, black, and silver. In the center of the crown was a dragon-like creature with winged feathers.

"May I?" Michelangelo asked.

Adrielle nodded. When he went to pick it up, Leonardo flinched.

"Be careful, it is very old."

Michelangelo slightly rolled his eyes. Leonardo lifted his hands up as if to say—*just had to mention it.*

After a deep sigh, Michelangelo picked up the book.

"There are several sections to this book," Adrielle explained, as he leafed through its many pages. "The hand sewn bands hold them together."

"I see that. And the pages are made of the finest papyrus," Michelangelo said, pausing every so often to absorb the particulars. "The edge text block has gold leaf mixed with mussel-shells. It is applied expertly. And the detail in these illustrations is exceptional. The expertise of the Calligraphy is also the finest I've ever seen. But I cannot read the script." He turned to Leonardo. "Have you seen this?"

"Yes, Adrielle showed me the book when she arrived."

"What language is this?" Michelangelo asked.

"An ancient Achaean text," Adrielle said.

"And you can read this?" he asked incredulously.

She nodded. "Yes. I'm not sure why, but I can."

"Very well then. What is the essence of the contents of this book?"

"The beginning explains the history of the Achaeans. How at one time, millions of years ago, they lived on this Earth. Before humans. They evolved from a dragon-like winged creature with feathered wings into what they are now. In their natural state, they look like birds, with feathered wings. Only they're larger and stronger. It's difficult to pick them out because they can take on human form and look like you or I. Usually, their feathers are hidden."

"That is incredible."

"Perhaps, but no more than many myths or beliefs passed down through the ages," Leonardo said.

"After the history section, the bulk of it is a collection of spells. I don't understand how they work, but I know they work. One of the spells is what sent me into the future. To Florida, where I was brought up."

"Sorcery?" Michelangelo shook his head vehemently. "I will have none of this." He pushed the book away and slid out from his chair. He turned to leave and wagged his finger, looking pointedly at Adrielle. "It is not for us to deal with the dark side."

Leonardo patted Adrielle's hand. "Michelangelo, for everyone's sake, keep an open mind and let her finish."

Adrielle saw Leonardo's desperation in his shaking hands. The tension was thick and palpable.

Michelangelo pressed his mouth into a scorn.

"If we don't stop him, everything is at stake. Your life. Your life's work. Even your precious David," Leonardo insisted.

"It's true. Domenikos has no regard for the physical laws. He defies them. He travels forward or back as he pleases, not caring if there are consequences.

And there are. Believe me, there are. Every time the teeniest detail changes, the imprint it leaves has a huge effect." Adrielle tugged at the collar of her shirt.

"Like ripples in water," Leonard said. "Michelangelo, I have spent hours studying the effects of the current. Life as we know it will cease to exist."

"And what exactly do you expect from me?"

"I have a plan," Adrielle said, her words coming out rushed. "He needs this book—without it he doesn't have the Achaean rituals. He can't tap into their powers. As long as this book is not in his possession, there is still a chance of defeating him."

Adrielle captured the eyes of each of them around the table, one of the few times in her life she didn't shy away from direct eye contact. The need to convey the importance of her mission burned in her. "If this is going to work, I need the support from every one of you."

"Do not take this wrong, but when you are confronted with an evil so terrible, you need to execute force. And you don't seem the type," Michelangelo said.

"Not by force, by wit. I need you to help me trick him."

"Trick him?" Michelangelo grunted. "How do you suppose to do that? Someone as deviant as you say, cannot be tricked easily."

"If he thinks he has the real book, he will stop pursuing it. We can reproduce an identical copy, changing the text in the chants to create a more powerful spell that will bind his powers."

The room grew quiet.

"Impossible," Michelangelo finally said. "It would take unmatched skill to create a forgery that would pass for the original. Only the very best artist could pull this off."

"Scusi." Leonardo straightened in his chair. His gaze bore into Michelangelo. He stroked his long beard with his bony fingers.

"No, no, no, no." Michelangelo roared. "I will have nothing to do with this."

Leonardo let the silence sit. "I can do the illustrations. But you are the best at gold leaf," he finally said. "I can teach Adrielle to produce the detailed calligraphy with my quill."

"That is only a small part of what needs to be done. We would still need to find a leather smith to tool the cover. And someone else to prepare the papyrus. No, no." Michelangelo shook his head. "You are on your own." He backed away from the table. "I will have no part of this."

A sharp rap at the window shattered the glass, a thousand shards exploding into the room like bullets. The blast stole everyone's breath. With no more impression than the soft glide of a feather, a silver bird landed on the floor in front of the door and transformed into human form.

"Angelo," Adrielle gasped, in relief and excitement.

Leonardo and Michelangelo froze. Their expressions were incredulous.

Angelo's eyes were wild with impatience. "Our time is running out."

Liz and Dave exchanged a look and whispered to each other.

"Ask him," Liz said.

"How long?" Adrielle asked.

"Seven nights until the solar eclipse."

"And if we don't finish?"

Angelo shook his head, his lips pressing into a fine line. "That is not an option. He has your friends."

"By friends you mean Scarlett, right?" Liz asked.

"Yes, and the others as well. Kate. Veda. Even Coco."

"No . . ." Adrielle breathed.

"Coco too?" Dave asked.

"He is leveling the playing field. Up until now, you had the advantage with the book. But now?" Angelo shook his head. "Now we need a miracle."

Michelangelo shut his gaping mouth and turned to Leonardo. "Now miracles, I believe in."

Leonardo and Michelangelo locked gazes. There appeared to be an invisibly charged conversation cycling between them.

With a small nod, Michelangelo backed away from the door, pulled the chair out from the table, and calmly took a seat. He slid *The Book of Feathers* squarely in front of him. He brushed roughly over the worn cover with his chaffed hands as he examined it closely. Adrielle could almost see the wheels of a plan forming in his mind as his eyes became effervescent.

"Very well then," he said brusquely, his face set with determination. "Someone will need to get Lorenzo. He is the best leather worker I have ever seen." As he spoke, he looked at each of them as if gauging each person as to their abilities. He stopped at Dave, his razor-sharp eyes instilling the importance of this task.

"You will find him by the Ponte Vecchio, next to the iron smith. Tell him we need him to reproduce an ancient book binding of the finest tooled leather. That it needs to be perfectly replicated. Not a similar likeness, but exact. He is to keep it in strictest confidence. And don't take no for an answer, tell him Michelangelo needs the favor repaid."

Dave smiled.

"Be right back," Adrielle said in a hushed tone, hoping Angelo wouldn't realize she planned on making an inconspicuous escape to go back for Coco. Back to a time before Domenikos had a chance to take her.

"No." Angelo snapped under his breath. "Dammit," he cursed. "Do not leave my side."

Adrielle left before he could stop her.

Chapter 19

Florida – Present Day

"COCO?" ADRIELLE WHISPERED. There was no *one* thing that stood out from ordinary, except for unsettling silence.

Seeking confirmation the chronometer had worked, her gaze drifted to the pile of dresses on the floor of Coco's room. Among the cast-offs was the sleeveless black dress Coco had wanted her to wear the night of the party. Immediately, she felt relieved. She was starting to get the hang of time-travelling, but there were so many things that could go wrong.

She stepped into the center of Coco's room and kicked over the mound, feeling a tinge of disappointment Coco wasn't there. She peeked in the adjoining bathroom and in the closet, where Coco could spend an exorbitant amount of time choosing outfits. *No one.* Why then did it feel like Coco was here?

On the dresser was the can of Coke. She picked it up. It was still cold. Red lipstick stains on top.

Everything appeared to be in order. Even the bottles of perfume still neatly arranged. Adrielle picked up the bottle Liz had sniffed. The lingering scent from being sprayed wasn't there. Nor were Liz's food wrappers on the floor. Meaning, Liz and the gang hadn't been there yet.

She glanced at the chronometer. She was right on schedule. Seven o'clock, party night.

The bed was still unmade. *Damn.* She'd made it herself that morning, before studying. By all rights, a version of herself should be lying there with her books scattered around, moping that Josh hadn't called.

What could've gone wrong to have changed this moment?

The creak of the stairs alerted someone was on the way up. Adrielle turned, fully expecting it to be Coco. *Huh?* She did a double take. It took a second to register . . .

"Josh?" She blinked. "It can't be." Her stomach clenched.

"Now what kind of greeting is that for your—what did you call me? Your *joie de vivre?"* he said, taking two long strides into the room.

"Joshy," she squealed, feeling a rush of relief. Tears sprang to her eyes, and she swiped them away quickly. She jumped up and wrapped her legs tightly around his waist.

"It's a good thing you're little," he teased, cuddling her in his arms.

Adrielle felt an enormous flood of emotions.

"You really are an emotional type, aren't you?" He set her down.

She clung to him and laid her chin on his shoulder. He was ok, she thought. She'd changed his murder. She'd missed him so much. She was about to kiss the spot on his neck that Domenikos had—*argg*. Directly behind him was Angelo, a stern expression on his face.

What? she mouthed, shooing him away with the wave of her hand.

Angelo pressed his lips together in disapproval and shook his head.

Dang. She was just registering how angry he seemed when all of a sudden it hit her—Angelo looked completely translucent, a hologram projected over the objects in the room.

How could this be? Haden's explanation popped in her head. Of course. Angelo had travelled as a spectator. *"Not cool!"* she mouthed over Josh's shoulder at Angelo.

"Why are you here?" Angelo mouthed back.

"Why is Josh here?" she mouthed silently. *"He's supposed to be dead."*

"There is no—supposed-to-be anything. You should know that by now.*"* The green in Angelo's eyes flashed.

Adrielle gasped. Angelo had said that out loud.

"Don't worry, he can't hear me. I'm in spectator mode. Totally legit. You, on the other hand, as usual, are breaking the rules."

"No, I'm not." *Oops. She hadn't meant to say that out loud.*

"Huh?" Josh asked, releasing his bear hug.

"Ouch!" Adrielle yelped, her gaze jutting to Josh's pocket. "*What* is that thing that just poked me?"

"This?" Josh pointed at a silver object sticking out of his pocket.

Adrielle nodded.

He pulled out an intricate silver-handled dagger with a long pointy blade.

Adrielle stared down at the knife, her heart pounding.

"Where did you get that?" It was the same one Domenikos used to slice Josh's throat.

"Sick, isn't it?"

Sick was right, but not the kind he meant.

"I won it in a poker game." He laughed and tilted the blade until the light caught the glint in much the same way Domenikos had. "Look, it's supposed to be made in Italy."

"Oh god, now I really *do* feel sick," she said, swiping at her forehead and squirming out of his embrace. She searched for Angelo, but he was gone.

"You play poker now?" she asked, feeling a rise of anger that Angelo had stayed long enough to be annoying, but left before this started getting complicated.

"Guess so. And I'm pretty good at it too." Josh grinned, gliding the blade of the knife along his palm and then sliding it back in his pocket. "Let's go. You ready?" His gaze drifted down to her jeans.

"Where to?"

"Nowhere, if Coco's gone," he said, searching the room. "You know, I thought you wanted to spend quality time." He grinned again, pulling her close.

She pushed him off. "Where's this guy now? The one who lost the knife?"

"The Goth? Who cares?"

"How did you meet him?"

"Look, are we gonna talk about him all night?"

"No, I—it's just weird okay? Suddenly you're gambling and—"

"Gambling? One poker game doesn't make me a gambler." He laughed. "Have you been talking to your sister?"

"No, why?"

"I know she's not my biggest fan, but that doesn't mean I'm not the right guy."

"Who said anything about the right guy?" Adrielle could not afford to get sidetracked. What she needed was to find out what kind of sick game Domenikos was playing. If he'd really taken Coco, she needed to find out where.

Josh tried to wrap his arms around her, and she pushed away again. He was being so annoying—acting as if all that mattered was their relationship.

"I get it. You'd rather go to the party."

"No, that's the last place I want to go."

"Let's hang then." He jumped on Coco's bed and picked up the remote. "I keep expecting your sister to walk in." He turned on the TV, relaxed back onto the fuchsia pillow, and stretched his arms behind his head. "Where is she?"

"Holy shit." He leaned forward. "Look, 144 people dead."

"What?" Adrielle spun around. The crawl on the screen turned her stomach. The regular programing was pre-empted with a news update.

Firefighters are struggling to keep the fires contained. Again, there are 144 confirmed dead, and over 300 missing.

"Quick, turn it up!" Adrielle said.

More sightings of bird murmurations. Authorities are investigating this strange phenomenon to see if there is a connection between the fires, and the increased bird sightings . . .

Adrielle darted to the window. It was so dark out she couldn't see anything with the window closed. "I've got to go."

"What? Haven't you been listening? It's not safe out there."

Adrielle opened the window and leaned out. The night air was warm. The news had it right. Overhead, the sky was swarming with birds. "Sorry, I really have to go," she said, heading for the door.

Josh wrinkled his brow. "Uh okay. I'll come with you." He jumped up.

"No." He would only slow her down. She scrambled for what to do next. How was this possible? This alternate reality brought back Josh, but what about the other lives? His possession of the knife proved he was just a pawn in Domenikos' plan. Domenikos was playing with her. Probably monitoring Josh and his whereabouts. Trying to jar her into making a mistake. The less important Domenikos believed Josh was to her, the safer he'd be. She couldn't afford more distractions. Detours would only slow her down and could worsen the situation.

The way to win this thing was to be pro-active and get on with her plan. In her head, Adrielle recommitted. First, she'd find Coco. Then she'd re-create a forgery.

She went to step out the door and turned back. "Hey, where was the Goth the last time you saw him?"

"We're back to that?"

"Just answer already," she shouted. Immediately, she felt sorry she'd been so brusque.

"The party."

"So you were there? At the party?"

Josh wore his poker face.

"And Scarlett?"

He grunted, lowering his eyes to the pattern on the bedspread.

Adrielle slammed the door on her way out. She was fuming. *Ahhh, where is Angelo when I need him!*

"Thought you'd never ask," Angelo said, re-appearing instantly.

He was out in the hall, leaning against the stair railing with one leg crossed over the other. Adrielle bit back a smile. His dress was ridiculous. He was wearing a French beret and skinny black jeans. She could almost imagine a thin moustache curling up at the corners. Angelo was adorable. For the first time in her modern day life, Adrielle felt a tug so strong towards him, it frightened her. *He's not human, not human* . . . she reminded herself.

"Let's go," he said, taking her hand. She was about to ask where when he said in a very French accent, "Paris."

Paris, France — Nov 13, 2015 — 21:40

THE BAND ON the stage was blaring. "Who's the band?" Adrielle yelled over the crowd. "They must be popular, it's sold out."

"Eagles of Death Metal."

Angelo barely got the words out before fireworks started blaring. Loud popping sounds came from all angles. Within seconds, Adrielle realized it wasn't fireworks at all, gunmen were shooting in all directions. Adrielle dropped to the ground. She covered her head with her arms. Someone shouted, "God is great" in Arabic. And people were dropping in mounds.

Adrielle's whole body trembled as panic spread. People pushed to escape. Some managed through an exit on the left side of the stage. The place was busting to the walls. Maneuvering was difficult around the hoardes of people.

A police officer shot one of the gunmen, and his suicide belt detonated. Adrielle pressed her hands to her ears. Two more exploded.

Adrielle trembled. A body next to her fell, blood seeping all around. She felt a spray of warmth on her hand and reached out. She caught him on his way down but it was too late. He was already dead. His eyes open in horror.

"How many?" Adrielle shouted, her body roiling in fury.

"Eighty-nine people dead. Ninety-nine in critical condition."

"WHY? WHY DID you take me there?" Adrielle yelled at Angelo.

"Because you are not taking this seriously."

"I am. I need to find Coco." She turned to run.

Angelo grabbed her arm. "Adrielle"—he shook her—"I know you don't want to hear this, but dammit, she is incidental. *Focus*. This is bigger that you and me. It affects everyone. Everywhere."

She stood silently trembling as the rage inside her flared. She wanted to scream at the unfairness of innocent lives lost. At having witnessed an act so heinous. Even with her new powers she'd been powerless. "How could this be allowed? He needs to be stopped!"

Angelo's face showed none of the turmoil she was feeling inside. He remained calm and collected. Though she wouldn't admit it, he was right. All along she'd been thinking of her friends, her family, with little regard for countless others that needed protection. And Coco? Sure, she was an insignificant ant in the grand scheme of things, but she cared about her. And that had to count for something.

Adrielle buried her head in her arms. She rocked as the tears flooded out, not caring if she looked weak. This was more than she could handle.

Angelo sat quietly beside her as she wept. When her sobs subsided, he placed one hand on her head and gently tousled her hair.

Finally, the tears stopped. She looked up, and Angelo was still there. The speckle of freckles on his cheeks made him look younger than Haden, but in many ways, he seemed more mature. More sensitive. Maybe more like her.

Although she was miles away from Florida, having Angelo next to her made her feel like she was home.

COCO TRIED TO see past the haze in the air. An unfamiliar stench permeated everything. She couldn't remember where she was, or why she was there. Only that she was.

Directly ahead, a constant stream of people entered through an open gate into the yard where she stood. Most of them were dressed in dark clothing. Middle aged. There were older men too, women and children.

Like her, they seemed disoriented. Sad. Heavy lines of distrust etched on their faces. They spoke a language Coco couldn't understand. She wished she had Adrielle's gift of language. Their voices weren't loud and boisterous, but quiet murmurings that buzzed like a soft hum, adding to the unnerving ambiance.

Trickling behind the masses was a group of elderly women. They looked exhausted. Almost at once, uniformed men directed everyone toward a building. The sign read: *To the baths and disinfecting rooms.*

A rush of goosebumps swathed Coco's skin. She had the unnerving feeling something terrible was about to happen. As though ordered by some unseen signal, the uniformed men instructed everyone to undress. Their voices sharp and menacing. People didn't immediately respond. They stood untrusting. Confused. The uniformed men swung their clubs. People fell to the ground. The ones who tried to help, got the worst of it.

Coco rushed to the corner of the yard, as far from the uniformed men as she could. Never had she seen so many people afraid. Fear was imprinted on their faces. Mothers clung to children. Children clung to one another.

At first, both men and women were embarrassed to strip off their clothes. But the uniformed men became frenzied. They swung their clubs full force. Bodies fell. Like trapped rats, there was no escaping the horror.

Quivering fingers trembled to undo buttoned collars. Women, terrified and self-aware, untied their shoelaces, hoping to buy time.

Coco stood motionless. A dark hole in her stomach clenching tight. In front of her, a mother had hopelessness painted on her face.

Uniformed men, dissatisfied with the speed with which people responded, became out of control. Two of them took their place at either side of the building's entrance. From there, they clubbed the group. Others mixed into the crowd chased naked people toward the entrance like cattle.

Others gave orders from the roof of the building, watching with impatience as the scene below unfolded. Confused and frightened, people tore off their clothes; embarrassment at being naked was no longer an issue.

One by one they were stripped of their dignity. Stripped of their hope. Beaten out of them and replaced by submission.

Coco found herself coping by watching a woman with her child. The mother undressed her child and then herself, a ritual for the last time. A ritual to remember. There was something sacred about the act. Haunting. Naked, she cradled her child in her arms and left the small heap of clothes at her feet. She walked slowly toward the building and disappeared inside.

The men on the roof smoked. A train of smoke rings disappearing into the air. This was an ordinary day for them.

A club hit the back of Coco's knees. Pain shot out, and she folded to the ground, the sting burning her skin. Coco thought of her mother. The flames licking at her face. *"Run,"* she'd said. Her final words as she dropped to the ground.

Coco peeled off her clothes as the others had. She left them in a pile.

She walked toward the iron gates and was the last to pass through them. Iron bars clanged shut. The sound shaking her eardrums. Inside the large room she was surrounded by hundreds of others. She shivered, wrapping her arms around her torso. She felt alone.

ADRIELLE CLUTCHED THE feather in her hand. She closed her eyes to shut out all extraneous thoughts. She had to concentrate on Coco. In her mind, she conjured up the moment Coco gave her the watch. The expression on Coco's face was full of melancholy and apprehension.

Thoughts tried to break through her concentration. Adrielle pushed them away. An image of Domenikos' face popped in her mind. Adrielle rejected it, pushing it away. If this was going to work, she couldn't afford distractions. Not even one.

Soon the familiar tingles swam in her veins. Adrielle grinded her jaw. She refused to acknowledge Angelo's fingers were wrapped tightly around her arms.

"Remember, you can't change a thing Adrielle, no matter what. Not if you want to win." Angelo's voice broke through her concentration barrier. It was a distant passing thought in her dreamlike state.

The tingling subsided and Adrielle opened her eyes.

The sky was gray with heavy clouds. There was a smell of something burning. Mounds of clothing, suitcases, and shoes littered the yard. A building in the near distance had uniformed men on the roof. And more uniformed men raking up the clothes, piling them in the corner of the fenced area until a great mound began to form.

Adrielle kicked at one of the heaps and wondered why she was here. She remembered her attempt to find her sister. Coco, where was she? Had it failed? Was this an associative thing because Coco threw her clothes in a heap? She couldn't be sure. A sickening smell burned her nose. Flesh. Her mother burning. Horrific screams came from behind the metal doors of the building. The moaning and wailing became intense.

"You can't interfere with history. Not for anything. Or anyone." Beside her, Angelo's face was stern and solemn. She'd never seen him like that. Her eyes drifted to the clothing at her feet. She picked up a coat and froze. A yellow star sewn on the right side of the chest.

"Oh my god. Tell me she isn't in there." Something inside her was breaking.

Angelo stood unmoving. His eyes locked resolutely onto hers.

Adrielle's heart thud in her chest. How was this possible? Moments before, they'd been in her bedroom. All of them: Veda, Kate, Dave, Liz . . . even Astraia and Haden. It seemed like years ago.

The banging against the door grew louder. It echoed in the yard. "No," Adrielle screamed, fighting to pull out of Angelo's grasp.

His hands tightened around her wrists. "Don't you see? That is what he wants. You need to be stronger."

"Let me go." Adrielle wrestled with his grip. "If she's in there, I couldn't live with myself."

"Your purpose is not to put a stop to this. This has already happened. Remember the horror. Put a stop to the abuse of power that travelling allows. *This*—is part of history. You can't change anything. The outcome could be worse."

"How? Thousands of people are dying." The agony was crushing her.

"Your place is to rein in Domenikos and his followers. It is the only way to achieve a sustainable victory."

Adrielle wrestled out of his grasp. She didn't care what he thought. He was infuriating. She was inside the building now. Her eyes stung. *"Coco!"* she yelled, her throat hurting. She was desperate to find her sister. A sea of faces stared back, many disfigured beyond recognition. The smell of sweat, urine, and blood was so powerful it was hard to concentrate on anything else.

On the ceiling were dummy showers installed to fool the people that this was a shower room. It was a gas chamber. The strongest of the people climbed over dead corpses. They realized too late the gas was coming up from the bottom. Gas was piped through perforations in the hollow sheet metal pillars. People coughed, their lungs sucking in poison. Some turned blue from it.

This was horrific. Even in Paris, as terrifying as that was, could not compare. This had been planned. It was appalling.

Among the twisted mangled bodies, Adrielle caught the vacant gaze of her sister, her arms wrapped around a pregnant woman hanging limply in her arms. She was about to rush over, burst through deadened bodies, to get to her.

Angelo was at her side. "You can't interfere."

"She's here. Please help," she pleaded. For an instant, she thought he was folding. His eyes betrayed his stoic stance. Something in them looked pained. She turned away from him, determined to reach Coco.

Liz's questioning eyes stared back at her. Dave was at her side, his face solemn. More serious than she'd ever seen him. He wore the look of disappointment. She'd let them down.

"No!" she screamed, furious she was back in Florence. Michelangelo's and Leonardo's shocked expression glared across the table.

"GO AHEAD, STICK her with it." Domenikos smiled.

A chill ran down Josh's back. "Are you serious? You can't be serious."

"I am." He grinned.

"You're crazy," Josh said, glancing back at Scarlett. She looked scared. The situation was escalating. "Look, I don't know what you're trying to prove here, but I won it fair and square. This isn't funny anymore."

"I'm laughing," Domenikos said, and he laughed raucously.

Josh turned to leave. This was bullshit. "I'm heading downstairs. My girlfriend didn't look happy when she saw I was here."

"Girlfriend?" Domenikos mimicked. He flicked his fingernail on his snaggle tooth and was very silent. He made no attempt for the knife. Josh headed for the door, but Brix was faster. He stood in front of it, blocking it with his body.

"Don't turn this into something ugly. Here, take your stupid knife. I just want to go." Josh tossed the pointy knife onto the floor but before it hit the ground, Domenikos scooped it up and had Scarlett by the throat.

"What the—is this some kind of sick joke?"

Domenikos shook his head. He appeared to be enjoying this. Scarlett squealed under his grip. "One of you is going to die tonight," he said, his voice chillingly calm. "It's going to be a quick, painless death. Now, tell me Josh, which one of you wants to live?"

Chapter 20
Florence – 1504

"WHAT DID YOU do?" Adrielle yelled at Angelo.

The instant she looked at his face, she realized what had happened. His appearance was transparent. She looked down at her hands; like him, her skin was filmy and translucent. Jeez. The disturbing surroundings had blocked her perception, and she hadn't been aware she'd travelled back to that horrific place as a spectator.

"How do I control this feather?" she yelled angrily.

Angelo inhaled a deep breath and released it slowly. He wore a solemn expression. "I've wrestled with teaching you the fine art of travelling. Every time it comes up for discussion, we always end with the same conclusion: you aren't ready for the full knowledge. You are using your power irresponsibly."

Adrielle was furious. And confused. How could her plan to save Coco have gone so wrong? How could she process this? She wanted to blame someone. Anyone and everyone. But mostly she was angry at herself.

"Adie, you have to get a grip," Liz said in a soft but firm voice. "Look at yourself, you're fraying at the seams and we're only just starting to prepare for the battle."

"I—I—" Adrielle choked on her words.

"You *need* to be strong. For all of us," Dave reasoned. "None of this is easy."

"The bodies, there were hundreds of them. Disfigured. Lifeless," she said, her voice coming out in jerks. She shook her head in defeat. "I couldn't save her, Lizzie." She broke down. Large tears spilling as she sobbed. "Coco was there in that terrible place, and I couldn't save her." She dropped into the chair beside Leonardo, the chair absorbing the weight of her defeat.

Adrielle buried her head in her arms and cried. She was drained. Tired. She raised her head and looked at the others.

"Where were you?" Dave said.

"The place where no one survives. Auschwitz." Adrielle took a shuddery breath.

"Oh, dear god." Liz slapped her hand to her mouth.

"You're here now." Dave said, resting one hand on her shoulder. He gave it a squeeze. "You have the power to change everything."

Inside, Adrielle felt utterly powerless.

THE LIGHT IN Michelangelo's guest room was dim. It came from a single lit candle at the bedside. Liz and Adrielle lay together on the same cot, light years away from one another, watching the flickering flame and the shadows it cast on the aged stucco walls.

"I can't figure it out. I thought I'd be able to bring her back. I couldn't," Adrielle whispered.

"What did Angelo do?" Liz asked. "I can't even imagine how he'd react to that."

"That's just it. He didn't do anything. He stood there beside me seeing the same horror I saw and said I couldn't change a thing." Adrielle turned to Liz, whose face was all skewed up with worry. "The worst part is, he was right. I couldn't. No matter how much I wanted to. I felt as helpless as I did the night Mom died."

Liz appeared to be quietly absorbing what she was saying. Adrielle wondered if Liz was thinking of her parents' divorce. She'd confided to her years before that she'd felt powerless. That their fights still haunted her.

Outside the wind howled. A branch tapped against the window, and they jumped, not knowing what danger lurked. It rapped again and cast a long shadow on the wall. "I've never had a sister, but Coco is practically my sister too. It hurts like hell having her gone. Not knowing if we'll ever see her again." Liz sat up and reached for her glasses on the night table. "About why Angelo wouldn't do anything—" She opened the journal and turned to a dog-eared page.

"It says here, you can't change anything as a spectator." She paused and looked at Adrielle. "That must be what happened when you travelled back in time."

"It's true." Adrielle sat up. "I hadn't realized it until after we got back. Angelo's appearance was transparent. I must have been too. That's why no one saw or heard me. The two of us were flies on the wall, watching the horror unfold. Not being able to do anything about it. I can't figure out how to make that distinction. Why sometimes I end up as a spectator and other times a participant."

Liz grinned. "That's the easy part." She underlined the tidy script with her finger. "It says here: *if at the time of departure the traveller focuses without a distraction on being a participant and concentrates only on experiencing the time epoch—everything about it: the smells, the way the air feels on your face, the general feeling of the times. Then the traveller will be able to participate.*"

She raised her eyes to Adrielle who was reading along in the journal with her. "Did Angelo go with you? At the same time, I mean?"

"Yeah."

"Well, there you go. I think he's as good of a distraction as I can think of."

"What do you mean?" Adrielle said.

"I mean . . . I've seen the way you two are with one another. I thought because it said in here you were marrying Haden, that you two were in love. But obviously, it's not true. At least not on your side."

"What?"

"I'm serious. I don't see you going gaga for Haden. I think you were crazier for Josh, and he wasn't even the right one for you. At least none of us thought so." Liz closed the journal and set it back on the table. She slipped her glasses off and blew out the candle. Then lay back down. The smell of melted wax lingered.

Adrielle settled onto her pillow. She watched Liz pull the covers up around her chin. She was going to sleep. And sleep was the furthest from her mind.

After some time, Liz said, "Adie, why were you going to marry him? Do you remember?"

"It doesn't matter now," Adrielle said.

"That's what I thought too, that it doesn't matter. But it does. It always does." With a deep inhale she relaxed into a lull and was beginning to doze off.

Liz bolted up and startled her. "Wait a minute, didn't you say Angelo said there was something he had to tell you?"

Adrielle thought back. "He did. But we never got that far."

"Maybe because you left without telling him you were leaving to find Coco. Give him a chance to explain. Maybe that's where you need to start, instead of running all over the place trying to do things by yourself. You keep alienating people, and one day there'll be no one left. You need to trust someone, Adie, so trust him. I think at this point, he's your best shot."

"Maybe," Adrielle said, turning onto her side. She closed her eyes. Liz had told her before she shut people out. Coco did too. Maybe she did. It wasn't hard to figure out why. Everyone she loved was ripped away from her.

Adrielle waited until Liz's breathing became heavy and rhythmic. The small window barely allowed enough moonlight to see. She tilted her chronometer's face until a sliver of light caught the glint of the hands. It was well past midnight. She closed her eyes tightly and slipped her hand under the pillow, where she kept her red feather, and felt for the soft downy barbs. With her fingers wrapped tightly around it, she concentrated on the decaying smell of the Auschwitz gas chambers. On finding Coco.

THE BODIES LAY in a tangled knot. Layers on top of layers of bodies. Some dead. Others grasping for their last breath.

Adrielle was the only one clothed, but no one seemed to notice or care. At first, she couldn't remember where she was. Or why. Her gaze drifted from one corner of the room to the other, as though she were having a dream. Then the tingles subsided.

The crowd pushed in around her. She couldn't breathe. The air in the room was stale and smelled of excrement. Panic rose in her chest. A rush of awareness came in one big boom—all her memories flooding back.

She was here for Coco. To save her life. Like the others around her, Adrielle headed for the doors, the only exit. They were trapped. People ahead pounded on the steel with their fists. With their bodies. The unforgiving metal held rigid. Their energy sapped by malnutrition and gas. Desperate cries drowned hope. She too felt desperate. As the minutes ticked on, her panic subsided. The life swimming in her veins drained from her body.

Where was she? Her body felt heavy. Her limbs unresponsive. It would be so easy to give up. Give in. And then she saw Coco. Standing in the corner. Her arms twined around a pregnant woman who lay limp in her grasp.

"Coco!" she wanted to yell. It was an effort to strain her voice. Her throat was dry. She pushed the sound out of her larynx with all her strength. *"Coco!"* she cried.

Coco turned and met her eyes with a vacant gaze. Adrielle's stomach twisted. Gone was the spark. The life that once shone from them had died. She'd given up hope of ever getting out. No. It wouldn't end this way. Adrielle couldn't accept that.

Gathering threads of strength, Adrielle trampled over the bodies that covered the floor ahead. Bodies that had fallen. The trek to reach Coco seemed impossible. Muffled cries from all sides of the room pleaded for help.

Cold stiff fingers wrapped around her ankles. Adrielle tried to scream but no sound came out. They gripped tighter. Someone was pulling on her right leg, using her for support. Adrielle shook her foot. She kicked and shirked wildly. When finally the fingers loosened their grasp, she bolted toward Coco, her heart thudding hard against her chest.

"We need to get out of here." She shrieked as she clung to Coco. "Let go of her."

"We can't leave her to die," Coco said. "She's expecting a baby."

"Coco, we can't. I don't think we can make it out of here with her too."

Coco tightened her grasp around the woman. "What's the point then, Adie? If we can't save them, then it's not worth saving ourselves."

The pit in Adrielle's stomach plummeted. She was in no condition to fight Coco on this. "God, I hope this works. Hang on to me tight." She concentrated as hard as she could on their Florida home.

EVEN AFTER THE initial memory lapse from travelling had worn off, nothing was recognizable. The lovely tree-lined street they lived on and remembered, looked like a desecrated graveyard.

There were no people in sight. The entire neighborhood was deserted. Cars were spewed and scattered like dice rolled in a craps game. Metal bodies bent and twisted out of shape. Other vehicles had been abandoned and stripped for parts. Tires, door panels, anything and everything was gone.

Instead of salty sea-spray and the scent of magnolias in the air, the rank smell of decay and char hung thickly, burning their noses and filming over their skin. Trees were charcoal shadows reaching to the sky. Homes were burnt down to the foundation. Black ashy remains were undecipherable. As far as they could see, the aftermath of fire lingered.

Some homes made out of cement block were only partially burnt, and most of those appeared to have been pillaged. Very few anomalies remained untouched by the flames. Those that survived had been boarded up. Broken windows and doors hung open.

Adding to the dread, in the middle of the road, a group of vultures picked at a carcass.

"What's happened?" Coco asked, bringing her hands up to shade from the sun.

The signpost on the corner read *Bunker Knolls*. Their street was around the corner. Adrielle lifted the chronometer out from inside her shirt. She looked at the date—nooooooo—she brought it closer and blinked. "Oh no." She'd thought her vision was blurred.

"What's wrong? Coco asked.

"Ah, we're in the future."

"What? I told you its broken."

"No, Coco," Adrielle said. "It's not."

"That's not possible."

"How is any of this possible?" Adrielle's anger rose. This was our town. Why hadn't she listened to Angelo? Her eyes drifted to the woman that had been in Coco's arms, now lying limply on the ground where Coco set her down. She was clasping at her stomach.

"You okay?" Adrielle asked her, but before the woman answered, Adrielle noticed blood pooling onto the pavement underneath her.

"OMG. You're hurt." She squatted down beside her. The woman had a large laceration on her arm. Adrielle tore her sleeve off and made a tourniquet to stop the bleeding. She wrapped it around and tied it. "We need to move you out of the street. You need clothes," Adrielle said, absorbing the baby bump. She'd never seen a pregnant woman, let alone a naked one. "Is the baby okay?"

The woman stared blankly ahead. She was in shock.

"Coco, let's get her into a house. Maybe someone's around."

"We're just around the corner. What are the chances Layla will be home?"

"Not good."

They supported the woman between the two of them and headed home. As they rounded the corner to their house, the desolate feeling of doom intensified. Adrielle couldn't believe devastation was all that remained of their neighborhood.

"I feel like we're in a Mad Max movie," said Coco.

Their home was one of three on their street untouched by the fire. When they reached the front door, it was unlocked. Someone had broken the window on the side of the door. They helped the pregnant woman inside and sat her down on the sofa.

"I'm afraid to go upstairs," Coco whispered, studying the interior. "Nothing looks the same."

This is how tomorrow moves, Adrielle thought, fighting a rise in hysteria. They left the woman to search the rest of the house.

Family pictures lined the stairs. "You're right. Another family lives here," Adrielle said, staring at a picture of twin freckled boys of about five and a teenaged girl of about fourteen. A mom and a dad stood behind them with proud looks on their faces.

Adrielle and Coco exchanged a look. They'd spoken about this. It was the picture-perfect family they'd never had.

Upstairs in Coco's room, a set of bunks sat against the wall. A felt play-mat filled a large portion of the floor. "Look at all the toy cars lined up along the parking spaces," Coco said. "Bet they never knew what was coming." On a shelf on the wall, t-ball trophies gleamed. Two baseball gloves and caps were hung on waist-high hooks.

"Hmmph," Coco grunted, stepping into the closet. "It's so strange to see all their stuff in here. It's like we've been erased."

The knot in Adrielle's stomach tightened. "God, don't say that." She exchanged a look with Coco, finding it hard to rein in her biggest fear—*what if they changed things and they'd never been born?*

Adrielle shed her clothes and found new clothes to fit them both in her old room. Coco and Adrielle slipped on clean jeans and t-shirts. The stench of death clung to their skin.

"Bet you're glad to be dressed again," Adrielle said.

Coco looked at her in surprise. "After Auschwitz, it's not about how you look anymore. It's about who you are."

Coco's sound advice always came at the right time. Despite setbacks, she always managed to get her priorities straight. Taking on the weight of the paradox, and in her sister's shadow, Adrielle felt inadequate.

They continued to explore the house. They found peroxide and bandages in the bathroom and took clothes down to the woman from the mother's closet. Coco tended to the wounds, and Adrielle set about dressing her in clean clothes. Once the woman was dressed and made comfortable, they headed into the kitchen for something to eat.

Dishes were piled high in the sink. An empty container with a meat sandwich and a mayonnaise jar sat on the cutting board. Fruit flies bounced around it.

"Ewww, gross," Coco said. She opened the fridge and slammed the door shut. The foul smell of rot and mold seeped out into the room. "Guess there's no electricity. Everything in there's gone bad. By the looks of it, the family left in a big hurry."

They checked the pantry and found it stocked with canned goods and crackers. A new jar of peanut butter. They opened a can of peaches and made peanut butter and crackers for lunch.

"Let's go," Adrielle said, filling a backpack with extra food supplies and bottled water. "We should get out of here."

"And go where?" Coco said. "This *is* home."

"Not anymore. We need to find the others. I have a plan." Adrielle told Coco of Florence, and how Liz and Dave were already there.

"It all sounds so up-in-the-air. What do you think happened to Layla?"

"I don't know. Let's go, I want to be gone before Domenikos finds out we're here."

"Why don't you just give him what he wants?"

"Yes, why don't you?" a voice said from behind.

They turned. Domenikos stood an arms-length away. His smile was cocky and triumphant. The other Goth from the party was there too. Neither looked surprised.

"You did this, didn't you?" Coco seethed.

"No, your darling sister did," Domenikos grinned.

"What? Me?" Adrielle blurted out. "How can you pin this one on me?"

"You've been a naughty girl, Adrielle." He paced around the room, his hands folded behind his back. "You are *so* stubborn. Always thinking you know best. Didn't they warn you not to tamper with the past?" He shook his finger at her and smiled broadly. Then he gestured to their surroundings with wide-open arms. "Everything you see here is the product of your meddling."

"I didn't, I—"

"You did," he laughed raucously.

He was insufferable. "How dare you blame this on me."

"You were warned there are consequences when you travel."

As much as she wanted to deny it, to shed blame for this future, Adrielle felt he was right. She shouldn't have gone back for Coco, but she couldn't trust Coco would have survived if she hadn't gone back for her either.

"Where are Kate and Veda? What did you do with them?" she asked.

Domenikos smiled, holding Adrielle's gaze. "Brix, show them."

Beside him, Brix held up a square black box.

"What's that?" Adrielle asked. She didn't trust him.

Brix opened the lid and tipped it forward so they could see.

"That's just a box of ashes."

Brix smiled. He exchanged a look with Domenikos.

"It was an unfortunate coincidence they were home when the fires started," Domenikos said flatly.

"My god." Adrielle took a quick step back. "You didn't!"

"Am I not making myself clear?" Domenikos pointed dramatically at her. "*You* did this."

"I don't believe you," Adrielle hissed. Could he be right?

"Go back and see for yourself."

"Is this some sort of trick?" Adrielle asked. Would he really let her go? Was this a test of trust?

Domenikos looked at Brix. They seemed to be having a wordless dialogue. "Very well, then don't. But it's the only way to find out."

"Not the on—" Brix began.

Domenikos cut him off with a glare.

Adrielle slipped her hand into her pocket, clutched her feather, and at the same time grabbed Coco's hand.

"Not so fast," Domenikos snapped. "If you change anything, anything at all, I will make sure Kate and Veda remain in this box. Back to ashes."

"What do you mean?" Adrielle needed to return to Florence in 1504, if she was going to set things right.

"Your travelling days are over. If you go anywhere, you will lose your friends forever."

How could she get out of this one?

"Silly girl. You are still thinking you are smarter than me." Domenikos sneered. "One mention of going back and you take the bait. Whether you admit it or not, you and I are not that different. Travelling is as much a part of me as breathing is to you."

"I'm not like you at all. I want to set things right. You keep changing things. Altering time and events from what they would naturally be."

"As do you," he said smugly. He lifted one eyebrow. "Was it not your intent to rescue Kate and Veda? What makes you think that is ok? And so sure you can? That it is not way things were meant to be. You act as though you believe the way you have seen it is the best history for everyone. Wouldn't it be better to go back and erase the Holocaust from ever happening? Snuff out Hitler before he has a chance to gain power? I saw you there, in Paris with Haden, the very first time you went to the Paris opera. You were thinking that very thing. How does it feel now that you've actually experienced it?"

"I see my mistake now. How easily the time sequence can be manipulated without meaning to. It isn't natural. The Achaean Act was set in place to prohibit tampering with history."

"It is natural for us Achaeans."

"And what about for us humans? It isn't right to play with their lives. Putty at your whim."

Domenikos leveled his gaze at her. "You can put a stop to this Adrielle. This post-apocalyptic future." He extended his arms. "All of this catastrophe can be undone in a single breath. All you need to do is hand over the chronometer. And you can go on living your life here in Florida, as before, where your biggest worry was what to wear for the next party. Or contemplating whether your boyfriend is your true soul mate."

Adrielle felt something inside her harden. He was a monster. She would never turn over the chronometer and give him that much power.

"Well?" He stretched out his hand palm side up, and mugged, puckering his lips as casually as though he were taking a selfie.

"No, never," she spat. She grasped onto Coco and closed her eyes.

COCO WAS QUIET, her mind slowly absorbing the details of the room. She breathed in deeply, inhaling the sweet scent of perfume she'd sprayed as she was getting ready for the party. She was surprised it lingered in the air as though she'd just pressed the atomizer.

"We're back." Coco grinned, euphoric as she drifted around the room, taking pleasure in all the little things she had missed: The old dresser she'd bought at a yard sale and refinished in her garage. The purple nail polish splatters on the chair when she'd hurriedly painted her toenails one night before a date. The super large button they'd won at the local fair, with the picture of all of them—Adrielle, Liz, Dave, Veda, and her. She'd fastened it to a crochet purse and hung it on a hook at the entrance to her closet next to her polka dotted robe.

The valance on the window she'd sewed for a school project hung unevenly because one side was longer than the other, and she'd been too lazy to fix it. Coco smiled. Together all these details provided the cozy feeling she called *home.* All intricately weaved and part of her history.

Excited to see her favorite dress tossed in the messy pile in the middle of the floor, she ran to pick it up, but her hands went through the clothes as though they were only air. "My hands! They're translucent!" Coco exclaimed.

"That's because we're only spectators. We're both transparent. Look, there you are." Adrielle pointed to the duplicate Coco from the past. "Remember we can't change anything this time around, we can only observe."

"I remember this," Coco said, inching closer to Adrielle as she studied her duplicate self.

Unlike the other occasions when they'd travelled, there was no momentary amnesia until the tingly feeling settled down.

"Gosh, it's weird to see everyone at the very moment you left with Haden. It's like hitting rewind and slipping into a movie while it's playing."

The sleeping bags were strewn on the floor, which was littered with candy wrappers from Liz's bingeing. In the corner where Liz had once sat, a half-eaten bag of Doritos lay abandoned. They watched Liz sit quietly next to Dave.

Then Veda, Coco, and Dave began talking all at once. Kate, partially hidden behind Veda, trembled on the bed while they discussed how disappearing into thin air could even be possible. Her messy bun shook as she cried.

And Astraia was there too, listening to the conversation and studying the dynamics between the group. Oddly, she didn't acknowledge them, Adrielle mused, remembering Haden had told her an Achaean could always spot a traveller.

Liz didn't participate in the debate, she only listened to the banter. Then without warning, she slipped her hand into her handbag and seconds later, she along with Dave also vanished into thin air.

"Oh my god. They're gone too," Veda exclaimed.

As soon as Liz and Dave disappeared, the Coco from the past shook her fist. "If Domenikos thinks he can pick us off one by one, he's mistaken. We will never side with him. He is delusional."

Out of nowhere, Domenikos appeared.

"If its war you want, then that's what you will get," he threatened.

"Wait," Astraia cried. "Think this through."

"Why? They will never understand us."

"Give them a chance," Astraia said.

Domenikos paced over to Veda and Kate. "If its death you fear, I can give you protection. Freedom from the chains of death."

Veda laughed as though it was an infantile proposition. The expression on Domenikos' face was chilling.

Domenikos turned and looked directly at Adrielle, his eyes glittering with hatred.

Coco shuddered under the harshness of his threat and pressed into Adrielle's body. Adrielle thought about her plan. Almost at once, she felt the tingles swim in her veins.

Chapter 21

Florence — 1504

"WHERE HAVE YOU been? We've been worried sick about you." Liz sounded accusatory.

Adrielle blinked. Across the room, a wedge of moonlight shone in through a small window. Once her eyes adjusted to the dim lighting, she realized she was back in Florence, lying in bed next to Liz. She was staring down at her, Liz's eyes narrowed and tightened. Adrielle had never seen her so angry.

"Chill. I'm back, okay? I brought Coco too." Coco didn't respond, and Adrielle jolted upright.

Coco was there, standing perfectly still at her bedside, seemingly deep in thought. Only her eyes moved, roving around the bedroom struggling to make sense of their surroundings.

"It's ok, we made it," Adrielle said. "The fogginess from travelling will go away soon."

Coco spotted her polka dotted robe hanging sloppily on the bedpost. Adrielle watched her closely. "How I've missed you," Coco murmured, pressing her face against the soft cotton. "Mmmm. Smells like home." She brushed her hand lightly over the nap of the fabric. "I smell bubble gum too." She reached into the robe's pocket and pulled out a *Bazooka Joe* gum and brought it up to her nose to inhale the sweet bubble-gum smell.

"Where did you find this? I haven't had one of these since—" She turned to the bed. "Eeeee." Coco's face lit up. "Lizzie—you're here! You're really here!" She jumped on the bed and hugged Liz tightly. "Where are we? Antique furniture, wood beamed ceiling, stucco walls."

"In Florence. Renaissance times," Liz said, reaching for her glasses on the night table. She sat up and pushed them high on the bridge of her nose. Then she squinted hard at Coco. "Wow. You really did it, Adie."

"Yep." Adrielle shifted over to make room for Coco between them then sank back into her pillow. She folded her arms behind her head. "Catch me up. Did Domenikos show up?"

"God no," Liz said as Coco slipped on her robe and wedged in between them. "Everyone was so upset you'd left." Coco began unwrapping the gum. "Please don't. It's my last piece."

"Wouldn't think of it," Coco said, quickly re-wrapping the gum and slipping it back into the pocket.

Liz blushed. "It's just that—I don't know. Maybe it's stupid. But the smell reminds me of home. And I'm a little homesick. That smell keeps me believing it really happened. That this isn't a bad dream. There's a reason we're here and one day there's a home to go back to." She swiped at her tears.

Coco and Adrielle exchanged a look. Maybe there would be a home. At this point, she didn't know.

"About that," Coco said. Adrielle jabbed her. There would be plenty of time to get into all of it.

"Everyone's upset," Liz continued. "You've put us in a pickle, Adie. Leaving like that. We've got five days left."

"Five? I thought there were seven until the eclipse."

"Exactly. You've been gone for two!"

"Two?" Adrielle searched her mind. "Are you sure?" She re-calculated how many times she'd gone back and forth: *Auschwitz. Future home. Past home . . . hmmmm . . .* "Guess you're right."

"Uh-hum," Liz assured. "When I woke up two days ago and you were gone, I didn't know what to do. I told Angelo, and he was very upset. He went to find you."

"He found me. And was kinda mad," Adrielle admitted.

"Kinda?" Coco challenged.

"What did you expect?" Liz said. "You come up with a plan and then leave before we have a chance to make plans."

"Sorry." Adrielle cringed, images of the bleak future flitting through her mind.

"So in the meantime, Dave—"

"Dave? Oh—thank goodness he's okay." Coco brightened.

"Yes, he's here and he's fine."

"And Veda and Kate? Are they here too?" she asked.

All Liz could do was shake her head *no*.

"Does anyone know where they are at least?" Liz bit her lip. "Someone has to know something."

Coco turned to Adrielle for confirmation, but Adrielle didn't trust Domenikos' box of ashes was really them.

"I'm pretty sure Domenikos has them. Remember, he offered them a chance to skip death if they joined him," Adrielle said.

"Skip death?" Liz pressed. "What the hell does that mean?"

Adrielle shrugged. "Who knows? We popped out, right about then."

"Typical." Liz grunted. "Anyways, Dave went to find the leather worker like Michelangelo suggested. To get started on the binding."

The bedroom door flung open.

"Wuz up?" Dave yawned in the threshold, a red silk robe tied around his waist. His hair was knotted and sticking up like he'd been in a windstorm.

"Nice." Coco giggled, gesturing for him to join them on the bed. She turned to Liz. "I thought you said he was fine. I don't think I've ever seen him without his hair coiffed."

"Shut up," he said, scooting onto the foot of the bed.

A warm syrupy feeling churned in Adrielle's tummy. She'd missed Coco's effervescent laugh. It was lilting and spontaneous like a child's and always made her feel happy.

"What now?" Adrielle asked.

Dave rubbed his face and shook it till his cheeks flapped. "Let me see . . . Leonardo started mixing the colors for the illustrations, but Michelangelo thinks they need more pigments. Especially gold leaf, which he's the best at. But Leo has the Calligraphy down."

"Leo? My, aren't we chummy." Liz laughed.

Dave grinned. "It's exactly like the original. You should see it. I mean *exactly* like the *Book*."

"Wait, Michelangelo? And Leonardo?" Coco asked.

"Yep." Dave smiled. "Mich and Leo. Two of the Renaissance greats."

Liz gasped. "I hope you're not calling them that to their face."

"Not to their face." Dave laughed. "Speaking of face, you should see who he's painting."

"Who?" Coco asked.

"Leo."

Liz chortled. Her face became very pink.

"*Really?* He's painting you?" Coco asked.

Liz jabbed Dave in the gut. "Yes, but let's not get ahead of ourselves."

"Stop acting as if it were inconsequential," Dave chided. "It's incredible."

"True. But let's not get hung up on that. We've got too much other stuff to go over. Have either of you been in touch with Haden?" Liz asked.

Adrielle shook her head. Despite the banter, maybe because of the banter, she was having a hard time not getting emotional. For the first time ever, she felt as if she was a part of something bigger than herself.

"Yikes. That's not good," Liz said. "Strange. Especially after he found you. I mean, don't you guys find it strange? He *did* genuinely look surprised and happy that you were there, Adie. That you were okay. So why disappear?"

They shrugged.

"C'mon. I can't be the only one that thinks that's strange."

"All right, yes. I think you may be onto something," Dave agreed. A deep furrow formed on his brow. "When was the last time you saw him?"

Adrielle thought back. "Honestly, I don't remember."

"Well, for a guy in love," Liz remarked.

"Paris," Angelo said, appearing at the foot of the bed.

"Haaaa." Dave jumped, then scuttled into the center of the bed. "How does one get used to that?"

"Trick of the trade," Liz commented.

Angelo turned to Adrielle, a pensive look crossing his face. "Think back. After Paris, did you see him again?"

Adrielle thought hard for a moment. "No, I guess I didn't."

"Who cares?" Coco said. "I wasn't impressed."

"Coincidentally, that's the last I've seen of him too," Angelo said, frowning.

"I don't know what more to do. I went back for the *Book*, just like you suggested and—"

"Adie, you getting defensive? No one's accusing you," Coco said.

"Except for going back and mucking with history," Adrielle said, feeling overwhelmed.

They all looked at her.

"Blame is not the solution," Angelo said, looking like he was refraining from adding more. He went to lay his hand on hers, and pulled back, his eyes remaining pinned on her.

Liz caught the gesture. "Anything else you want to tell us about?"

Adrielle thought back to her past travels. Angelo was more right than she cared to admit. "Oh, I forgot. I saw Josh."

Everyone was stunned.

"Josh? He's okay?" Coco asked. "I thought you said he was dead. That Domenikos killed him."

"He did. I saw him when I travelled back."

"Maybe someone else changed it, too," Angelo said.

"But that's a good thing, right?" she asked Angelo.

"Depends."

"On what?" Liz pressed.

"This is not the time. I have my suspicions, but they are just that. Uncertainties. We need distance and perspective. With Domenikos running back and forth, there's no telling what will become of this fragile world."

Adrielle swallowed a lump. Her mind was already going to the worst.

"Dismal," Coco stated. "Tell him, Adie. The future we saw was horrible. A total nightmare."

"What do you mean?" Dave and Liz asked.

"Dystopian. A bad dream you can't wake up from," Adrielle said. She regretted messing with anything.

"Think *Mad Max*."

"No!" Dave gasped.

"The homes were burnt. Everything was different. I wonder if we even erased ourselves?" Coco said. "Is that possible?"

"Unfortunately, yes," Angelo confirmed.

"And if we did?" Adrielle whispered. She had a terrible feeling she hadn't seen the worst of it.

"You can never go back."

"But we're here now. Doesn't that mean we exist?" Dave asked.

"Yes, you exist here. So you could always make this your home."

Dave buried his head in his hands. "That's all I need. To be stuck, years before."

He didn't need to finish. Everyone knew exactly what he meant.

"What about our memories?" Adrielle asked. "If we can remember, then it is."

"It doesn't work that way," Angelo said. "There's a time vault. Memories, all memories of occasions that happened in any time, are placed in it, and eventually fade. As the portal locks, they will be erased because they never occurred."

"Goodness." Liz gulped. "That's not good."

No one pressed the further explanation or ventured to discuss the eight-hundred-pound gorilla in the room, though Adrielle was certain they were all thinking it. *Their life would be wiped away after the eclipse.*

After a long silence, Coco turned to Liz. "Right before we left, this last time, when we were all in my room"—she looked around to make sure everyone was listening—"I'm talking about after Adrielle and Haden left. Liz, before you and Dave disappeared, Domenikos propositioned Veda and Kate to side with him, promising they would never have to experience death." She turned to Angelo. "What did he mean by that? Is that possible?"

Angelo's jaw clenched. He opened his mouth and then shut it. The skin around his eyes tightened, and Adrielle knew Coco had touched a nerve.

"Fast forward to *Mad Max*. Domenikos' buddy, Brix—the other Goth from the party," Coco clarified. "He held up a box full of ashes, and Domenikos said it was Kate and Veda."

"The ashes?" Liz and Dave asked, terror on their faces.

"Yep." Coco shrugged.

Still, Angelo didn't respond.

Liz punched Angelo in the arm. "That's it? You're just going to sit there and look all solemn like that without any more explanation? Just like Domenikos did?"

Dave cringed.

"Don't compare us. I am nothing like him," Angelo said, the flecks in his eyes blazing.

"Then help us understand. For all we know, the five of you, Domenikos, Brix, Astraia, Haden, and you, are in it together."

Angelo shook his head. "Only four of us remain—out of several thousand Achaeans—that's it. Domenikos destroyed the others. Including our governing leaders. If Brix was there, it can only mean one thing."

"That he's gone to the past and brought them back? Tell us about the effect of doing that," Dave said sarcastically.

Angelo glanced at him, then gazed at Adrielle. He gestured for her to follow him out into the hall.

Once they were outside the bedroom, Angelo whispered, "Adrielle, there was a reason you agreed to marry Haden."

Liz closed the journal and perked up. Even low voices carried if you were quiet.

"I have information I was trying to tell you before you disappeared. The morning of the coup," Angelo said.

Liz nudged Dave. "To be honest, this has never made sense. I see the way Angelo looks at her. And the way Adrielle's skin turned a shade pinker," she whispered.

With ears pricked, they listened.

Since Adrielle travelled back to retrieve the *Book*, fragments of that time had seeped into her dreams, blurring reality. It was frightening. If her life wasn't a linear sequence of events, how would she ever grasp her mortality?

Adrielle's breathing became shallow as her mind evoked that moment . . . *The tolling bell had interrupted her sleep. It had been a good dream. The letter. A.*

"A for Angelo?"

"Remember," he urged, placing his hands on hers.

A current of warmth moved from his touch, up her arms. She looked up at him and there it was, well hidden behind his eyes. He loved her. She felt the climate of trust and intimacy and lowered her gaze, feeling embarrassed at the rush of emotion she felt. She pulled her hands away. It was impossible. There was no time for love. No time for anything but the plan.

Angelo shifted his weight. He cleared his throat, looking away and trying to mask his dejection.

"That morning, before Domenikos started the fires that set the coup in action, we had agreed to meet. You refused to leave Achaea, though Haden wanted you to. Not because you believed it was safe, but because you and I were working together with the Unity. To provide proof of Haden's treason."

Gasps echoed in the room.

Adrielle put her hands to her head. Memories rushing. "No, it can't be true."

"Listen to me, you have sacrificed so much already. A heavier weight than you originally thought. Perhaps more than you can handle. And so, you've blocked it from your memory. Not a case of the travel memory lapse; this is voluntary, Adrielle."

What?

"Your way of dealing or not dealing with a lifetime of guilt, resulting in nightmares. Until you come to terms with the truth."

Coco, listening, said under her breath, "How could he know about her nightmares?"

Angelo turned to the door. "I wanted privacy," he said, looking upset. He turned back to Adrielle. "This is not your fault, but it was a risk you took, when you vowed to stop him."

"What risk?" Adrielle asked, horrified at the insinuation.

"Your mother's life."

"It's not her fault. No one could predict the fire," Coco shouted in a strained voice.

"Listen to me," Angelo said in an urgent voice. He searched out her gaze and held it. "Domenikos set that fire. He was looking for you ever since he discovered you had the chronometer, hoping to destroy you."

"It wasn't mine until the eve of my birthday."

"Make no mistake, it was always yours. Domenikos coveted it. Haden was in charge of protecting you until you were of age. His assignment included guarding the chronometer and the *Book of Feathers*, the two obstacles able to take you down."

"Bullshit."

"It's true. Aaron suspected Domenikos would try to steal it. And you needed it for your protection." Adrielle stood dumbfounded. Angelo appeared to have more to say, but Adrielle had enough. Haden a traitor? Was this true, or two brothers rivaling? She pushed away and paced down the hall.

Leonardo and Michelangelo, looking puzzled, stood in their nightdresses at the bedroom doorway.

Angelo followed her. By now everyone in the house was listening.

"Adrielle, when you accepted Haden's marriage proposal, you were only seventeen. The spell he used to cast you forward included a cloaking spell that turned you into a small child as a decoy, so Domenikos wouldn't find you. But your mother—she worried. She knew how deviant Domenikos was, so she went along with you and brought Coco. Your father cast a spell that linked you to her until you were of age, and able to care for yourself. *That* is how Domenikos traced you to Florida. Through her."

"But why did he kill her?"

"Without her, you were left vulnerable."

"I still don't understand. Why would Domenikos want to hurt me? I would have gladly given him the chronometer, if I'd known it cost my mother her life."

"Would you have?" he asked. "Coupled with the Chronometer, Domenikos would be unstoppable. You are the last remaining obstacle to his power. He has grown too strong for anyone else to match."

"But I don't have any powers. I'm just me."

"You can travel," Liz said.

"Only because of this feather." Adrielle pulled it out of her pocket and placed it in Angelo's hand. "This is too much. I'm not a match for him."

Angelo stared at the feather. "This is Haden's, he never should have given it to you."

"Why did he?"

Angelo grew quiet.

"He fell in love with her, obviously," Liz whispered.

"Shhh," Dave warned.

Reaching for the back of her t-shirt, Angelo asked, "May I?"

Adrielle nodded. The others looked on as Angelo pulled the neck of her shirt down and exposed her shoulder blades.

"The mark's grown," Liz whispered. "It looks like a tattoo, a crimson-feathered crest burned into her skin. Identical to the embossing on the cover of the *Book of Feathers*."

"This feather is a part of you now," Angelo said. "You no longer need it. You've earned the right to time travel. But don't forget, there are three other seal judgments you must pass."

"How?"

"By upholding the Achaean Act—at all costs."

"I can't make that promise. Not now. I need to think about Kate and Veda. How to get them back."

Angelo shook his head. "Adrielle Maddox, I don't know when you've ever played by the rules. But you must. Everything hinges on it. If you don't stop travelling, you're no better than Domenikos. Collateral damage comes from doing the right thing. Come to terms with it."

"I'm not willing to accept that."

Chapter 22

Florence —1504
Three Days to the Eclipse

THEY GATHERED AROUND the table in Michelangelo's small kitchen. Ordinarily, a cook came in the mornings to fix breakfast, but with the secrecy needed to implement Adrielle's plan, Salai had taken over the meal preparations.

Breakfast consisted of struffoli—fried dough balls drizzled with honey and sprinkles, from the local market—and a new and rare delicacy, very strong coffee, which Salai made to everyone's specifications. The dark Italian roast had an earthy aroma that infiltrated everything in the room. So strong, one whiff had enough caffeine to jack anyone up for an entire day.

Salai poured the liquid gold into tiny porcelain cups, no larger than a child's tea set, and set them in the center of the table along with the tray of struffoli.

Leonardo and Michelangelo tipped their tiny espresso cups casually back. The others, used to the American gargantuan version, exchanged looks of wonderment. Only Liz licked at the rich thick head of crema and asked for a second cup before Salai was finished pouring his own.

They ate silently. Liz was sure each was contemplating the very real changes in the future—at least as it presently stood. It meant they could never go back. That place in time they once called home was gone. They were tired, cranky, and uneasy about the whole thing.

Liz finished her pastry and was about to scoop the remaining dough balls on the large platter in the center of the table onto her plate, when it occurred to her that she stress ate. And it wasn't working. Though the struffoli was delicious, in light of their prognosis, no amount of pastries could lift the impending feeling of doom. Things were hightailing from bad to worse. And time was running short.

She looked at the sticky pastry in her hand and set it back on the dish, committing to do whatever it took to help set Adrielle's plan in motion. If Adrielle didn't get her act together and start taking advice from those who knew more, they were all condemned to spend the rest of their days without electricity and TV. And of course, that meant putting an end to her dreams of being a TV anchor.

DAVE, WHO HAD taken on the chore of gathering firewood in exchange for a warm bed, downed his cappuccino in three gulps. He set about his morning routine to stock the firebox for their evening fire. Fall was quickly approaching and the night air was cooler than expected. If he concentrated on menial tasks and kept busy, he could postpone thinking about what it would truly be like to be stuck in a time before coming out of the closet was as second nature as which side you parted your hair on. Blindness was bliss. At least it made the immediate present, bearable.

AFTER MUCH CONTEMPLATION, Leonardo put the completion of Liz's portrait on hold. The forgery was a daunting task. So much text to copy. Even if he worked straight through without sleeping, he couldn't possibly do it all himself. There simply wasn't enough time.

He dabbed at his beard with a white napkin, sat it on the table, and pushed out of his chair. Adrielle would have to become an expert on the art of Calligraphy.

They cleared a large area on the table and Leonardo laid two clean sheets of Papyrus, one for him and one for Adrielle. Two inkwells sat on the left side of each sheet. "Salai, fetch Adrielle a feather quill." When Salai returned with her writing instrument, Leonardo showed her how to dip the tip in the ink, blot any excess, and glide the point over the papyrus until the desired stroke was executed.

He reproduced both the upper- and lower-case formations of the script, and scrutinized the dipping of the quill into the ink. "Be careful, too much ink and it will seep out." Adrielle hesitated. He tapped on her side of the ancient manuscript. "What's wrong? Why aren't you trying this?"

"I'm not left-handed. I'll dribble ink all over the place."

"Ah." He nodded. "Move the jar to the other side."

She did as instructed and looked up at him.

"Go on. There is no time to spare. Dive in and set your mind to it," he said.

AT FIRST, ADRIELLE was self-conscious that Leonardo supervised her so closely, as she carefully reproduced every curve. But soon, he seemed satisfied she was exceptionally detail oriented and managed to copy with astounding ease. At least he told her so. "Well done," he said nodding with encouragement, then he set about his own toil. And Adrielle felt relieved.

After hours of practice, the time arrived to begin the forgery. They placed the *Book of Feathers* between them and opened it to the first page of script.

Adrielle was pleasantly surprised with her language talents. Deciphering the text came naturally. She discovered Achaeans used their own encrypted language to keep the ordinary eye from understanding the information.

If they copied the text exactly as is, Domenikos would get a hold of the ancient spells that had been so carefully guarded. So Adrielle worked on rewriting them, changing the words just enough so they would backfire if he tried to use them.

Adopting the same layout as the original book, they began the process of combining the old text with the new falsified version. The task was intricately tedious. In order to simplify things, Leonardo copied the pages on the left side, while Adrielle worked on the right.

Leonardo's hands were dry and veiny with splatters of oil paints embedded in his nails. They didn't look that different from other hands, yet when he traced his quill on the papyrus, the result looked like a lithograph. It was magical to see him at work.

Adrielle worked diligently beside him, concentrating on making each stroke exactly as Leonardo had taught her. She was just thinking how well it was going and curling the end of the letter halfway down the page, when a blob of ink gushed out of the tip, soaking into the papyrus.

"Damn. I ruined the entire page," she gasped, watching the ink spread and feather into the paper. She felt a rush of heat and embarrassment. It was all she could do to hold herself together.

Leonardo looked at the ink stain and shook his head in frustration. He lifted her hand to inspect the quill. The ink had leaked onto her fingers too.

"No, no, no. This will never do," he complained, narrowing his eyes to inspect the tip closely. "The tips are not fine enough. They need to be cut more accurately, on the exact angle so the ink doesn't run out of the calamus."

"Salai," he called, searching for him over his shoulder.

Salai was at the other end of the room, sweeping debris from around Michelangelo's workbench. "Bring Adrielle another quill. The ink is seeping out the tip."

"At this rate, we'll be out of feathers before sundown," Salai mumbled.

"Be careful how you trim them. They must be shaped more precisely. And bring us more paper too," Leonardo ordered, shaking his head in disapproval.

Adrielle knew Salai didn't take offense. He'd told her he'd been his assistant for many years and knew Leonardo was meticulous to a fault. His scrupulousness had long ago become second nature. He propped the broom against the wall and reached for the basket on the shelf where he kept the supply of finished quills.

"Oh, mama mia. That was the last one," he cried, tipping the empty basket for Leonardo to see. He walked toward the worktable and dropped his eyes to the floor.

"Look," he said, "quills are scattered everywhere." Adrielle had been tossing them into a bin by her feet. "Her garbage is overflowing."

Leonardo glanced down and leveled a look at him. "Make more."

"I bought all they had at the market yesterday, the last batch of feathers. I don't know where we'll find more."

Adrielle suspected there was more behind Salai's testiness. It was his job to prepare the quills and go to the market for supplies. Paints, paper, conte. He even stretched canvases, anything that Leonardo needed him to do. But she'd never heard him complain before.

"What is wrong Salai? Are you still upset I put the portrait on hold?"

"It's outrageous. Copying someone else's work. Especially when Francesco is paying such a handsome sum."

"Now, Salai, we have gone over this."

"But you are a creator, not a forger. This is too big a compromise."

Leonardo wouldn't hear of it. Adrielle wondered if it was because the prospect of learning more about time travel and the time continuum was fascinating to him and took precedent over everything else.

"I'll go to the market and see if there are more," Adrielle offered, pushing away from the table. "Dave is headed there after his chores and my hand is starting to cramp."

"Fine," Leonardo agreed. "Bring back news of the leather smith. See if the outer cover is completed."

Adrielle wiped the ink off her hands with a cloth soaked in turpentine and headed for the kitchen.

The smell of fresh baking was a welcome change from the solvents and oils of the studio. She inhaled the sweet yeasty aroma and peeked in the stone oven where two loafs of bread were rising. "Mmmm . . . it smells *so* good. How can you stand working in here without eating everything in sight?" she asked Liz, who was sitting at the kitchen table scribbling something into her notebook.

Liz didn't even look up.

Adrielle bent down and whispered in her ear, "Earth to Liz. Hello?"

"What?" Liz looked up.

"Never mind. Where's Dave? I thought he'd be in here re-stocking the firebox."

"You just missed them." She waved without taking her eyes off her notes.

"Them?"

"He left with Coco. Papyrus."

"How long ago? We need feathers for quills," Adrielle said, looking at the ballpoint pen in Liz's hand.

"Only by minutes. If you hurry, you can catch 'em."

Adrielle pulled a cape from a hook by the door. "Ever think what's going to happen when that dries out?" She slipped on the cape. "It's not like we can go to Walmart and pick up more pens."

Liz sighed, finally looking up. "I know." She clicked on the end of her retractable pen. "It's the little things that mean the most."

"Who knows? John Loud may not be the one taking credit for that discovery if Leonardo gets a hold of your pen," Dave interjected.

Liz and Adrielle turned to the door. Dave walked through the doorway, his arms loaded with trays of colorful jars.

"That was fast. Feels like you just left," Liz said.

"I did. But we ran into Michelangelo. He wants Coco to stay." He sat the trays on the table. Michelangelo and Coco were right behind him, carrying more jars.

"What are those?"

"Pigment containers," Coco said, her face beaming. "He's going to teach me how to paint. I think I might actually like it. I mean, how different could it be than applying makeup?"

"Oh, no difference. I'm sure it's exactly the same," Liz said, an amused look on her face. She'd watched Leonardo mix the paints for her portrait and told Adrielle how tedious it was. One wrong addition threw the color off completely.

"I'll go with you then," Adrielle suggested. "We need feathers for quills. And we should check on the leather smith."

"WHERE IS IT?"

"I don't know." Why don't you ask Haden? I have a feeling you may never see it," the woman said smugly.

Domenikos paced a tight circle around her. "She's just wasting time. Nothing she does is going to make a difference. I've always been the stronger one."

"It doesn't have to be like this. There's a better way."

Domenikos grinned. "My way."

"There are boundaries. Consequences."

He slipped his hand out of his pocket and pulled on the tips of his leather gloves. Finger by finger he made small even tugs until the gloves glided off. With two fingers he gestured for Vladik to approach. Vladik stepped forward, carrying an assortment of torture devices on a silver tray.

"Now, darling, which one is to your liking?" Domenikos asked and waited as Vladik tipped the tray so she could see.

The woman turned her head away and jiggled her hands, but they were tied behind her back. Her feet too, the rope woven around the chair and secured to her wrists.

"Hmm?"

She breathed in a long breath and closed her eyes.

"I'll pick then," he said, drawing circles in the air with his fingers until he darted for the brass knuckles. He slipped them on, took a step to the side, and with the expertise of a tennis backhand, hit her in the jaw.

The woman moaned. Her chair tipped back, teetering on one leg, then settled back on the floor. She wouldn't look at him. Not ever again.

Domenikos slipped the knuckles off. The blow had broken the woman's skin. He licked off the blood and rubbed the brass on his cloak. Taking a moment to re-inspect them, he said, "There. Good as new." And replaced them on the tray.

He ambled to the door and paused, waiting for a reaction. Any reaction, but the woman was silent. "We'll see if you have some news for me when I return. Don't wait up. I have an appointment."

THE SNAP OF a cold wind whistled through the narrow streets. The sky had clouded over since morning and was threatening vengeance. Adrielle shivered and wrapped her cloak tighter around her shoulders. "I swear it feels like it's going to snow. I miss that balmy Florida weather."

"Me too. Among other things," Dave admitted, inhaling a waft of garlic and tomatoes as they passed by an open window. "But you have to admit, the food here is *the* best. I'll bet they're making spaghetti alla puttanesca for lunch in that place." He pointed with his thumb at the window.

Adrielle looked back. A laundry line with fresh cleaned linens hung out to dry in the next story up from it.

"What's *alla puttanesca?*"

"Spaghetti in a tomato sauce with garlic, olives, and capers."

"Oh," she said, thinking how Dave was an endless information bank. "How do you know *that?*"

"I've been helping Salai in the kitchen," he admitted. "I'm really liking it too."

They worked their way down the narrow cobbled path, weaving from one side of the street to the other in order to sidestep the local merchants who tried their best to attract their attention. Finally, they reached the leather smith at the other end of town.

Not unlike Michelangelo's studio, the leather smith's shop also had the underlining scent of solvents, but here the odor was masked with a very strong smell of leather goods.

Dave cleared his throat and stepped forward to address the worker at the front counter, since he'd been the one to place the order. The worker said the book cover wasn't ready.

Dave raked his hands through his hair as he did whenever he was at a loss and bounced on the balls of his feet. Although he was studiously trying to master the language, he was struggling. Adrielle had watched him pour over Italian language manuals and understood what a challenge it was for him.

"There was a rush on it," he said and asked for an approximate completion date.

The worker shrugged. "Try in two weeks."

"We need it now," Dave said.

Adrielle could see him grow more and more frustrated with the language barrier. How could they go back empty-handed? He tried explaining how important it was and began making catastrophic mistakes with his words. Instead of *libro,* meaning book, he was asking for *bambino,* which means boy. And soon the worker was laughing loudly because Dave started using hand gestures making it fairly obvious that he was gay.

Adrielle stepped in. She explained that when the order was placed, the owner had put a rush on it because it had been a favor requested by Michelangelo and emphasized the work itself was to be kept under the strictest confidence. When the worker finally understood, he disappeared into the back of the shop.

The owner of the shop walked through the back doorway with the leather cover. Both Dave and Adrielle inspected the work closely. It was perfect. Adrielle felt a nervous flutter. They were really doing this. The leather was hand tooled with the same design as the original manuscript and was darkened with oil that made it look like it had been aged for a zillion years. Minor defects had also been added to make it look more authentic.

"Perfecto," Adrielle said, elated. She wrapped the binding under her cape and went outside, while Dave settled the account with the coins Michelangelo had given him.

Most of the passers-by were men. Apparently, this was the industrial part of town. Instead of the colorful displays in the retail center of Florence, these storefronts were bleak and uninviting. Some of the doors only bore a knocker with no other explanation for the type of business it was.

Out of her peripheral vision, Adrielle caught the flutter of a long cape, reaching almost to the ground. It seemed familiar. She looked across the street but couldn't see the face of the cape wearer, who walked with long and quick strides. Purple lining peeked out as wind caught the black cape.

Haden. She'd recognize his cape anywhere. Made of the finest wool, it had a full hood with a silver button closure on the neck.

He approached the blacksmith shop two storefronts away, and Adrielle was hoping he'd look up so she could signal to him. But he kept his head low.

She felt herself getting angry. The least he could do was acknowledge her. A simple tip of the head would do. But he strode past. She took a step to dart across the street and call out to him, but someone grabbed her by the arm.

"Not so fast," Angelo whispered, pulling her back.

She threw a quick sideways glance. "What are you doing?"

"Look who he's with." He pulled her further out of sight and ducked behind a display of leather saddles. "We can watch from here without being seen."

She squinted at the darkly dressed man at Haden's side and inhaled a quick breath. "It can't be."

It was Domenikos, with that smug insolent grin. And next to him, were Brix and Astraia. They looked like hoods. The mob even. Adrielle shivered, inching closer to Angelo.

Haden slid his hood off as he was about to enter the shop and began chatting with Domenikos. No surprise on his face, only a welcomed greeting. Fury built inside Adrielle.

Brix pointed to a prominent display of knives in the window and soon, they appeared to be joking, like they didn't have a care in the world but to window shop.

After several moments, they pointed at the various knives and seemed to be discussing them. Then someone from the back stepped out wearing a black apron and unfurled a long pouch with an assortment of knives tucked neatly into pockets.

Domenikos slid a dagger out from one of the compartments, and Adrielle froze. "It's the same knife he used on Josh. I'd recognize the tooling on the handle anywhere."

"Keep looking," Angelo insisted.

The blacksmith pulled out four other identical knives and handed them each one.

"They're all identical. The same twisted handles and needle thin blades."

"It is not uncommon to order identical knives, especially if they belong to the same gang," Angelo said.

One by one, they slipped the knives out of the sheaths, held them up to the sky, and turned the blades until they caught the glint of light breaking through a cluster of clouds. In that moment, the sky became dark, angry clouds banding overhead. They chanted something undecipherable, a low hypnotizing hum, and clinked the blades together much like in a toast, continuing to keep their blades crossed until thunder rumbled and rain poured down.

"It almost looks like they're in collaboration," Adrielle said, finding it difficult to breathe.

Angelo pulled her toward him, his eyes boring into hers as if everything depended on it. "Not almost, Adrielle, they are."

Adrielle couldn't wait to get back to the studio. The feeling of betrayal burning inside her was burrowing deep. It was incomparable to the feeling she'd felt when she thought Josh was cheating with Scarlett. This pain was much worse. And yet, she reasoned Haden meant nothing to her. Why then, did she have these intense feelings of loss and abandonment?

BY THE TIME Dave came out from the leather smith's, the group had disbanded and gone their separate ways. He didn't see Adrielle right off as he stood at the doorway, looking up and down the street, trying to see past the rain that was coming down in pellets.

Adrielle flagged him down and Dave ran over to where she and Angelo stood, tucked under an awning. Though he pulled his shirt over his head, he was drenched. He was about to say something—remark how dark everything looked and how quickly the clouds had appeared, but the tension between them was so thick, he realized something was going on.

Adrielle didn't elaborate, and that was fine with him. He had no intention of getting in the middle. He'd been around Adrielle and Coco often enough when they'd had their disagreements to know how stubborn Adrielle could be. No matter what anyone said, she had her own opinion on things. Nothing would sway her.

They waited wordlessly under the awning, watching the rain as it pooled and ran in small currents into the drains. Finally, it settled to a light drizzle and they headed back.

Adrielle walked several paces ahead, the newly tooled cover tucked protectively under her cloak. Angelo followed closely behind her.

Dave trailed behind, to give them space. He wondered if Liz could be right. She'd mentioned that though Adrielle would never admit it to anyone, she believed Adrielle had strong feelings for Angelo. If she did, she'd tell him about it in her own time. If she didn't, Liz would get to the bottom of it like she always did, and he'd find out anyways.

Clearly, Adrielle was shaken as they hurried back to the studio. Hot tears ran down her face, but Angelo kept a solemn expression and pretended they were only streaks of rain, dripping from her hair. She swiped at them periodically and pulled the cloth of her cloak high around her cheeks.

OVER THE PAST few weeks, Angelo had seen Adrielle struggle with her feelings. She was going through countless adjustments, and he understood how difficult a time she was having juggling everything that was being thrown on her: coming to terms with the changes in her body, realizing the negative effects of time travel, and trying her best to restore her life in Florida to what it once was. He wasn't sure now, that would ever be possible.

If he was being brutally honest, he knew he would do whatever it took to make her happy, everything short of breaking his oath to uphold the Achaean Act, even if it meant losing her love.

He differed from Haden in that way. Rules were meant to be followed. And when they weren't, everyone got hurt. He thought about Haden and wondered what had gotten into him. What he was up to. He'd gone too far. Perhaps he believed by siding with Domenikos, Adrielle would be free to live a simple life. That wasn't possible. Not ever.

When the ache of deception proved too bitter, Angelo turned his thoughts to Adrielle.

He had every intention of being a support to her, but she was so damned stubborn. He knew that about her. It had worsened since living in Florida. She had grown more opinionated than ever and was hell bent on doing things her way. On leaving her mark.

He supposed that was part of what he loved about her, but her naivety could leave scars that he wouldn't be able to erase.

THE CRACKLING FIRE was a warm welcome from the cold. Adrielle hung her cape on the hook and handed the binding to Michelangelo. Dave and Angelo were steps behind, both seemed anxious to see Michelangelo's response.

He took the binding and studied it for a moment before heading to the studio.

The smell of melting wax was overpowering. Because the light coming in from the window was dim, Leonardo had lit a candle close by. Michelangelo laid the cover gently next to Leonardo, who put down his quill to have a look and slid it closer. The two studied it intently, their heads bent in concentration for some time.

"Molto Bene." Meaning, *very good*, was Michelangelo's only comment, but it was clear he was pleased.

Leonardo's satisfaction was apparent only by the slight lifting of the corners of his lips. "And the feathers for the quills?" he asked, resuming the transfer of the text onto the papyrus.

"Oh darn." Dave's face went pallid. "It was raining so hard we forgot to get them."

Leonardo shook his head in disappointment and spoke very quickly. Dave was lost in his flurry of words, he seemed to only be getting the gist of it. *Without the quills, they would never finish in time.*

Angelo dropped an armful of silver feathers onto his lap. The smile on Leonardo stretched across his face like a half moon. No one had seen Angelo leave. And no one dared ask how they were simply there.

"I STILL DON'T understand why you find it so upsetting that they were all together. You know we can't trust any of them," Coco said, stripping down to her bra and underwear to get ready for bed.

"It's such a betrayal," Adrielle insisted, pulling back the thick velvet bedspread and climbing in. She settled back onto her pillow and stared up at the wood beamed ceiling.

Liz had opted to take the extra mattress on the floor so Coco could share the bed with Adrielle. She'd been listening to them going back and forth. The two sure went around the issue, she thought, pulling her bedspread up and tucking it snuggly under her arms.

"Are you sure you're not mad 'cause he lied to you?" she finally asked.

"Lizzie, have you *even* been listening? Haden *didn't* lie to me, he just didn't tell me he hung out with him."

"Guilty by omission," Liz stated, turning onto her side and leaning onto her elbow. "Can't be any clearer to me."

"Or me," Coco agreed.

"It's so—" Adrielle flailed her arms searching for the right word.

"Disconcerting?" Liz asked.

Adrielle shook her head.

"Disheartening?"

"Nah-uh. That's not it—exactly."

"Frustrating?" Liz added, looking at her over the rim of her glasses. She could see Adrielle was getting more and more agitated. "Adie, what is it really that gets you the most?" She didn't know if she was helping, but at least Adrielle was exploring her feelings.

"Lame maybe."

"Lame? That's such a weak adjective."

"Ahrgggg." Adrielle squawked.

"No, I think it's more like—betrayed," Coco finally said, searching out Adrielle's eyes. "And not by Haden. But by Angelo. Because he hadn't told her of the alliance."

Chapter 23

FLORENCE – 1504
Two days to the Eclipse

A SHRILL SCREAM echoed through the house.

"Adie, Adie wake up!" Coco shook Adrielle gently, but she didn't answer. "Adrielle!" Coco shouted, shaking her harder and fighting a rise of hysteria. "Omigod. She's not waking up!" No matter how loudly she called out, Adrielle didn't respond.

Outside their room, loud footsteps clapped against the wood treads. The door to their bedroom slapped open, banging against the wall. A piece of stucco crumbled to the floor and scattered a light dusting of powder.

"Quello che e successo?" (What happened?) Michelangelo roared from the door frame. He wore a piercing, heated expression as he searched the room. Coco winced. His balled-up fists announced he was ready for a fight. His anger dissolved when he saw Adrielle curled in a fetal position, trembling on the bed.

"What's wrong with her?" he asked, rushing to her bedside. Leonardo and Dave followed closely behind. They stared at Adrielle, their faces creasing with worry.

"She's having a nightmare." Coco leaned in closer to Adrielle and said in a hushed tone, "This fear is irrational, Adie. It's not real." She brushed her hair off her face. She'd woken Adrielle a hundred times from nightmares. Why wasn't she waking up now?

Adrielle shuddered.

"Wake up. All you have to do is wakeup." Coco looked up at the others. "I can't get her to respond. She's burning up." Her biggest fears were coming to life. She pressed the palm of her hand flat against Adrielle's chest and pulled herself a little straighter. "Her heart is pounding."

"Has this happened before?" Michelangelo asked.

"I've always been able to wake her," Coco said, panic sinking its claws. "I don't understand, it's like she's trapped in her dream."

HE WAS LEANING over her face, his hot breath brushing against her skin. The smell of cigarettes was so pungent it was nauseating.

"You're lying. You're lying!" Adrielle spat.

"I am not."

"I don't believe you," she said, her eyes locking onto his. The green flecks shimmered inside his iris. "I can see it in your eyes."

"How can you say that? Knowing what you now know?" he asked. His mouth twisted into a snarl.

"I don't know how I know. I just do." Adrielle shook her head in disapproval. "Look what you've done. We're supposed to be on the same side, and now you're consorting with the enemy. Destroying everything worthwhile." Her gaze drifted off into the distance. "Nothing good can come of this," she murmured.

"Don't say that. I'm only doing this for you." Haden grabbed her arm and turned her toward him, thick tension between them. He narrowed his eyes. "I can save you, you know."

"Save yourself. If it's not too late."

COCO TOUCHED ADRIELLE'S forehead. "She feels cold. Clammy."

"She needs body heat," Angelo said. He pressed his body onto hers and dissolved into tiny silver particles.

Everyone gasped. Coco ran her hand along the bedspread and cupped a handful of the powdery residue.

"Silver sprinkles. Like Christmas glitter. The kind you mix with glue to make ornaments." She blew on the tiny mound twinkling in the palm of her hand. The shimmer scattered and swirled around the room invoking a magical feeling. It was like looking onto a field of snow and seeing tiny snowflakes glistening in the sunlight.

Though Adrielle was still laying in fetal position, she had stopped shivering.

LIZ LICKED AT the golden foam of her espresso before tipping the entire contents of the tiny porcelain cup back.

"You drink your coffee like whiskey," Dave said.

The quick shot of caffeine jolted through her body. These days, she preferred the tanginess that hit the front of her tongue, to the sweet coating of milk residue left on the roof of her mouth from a cappuccino. Maybe it was her nerves, but she'd lost the taste for the struffoli too. She could only take so much of that syrupy dough, and she'd had enough to last a lifetime.

"I think we have to confront him," Coco said, reaching for the juice.

"Bad idea. Very bad idea," Liz said, then flicked her tongue along the inside of her cup.

"That's so gross," Dave said. "Is that what you do when Francesco takes you out?"

Liz raised her eyebrows slightly and without taking umbrage at his comment, contemplated his question. She sat her cup primly down, her pinky waving out to the side. "No, definitely no." David was watching her curiously. "What's up? Why are you staring?"

"I was just thinking how different you look without the long bushy caterpillar crawling along your forehead."

"Thanks. Thanks a lot,"

"It's not bad. You have two identical arched lines hovering over each eye. They're so fine, they could have been sketched by Leonardo."

"About Francesco . . . I thought you were breaking up with him," Coco said, wiping her hands on a dishtowel and slipping on her painting apron.

"Was working on it, but he's grown on me."

"That's what you said at the start," Dave interjected, "and look where *that* got you!"

Liz brushed her hands over her lap to smooth out her silk skirt. "Yes, you're right," she said, mesmerized by the light diffracting from the gems on her rings onto the white stucco wall. "Look where it's gotten me."

Coco rolled her eyes. "I'm getting back to work, coffee break's over." She handed her juice cup to Salai, who was washing the dishes in the sink. "You two coming?"

They nodded.

"Okay. Keep in mind we're running out of time." Coco headed toward the studio. Before disappearing into the hall, she turned back. "So we're all on the same page? That confronting Haden is a bad idea?"

"Yes," Liz and David answered in unison.

"Why?" Salai asked. He set the clay jug to drain.

"It's like R2D2 taking on Darth Vader," Liz said.

"I'm not so sure Haden's Darth Vader. I thought Domenikos was," Dave added.

"Who's Darth Vader?" Salai asked, wiping the crumbs off the table.

Liz exchanged a look with Dave. If they didn't get it right, they would never get back home.

IN ORDER TO finish before the eclipse, they formed a chain of productivity—everyone doing their part. Dave smoothed out the prepared sheets of papyrus on a wood board and set out to cut more strips. They kept a basket stocked with papyrus reeds Angelo had gathered in the center of the studio. He grabbed one from the top of the pile and stripped the reed with a sharp knife until the inside center was visible, then cut along the length to make long thin strips. He laid the broader ones side by side onto a new piece of wood to form a rectangle, and the others he pressed on top, across at right angles.

Once they were wetted and hammered flat until the two surfaces were bound together, they were ready to be dried. Under normal circumstances, the papyrus would have been dried out in the sun and the surface smoothed with a shell, but they were short on time, manpower, and energy. So they improvised.

Dave set the prepared papyrus strips onto the wood slabs. Salai took them and laid them in the kitchen by the fireplace to dry. He used a fan to spread the heat from the flames as evenly over them as possible, and when the sheets were dried, he took them in to Michelangelo who smoothed out the surfaces with a shell so they could write on them.

Michelangelo boasted how easily Coco had taken to painting, but she set aside any egotism, believing it had less to do with being a quick learner than the breadth of knowledge and skill her instructor passed on. In any case, she was delighted to be a part of the process. She worked tirelessly along with the others, mixing paints, and creating the *base under-painting* for the illustrations as best as she could.

Though Adrielle was still in that dormant unreachable state, she was stable. And so, the work continued. Leonardo trained Liz to help him with the Calligraphy. He worked tirelessly, alternating between the text, and the illustrations with Michelangelo.

Once the sheets were completed with both text and illustrations, Salai cleared the back shelves on the far wall in the studio and laid them out to dry.

Fearing they would run out of time, they pushed themselves beyond exhaustion. The forgery had to look as authentic as the real book.

Liz's tummy growled and she ignored it, pressing on, often working through until well after long shadows turned to night.

Coco wiped her brow with the back of her hand. "Ahh . . . the smell of the solvents is getting to me. It's making me nauseous," she said, folding over at the waist and grabbing at her stomach.

"Go over to the window and get some fresh air," Michelangelo instructed.

Coco slid out from her chair, the sound of the wood scraping against the stone floor filling the room. She padded over to the window and opened the glass pane. It was twilight. In the distance, the sun cast an orange streak across the sky. She leaned out and inhaled the fresh air. The cool breeze against her skin reminded her of home in the winter.

Home . . . if she'd never known what it was like to walk along the Palm Coast beach as the sun went down, this may have been the most beautiful sunset she'd ever seen. But she missed the sound of the waves lapping onto the shore. The salty mist spray clinging to her face and skin. Scrunching her toes in the sand and feeling them sink as the water lapped over them and back into the ocean. She hated to admit it, but she was homesick.

She turned around and looked at the others, their heads bowed in concentration to complete their assignment. She wondered if they believed this plan could actually work. Or if burying oneself into this task was one way of coping with an impossible situation.

A wave of fear bit her hard and sank its angry teeth. How could this plan really work? If Domenikos was cunning enough to overtake the Unity and able to destroy all the other Achaeans, then how could Adrielle possibly believe she could win this war?

"I'm going up to check in on Adrielle," she said, masking her alarm with a smile. Her legs grew wearier with every tread she climbed. She hesitated at the bedroom door and pressed her forehead into the wood. Promising herself not to show her weakness.

"WHAT IS IT you want, Adrielle?" Monika's eyes were black shiny marbles.

"I want this all to stop."

Monika shook her head. Her red lips formed a hard line across her face. "I warned you: The moment you took your first step along the path of truth, there was no going back."

"But I didn't understand the consequences. I didn't know innocent people could lose their lives because of me."

"Not because of you, in spite of you. There *is* a difference you know. And everyone is innocent, until they aren't."

"Domenikos isn't innocent."

"No, not now. But once he was as innocent as the driven snow."

"What happened? Why doesn't life hold any value to him?"

"On the contrary, Adrielle, he values life. He believes every Achaean's life was breached and compromised by the enforcement of the Achaean Act. That to prevent travel is like clipping a bird's wings.

"Kraaa, Kraa." The black bird on Monika's shoulder spread its wings and swooped toward her. Adrielle ducked, blocking her face with her forearms. She screamed as the feathers grazed against her skin. The bird lunged again and again.

"Stop! Stop it!" Adrielle cried. She felt her anger rise until she thought she might explode. Swift as the unfolding of a hand-held fan, the skin on her back molted and she found herself hovering over the floor, flying along the circumference of the room.

For the first time in a long time, as the cool air brushed against her skin, Adrielle felt free.

THE BLADES OF the daggers clinked in a toast. Domenikos' gaze drifted around the circle, demanding allegiance, not moving from one to the next until he was certain of their utmost devotion. When all present swore their fidelity, Domenikos twisted his filigree handle between his fingers. "As an initiation and proof of your loyalty, you must bring back your knife, stained with the blood of an innocent."

Brix snickered. "I'll get the pregnant wench and her baby. First, I'll sink my blade into her flesh, and then I'll burn the both of 'em."

The other three blades met his with a clang.

"Astraia, who will be your choice?"

"Coco," she said without hesitation, her eyes locking onto Domenikos'.

"Coco?" Domenikos asked, his eyes widening.

"Yes. Blood ties run deep. By severing the links that bind, she will be weakened."

Domenikos paused before responding, the flecks of his eyes blazing green. He inhaled a quick breath. He turned to Haden who stood at his side. "And you? How will *you* pledge your commitment?"

"I have not yet chosen," he lied, cursing the turn of events that had led to this moment. A thread of understanding flowed between them that didn't need to be voiced. Haden knew what Domenikos wanted to hear. He lowered his eyes to the ground. Domenikos had grown too strong. There would be no chosen innocent if it was within his power.

"Very well then," Domenikos said, the skin around his eyes tightening. Without breaking his gaze, he slid his dagger into the sheath fastened around his waist. "You have until the solar eclipse."

Haden turned to leave. Domenikos grabbed his arm. "Bring me back the stained blade. And I will grant your wish."

"And you?" Haden asked, "You have not yet divulged your victim."

"I think you will be quite surprised at the plans I have in store," Domenikos said, his eyes glinting. His hand went back to the sheath. "Astraia may be right." He tapped the silver handle of his dagger and smiled, his snaggle tooth gleaming. "The ties that bind may be the best ones severed."

A shiver ran up Haden's spine. He hoped it wasn't too late to warn her.

ADRIELLE RAN TO her mother's side. "It's not fair. Why does *he* always get his way?"

"Not always," her mother said, picking up her young daughter and lifting her onto her lap. She traced her finger around the bottom of her chin and tapped the tip of Adrielle's nose lightly. "Have you done your exercises today?"

Adrielle nodded.

"Very good. Now tell me about your travels. Where did you go today?" she asked, tucking a platinum strand behind her ear.

"I went to Rome."

"And?"

"I saw Julius Caesar sit on his throne."

"Was he surrounded by his subjects?"

"No, only his generals."

"What was he doing?"

"He gave the command for a new battle."

"And how did that make you feel?"

"Sad."

"Why?"

"I don't like battles."

"No one does, sweetheart, but they are necessary to keep the peace."

"That's what my new friend said, too."

"What friend?"

"A friend."

"Does this friend have a name?"

"Yes, but he wouldn't tell me. He said leaders have to do what they believe in."

"He's right. And *you* are no exception. Caesar is one of the greatest military minds in history." She pulled Adrielle close. "What else did you and your friend do?"

"We had a snack. Daisies."

"Daisies?"

"Uh-huh. They're yummy."

"Oh." Adrielle's mother laughed. "Canestrelli. They do look like daisies."

"He said it reminds him of Italy. And the day when everything he imagined, became real."

Adrielle ran her hand along the chain hanging around her mother's neck. "Is this really mine?" she said, twirling the gold pendant.

"Yes, Adrielle." Her mother set her down. "One day, when you're older, you'll understand why it's important to keep peace."

"All he wants to do is fight. I hate fighting."

She cupped Adrielle's chin in her hands and said pointedly, "One day, when you're all grown up, the hands of fate will stop spinning. Always remember, Adrielle, you will need to control your own future.

Chapter 24

Florence – 1504
The Day Before the Eclipse

AS SHE SLEPT, the tremors started in her chest and seeped into her limbs. Adrielle tensed, like an animal in the wild hearing the snap of a twig. Even after numerous trips, the tremors—the precursor signaling the commencement of travel—sent a silent alarm blaring though her body that warned: *watch out, here it comes,* that thing that takes you away from the here and now into unrevealed territory.

Uncertain if she was going to face her biggest nightmare or be able to get back, was terrifying. So was the constant fight to survive, improvising with the unknown. The first tremor always meant the onset of something gargantuan.

A wave of dizziness unsteadied her. Adrielle opened her eyes as soon as she was somewhat coherent before her body lost that listless numbness and the memory bank had replenished itself. The world around was still blurry, unfocused as if a thick swath of Vaseline had been slathered inside her eyelids.

She fought to make out unfamiliar sounds and chattering. Visually, forms were speckled, perforated with light points in motion making them appear as though they weren't solid. Adrielle rubbed her eyes and blinked. Telling herself not to panic, she waited for the temporary dulling transition-period to pass.

After several minutes, her surroundings came into focus. She sighed with relief and watched a chicken cross the road. It was trying to get away from a merchant who ran after it, basket in hand.

Run for your life, she thought, taking pleasure as the chicken rounded the corner and disappeared. The merchant raised his hands in surrender and returned to his kiosk. Adrielle twitched her nose. The smell of burning metal tainted with spices and different foods hung heavily in the air. She raised her hands up to her brows to shade her eyes from the sun. Rows of vendors and shops lined narrow cobbled streets as far as she could see. Florence. She was in Florence at the blacksmith's. She smiled, overwhelmed with joy at knowing where she was. From what she could tell, it was still 1504.

But what was she doing here, back at the blacksmiths?

A dark presence descended over top of her like a black cloud in a flash storm. Adrielle looked up and froze. Domenikos hovered over her in a translucent state. He was dressed in a long black cape, his ominous vibes enshrouding him.

He was staring at her curiously, brows furrowed. His cold and calculating eyes disheveling her, making her feel vulnerable. Incapable. His stance, legs shoulder width apart, hand on sheath ready to pounce, conveyed he was the hunter: a raptor who tracked and fed for fun.

Adrielle's instinct was to run. To put as much distance between them as possible. But a tidal wave of truths came rushing to her. Her blood ran cold. She could see the extent to which Domenikos jeopardized them all. Not just her and her friends, but mankind. His gross abuse of power could turn life on earth into a living hell. Could cause a lifetime of captivity for everyone. If she didn't stand up to him soon, he would become unstoppable. She shuddered, fear shooting through her.

"Go!" someone shouted. A strong force interlaced their stiff fingers with hers and began pulling her. Away from Domenikos. Away from the blacksmiths. She was a vortex spinning out of control.

COCO BURST INTO the room and stopped at Adrielle's bedside. "How is she?" Adrielle lay on her side, crunched in fetal position. Coco felt sick. She'd hoped this would pass but Adrielle hadn't moved.

"She's stopped twitching," Angelo said, reaching for Coco's hand and giving it a squeeze. He brushed Adrielle's hair gently off her face with his fingers and lay his hand back on Adrielle's, his large hands enveloping hers.

What could he say? Time was suspended until she returned. He resigned to the business of doting over Adrielle.

"Shouldn't we do something? Isn't there a way to wake her up?" Coco hated that her voice came out tremulous and weak. It exposed her vulnerability; everything hinging on his response. Angelo raised his eyes and met hers. This time, they communicated what words dared not. He was helpless. He couldn't reach her any more than she could. He shook his head and returned to his vigil.

Angelo's expression caught Coco off guard. He was terrified. He no longer looked like the valiant undefeated warrior. The way his eyes lingered on Adrielle's face revealed unspoken truths. Angelo was a man on the edge of losing his true love.

Coco watched him surreptitiously, busying herself by smoothing out the wrinkles of the bedspread. Angelo was so absorbed in Adrielle he didn't seem to notice.

The light speckling of freckles on his cheeks made him appear younger than his maturity level. Eighteen. No, maybe twenty. She wanted to ask how old he was but didn't.

Coco thought back to the journal. Liz had said she'd read Angelo and Adrielle were lovers in the past. She'd even shown Coco the exact passage. Coco hadn't believed it. The whole thing seemed impossible. *Wasn't it?* That the journal had ever belonged to Adrielle? That Adrielle was anything more than her kid sister? But now, after everything they'd experienced . . . and seeing how broken Angelo was. She wondered if it was true. If he could really be in love with her? And if he would do anything to save her?

Wasn't there some sort of universal law against cross-mixing of the species? He was Achaean. They were—god, who knew what they were. Aliens? Birds? Different than humans. Definitely different. And yet, to look at him . . .

As she pondered, Angelo turned to her, his eyes betraying his pursuit for privacy. He was vulnerable and scared. Coco was uncomfortable knowing this and embarrassed she'd been staring. That she'd been thinking those things. He wasn't that different from her. She lowered her eyes and brushed her hand over Adrielle's face as she had so many times when Adrielle had nightmares. Thinking those things about Angelo made her feel like a hypocrite. A racist. *He couldn't read her thoughts. Could he?* She felt her face warm. God, and she'd always prided herself on not being judgmental. A free spirit who believed everyone should live and let live.

"I have to get downstairs," she said nervously, wiping her hands on her painting apron. "Gotta—" She tilted her head toward the door. "There's so much left to do—I don't see how we're going to finish in time."

"We have to," Angelo said, his voice cracking. "If we want to see her again."

"CLOSE YOUR EYES, Adrielle. Do not be afraid." The woman took Adrielle's hands in hers and leaned in until their foreheads touched. She smelled like incense and smoke. Her voice was a low murmur. A rhythmic cadence like ocean waves rolling onto the sand. She was reciting a chant. And then, Adrielle recognized the voice. It was her, the old woman with the scepter.

Like a film projecting in her mind, Adrielle remembered how once she'd thought this woman was part of a hoax. At Scarlett's party, before any of this happened. God, that felt like years ago. The memory came with a heaviness, a longing for simpler times when the whole world didn't depend on her. When her biggest worry was Josh and what she would do with the rest of her life. She became melancholy, drowning in the memory of that night and was fully prepared to loiter there.

Then a burst of energy ignited from all points of contact with the woman—the forehead, her hands; a jarring rush of power like a zap from a defibrillator. A centrifugal force so powerful Adrielle's hair stood on end. A syrupy fragrance with the sweetness of a honeysuckle saturated the air and filled her lungs.

In her mind, she saw a spot of light inflame. It swelled until it was blazing and radiated heat. Afraid it would scorch her skin, she almost cried out when the heat mellowed and simmered. The draw was intoxicating: a river of warm tingles swimming in her veins. Stronger than the bubbling effervescence she'd felt when she'd travelled using the feather.

Now fully aware of what was happening, Adrielle asked the woman, "How can this be when I left my feather at home?"

Somewhere in the back of her mind, Adrielle remembered someone telling her she no longer needed it. Was it Angelo? Angelo—the thought of him tugged at her core.

Before the woman answered, a dark mist leached in. A vaporous smoky film that swallowed the daylight. Adrielle's hair rose and whipped violently around her face. The force increased like a cyclone, a whirling mass sucking all the energy. It tried to rip Adrielle away from the old woman.

The woman clasped her hands firmly onto Adrielle's, clutching tighter as the darkness descended upon them. Adrielle stared at the woman's white knuckles, petrified she would let go. The turbulence was so powerful Adrielle's feet lifted out from underneath her. She tumbled in the air, tossing like a rag doll, her hair whipping like reins around her.

Somewhere, glass beads clinked together—reminding her of the ones Coco hung over her window during summer storms. They'd lie in bed, listening to them tinkle and chime as they fell asleep.

But those moments of calm storms were in the past. And this was more than a storm. It was a vengeful and ferocious force. She needed to see what she was up against. Catching her breath and summoning all her courage, Adrielle strained to see past the darkness. With her eyes open a sliver, she saw far below them her bed in Michelangelo's guest bedroom. And she was on it, lying perfectly still in fetal position. She looked like a wax resemblance of herself.

Something inside her twisted. How could that be her? She was in the air with the old woman. Monika, she remembered suddenly. She looked ahead and saw her blowing in the opposite direction as her. Her pointy gold shoes floating behind her small body, high over her head. Adrielle closed her eyes and imagined she was in a speeding plane, her body flapping like a flag out the window.

She went to scream but all that came out was a squeak. The moisture had been sucked away from her throat. The only thing holding her in place was their inter-clasped hands. If either of them let go, they would die.

Monika squeezed her hands onto hers. "Concentrate, Adrielle. You have the strength to stop this."

Adrielle tried to speak but the force against her skin was so strong she couldn't move her lips.

"Think of something good," the woman said.

Adrielle squeezed her eyes shut. She wanted to go home. Home. Home. In her desire for safety she conjured up a memory of Coco's feather duvet. She could almost feel the warmth. Smell the Tide laundry detergent Layla used.

Abruptly the force stopped. Her body was floating. Adrielle opened her eyes. They were in Coco's room. Their room. She felt a surge of relief and joy. It was nighttime; a light wedge of moonlight filtered in through the curtains and formed a rectangle on the wood floor. She searched for the pile of clothes in the center of the room, but it wasn't there. It had to be before the party.

Still, she was home. Really home. She reached around her neck and felt for her gold chain. It was there. She released a breath.

Then it hit her: How could she have the chronometer if Coco hadn't given it to her yet? Adrielle pushed the thought out of her mind. She wanted to believe. She needed this to be real. Damn. Her stomach clenched. This couldn't be real.

She closed her eyes quickly, afraid if she kept them open everything would vanish like vapor. She felt terror. She opened her eyes and found she was lying in bed, the cool crispness of white cotton sheets pressed against her skin. She was facing Coco, their knees touching as they did when they had a heart-to-heart. The room was dark with only the occasional flash of lightning lighting it up and they were listening to pellets of rain hammer on the glass. Neither of them made an attempt to get up. Coco slipped her hand into Adrielle's and gave a long squeeze. God, it had been forever. She hadn't done that since they were little.

Without warning, the hand holding hers was Angelo's. She felt a thread of warmth swim through her. It felt good. She was safe. She didn't dare speak.

HER MOTHER DROPPED her legs over the side of the bed. She wiggled her toes, stood, and worked her way across the room toward her. She was dainty, the epitome of femininity, just as Adrielle remembered. "Adrielle? How are you coping?" she asked.

"Some nights are better than others," Adrielle murmured, trying to gauge if this was real or a memory.

"I understand your fear." Her mother paused. "There are no words to erase the terror of losing a loved one. These kinds of scars weave through you and choke. But you can't let fear paralyze you. I did, for a time. I resigned to the fact that sleeping through the night was impossible for me, because we were separated by the veil of time. And now here you are." Her mother laughed then, the sound a light frothy version of Coco's.

Adrielle stared into her mother's eyes. They were doe-like, brown like melted chocolate. Adrielle could see the resemblance to Coco: the large eyes, the smile that burst despite everything. Despite the pain reflecting in them. A sting of pain stabbed her chest. My god she'd missed her. "I'm so sorry. I couldn't save you." Adrielle concentrated on keeping her tears in. If she started crying, she might not be able to stop.

"And I you."

Her mother brushed Adrielle's cheek. "Why are you so sad?"

"Because I can't win. I've already lost you, and I'm about to lose Coco too."

Her mother cupped her chin toward her, as she had when she was a child. "What makes you think you've lost me?"

Adrielle stared into her mother's eyes. "It's amazing how real this feels."

Her mother laughed again, the lilting sound taking some of the weight from her chest. "I see you got this okay." She smiled, lifting the gold chain around Adrielle's neck to eye level. She studied the chronometer's face. "I'm so glad. I worried I hadn't been firm enough with Coco about going back for it."

Adrielle was confused.

"You see, darling, this chronometer was made for you. Only you. A cloaking spell kept it safe from Domenikos—and kept you safe, on the odd chance he'd find us."

"Find us?" Adrielle grew suspicious. "How did you know to tell her to get it?"

"I knew Domenikos would do anything for this," she said, letting go of the chain. "So I hid it from him. He'd always wanted it, but it was *your* birthright. Not his."

"The dreams—nightmares. Is this one of them?"

"No, Adrielle." She placed a hand on Adrielle's cheek. It felt warm. Good. "You are really here with me."

Adrielle placed her hand over her mother's, pressing it to her skin. "It feels real, like mine, made of flesh and bones. But it can't really be you—you died in the fire."

To get a better look at her mother's face, Adrielle moved a layer of hair partially covering one eye and went to tuck it behind her ear. There was a jagged scar across her mother's cheek.

"What is that? Who—"

Her mother shook her head dismissively. "Adrielle, face your fear."

Adrielle felt an ethereal feeling about them. She searched the room and realized there were no walls defining the space. It wasn't a house or a building. Only a vast openness as far as she could see. "Where are we? This place—it doesn't feel *real.*"

For the first time since seeing her mother, a flicker of sadness reflected in her mother's eyes.

"Adrielle, you need to remember—everything."

Suddenly she was a little girl, back in her mother's bedroom sitting on her chair at the dresser. Her mother was standing behind her, brushing her hair. "You're beautiful, Adrielle. Don't let anyone judge you by the way you look."

"Mom! Mom!" Coco ran into the room. Adrielle turned and saw Coco was jumping up and down, her turquoise necklace jiggling as she spoke. "There's a blue light glowing outside. It looks like a comet."

Her mother froze; the horror in her eyes reflecting in the mirror as they flicked to the window and back to meet Coco's gaze. "You will remember what I told you?" she asked Coco, her voice strained.

"Oh, Mom. Why do you always bring that up? Come see the comet." Before Coco got the words out, giant flames sprang into the room from the hall. "Fire, we're trapped!" Coco screamed, thick black smoke coiling around them.

The hairbrush dropped to the floor and bounced. "Run, Adrielle, run," her mother yelled.

"No, Mommy—the fire is blocking the door," Adrielle cried. She ran to the window. The blue glow lit up the sky, silhouetting a multitude of birds.

"You need to go. NOW!" her mother shrieked. "Both of you."

"We'll burn."

"No, Adrielle, you won't. Neither will Coco."

Adrielle turned to look. Flames licked at the door. This went against everything she'd been taught about fire. When she turned back to her mother, she was gone.

"You were wrong. She *did* burn," Adrielle said, the memory of that horrific day bludgeoning its way in. "Coco has scars. Hideous scars."

Her mother nodded. "We all do. But she survived."

"How could you risk her life?"

"I knew as long as she got the chronometer, you would both be okay."

"You couldn't possibly know that. But you knew something terrible was about to happen. I saw your horror in the mirror as soon as Coco mentioned the blue light."

Her mother stared off into the distance, pain twisting her features.

Adrielle's heart pounded. Recalling that day was the thing of her nightmares. "Mom? How did you know?" she asked, tugging on her shirt. She realized her mother was wearing the same clothes. "This shirt—" She gasped.

"The embroidered trim around the sleeves . . . I remember watching it while you were brushing my hair. Why isn't it burnt?"

Adrielle's mother slid her eyes to meet hers. "The Doppler effect. That's how I knew. As soon as Coco mentioned the blue glow, I knew it was over. Domenikos had found us."

"What's the Doppler effect?"

"When Achaeans travel, they tap into energy around them, using it to propel themselves through time. Their bodies absorb and transform it, much as humans do food, and it produces a blue glow. The transformed energy escapes through the barbs of their feathers, the tiny perfectly divided sections. With enough travellers, there is a more saturation of light. That's what Coco saw, what she took to be a comet. The Doppler effect."

"But how could she? She's mortal."

"No, Adrielle, only part mortal. You both are."

"No. Impossible. Coco and I—"

"Your father is Achaean. I never talked about him after we—well—when we transported to the future. We both decided it was better that way."

Adrielle shook her head. "It can't be true."

"Look around you, Adrielle. Really look."

Adrielle turned her focus to the vast space surrounding them.

"What do you see?" her mother asked.

For the first time since arriving, she saw faces. Thousands of them. As far as her eyes could see. "Who are they? They're filmy and translucent. It's creepy. Why do they look like that? So dull and lifeless."

"They are deadened-versions of their vibrant counter parts."

"I'm not getting a good feeling about this, we need to get out of here!" said Adrielle.

"I can't leave, I'm a prisoner here. We all are."

"*Whose* prisoner?"

"Domenikos'."

"Domenikos? You can't possibly mean—"

"I do. He taps into their energy and uses it for his own. That's how he controls them. Sapped of their energy, they have no strength to fight back. Their sole purpose is to supply Domenikos the energy he needs for unlimited travel."

Adrielle felt rising anxiety. "Tell me this isn't possible. That he can't be holding everyone hostage."

"Do I need to tell you what you already know, Adrielle?"

Adrielle shook her head, her fingers tracing over her mother's scar. "I'm having a hard time wrapping my head around this. It's *too much.*"

"It's not. You wanted the truth, I saw you tell Monika so, yourself."

"You were there? On my birthday?"

"Yes, Adrielle, I've always been there, behind the veil of time. Watching you grow into your destiny."

"Destiny? Ha. You make it sound like an honor, but it feels more like a curse."

"It *is* an honor. Adrielle, you have been preparing for this moment your entire life. What greater honor is there, than committing to the greater good? Think about it, *you* are the only one who can lift the shackles of fear. I shouldn't have to tell you that if Domenikos isn't stopped, life as we know it will disappear. Time travel *has* to stop. This isn't a mortal or Achaean issue, it's both. Everyone deserves to live freely, in peace, without worrying about someone tampering with their timeline."

"Now you're starting to sound like Coco. What ever happened to free choice?"

"There's always a choice, you know that. And you have to defend it." Adrielle's mother turned away, casting her eyes into the infinite space beyond. But not before Adrielle saw the clear imprint of disappointment settle on her face.

Adrielle felt like screaming. All her pent-up anger bursting within her. She felt betrayed. Lied to. "How could you let me suffer like that? Both of us? We thought you were dead. Some people even believed I had something to do with it, because I was unharmed in that fire. They wondered why. *How,* I survived unblemished. I had to live with that."

"We all have to live with how others see us. No matter how wrong they may be, we have no control over another's opinions. But when it comes down to it, all that really matters is what we think of ourselves. Our own approval. Believe me when I say, I am truly sorry you were hurt. But it was the only way to save you. Once Domenikos had tracked you, there was no stopping him. We had already decided if that were to happen, I would do whatever it took."

"*Who* is we?"

"Your father and me. We knew your role and understood it could mean bargaining away my life for yours. For the greater good. That one day you would come to understand the simple truths."

Adrielle stared at her mother, overwhelming sadness sweeping over her. A surge of tears sprang to her eyes. She swiped at them, suddenly embarrassed to show her emotions. "We can get out of here. You don't have to be his prisoner anymore."

Her mother shook her head. "No, Adrielle, we are trapped between time. There's only one way out of *this* prison," she said, opening her arms and gesturing to the others around her. "You need to face Domenikos and fight for our freedom, or no one will ever be free to do anything again. It's your choice."

"If there was a choice, then I would have chosen not to grow up without a mother. Not to be singled out as different. All I wanted to be was normal."

"Is that what you really want, Adrielle? Would you give up everything you know now, to be like everyone else?"

Adrielle stared into her mother's face. Those placid brown eyes that had once brought her peace, now brought turmoil. They were like Coco's, unwavering in their view of the world. Steadfast. She was wrong.

Fitting in was what she'd always wanted. *Wasn't it?*

Words could not describe the heavy chains pressing down on Adrielle in that moment. The knot in her stomach twisted. She lowered her eyes. It was difficult for her to let anyone see her true emotions, even if it was her mother. She realized then that she'd always let her anger be a shield for her vulnerability.

Adrielle peered at the swarms of faces around them.

"Who are they?" she whispered, her hunger for truth insatiable now.

"They are his shadows. Achaeans, for the most part. Some mortals too."

"How were they imprisoned?"

"He tricked them. Promising they would escape the chains of death if they would succumb to him. Instead, he gave them an eternity of nothingness. Pawns for his bidding."

"But I thought Achaeans were immortal. That they couldn't die."

"Not in the sense a mortal does. Achaeans have existed for eons, millions of years before mortals. They evolved from the earth's core—the molten fires from which the mountains and the oceans were formed—destined to one-day return to it. Once, long ago, Achaeans breathed fire and had feathered wings."

"Domenikos doesn't look like that. Neither do Haden and Angelo."

"Well, like all other living things, they evolved into what they are today; able to shape-shift from their natural bird-like state—into human form."

"Tell me about my father. Why can't I remember him?"

"A veil—a chant or spell some call it—was put over you to keep you safe."

"How did you—I mean, if I am half-Achaean, then, you two must have . . ."

"His name was Aaron. He was one of the leaders in the Unity. When we fell in love, some thought it was blasphemy. They believed it was wrong to interbreed. But Aaron didn't care what others thought. Our union was not always easy, but it helped him gain greater insight into humanity. We never expected he could father a child. And when he did, there was so much controversy. So many against us."

"Why?"

"Because when mortals stepped into the picture, everything changed. Travelling caused a paradox to man. In order for both races to co-exist, it became obvious that travelling needed to be outlawed. And when you were born, when your father held you in his arms . . . well, that's when it all became crystal clear to him. Your father penned the Achaean Act and formed the Unity to uphold the new law."

"And the Achaeans didn't like this."

"Actually, most were ok with it. They wanted to live in peace. And they could, if they abided by the new guidelines. But there were some who opposed it. One of them was Domenikos. He wanted his freedoms at all costs. He slaughtered the leaders—your father included."

"Wow." Adrielle inhaled a long thin breath and struggled to steady herself.

"Your father gave his life for a cause he believed in. There's no nobler thing than that."

"Are there others like me? Hybrids?"

"Adrielle, his children, our children, are the only known offspring between mortals and Achaeans. There's mention of this rarity, among other things, in the *Book of Feathers*. If it were to get in the wrong hands—"

"I've got the book. I'll keep it safe," she said, looking at her mother pointedly. "But if it's so important, why did Haden have it?"

"Haden is the leader of the Achaean army. When your father learned of the revolution, he entrusted it to him only for a time, until the day his heir was old enough to take over. That's how he became the protector of the *Book* of ancient spells."

"Wait. Are you saying I'm Aaron's heir? I don't understand."

Her mother nodded.

"Why isn't Coco the heir?"

Adrielle's mother fumbled for the right words. She reached forward, picked up a stray hair dangling over Adrielle's face, and rubbed it between her fingers. "There is more to being a leader than birth order. It is more about who we are."

"But Coco is more—"

"Coco is as different from you as dark is to light. Though you both carry the Achaean gene, *you* are the one who takes after your father. You are stronger and far more pragmatic than her."

"What if I can't—?"

"Don't doubt." Her mother placed a finger on her lips. "There's too much riding on it."

Adrielle drifted back to the myriad of faces around them. She would do anything to set things right.

"Ouch." Piercing pain stung her back. "It feels like a bullet. Hot and stinging." Adrielle pulled on her t-shirt, twisting her neck around to see, but it was too far up.

"Let me see." Her mother scooped the neck down. "A new link is branded onto your skin. The black feather."

"What does it mean?"

"It's the second mark of the traveller," she said, raising her eyes to meet Adrielle's. "The scales of justice. You've earned it from your thirst for truth. It means from now on, you will be able to see the truth in all things and know when someone is lying to you. Adrielle, we are out of time. Go now and be brave."

Her mother and the others began to fade.

"Wait, don't go," Adrielle pleaded. She had so many unanswered questions. "How do I see my father?"

Her mother shook her head. "You can't. He has returned to the earth."

"There has to be a way. I can travel back in time."

"Adrielle, haven't you been listening?"

"I understand, but if I could only see him. Get his advice."

Her mother shook her head. "You have always been stubborn. It is your curse and your blessing. Trust yourself. That is the only way."

Suddenly, the vast space that enveloped them felt oppressive. It threatened to suck all the oxygen from her lungs.

THE SOUND WAS no louder than the snap of a twig. Liz cracked her eyes open and lay still. Holding her breath, she listened. It was the creak of the chair by Adrielle's bed. *Angelo.* She exhaled. A low murmur followed and ripped at her heart. He was at her side again. Begging her to return. Vowing undying love.

Toasted chocolate almonds! She couldn't bear it. Liz turned onto her side. She'd wrestled with insomnia for what seemed like hours, and now this . . . just when sleep had come.

Having Angelo constantly around was an awkward adjustment. She didn't know him very well, and it seemed like he was always there. Admittedly, she was more private than other girls her age. *A prude,* Veda had called her. But in her defense, she was an only child.

Though she was close to Dave, she missed her quiet-evening-whisperings with Coco. They calmed her. Ever since Adrielle and Coco had returned from the future, she'd felt a sisterhood she'd never sensed before.

Learning that Veda and Kate had been reduced to ashes spurred a series of panic attacks. Crushing moments of helplessness fueled by rampant thoughts that would arise unexpectedly. These fears usually spiked at night. Liz scuffled with them, justifying the fears were irrational. But they taunted her. As the days slipped by, they came more often, making sleep impossible.

At first, Liz refused to discuss anything in front of Angelo. Not her fears, and not her apprehension about going back to her life in Florida—if everything went as planned, that is. But in her sleeplessness, she learned of Angelo's devotion to Adrielle, and this changed everything for her. This was a man in love. So deeply in love, and so devoted to Adrielle, she felt sorry for him. And she wanted this for herself.

Chapter 25

FLORENCE – 1504
DAy of tHE EclipSE

THE DAY ARRIVED everyone had both hoped for and feared. It didn't bully its way with tolling bells or ground-shaking earth but announced its arrival with a brilliant slant of light that lit the entire room.

Somewhere outside a cock crowed and Angelo stirred, raising his head from where it had dropped onto the edge of Adrielle's bed. His gaze went directly to her face, and immediately a slow breath deflated his diaphragm. No change.

From her bed on the floor, Liz pushed her hair out of her eyes and watched as Angelo studied Adrielle intently. Adrielle lay motionless, trapped worlds away from him. She looked paler that usual. Her skin and hair glowed against the pillowcase. Liz caught the rise and slump of his chest as he registered her condition. The fact that she was still asleep seemed to snuff something inside him.

Liz turned to the spot next to her to see if Coco was awake. *Empty.* She felt the sting of disappointment, she would have liked someone to confide in. By the day's end they'd know if they were trapped or if they'd be returning to that place called home. And that scared the hell out of her.

The bedding next to her was un-slept in, so once again, Coco had stayed up all night. She drove herself to exhaustion working side by side with Leo and Mich, Dave's nicknames. Liz sniggered, amused simple nicknames brought joy these days.

She turned back to watch Angelo who was now stretching, twisting his torso from one side to the other. His muscles were stiff and no wonder, he'd slept in that chair for days, guarding Adrielle's body ever since she'd gone comatose.

Liz rubbed her eyes and listened to the low murmur of his voice . . . *"I tried to warn you, but you wouldn't listen. I am here for you, but you can face this—you are strong."*

She tuned him out, embarrassed to be eavesdropping. Angelo was the entire package; everything she'd ever hoped for in a guy. Devotion. Sincerity. Steadfastness. He even had the looks, but that had never been a priority for her. She thought about Francesco and wondered if the roles were reversed, how he'd measure up? If he'd believe her, if she told him the truth. That she was a time traveller from the future.

Angelo was unyielding. Even when she and Coco complained of their much-needed privacy, or reminded him this was *their* bedroom, he kept his post, only leaving Adrielle's side when he deemed it indispensable he be somewhere else. And then he'd return immediately.

There was something gentle about him. It reminded her of sitting on the beach, watching the waves roll in. The way he'd stroke Adrielle's hand when he thought everyone was asleep and murmur things of their past life together. He'd whisper hopes for their future together. He was the wave, the crest, and the trough.

Dave confided he too, was touched by Angelo's devotion. Said he'd often felt his sexual orientation made him more susceptible to feelings than other males, but Angelo proved him wrong. He believed Angelo was every bit as sensitive as he was. So different from anyone Dave had ever been close to.

The robust smell of coffee and baking radiated from the kitchen and filtered into the bedroom. Liz jumped up and slipped on Coco's robe, tied it at the waist, and met Angelo's gaze fleetingly before tiptoeing out the door.

Fear? Was that what she'd seen in his eyes? She couldn't be sure. She broke contact quickly and closed the door behind her. She pressed her forehead against it. How would she tell everyone Adrielle hadn't awakened?

LIZ ENTERED THE kitchen and saw Salai, nervous as could be, had risen early. He baked. And baked. And baked. Three dozen spongata di brescello (an Italian pastry with a honey and currant filling). Check. Two tortas ricciolinas (sweet cakes made with butter, sugar, and Amaretto). Check. A bowl-full of canestrelli (thin crumbly biscuits the shape of daisy flowers). Check. Check. Liz caught him rubbing his breastbone as he glanced at the spread he'd prepared and then go into the pantry for more flour. No amount of busy work could relieve the tension in his chest, but he seemed resigned to try. Nothing short of Adrielle's victory could do that.

He filled two carafes with espresso and set them in the center of the wooden table, alongside the baking.

"*Mama mia—che cosa e tutto questo?* What is all this?" Michelangelo roared from the doorway, his hands pressed to his head in surprise. Leonardo, stepping into the kitchen directly behind him, acknowledged the exhaustion on Salai's face. He maneuvered past Michelangelo, walked directly to Salai, and gave his shoulder a squeeze.

"It is almost complete," Michelangelo said, collapsing onto the chair at the head of the table. Coco trailed behind, her hands and apron stained with ink and paints. She went to the sink and scrubbed the paints off with a brush kept on the sill for that purpose, but the tips of her fingers were stained blue with traces of ink, and it had hardened along her cuticles.

"Turpentine. It's the only thing that will take the ink off," Salai suggested, handing her a rag and a jar. She unscrewed the lid and tipped the jar until the pungent solvent soaked the rag. The others were unfazed by the overpowering smell. It had become a mainstay.

Dave bolted in the back door with an armful of logs and dropped them onto the basket by the firebox. He wiped his forehead with his sleeve and scanned the room. When Adrielle was nowhere in sight, he selected small wood chips and kindling for fire.

"Any change?" Coco asked as she sat at the table. Liz, not trusting her voice, nor wanting to acknowledge the worried look frozen on everyone's face, only shook her head and let her gaze drift past them to the pastries filling the table, and then down to her lap, where she smoothed out the wrinkles of her nightgown.

"Angelo's not coming down?" Coco asked. She sounded disappointed.

Liz shook her head and bypassing the sweets altogether, slid the tiny porcelain cup toward the carafe, surreptitiously studying everyone's reactions, from Leonardo to Michelangelo, hoping to assess the progress: pointless now, without Adrielle to execute the plan.

Salai reached for her cup and filled it, adding milk and sugar before handing it back. He turned away from the table and fussed with the dishes stacked on the shelves on the wall. He moved a row of bowls a fraction to the left and then stopped. With his hands resting on his hips, he looked straight ahead and sighed a low whistle. Liz believed he was thinking the same thing everyone else was. How long must they wait before someone brought up the ghost of a girl lying lifeless upstairs?

HADEN CLOSED HIS eyes, wanting desperately to revisit that place, that occasion, when Adrielle accepted his marriage proposal. It was a sweet moment, even if tainted with ignorant wistfulness. For a time, he'd envisioned what their future could hold: acceptance from her. He believed she was his match, able to grasp both sides of the coin, leader, and lover and partner. Not many had that breadth of versatility.

But looking back, he'd been naïve. Knowing what he now knew, after pouring over the ancient manuscripts, he should have realized he could no more ignore the pull of the universe than she could. There were so many obligations. But he'd tried, and that had to count for something.

Armed with the knife Domenikos had given him as part of their treaty, he concentrated on changing into his natural form. As his muscles rippled and twitched, his mind raced. He had one last shot at sparing Adrielle's life. He'd use the very dagger Domenikos had given him and turn it on Domenikos. Only by killing him, would Adrielle be freed from his demonic nature. If he was successful, he only hoped that with time, Adrielle would forgive him.

"THE HOUR IS nigh," the old woman hissed. She lifted her face to the sky. Already the light was dimming, but a faint splash of sunlight illuminated the horizon.

She raised the scepter high and saw her hand tattered and pickled by age. She'd been guarding the diamond all her life, and this was the moment she'd waited for. She lowered the scepter and rapped the ground with great force. "Kraa. Kraaa." The black bird on her shoulder spread its wings and dove into the center of the diamond and disappeared.

Swirls of colors flared from the center. A great wind rose, gaining momentum like a giant cyclone sweeping over the land. Monika braced against the elements, her eyes narrowing to thin slits. She chanted the ancient spell that would summon souls from the four corners of the earth. Murky shadows leached out of the ground like early morning fog, the vaporous mist taking the form of thousands of birds. A murmuration. Their feathers brilliant and iridescent; every hue found in nature. They flapped their wings forcefully, navigating against the current and plotting their course eastward.

ANGELO TOOK ADRIELLE'S hand and covered it with his. He wondered if he should have told her, if she'd even believe him. Perhaps it was best she didn't remember everything . . . it would make it that much harder for her.

He lifted her hand close to his mouth and held it there for a moment, his lips brushing along her skin, then leaned over her body and pressed his cheek to hers. Her body felt warm. He was overcome with a longing so deep it pulled at his core. "I love you, Adrielle, more than life itself." He crushed his lips to hers, feeling the softness of her mouth. "It's time," he whispered, "The book is complete. Come back, Adrielle. Come back and face your destiny."

ANGELO'S WORDS SPARKED a thrumming in her heart, like the steady roll of a drum. The sound of her blood swimming through her veins pumped in her ears. One thought blared above all others: Domenikos had committed unspeakable crimes. And for this, he would pay.

Adrielle opened her eyes with a start. Angelo was at her bedside. He stared back at her with such intensity, an overwhelming surge of emotion swept over her. He seemed troubled and relieved all at once. He wiped moisture from the corners of his eyes and smiled. Adrielle fought to suppress her feelings. She couldn't let him see how she truly felt. How much she loved him. She cursed inwardly, afraid to let anyone see inside.

Angelo seemed to know this about her. He leaned down and kissed her mouth slowly, his lips warm against hers. A longing more profound than she'd ever remembered stirred inside her. She felt herself melting into him, and then as she was about to lose herself in the rapture, he lifted away, his eyes probing hers.

Adrielle struggled to sit up and wordlessly, Angelo pressed his hand against the small of her back. He waited while she reconnected with her physical self. Despite the immobility, her body felt invigorated.

Adrielle slid her legs to the side of the bed and stood up, gravity centering her.

"Hungry?" he whispered, trying to assess her.

"Starved. But I'm going to the studio first."

Angelo nodded, the pressure of his hand steadying her.

"I can do this," she said, removing his hand and hobbling toward the hall. Her legs were stiff and weak but she was determined to walk on her own. They fell into step, Adrielle leading, each one lost in their own thoughts. At the bottom of the stairs, she took a left toward the studio. He followed. Every step sped up her heart. She reached the paint-splattered door. It was open a crack and bright daylight poured out of the studio. Adrielle pushed the worn door open and entered. The creak of the door filling the room.

Leonardo and Michelangelo were bent over the worktable. Michelangelo looked up. *"Madre Santisima."*

"Are you all right? You were in that bed for days," Leonardo said.

"Yes," Adrielle said, anxious to minimize the fuss.

After their initial perusal, they seemed satisfied she was all right, and relief replaced their worry. They pushed away from the table to make room for her to inspect their work. A hush silenced the room as she headed toward them.

Adrielle could barely breathe, so much was riding on this. The worktable was cluttered with dishes, paints, used quills and brushes, and in the center, were the two books side-by-side, along with the tray of Canestrelli left over from breakfast that Salai had brought in for snacks. Seeing the tray of daisy-shaped cookies lightened her mood. It made her feel like everything and anything was possible.

Both she and Angelo reached for the pastry at the same time, their hands colliding mid-air. They exchanged a knowing look as a warmth cycled between them. They'd come a long way.

Adrielle lowered her eyes to the worktable. There they were, the two leather bindings, side by side. A strand of her platinum hair fell onto the worn leather cover as she bent over the books, and she tucked it quickly behind her ear. Her fingertips tingled with vigor as she brushed over the covers.

"Amazing," she said, in an almost reverent tone, "the books look identical."

She opened the cover to the original *Book of Feathers* first and scrutinized every detail, then quickly turned to examine the forgery. She did this for every page, scrolling down the length and comparing: the illustrations, the formatting, the text. Finally, she closed both covers and stood silent.

Leonardo, paralyzed with concentration, suspended his breath. Adrielle picked up the original volume to the left and inspected closely the gold foil on the fore-edge, her eyes absorbing every detail. Then she did the same for the other.

"Michelangelo is a master at the gold foil. It is identical." Leonardo beamed, scouring her face for approval.

"Nearly perfect," she said, her eyes meeting his. Then picking up the first book, she fanned the fore-edge slightly until it exposed a hidden painting. Michelangelo and Leonardo appeared speechless. There was a painting of a white bird-like creature with wide wings and brilliant white feathers on the fore-edge. Adrielle met their gaze.

"That's not all." She flipped the book over and fanned the pages in the opposite direction, exposing a second painting. This one was of a cave high in a mountain.

"Unbelievable. A double fore-edged painting!" Leonardo exclaimed. "How could we have missed it?"

Adrielle slid her focus from the original to the forgery and back.

Outside Michelangelo's studio, the moon almost completely covered the sun. A halo of light surrounded it. "There's no time to reproduce this. The sky is already darkening," Michelangelo moaned, agitation grinding his voice.

"We have to *make* time," Angelo snarled. "If Domenikos suspects this is a forgery, it's all over."

Coco bolted full speed into the studio. "I heard voices. Adie, thank goodness."

"Are you okay?" Dave, Liz and Salai, cried at once, trailing in behind Coco. Adrielle nodded. She returned to fixating on the books.

"Oh-oh. What's wrong?" Coco asked.

"We need to add these images, Adrielle said, pointing to the fore-edge paintings, and then turning to the foreword, she scrolled half-way down the first page. "I knew they must be somewhere because here, the text references the double-edged image. I'm sure if we copy these onto the forgery, Domenikos will believe it's the original manuscript." She met Leonardo's eyes. "We have to reproduce it. It's the only detail missing."

He slapped his hand to his forehead and sighed heavily. "It would take days."

"How will they dry?" Salai asked.

"Paint it and I will dry them," Angelo assured.

Leonardo backed away from the table and crossed the room in quick long strides toward the back shelves, where he had already retired the paints. He selected an assortment of jars and hurried back with an armful of pigments.

"Everybody move back. I need space," Leonardo growled.

Everyone scattered except for Michelangelo, who stayed behind. He began mixing the paints with acute precision, while Leonardo worked on the ink sketch.

"THEY AREN'T GOING to do it. There's no way," Salai objected. He was standing in the center of the kitchen, compulsively wringing his hands.

Coco paced up to him and placed her hands on his. "Salai," she started, shaking her head slowly. "Have some faith. Don't you believe after everything you've seen—with the time travelling and everything else—that the cosmos has a greater plan?"

"Destiny?" he asked, staring back at her.

"Call it what you will."

"Make plans and destiny laughs," he said.

"Or, if it's destined to be, it will be."

Coco saw plainly on his face he wondered how a sprig of a girl could have such optimism. He sighed. "I want to. I really want to. But I know how much time it takes for the oils to dry. It will never happen."

"NEVER SAY NEVER," Dave said, his stomach clenched in knots. It had to happen. "Crap. So many *ifs.*" He couldn't imagine being trapped here before the LBGTQ movement. He'd never have a normal life again. Be free to express his sexuality. Free to pursue his love of fashion. He slipped his iPhone out of his pocket and stared at the blank screen. "Out of juice," he mumbled in a low voice. How he missed his phone. It would take centuries until this technology was discovered. And he'd be long gone by then.

LIZ WATCHED DAVE surreptitiously. He was upset. She didn't approach to comfort him. He'd hate knowing she'd been watching him. A part of her felt guilty she'd dragged him here with her. She shoved her hands in her robe's pocket and nervously balled and un-balled her fists. *Wait* . . . the stiff end of Adrielle's feather she'd snipped was tucked in the corner.

She turned her back to the others and ran her fingers over the bristly end of the spine, then ruffled the soft barbs. She entertained for a moment what would actually happen if she tried to flee now? Would it work? Could she manage to get back to the night of the party? Would she be happy back there, now, knowing what she'd learned?

She let the feather slide through her fingers and drop back to the bottom of her pocket, slipped her hand out, and tapped it firmly against her body.

She sidled up to Adrielle. "Can you kick his ass?"

Adrielle was taken back. "I—I—Huh?"

"You'd better. The thing is, Adie, I don't know how this is going to end. And I have to tell ya, I haven't decided yet if Florence is the best thing that ever happened to me, or the worst. But you gotta kick ass 'cause I sure as heck want to keep my options open."

Adrielle nodded.

"For the record," Dave said, "Florence is my worst."

THE MOON TOOK a small bite out of the sun and thus it had begun. Adrielle's stomach twisted into a painful knot. They were out of time.

"It's done," Leonardo said. "Both scenes are now on the fore-edge. But the paint still needs to dry."

Adrielle turned away from the window and trekked over to the table, where Leonardo had just handed Angelo the book.

Angelo took it in his hands and lifted it eye level. Then, opening his mouth a crack, exhaled onto the painted edge. A dry heat blustered out more intense than a raging fire.

Feeling the sudden blast of extreme temperature, Leonardo's hands fluttered to his beard. He took a step back, stuffing his beard into his shirt and almost tripping on his chair.

"Oh mio Dio! Che cosa e questo?" Michelangelo thundered. Backing quickly into a corner, his expression reflected what his mind couldn't grasp: *who was this ungodly creature?*

Angelo, seemingly unaffected by the outburst, continued to blow, slowly turning the book over to the opposite side. When he was done, he inspected the edges and tapped it lightly with his fingertips. "Dry," he said, handing the book to Adrielle with a satisfied expression.

Adrielle took the forgery in her hands. She inspected the details quickly, fanning the fore-edge and riffling through the pages until she was convinced the image looked exact. She drew in a deep breath and met Angelo's gaze. It was time.

"You sure you can do this alone?"

"I have to," Adrielle said.

"Do you know where to go?" he asked.

"Oh my god, this? Now?" Dave cried out, turning his head away from the window to face them. "Please tell me you've gone over the plan."

"Calm down. If you're scared, you might wanna keep that to yourself," Liz warned. "Adrielle has a lot to deal with as it is."

Dave lowered his eyes to the ground.

"Think back. Way back," Angelo urged. "Strategy was always your strongest trait. You would go on trips to study world leaders by simply closing your eyes."

"How does he know this?" Dave whispered.

By the time Liz looked up, Adrielle had vanished.

Chapter 26

The Eclipse

"THIS IS HAPPENING. This is really happening," Adrielle whispered to herself, pausing to catch her breath. Up ahead was the part of the cave matching the fore-edge image. The fissure in the side of the rock had not been visible from below. She swallowed hard, gripping onto the stone, her nails feeling as though they'd rip off.

She pressed her torso to the rockface and felt the forged book tucked into her jacket. She exhaled a sigh of relief and dread. The last thing she wanted was to confront Domenikos, but here she was. Going to the place her crest told her she'd find him.

She peered over her shoulder. Even more terrifying than going up was going down. The sheer height was heart stopping. An almost vertical drop. If she fell, she'd hit the side of the cliff and plunge to her death, the angry ocean below claiming her body.

"Just a bit further," she muttered, hoping hearing the words would spur courage.

Along the rock face were stones that jutted out. Adrielle used them to propel herself upward. She stretched her right arm, struggling to reach the next rock nub, trying not to think of falling. She swung and clung to it, then pulled herself higher.

Her chest was tight. Every breath a strain. She clung to the rock's surface and reached again. One misstep and she lost her balance, her body dangling. She swung and thrust her foot, hitting the rock ledge too hard. Rocks and shards cascaded down. Her heart pounded in her ears. She couldn't hang here for long. Her arms felt heavy. Sweat stung her eyes. She blinked, trying to rid the burning. Her vision blurred and then cleared.

There . . . another ledge a ways up. The fissure was in reach. If she could just . . . *one, two* . . . she swung her body dangerously side-to-side with increasing force. One last hurl, and she heaved her torso onto the cave's entrance. She swung her legs over the edge and laid there, her lungs heaving, flat against the cold surface. She was exhausted.

A dank smell permeated everything. She stood up, her fingers and forearms aching, and backed against one wall. She couldn't afford any surprises. This way no one could sneak up on her. It took a moment for her eyes to adjust. There wasn't much room to maneuver in this tight space. The cliff's edge was dangerously close. Then her heart stopped. Further in the shadows stood Domenikos. Brix at his side.

Adrielle felt a revulsion to Domenikos so strong it took all her concentration not to run. His stance was intimidating. Legs wide, hands resting on his hips with his fingers grazing the silver handle of his dagger. He kept his eyes pinned on her, the corners of his lips curling.

"Look who made it," he said.

Adrielle balled her fists, slighted by his allusion to her weakness. She glanced fleetingly at Brix with his arms folded across his chest. A thug like him with delusions of grandeur could spark a reckless response, making him that much more dangerous. She swung her focus on Domenikos while keeping an eye on Brix. It was too dark to determine if Domenikos' *big dogs* would dart out from behind shadows.

Adrielle felt inside her jacket, where *The Book of Feathers* was strapped securely. She gathered her shoulders in a quarterback's hunch and raised her eyes to Domenikos. Their eyes locked. His confidence heightened her insecurities. She flashed to how powerless she'd felt in Scarlett's den. Fear had paralyzed her. She pushed past her terror. She couldn't afford any distractions.

"Domenikos, release the prisoners."

Domenikos stared icily. Her warmth leached out with his frozen glare and anger took hold.

"I have no ethical obligation to play by the rules," he said.

"Tell me something I *don't* know," Adrielle said.

Domenikos smirked. Brix laughed like this was the punch line to a joke.

Domenikos slid one hand over his glossy coif. He primped like a red-whiskered bulbul. He patted the point on its top. Though no taller than Adrielle, the added height from his hairdo was meant to intimidate.

They didn't have time for games. Adrielle slid her eyes to the sky. Only a small crescent of the sun remained. Points of light surrounding the edges of the dark moon resembled a string of Coco's beads. *Concentrate Adrielle . . .* she cursed inwardly. Her frustration seemed to empower Domenikos.

He lowered his eyes to her necklace. "Hand it over."

Adrielle unzipped her jacket, exposing a corner of the book. When he saw it, she began chanting a spell.

At that moment Haden emerged from the cave's depth. "Stop her, she's got the *Book of Feathers* in her jacket."

What? Had Angelo been right? Haden had been colluding with the enemy?

Domenikos flicked to the book protruding. "Is that . . . my god . . . I thought it was destroyed!"

"She's chanting a spell," Brix shouted, ready to pounce, his gaze jumping from Haden to Adrielle.

Domenikos pounced for the book. Haden pulled out his knife and charged toward him. Brix caught the glint of Haden's blade and lurched in front, shielding Domenikos. Haden's knife sunk into Brix's chest. He hissed. His eyes rolled back, he transformed into bird form, and dropped to the ground dead.

Domenikos thrust his blade into Haden's side. Haden folded at the waist. He turned to Adrielle as the blade sunk in.

"No!" Adrielle screamed. He'd been trying to save her. Haden staggered backward, crimson seeping onto his billowy shirt. Adrielle reached for him, but Haden tumbled over the edge, disappearing to the depths below.

Adrielle shook with rage.

Domenikos lunged at her, his weight knocking her down. Adrielle swung her fists. She delivered a barrage of vicious blows, but Domenikos grabbed her throat. Her air passages constricted. She clamped both hands around his hand. His grip tightened, cutting her oxygen off.

"Father should have given this to me," Domenikos said, snatching the book and releasing his hold. He stood up, backing away with the book.

Adrielle gasped for air. "What? What did you say? Father?"

"I am your twin. Born seconds before you. I am the rightful heir."

Adrielle's adrenaline pumped. "You can't be . . . you're a monster. We couldn't share the same parents!"

"It was sickening, the way Dad groomed you—his chosen one. Lessons on how to read Achaean. Time travel to see leaders . . ."

Domenikos' words were sinking in. The look on her mother's face the night of the fire. The veil of sadness dulling her mother's eyes was a mother's regret. Then a barrage of memories assaulted. Her stomach contents lurched up, and she bent at the waist, heaving. *My god, he is my brother.* The cloaking spell had made her forget.

Her eyes went to the knife on the floor. It must have fallen in the tussle. She grabbed it and jumped to her feet. She shook the knife, holding it with both hands, rage and revenge rising in her gut. "How could you? You killed our father. Your father!"

"We are not so different, you and I." He backed away, keeping a safe distance between them and opening the book. He flipped through the pages while eyeing her. "You won't kill me. We're bound. We shared the same womb."

Adrielle tightened her grip on the handle. The knife had Haden's blood. It was on her hands. "This is the same knife you used to torture father, isn't it?"

Domenikos' flicked to the blade and back to the book. The expression on his face said he didn't think her much of a threat. He searched the book hungrily, his eyes zigzagging feverishly through the pages. "I wasn't going to allow him to ban time travel. Take away my freedom. Our Achaean birthright from our beginnings."

Adrielle didn't want to make sudden moves while Domenikos decided if the book was authentic.

"What's this?" he spat. "You think I'm a fool?"

The pit of Adrielle's stomach dropped. They'd failed. All that work . . .

Domenikos flipped the page. Then another. And another. He stopped, reading the portions regarding the hidden image. He bent the fore-edge until he saw the image. He looked up, a seriousness overcoming him. "Give me the chronometer."

He'd bought it? Adrielle felt partial relief from the pressure. She shook the knife still clutched in both hands, not knowing if she could follow the threat. "You tortured mother, killed father. You hurt thousands of others. Set—them—free!"

The book clutched in one hand, Domenikos lifted it to the night. From the depths of the cave, a murmuration emerged. Thousands upon thousands of black birds. A dark cloud spinning in unison headed straight for her.

High-pitched screeches screamed in her ears. Adrielle cupped her hands over her ears, the knife dropping. The birds zoomed around her in layers. It was the image from her nightmares: A tapestry of feathers, one form indistinguishable from the next. She swatted and cowered. Her ears splitting with pain. There were too many. She didn't stand a chance.

Adrielle recoiled, tightening her grip around her chronometer. She could flee. But everything depended on her. The spell she'd memorized for this moment came to her and she recited the words. They empowered her. The crest on her back seared and the murmuration retreated. She continued chanting.

Domenikos folded over in pain, his hands springing to his temples. "Stop," he cried, staggering back, his palms pressing against his skull.

Adrielle's crest burned. The black feather in the wreath confirming the spell was working.

Domenikos turned to another spell. "A promise for the *Time Keeper.*"

Adrielle sucked in a breath. She recognized the spell. She'd changed the words to imprison him. He was mistaking it to mean the Time Keeper would get everything they wanted.

The sky darkened. A fierce wind rose from the depths of the earth. "Will you give your life for freedom?" a voice echoed. Domenikos paused, his gaze searching the space around them.

Adrielle recognized the old woman's voice. She turned to search the sky.

"Yes. God, yes," Domenikos shouted. He continued reciting the spell, believing he was winning.

Deep guttural noises rose from the depths of the earth. Howling winds increased at a dizzying pace. A cyclone swirled around Domenikos, pinning his arms to his side. His eyes locked onto Adrielle's. There was confusion. And then he knew she'd tricked him.

"Stop. Sister. Have mercy."

Adrielle broke his stare. He would do anything to escape. Say anything. "You will pay."

"Let the balance of the universe be restored," Monika declared.

Adrielle could see her now, waving her scepter. A whirlwind sucked Domenikos into the scepter diamond.

The Moon slid in front of the sun and in the total eclipse, an explosion of colors reflecting every color of the rainbow shot out of the diamond. Red, yellow, blue, green, violet, and orange.

Adrielle was stunned. It was over. She had won the war. She thought of her father. The sacrifices her parents made to save humanity. To save the world. Her quest for the truth had led her here. Everything was stripped down to this one truth. Without the Achaean Act, the world would never survive. Her father had sacrificed his life for this truth. It was her turn now. She accepted her destiny. She'd do whatever it took to save the world from the shackles of time travel. She was the Achaean leader.

A quiet calm spread within her. For the first time in her life, she didn't care what anyone thought. She was at peace with her past.

The diamond in the scepter grew brilliant. A blinding bolt escaped and stabbed Adrielle between her shoulders.

What was happening? Her back arched in pain. She lost her balance and stumbled, over-stepping the edge of the cliff. She tumbled into a downward death spiral. She screamed, her horror echoing in the darkness.

The old woman shook her scepter vehemently and held it high. As she was falling, a ray from the diamond pierced Adrielle's body and split the sky.

FROM THE STUDIO'S window, Leonardo and the others gazed up. A lightning bolt lit the sky and a thunderous rumble shook the earth. Then a white bird emerged from the whirlwind. Its strong wide wings soared across the vast space, its white feathers gleaming. The luminous bird swooped over the landscape in wide circles and neared close enough for them to see a four feathered crest glowing on the middle of the bird's back: red, black, silver, and pale green.

"Mama Santisima," Michelangelo said, tracing the sign of the cross.

"It's the painting on the fore-edge," Leonardo exclaimed.

"It's Adrielle. The time keeper," Liz said, reaching into her robe pocket and feeling the snippet of feather. In the commotion she saw Angelo had vanished. A silver bird swooped next to the white one and they flew.

"The silver bird behind her is Angelo."

Everyone turned to Liz questioningly. She shrugged sheepishly. "It's in the journal."

In the palm of her hand Liz stared at her thick, black-rimmed glasses. She was about to unfold them when she had a thought. She didn't need them to see what she'd known all along. Adrielle finally accepted herself. That was all they needed to get them home.

Epilogue
Florida – Present Day

"C'MON, JUST GO," Dave pleaded.

"Who can think of eating at a time like this?" Liz laughed.

"I'll get it," Adrielle offered, putting the Netflix mystery on hold. She handed Coco the remote and skirted off the bed. "Drinks too?" Coco jiggled her glass until the ice clinked.

"Sure," Adrielle said, "I'll bring up the Coke."

"Don't forget the lemon."

"Never," Adrielle said, a warmth stirring inside. She stepped into the hall and paused, glancing into Coco's room.

Dave was sprawled on the chair by the window in his wrinkled flannel pajama bottoms, licking his fingers and dumping the remaining Dorito crumbs onto the palm of his hand. He'd let his hair grow past his ears and was far more relaxed these days.

Liz's eyes remained pinned on the TV screen, her journal and pen within arm's reach. She was in her sleeping bag on the floor, wearing an emerald silk robe and had traded in her fuzzy slippers for gold-heeled strappy sandals. Gone were the black-rimmed glasses, replaced with contacts.

Adrielle missed Liz's frizzy hair, though it had always looked in disarray, strange as that may sound. Since Florence, Liz wore it straight, shoulder length with golden highlights. As much as Liz complained she hated the upkeep, she said she didn't want to risk anyone mistaking her for the Mona Lisa.

She thought back to Veda and Kate and wondered if those really were their ashes, or if it was another one of Domenikos' tricks. There was still a chance they were among the thousands of mortals he'd captured and held as prisoners, in the outer region. Her mom had taken over the task of working alongside Angelo and Astraia to free the countless others. She said it would take time to sort through everyone and return the captured mortals to their proper time frame.

A warm feeling swam in Adrielle's chest. It felt like Christmas. Though they weren't all connected by blood, for better or worse, they were family. Her family.

Adrielle was halfway down the stairs when Dave and Liz's bickering carried out into the hall. Apparently, Liz, with complete control of the remote, had exited out of Netflix and tuned into a news program. Liz reassured it was only until Adrielle returned, but this reasoning didn't appease anyone.

Some things never change, Adrielle thought thankfully, as the lilting sound of Coco's laugh trailed out.

THE COUNTER IN the kitchen was a mess of chip bags, dips, leftover Pizza, red plastic cups, and an array of soda bottles. Adrielle grabbed the pizza box and set the chip bags on top. She was about to carry them up along with the Coke when the crest on her back began to sting. Someone was attempting to breach the Achaean Act.

An alarm went off inside her. She stared down at her chronometer. The dials were turned to Florence 1504. She could do this. She could set the universe on the right track.

With a quick glance toward the stairs, Adrielle made a split-second decision. They'd have to grin and bear—whatever Liz had decided to watch—until she corrected the situation.

Adrielle closed her eyes and braced for the tingling sensation to stop. When she opened her eyes, Leonardo was staring ahead, a small snippet of her white feather clutched in his fingers.

Adrielle giggled. Leonardo turned to his left and exhaled with relief. "Oh, there you are," he said, his eyes absorbing her the way only an artist does. He watched her silently for several moments.

"What's wrong?" Adrielle asked.

"Wrong? Nothing. The future agrees with you. You are beaming with light," he remarked.

Adrielle laughed. "Leonardo, you *do* remember what I told you. Don't you? You see me as a translucent version of my real self when you use the feather."

"Oh yes, yes, I remember. But that's not what I mean. Have you fallen in love?"

"Love?" Adrielle bit her lip. She wasn't going to encourage him. And besides, she hadn't heard from Angelo recently.

"You look happy," he said, turning to Michelangelo on his right. His brow furrowed as his eyes danced around the room.

"I don't see a thing," Michelangelo said.

"Oh, here, touch a corner of this." Michelangelo stretched out his hand and grasped a small piece of white fluff protruding from Leonardo's fingers.

"I see you now, Bellisima." He smiled.

"What's up? I was sure someone was trying to breech the time fabric."

Leonardo pressed his lips into a thin line. "Well, if you must know, we were having a discussion." He sauntered over to the table and shuffled through a stack of papers. He pulled out a large thin sheet with sketches and pointed with his finger.

"You see over here, if a person were to lie on this central board and wear a head piece for steering, he could crank this—it's connected to this rod and pulley, it would flap the wings. The main frame is made of pine covered with silk to create a sturdy membrane."

As he directed her to the different aspects of the drawing, he became more animated. "This has a wingspan of over thirty-three feet. I've sketched the wings with pointed ends like the ones you had when you were flying around up there . . ." He fluttered his hands. "Once up in the air, the wings spin and flap. It should have no problem."

"That's where we disagree," Michelangelo interjected. "I don't see how a person can create enough power to get this machine off the ground."

Adrielle folded her arms and gave them both a stern gaze. "Guys, c'mon, you know I can't interfere."

Leonardo sighed. He exchanged a look with Michelangelo. "Very well."

"And?" Adrielle, seeing the interchange, asked.

"Have you seen Angelo?" Michelangelo asked.

Adrielle thought back. "No. Not since . . . but he's busy restoring chaos."

"There's been an alarming number of birds around the Arno. We were wondering if it had something to do with him?"

"I don't think so," Adrielle said. Damage control from Domenikos would take time. And Angelo would have contacted her if—

"I have to go," she said, pushing it out of her mind. She set her chronometer to get back home. She felt empowered. Things were under control. And most of all, she felt happy. She knew her purpose.

When she returned, Liz had the news turned up. Angelo's picture flashed on the screen. Adrielle froze. The flashing red news band said, "Breaking news. A man was found wandering the streets in Jacksonville with no recollection of who he is. Where he lives. Call local authorities if you have information."

Montana Wakefield, author of the Adrielle Maddox series and other forthcoming books, her illustrated children's book series, *Squiggley Wiggley: The Magical Blue Bear*, and mystery novel, *Twist in Fate*, is a lover of life and has an unquenchable thirst for the next adventure. As an avid reader and writer, she's a firm believer that stories unite us all on a deeper level and will enrich our lives if we embrace the imagination within us.

Montana studied fine arts and writing at the University of Calgary, attended the Royal Conservatory of Music for classical guitar, paints, writes songs, and loves to play with her dog Scarlatti. This mother of three is happily married to her husband, close to all her siblings, is an avid TV binger, and is constantly surprised by life's turn of events. Her mission in life is to spread a little fun, love deeply, and stay true to her belief that each of us can reach unfathomable heights if we learn to believe in ourselves and each other.

Visit Montana's website: https://montanawakefield.com